TWISTED GAMES

TWISTED BOOK TWO

ANA HUANG

TWISTED GAMES:

Cover Designer: E. James Designs

Editor: Amy Briggs, Briggs Consulting LLC

Proofreader: Krista Burdine

To all the girls who said fuck Prince Charming,
give me a scarred knight.

Playlist

"Queen"—Loren Gray
"Castle"—Halsey
"Arcade"—Duncan Laurence
"You Should See Me in a Crown"—Billie Eilish
"Telepatía"—Kali Uchis**
"Stay"—Rihanna
"Uncover"—Zara Larsson
"Secret Love Song"—Little Mix
"They Don't Know About Us"—One Direction
"Minefields"—Faouzia & John Legend
"Wildest Dreams"—Taylor Swift
"Princesses Don't Cry"—Aviva
"Fairytale" (Slowed Version)—Alexander Rybak
"I Guess I'm in Love"—Clinton Kane

For the Chapter 18 vibes more than the lyrics

NOTE TO READERS:

This story takes place over four years and includes several time jumps, especially in Part I, in order to bring us to the present. It has overlapping timelines with the preceding book, *Twisted Love*.

Part I takes place through the epilogue of *Twisted Love* (the past); Part II takes place after (the present).

It is recommended but not necessary to read *Twisted Love* first in order to understand what happens.

PART I

1

BRIDGET

"SPANK ME! MASTER, SPANK ME!"

I stifled a laugh at my bodyguard Booth's face as Leather the parrot squawked in his cage. The parrot's name said all you needed to know about its previous owner's sex life, and while some found him amusing, Booth did not. He hated birds. He said they reminded him of giant flying rats.

"One day, he and Leather are going to get into it." Emma, the director of Wags & Whiskers, clucked her tongue. "Poor Booth."

I held back another laugh even as I felt a small pang in my heart. "Probably not. Booth's leaving soon."

I tried not to think about it. Booth had been with me for four years, but he was leaving for paternity leave next week and staying in Eldorra after to be closer to his wife and newborn. I was happy for him, but I would miss him. He was not only my bodyguard but a friend, and I could only hope his replacement and I had the same rapport.

"Ah, yes, I forgot." Emma's face softened. She was in her

early sixties, with short, gray-streaked hair and warm brown eyes. "Lots of changes for you in a short time, my dear."

She knew how much I hated goodbyes.

I'd been volunteering at Wags & Whiskers, a local pet rescue shelter, since my sophomore year of college, and Emma had become a close friend and mentor. Unfortunately, she, too, was leaving. She'd still be in Hazelburg, but she was retiring as the shelter director, which meant I would no longer see her every week.

"One of them doesn't *have* to happen," I said, only half-joking. "You could stay."

She shook her head. "I've run the shelter for almost a decade, and it's time for new blood. Someone who can clean the cages *without* her back and hips acting up."

"That's what volunteers are for." I gestured toward myself. I was belaboring the point, but I couldn't help it. Between Emma, Booth, and my impending graduation from Thayer University, where I was majoring in international relations—as expected of a princess—I had enough goodbyes to last me for the next five years.

"You are a sweetheart. Don't tell the others, but..." She lowered her voice to a conspiratorial whisper. "You're my favorite volunteer. It's rare to find someone of your stature who does charity because she wants to, not because she's putting on a show for the cameras."

My cheeks tinted pink at the compliment. "It's my pleasure. I adore animals." I took after my mother in that regard. It was one of the few pieces of her I had left.

In another life, I would've been a veterinarian, but in this life? My path had been laid out for me since before I was born.

"You would make a great queen." Emma stepped aside to allow a staff member with a wriggling puppy in his arms to pass. "Truly."

I laughed at the thought. "Thank you, but I have no interest in being queen. Even if I did, the chances of me wearing the crown are slim."

As the princess of Eldorra, a small European kingdom, I came closer to ruling than most people. My parents died when I was a kid—my mother at childbirth, my father in a car accident a few years later—so I was second in line to the throne. My brother Nikolai, who was four years my senior, had been training to take over for our grandfather King Edvard since he was old enough to walk. Once Nikolai had children, I would be bumped further down the line of succession, something I had zero complaints about. I wanted to be queen as much as I wanted to bathe in a vat of acid.

Emma frowned in disappointment. "Ah, well, the sentiment is the same."

"Emma!" one of the other staff members called out. "We've got a situation with the cats."

She sighed. "It's always the cats," she muttered. "Anyway, I wanted to tell you about my retirement before you heard it from anyone else. I'll still be here until the end of next week, so I'll see you on Tuesday."

"Sounds good." I hugged her goodbye and watched her rush off to deal with a literal catfight, the pang in my chest growing.

I was glad Emma hadn't told me about her retirement until the end of my shift, or it would've been in my head the whole time.

"Are you ready, Your Highness?" Booth asked, clearly eager to get away from Leather.

"Yes. Let's go."

"Yes, let's go!" Leather squawked as we exited. "Spank me!"

My laugh finally broke free at Booth's grimace. "I'll miss

you, and so will Leather." I stuffed my hands in my coat pockets to protect them against the sharp autumn chill. "Tell me about the new bodyguard. What's he like?"

The leaves crunched beneath my boots as we walked toward my off-campus house, which was only fifteen minutes away. I adored fall and everything that came with it—the cozy clothes, the riot of earthy colors on the trees, the hint of cinnamon and smoke in the air.

In Athenberg, I wouldn't be able to walk down the street without getting mobbed, but that was the great thing about Thayer. Its student population boasted so many royals and celebrity offspring, a princess was no big deal. I could live my life like a relatively normal college girl.

"I don't know much about the new guard," Booth admitted. "He's a contractor."

My eyebrows shot up. "Really?"

The Crown sometimes hired private security contractors to serve alongside the Royal Guard, but it was rare. In my twenty-one years, I'd never had a bodyguard who was a contractor.

"He's supposed to be the best," Booth said, mistaking my surprise for wariness. "Ex-Navy SEAL, top-notch recommendations, experience guarding high-profile personalities. He's his company's most sought-after professional."

"Hmm." *An American guard. Interesting.* "I do hope we get along."

When two people were around each other twenty-four-seven, compatibility mattered. A lot. I knew people who hadn't meshed with their security details, and those arrangements never lasted long.

"I'm sure you will. You're easy to get along with, Your Highness."

"You're only saying that because I'm your boss."

Booth grinned. "Technically, the Director of the Royal Guard is my boss."

I wagged a playful finger at him. "Backtalking already? I'm disappointed."

He laughed. Despite his insistence on calling me *Your Highness,* we'd settled into a casual camaraderie over the years that I appreciated. Excessive formality exhausted me.

We chatted about Booth's impending fatherhood and move back to Eldorra for the rest of our walk. He was near bursting with pride over his unborn child, and I couldn't help a small stab of envy. I was nowhere near ready for marriage and kids, but I wanted what Booth and his wife had.

Love. Passion. *Choice.* Things no amount of money could buy.

A sardonic smile touched my lips. No doubt I'd sound like an ungrateful brat to anyone who could hear my thoughts. I could get any material thing I desired with a snap of my fingers, and I was whining about love.

But people were people, no matter their title, and some desires were universal. Unfortunately, the ability to fulfill them was not.

Maybe I would fall in love with a prince who'd sweep me off my feet, but I doubted it. Most likely, I'd end up in a boring, socially acceptable marriage with a boring, socially acceptable man who only had sex missionary style and vacationed in the same two places every year.

I pushed the depressing thought aside. I had a long way to go before I even *thought* about marriage, and I'd cross that bridge when I got there.

My house came into sight, and my eyes latched onto the unfamiliar black BMW idling in the driveway. I assumed it belonged to my new bodyguard.

"He's early." Booth raised a surprised brow. "He's not supposed to arrive until five."

"Punctuality is a good sign, I suppose." Though half an hour early *might* be overkill.

The car door opened, and a large black boot planted itself on the driveway. A second later, the biggest man I'd ever seen in real life unfolded himself from the front seat, and my mouth turned bone dry.

Holy. Hotness.

My new bodyguard had to be at least six foot four, maybe even six-five, with solid, sculpted muscle packed onto every inch of his powerful frame. Longish black hair grazed his collar and fell over one gunmetal-gray eye, and his legs were so long he ate up the distance between us in three strides.

For someone so large, he moved with surprising stealth. If I hadn't been looking at him, I wouldn't have noticed him approach at all.

He stopped in front of me, and I swore my body tilted forward a centimeter, unable to resist his gravitational pull. I was also strangely tempted to run my hand through his thick dark locks. Most veterans kept their hair military-style short even after leaving the service, but clearly, he wasn't one of them.

"Rhys Larsen." His deep, gravelly voice rolled over me like a velvety caress. Now that he was closer, I spotted a thin scar slashing through his left eyebrow, adding a hint of menace to his dark good looks. Stubble darkened his jaw, and a hint of a tattoo peeked out from both sleeves of his shirt.

He was the opposite of the preppy, clean-shaven types I usually went for, but that didn't stop a swarm of butterflies from taking flight in my stomach.

I was so flustered by their appearance I forgot to respond until Booth let out a small cough.

"I'm Bridget. It's nice to meet you." I hoped neither man noticed the flush creeping over my cheeks.

I omitted the *Princess* title on purpose. It seemed too pretentious for casual, one-on-one settings.

I did, however, notice Rhys didn't address me as *Your Highness* the way Booth did. I didn't mind—I'd been trying to get Booth to call me by my first name for years—but it was another sign my new guard would be nothing like my old one.

"You have to move."

I blinked. "I beg your pardon?"

"Your house." Rhys tilted his head toward my spacious but cozy two-bedroom abode. "It's a security nightmare. I don't know who signed off on the location, but you have to move."

The butterflies screeched to a halt.

We'd met less than two minutes ago, and he was already ordering me around like *he* was the boss. *Who does he think he is?* "I've lived here for two years. I've never had an issue."

"It only takes one time."

"I'm not moving." I punctuated my words with a sharpness I rarely used, but Rhys's condescending tone grated on my nerves.

Any attraction I'd felt toward him crumbled into ash, dying the quickest death in my history with the opposite sex.

Not that it would've gone anywhere. He was, after all, my bodyguard, but it would've been nice to have eye candy *without* wanting to drop-kick him into the next century.

Men. They always ruined it by opening their mouths.

"You're the security expert," I added coolly. "Figure it out."

Rhys glowered at me beneath thick, dark brows. I couldn't remember the last time anyone had glowered at me.

"Yes, *Your Highness.*" His inflection on the last two words made a mockery of the title, and the embers of indignation in my stomach stoked brighter.

I opened my mouth to respond—with what, I wasn't sure, because he hadn't been outright hostile—but Booth cut in before I said something I would regret.

"Why don't we go inside? It looks like it's about to rain," he said quickly.

Rhys and I looked up. The clear blue sky winked back at us.

Booth cleared his throat. "You never know. Rain showers come out of nowhere," he muttered. "After you, Your Highness."

We entered the house in silence.

I shrugged off my coat and hung it on the brass tree by the door before making another stab at civility. "Would you like something to drink?"

Irritation still stabbed at me, but I hated confrontation, and I didn't want my relationship with my new bodyguard to start on such a sour note.

"No." Rhys scanned the living room, which I'd decorated in shades of jade green and cream. A housekeeper came by twice a month to deep clean, but I kept the place tidy myself for the most part.

"Why don't we get to know each other?" Booth said in a jovial, too-loud voice. "Er, I mean you and Rhys, Your Highness. We can talk needs, expectations, schedules..."

"Excellent idea." I mustered a strained smile and gestured Rhys toward the couch. "Please. Sit."

For the next forty-five minutes, we ran through logistics for the transition. Booth would remain my bodyguard until Monday, but Rhys would shadow him until then so he could get a feel for how things worked.

"This is all fine." Rhys closed the file containing a detailed breakdown of my class and weekly schedules, upcoming public events, and expected travel. "Let me be frank, Princess Bridget.

You are not my first, nor will you be the last, royal I've guarded. I've worked with Harper Security for five years, and I've never had a client harmed while under my protection. Do you want to know why?"

"Let me guess. Your dazzling charm stunned the would-be attackers into complacency," I said.

Booth choked out a laugh, which he quickly turned into a cough.

Rhys's mouth didn't so much as twitch. *Of course it didn't.* My joke wasn't Comedy Central worthy, but I imagined finding a waterfall in the Sahara would be easier than finding a drop of humor in that big, infuriatingly sculpted body.

"The reason is twofold," Rhys said calmly, as if I hadn't spoken at all. "One, I do not become involved in my clients' personal lives. I am here to safeguard you from physical harm. That is all. I am not here to be your friend, confidant, or anything else. This ensures my judgment remains uncompromised. Two, my clients understand the way things must work if they are to remain safe."

"And how is that?" My polite smile carried a warning he either didn't notice or ignored.

"They do what I say, when I say it for anything security-related." Rhys's gray eyes locked onto mine. It was like staring at an unyielding steel wall. "Understand, Your Highness?"

Forget love and passion. What I wanted most was to slap the arrogant expression off his face and knee him in the family jewels while I was at it.

I pressed the pads of my fingers into my thighs and forced myself to count to three before I responded.

When I spoke again, my voice was frigid enough to make Antarctica look like a beach paradise. "Yes." My smile sharpened. "Luckily for us both, Mr. Larsen, I have no interest in being your friend, confidant, or 'anything else.'"

I didn't bother dignifying the second part of his statement—the one about me doing what he said, when he said it—with a response. I wasn't an idiot. I'd always heeded Booth's security advice, but I'd be damned if I fed into Rhys's inflated sense of self.

"Good." Rhys stood. I hated how tall he was. His presence obliterated everything else in the vicinity until he was the only thing I could focus on. "I'll assess the house before we discuss next steps, including upgrading your security system. Right now, any teenager with access to YouTube tutorials can bypass the alarm." He shot me a disapproving glare before he disappeared into the kitchen.

My jaw dropped. "He—you..." I sputtered, uncharacteristically speechless. "Why, I never!" I turned to Booth, who was trying to melt into the giant potted plant by the front door. "You're not leaving. I forbid it."

Rhys *could not* be my bodyguard. I would murder him, and my housekeeper would murder *me* for staining the carpet with blood.

"He probably has first-day jitters." Booth looked as uncertain as he sounded. "You'll get along just fine after the, ah, transition period, Your Highness."

Perhaps...*if* we made it out of the transition period alive.

"You're right." I pressed my fingers to my temple and took a deep breath. *I can do this.* I'd dealt with difficult people before. My cousin Andreas was the spawn of Satan, and a British lord once tried to grope me under the table at Monaco's Rose Ball. He only stopped after I "accidentally" stabbed his hand with a fork.

What was one surly bodyguard compared to entitled aristocrats, nosy reporters, and evil family members?

Rhys returned. Surprise, surprise, his glower hadn't melted.

"I've detected six security vulnerabilities we need to

address ASAP," he said. "Let's start with number one: the windows."

"Which ones?" *Stay calm. Stay reasonable.*

"All of them."

Booth covered his face with his hands while I contemplated turning my hairpin into a murder weapon.

Rhys and I *definitely* weren't making it out of the transition alive.

2

RHYS

Princess Bridget von Ascheberg of Eldorra would be the death of me. If not literal death, then the death of my patience and sanity. Of that, I was certain, and we'd only been working together for two weeks.

I'd never had a client who infuriated me as much as she did. Sure, she was beautiful (not a good thing when you were in my position) and charming (to everyone except me), but she was also a royal pain in my ass. When I said "right," she went left; when I said "leave," she stayed. She insisted on spontaneously attending crowded events before I could do the advance work, and she treated my security concerns like they were an afterthought instead of an emergency.

Bridget said that was the way things had worked with Booth, and she'd been fine. I said I wasn't Booth, so I didn't give a damn what she did or didn't do when she was with him. I ran the show now.

She didn't take that well, but I didn't give a shit. I wasn't here to win Mr. Congeniality. I was here to keep her alive.

Tonight, "here" meant the most crowded bar in Hazelburg.

Half of Thayer had turned out for The Crypt's Friday night half-off specials, and I was sure the bar was over max capacity.

Loud music, loud people. My least favorite kind of place and, apparently, Bridget's *most* favorite, considering how vehement she'd been about coming here.

"So." Her redheaded friend Jules eyed me over the rim of her glass. "You were a Navy SEAL, huh?"

"Yes." I wasn't fooled by her flirty tone or party girl demeanor. I'd run in-depth background checks on all of Bridget's friends the moment I took the job, and I knew for a fact Jules Ambrose was more dangerous than she appeared. But she didn't pose a threat to Bridget, so I didn't mention what she did in Ohio. It wasn't my story to tell.

"I love military men," she purred.

"Ex-military, J." Bridget didn't look at me as she finished her drink. "Besides, he's too old for you."

That was one of the few things I agreed with her on. I was only thirty-one, so I wasn't ancient by any means, but I'd done and witnessed enough shit in my life to *feel* ancient, especially compared to fresh-faced college students who hadn't even had their first real job yet.

I'd never been fresh-faced, not even when I was a kid. I grew up in dirt and grit.

Meanwhile, Bridget sat across from me, looking like the fairytale princess she was. Big blue eyes and lush pink lips set in a heart-shaped face, perfect alabaster skin, golden hair falling in loose waves down her back. Her black top bared her smooth shoulders, and tiny diamonds glittered on her ears.

Young, rich, and regal. The opposite of me in every way.

"Negative. I love older men." Jules upped the wattage of her smile as she gave me another once-over. "And you're hot."

I didn't smile back. I wasn't dumb enough to get involved with a client's friend. I already had my hands full with Bridget.

Figuratively speaking.

"Leave the man alone." Stella laughed. *Fashion design and communications major. Daughter of an environmental lawyer and the chief of staff to a cabinet secretary. Social media star.* My brain ticked off all the things I knew about her as she snapped a photo of her cocktail before taking a sip. "Find someone your own age."

"Guys my age are boring. I'd know. I dated a bunch of them." Jules nudged Ava, the last member of Bridget's close friend group. Aside from Jules's inappropriate come-ons, they were a decent bunch. Certainly better than the friends of the Hollywood starlet I'd guarded for three excruciating months, during which I saw more "accidental" genital flashings than I'd thought I would ever see in my life. "Speaking of older men, where's your boo?"

Ava blushed. "He can't make it. He has a conference call with some business partners in Japan."

"Oh, he'll make it," Jules drawled. "You in a bar, surrounded by drunken, horny college guys? I'm surprised he hasn't—ah. Speak of the devil. There he is."

I followed her gaze to where a tall, dark-haired man cut a path through the crowd of said drunken, horny college guys.

Green eyes, tailored designer clothing, and an icy expression that made the frozen tundra of Greenland look like tropical islands.

Alex Volkov.

I knew the name and reputation, even if I didn't know him personally. He was a legend in certain circles.

The de facto CEO of the country's largest real estate development company, Alex had enough connections and blackmail material to bring down half of Congress and the Fortune 500.

I didn't trust him, but he was dating one of Bridget's best friends, which meant his presence was unavoidable.

Ava's face lit up when she saw him. "Alex! I thought you had a business call."

"The call wrapped up early, so I thought I'd swing by." He brushed his lips over hers.

"I love when I'm right, which is almost always." Jules shot Alex a sly glance. "Alex Volkov in a college bar? Never thought I'd see the day."

He ignored her.

The music changed from low-key R&B to a remix of the latest radio hit, and the bar went wild. Jules and Stella scrambled out of their seats to hit the dance floor, followed by Bridget, but Ava stayed put.

"You guys go. I'll stay here." She yawned. "I'm kinda tired."

Jules looked horrified. "It's only eleven!" She turned to me. "Rhys, dance with us. You have to make up for this...blasphemy." She gestured at where Ava was curled into Alex's side while he wrapped a protective arm around her shoulders. Ava made a face; Alex's expression didn't so much as budge. I'd seen blocks of ice show more emotion than him.

I remained seated. "I don't dance."

"You don't dance. Alex doesn't sing. Aren't you two a bundle of joy," Jules grumbled. "Bridge, do something."

Bridget glanced at me before looking away. "He's working. Come on," she teased. "Aren't Stella and I enough?"

Jules let out an aggrieved sigh. "I suppose. Way to guilt-trip me."

"I learned the subtle art of guilt-tripping in princess school." Bridget pulled her friends onto the dance floor. "Let's go."

To no one's surprise, Ava and Alex called it a night soon after, and I sat at the table by myself, keeping half an eye on the girls and the other half on the rest of the bar. At least, I tried. My gaze strayed back to Bridget and Bridget alone more often than I'd like, and not just because she was my client.

I'd known she would be trouble the minute Christian told me about my new assignment. Told, not asked, because Christian Harper dealt in orders, not requests. But we had enough of a history I could've turned down the assignment had I wanted to—and I'd really fucking wanted to. Me guarding the Princess of Eldorra when I wanted nothing to do with Eldorra? Worst idea in the history of bad ideas.

Then I'd looked at the picture of Bridget and saw something in her eyes that tugged at me. Maybe it was the hint of loneliness or the vulnerability she tried to hide. Whatever it was, it was enough for me to say yes, albeit reluctantly.

Now here I was, stuck with a charge who barely tolerated me, and vice versa.

You're a goddamned idiot, Larsen.

But as infuriating as I found Bridget, I had to admit, I liked seeing her the way she was tonight. Big smile, glowing face, eyes sparkling with laughter and mischief. None of the loneliness I'd spotted in the headshot Christian gave me.

She threw her hands in the air and swayed her hips to the music, and my gaze lingered on the bare expanse of her long, smooth legs before I tore it away, my jaw tightening.

I'd guarded plenty of beautiful women before, but when I saw Bridget in person for the first time, I'd reacted in a way I never had for my previous clients. Blood heating, cock hardening, hands itching to find out how her golden hair would feel wrapped around my fist. It'd been visceral, unexpected, and almost enough to make me walk away from the job before I started, because lusting after a client could only end in disaster.

But my pride won out, and I stayed. I just hoped I wouldn't regret it.

Jules and Stella said something to Bridget, who nodded

before they left for what I presumed was the bathroom. They'd been gone for only two minutes when a frat boy-looking type in a pink polo shirt beelined toward Bridget with a determined expression.

My shoulders tensed.

I rose from my seat right as Frat Boy reached Bridget and whispered something in her ear. She shook her head, but he didn't leave.

Something dark unfurled in my stomach. If there was one thing I hated, it was men who couldn't take a fucking hint.

Frat Boy reached for Bridget. She pulled her arm away before he could make contact and said something else, her expression sharper this time. His face twisted into an ugly scowl. He reached for her again, but before he could touch her, I stepped in between them, cutting him off.

"Is there a problem?" I stared down at him.

Frat Boy oozed the entitlement of someone who wasn't used to hearing no thanks to Daddy's money, and he was either too stupid or too arrogant to realize I was two seconds away from rearranging his face so thoroughly a plastic surgeon wouldn't be able to fix it.

"No problem. I was just asking her to dance." Frat Boy eyed me like he was thinking of taking me on.

Definitely stupid.

"I don't want to dance." Bridget stepped around me and stared Frat Boy down herself. "I already told you twice. Don't make me tell you a third time. You won't like what'll happen."

There were times when I could forget Bridget was a princess, like when she was singing off-key in the shower—she thought I couldn't hear her, but I could—or pulling an all-night study session at the kitchen table.

Now was not one of those times. Regal iciness radiated

from her every pore, and a small, impressed smirk touched my mouth before I squashed it.

Frat Boy's ugly scowl remained, but he was outnumbered, and he knew it. He shuffled off, muttering *"Stupid cunt"* under his breath as he did so.

Judging by the way Bridget's cheeks pinkened, she heard him. Unfortunately for him, so did I.

He didn't make it two feet before I grabbed him hard enough he yelped. One strategic twist of my wrist and I could break his arm, but I didn't want to cause a scene, so he was lucky.

For now.

"What did you say?" A dangerous edge bled into my voice.

Bridget and I weren't each other's favorite people, but that didn't make it okay for anyone to call her names. Not under my watch.

It was a matter of principle and basic fucking decency.

"N-nothing." Frat Boy's puny brain had finally caught up with the situation, and his face reddened with panic.

"I don't think it was nothing." I tightened my hold, and he whimpered in pain. "I think you used a very bad word to insult the lady here." Another tightening, another whimper. "And I think you better apologize before the situation escalates. Don't you?"

I didn't need to spell out what *escalates* meant.

"I'm sorry," Frat Boy mumbled to Bridget, who blinked back at him with an icy expression. She didn't respond.

"I didn't hear you," I said.

Frat Boy's eyes flashed with hate, but he wasn't stupid enough to argue. "I'm sorry," he said louder.

"For what?"

"For calling you a..." He shot a fearful look in my direction. "For calling you a bad name."

"And?" I prompted.

His brow creased in confusion.

My smile contained more threat than humor. "Say, 'I'm sorry for being a limp-dicked idiot who doesn't know how to respect women.'"

I thought I heard Bridget choke back a small laugh, but I was focused on Frat Boy's reaction. He looked like he wanted to punch me with his free hand, and I almost wished he would. It would be amusing to see him try to reach my face. I towered over him by a good eight inches, and he had shrimp arms.

"I'm sorry for being a limp-dicked idiot who doesn't know how to respect women." Resentment poured off him in waves.

"Do you accept his apology?" I asked Bridget. "If you don't, I can take this outside."

Frat Boy paled.

Bridget tilted her head, her face pensive, and another shadow of a smile ghosted my mouth. *She's good.*

"I suppose," she finally said in the tone of someone who was doing someone else a huge favor. "There's no use wasting more of our time on someone insignificant."

My amusement tempered some of the anger running hot in my veins at Frat Boy's earlier comment. "You got lucky." I released him. "If I ever see you bothering her or another woman again..." I lowered my voice. "You might as well learn how to do everything left-handed because your right one will be out of commission. Permanently. Now leave."

I didn't have to tell him twice. Frat Boy fled, his pink shirt bobbing in the crowd until he disappeared out the exit.

Good riddance.

"Thank you," Bridget said. "I appreciate you dealing with him, even though it's frustrating it took someone else to intervene before he got the hint. Isn't me saying no enough?" Her brow puckered with annoyance.

"Some people are idiots, and some people are assholes." I stepped aside to allow a group of giggling partygoers past. "Just so happened you ran into one who was both."

That earned me a small smile. "Mr. Larsen, I do believe we're having a civil conversation."

"Are we? Someone check the weather in hell," I deadpanned.

Bridget's smile widened, and I'd be damned if I didn't feel a small kick in my gut at the sight.

"How about a drink?" She tilted her head toward the bar. "On me."

I shook my head. "I'm on the clock, and I don't drink alcohol."

Surprise flashed across her face. "Ever?"

"Ever." No drugs, no alcohol, no smoking. I'd seen the havoc they wreaked, and I had no interest in becoming another statistic. "Not my thing."

Bridget's expression told me she suspected there was more to the story than I was letting on, but she didn't press the issue, which I appreciated. Some people were too damn nosy.

"Sorry that took so long!" Jules returned with Stella in tow. "The line at the bathroom was insane." Her eyes roved between me and Bridget. "Everything okay?"

"Yes. Mr. Larsen was keeping me company while you guys were gone," Bridget said without missing a beat.

"Really?" Jules arched an eyebrow. "How nice of him."

Neither Bridget nor I took the bait.

"Calm down, J," I heard Stella say as I returned to the table now that I'd handled the situation with Frat Boy and her friends were back. "It's his job to look after her."

Damn right. It was my job, and Bridget was my client. Nothing more, nothing less.

Bridget glanced at me, and our eyes locked for a split second before she looked away.

My hand flexed on my thigh.

Sure, I was attracted to her. She was beautiful, smart, and had a spine of steel. Of *course* I was attracted to her. That didn't mean I should or would act on it.

In my five years as a bodyguard, I'd never once crossed my professional boundaries.

And I wasn't about to start now.

3

BRIDGET

One of the worst things about having a round-the-clock bodyguard was living with them. It hadn't been an issue with Booth because we'd gotten along so well, but living in close quarters with Rhys put on me on edge.

Suddenly, my house seemed too small, and everywhere I looked, Rhys was *there*.

Drinking coffee in the kitchen. Stepping out of the shower. Working out in the backyard, his muscles flexing and his skin gleaming with sweat.

It all felt strangely domestic in a way it hadn't felt with Booth, and I didn't like it one bit.

"Aren't you hot in those clothes?" I asked one unseasonably warm day as I watched Rhys do push-ups.

Even though it was fall, the temperature hovered in the high seventies, and a bead of sweat trickled down my neck despite my light cotton dress and the ice-cold lemonade in my hands.

Rhys must be roasting in his black shirt and workout shorts.

"Trying to get me to take my shirt off?" He continued his pushups, not sounding the least bit winded.

Warmth that had nothing to do with the weather spread across my cheeks. "You wish." It wasn't the most inspired answer, but it was all I could think of.

Honestly, I *was* curious about seeing Rhys shirtless. Not because I wanted to sneak a peek at his abs—which I grudgingly admitted had to be fantastic if the rest of his body was anything to go by—but because he seemed so determined *not* to be shirtless. Even when he left the bathroom after a shower, he was fully dressed.

Maybe he was uncomfortable getting half-naked in front of a client, but I had a feeling not much discomfited Rhys Larsen. It had to be something else. An embarrassing tattoo, maybe, or a strange skin condition that only affected his torso.

Rhys finished his pushups and moved on to the pull-up bar. "You gonna keep ogling me, or you got something I can help you with, princess?"

The warmth intensified. "I wasn't ogling you. I was secretly praying for you to get heatstroke. If you do, I'm not helping you. I have...a book to read."

Dear Lord, what am I saying? I didn't make sense even to myself.

After our moment of solidarity at The Crypt two weeks ago, Rhys and I had settled right back into our familiar pattern of snark and sarcasm, which I hated, because I wasn't a typically snarky and sarcastic person.

A shadow of a smirk filled the corners of Rhys's mouth, but it disappeared before it blossomed into something real. "Good to know."

By now, I was sure I was beet red, but I lifted my chin and reentered the house with as much dignity as I could muster.

Let Rhys bake in the sun. I hoped he *did* get heatstroke. Maybe then, he wouldn't have enough energy to be such an ass.

Sadly, he didn't, and he had plenty of energy left to be an ass.

"How's the book?" he drawled later, when he'd finished his workout and I'd grabbed the closest book I could find before he entered the living room.

"Riveting." I tried to focus on the page instead of the way Rhys's sweat-dampened shirt clung to his torso.

Six-pack abs for sure. Maybe even an eight-pack. Not that I was counting.

"Sure seems that way." Rhys's face remained impassive, but I could *hear* the mocking bent in his voice. He walked to the bathroom, and without looking back, he added, "By the way, princess, the book is upside down."

I slammed the hardcover shut, my skin blazing with embarrassment.

God, he was insufferable. A gentleman wouldn't point something like that out, but Rhys Larsen was no gentleman. He was the bane of my existence.

Unfortunately, I was the only person who thought so. Everyone else found his grumpiness charming, including my friends and the people at the shelter, so I couldn't even commiserate with them over his bane-of-my-existence-ness.

"What's the deal with your new bodyguard?" Wendy, one of the other long-term volunteers at Wags & Whiskers, whispered. She snuck a peek at where Rhys sat in the corner like a rigid statue of muscles and tattoos. "He's got that whole strong, silent thing going on. It's hot."

"You say that, but you're not the one who has to live with him."

It was two days after the upside-down book debacle, and

Rhys and I hadn't exchanged any words since except *good morning* and *good night.*

I didn't mind. It made it easier to pretend he didn't exist.

Wendy laughed. "I'll gladly change places with you. *My* roommate keeps microwaving fish and stinking up the kitchen, and she looks nothing like your bodyguard." She tightened her ponytail and stood. "Speaking of changing places, I have to head out for study group. Do you have everything you need?"

I nodded. I'd taken over Wendy's shift enough times by now to have the routine down pat.

After she left, silence descended, so thick it draped around me like a cloak.

Rhys didn't move from his corner spot. We were alone, but his eyes roved around the playroom like he expected an assassin to pop out from behind the cat condo at any minute.

"Does it get exhausting?" I scratched Meadow, the shelter's newest cat, behind the ears.

"What?"

"Being on all the time." Constantly alert, searching for danger. It was his job, but I'd never seen Rhys relax, not even when it was just the two of us at home.

"No."

"You know you can give more than one-word answers, right?"

"Yes."

He was impossible.

"Thank God I have you, sweetie," I said to Meadow. "At least you can carry on a decent conversation."

She meowed in agreement, and I smiled. I swore cats were smarter than humans sometimes.

There was another long stretch of silence before Rhys surprised me by asking, "Why do you volunteer at an animal shelter?"

I was so startled by the fact he'd initiated a non-security-related conversation I froze mid-pet. Meadow meowed again, this time in protest.

I resumed my petting and debated how much to tell Rhys before settling on the simple answer. "I like animals. Hence, animal shelter."

"Hmm."

My spine stiffened at the skepticism in his voice. "Why do you ask?"

Rhys shrugged. "Just doesn't seem like the kinda thing you'd like to do in your free time."

I didn't have to ask to know what types of things he *thought* I liked doing in my free time. Most people looked at me and made assumptions based on my appearance and background, and yes, some of them were true. I enjoyed shopping and parties as much as the next girl, but that didn't mean I didn't care about other things too.

"It's amazing how much insight you have into my personality after knowing me for only a month," I said coolly.

"I do my research, princess." It was the only way Rhys addressed me. He refused to call me by my first name or *Your Highness.* In turn, I refused to call him anything except Mr. Larsen. I wasn't sure if it accomplished anything, since he gave no indication it bothered him, but it satisfied the petty part of me. "I know more about you than you think."

"But not why I volunteer at an animal shelter. So, clearly, you need to brush up on your research skills."

He flicked those steely gray eyes in my direction, and I thought I spotted a hint of amusement before the walls crashed down again. "Touché." He hesitated, then added reluctantly, "You're different from what I expected."

"Why? Because I'm not a superficial airhead?" My voice

chilled another degree as I tried to cover up the unexpected sting of his words.

"I never said you were a superficial airhead."

"You implied it."

Rhys grimaced. "You're not the first royal I've guarded," he said. "You're not even the third or fourth. They all acted similarly, and I expected you to do the same. But you're not..."

I arched an eyebrow. "I'm not...?"

A small smile ghosted across his face so fast I almost missed it. "A superficial airhead."

I couldn't help it. I laughed.

Me, laughing at something Rhys Larsen said. Hell must've iced over.

"My mom was a huge animal lover," I said, surprising myself. I hadn't planned on talking about my mother with Rhys, but I felt compelled to take advantage of the lull in our normally antagonistic relationship. "I got the gene from her. But the palace didn't allow pets, and the only way I could regularly interact with animals was by volunteering at shelters."

I held out my hand and smiled when Meadow pawed at it like she was giving me a low five. "I enjoy it, but I also do it because..." I searched for the right words. "It makes me feel closer to my mom. The love for animals is something only we shared. The rest of my family likes them fine, but not in the same way we do. Or did."

I didn't know what prompted my admission. Was it because I wanted to prove I wasn't volunteering as a PR stunt? Why did I care what Rhys thought of me, anyway?

Or maybe it was because I needed to talk about my mom to someone who hadn't known her. In Athenberg, I couldn't mention her without people shooting me pitying looks, but Rhys was as calm and unruffled as ever.

"I understand," he said.

Two simple words, yet they crawled inside me and soothed a part of me I hadn't known needed soothing.

Our eyes met, and the air developed another layer of thickness.

Dark, mysterious, piercing. Rhys had the kind of eyes that saw straight into a person's soul, stripping past layers of elaborate lies to reach the ugly truths underneath.

How many of my truths could he see? Could he see the girl beneath the mask, the one who'd carried a decades-long burden she was terrified to share, the one who'd killed—

"Master! Spank me, Master!" Leather chose that moment to let loose one of his notoriously inappropriate outbursts. "Please spank me!"

The spell shattered as quickly as it had been cast.

Rhys flicked his gaze away, and I looked down, my breath gusting out in a mixture of relief and disappointment.

"Mas—" Leather quieted when Rhys leveled it with a glare. The bird ruffled its feathers and hopped around its cage before settling into a nervous silence.

"Congratulations," I said, trying to shake off the unsettling electricity from a moment ago. "You might be the first person who's ever gotten Leather to stop mid-sentence. You should adopt him."

"Fuck no. I don't do foul-mouthed animals."

We stared at each other for a second before a small giggle slipped from my mouth and the iron curtain shielding his eyes lifted enough for me to spot another glimmer of humor.

We didn't talk again for the rest of my shift, but the mood between us had lightened enough that I'd convinced myself Rhys and I could have a functional working relationship.

I wasn't sure if it was optimism or delusion, but my brain always latched onto the smallest evidence things weren't so bad to cope with discomfort.

The wind nipped at the bare skin on my face and neck as we walked home after my shift. Rhys and I had fought over whether to walk or drive, but in the end, even he had to admit it would be silly to drive somewhere so close.

"Are you excited to visit Eldorra?" I asked. We were leaving for Athenberg in a few days for winter break, and Rhys had mentioned it would be his first time in the country.

I'd hoped to build on our earlier flash of camaraderie, but I'd misjudged because Rhys's face shut down faster than a house party raided by cops.

"I'm not going there for vacation, princess." He said *there* like I was forcing him to go to a prison camp, not a place *Travel + Leisure* had named the ninth-best city in the world to visit.

"I know you're not going for vacation." I tried and failed to keep the annoyance out of my voice. "But you'll have free ti—"

The high-pitched squeal of tires ripped through the air. My brain didn't have time to process the sound before Rhys pushed me into a nearby alleyway and pressed me tight against the wall with his gun drawn and his body covering mine.

My pulse kicked into high gear, both at the sudden spike of adrenaline and the proximity to him. He radiated heat and tension from every inch of his big, muscled frame, and it wrapped around me like a cocoon as a car sped past blasting music and leaking laughter out of its half-open windows.

Rhys's heartbeat thumped against my shoulder blades, and we stayed frozen in the alleyway long after the music faded and the only sound left was our heavy breathing.

"Mr. Larsen," I said quietly. "I think we're okay."

He didn't move. I was trapped between him and the brick, two immovable walls shielding me from the world. He'd braced one hand protectively against the wall next to my head, and he stood so close I could feel every sculpted ridge and contour of his body against mine.

Another long beat passed before Rhys re-holstered his gun and turned his head to look at me.

"You sure you're okay?" His voice was deep and gruff, and his eyes searched me for injuries even though nothing had happened to me.

"Yes. The car took a turn too fast. That's all." I let out a nervous laugh, my skin too hot for comfort beneath his fierce perusal. "I was more startled by you throwing me into the alley."

"That's why we should've driven." He stepped back, taking his heat with him, and cool air rushed to fill the void. I shivered, wishing I'd worn a thicker sweater. It was suddenly too cold. "You're too open and unprotected walking around like this. That could've been a drive-by."

I almost laughed at the thought. "I don't think so. Cats will fly before there's a drive-by in Hazelburg." It was one of the safest towns in the country, and most of the students didn't even *own* cars.

Rhys didn't look impressed by my analogy. "How many times do I have to tell you? It only takes once. No more walking to and from the shelter from now on."

"It was literally nothing. You're overreacting," I said, my annoyance returning full force.

His expression turned to granite. "It is my *job* to think of everything that could go wrong. If you don't like it, fire me. Until then, do what I say, when I say it, like I told you on the first day."

Any trace of our semi-truce from the shelter vanished. I wished I *could* fire him, but I didn't have a say over staffing decisions and no good reason to fire Rhys other than we didn't get along.

I'd been so sure our shelter interaction marked the beginning of a new phase in our relationship, but Rhys and I had taken one step forward and two steps back.

I pictured us flying to Athenberg with nothing except our familiar icy silence keeping us company for hours and grimaced.

It was going to be a *long* Christmas break.

4

RHYS/BRIDGET

RHYS

Bridget and I arrived in Athenberg, Eldorra's capital, four days after my no-more-walking decree opened a second front in our ongoing cold war. The plane ride had been chillier than a winter dip in a Russian river, but I didn't care.

I didn't need her to like me to do my job.

I scanned the city's near-empty National Cemetery, listening to the eerie howl of the wind whistle through the bare trees. A deep chill swept through the cemetery, burrowing past my layers of clothing and sinking deep into my bones.

Today was the first semi-free day on Bridget's schedule since we landed, and she'd shocked the hell out of me when she insisted on spending it at the cemetery.

When I saw why, though, I understood.

I maintained a respectful distance from where she knelt before two tombstones, but I was still close enough to see the names engraved on them.

Josefine von Ascheberg. Frederik von Ascheberg.

Her parents.

I'd been ten when Crown Princess Josefine died during childbirth. I remembered seeing photos of the late princess splashed across magazines and TV screens for weeks. Prince Frederik had died a few years later in a car crash.

Bridget and I weren't friends. Hell, we weren't even friendly most of the time. That didn't stop the strange tug at my heart when I saw the sadness on her face as she murmured something to her parents' graves.

Bridget brushed a strand of hair out of her face, her sad expression melting into a small smile as she said something else. I rarely gave a damn what people did and said in their personal lives, but I almost wished I were close enough to hear what made her smile.

My phone pinged, and I welcomed the distraction from my unsettling thoughts until I saw the message.

Christian: I can get you the name in less than ten minutes.

Me: No. Drop it.

Another message popped up, but I pocketed my phone without reading it.

Irritation spiked through me.

Christian was a persistent bastard who reveled in digging into the skeletons of other people's pasts. He'd been bugging me since he found out I was spending the holidays in Eldorra—he knew my hang-ups about the country—and if he weren't my boss and the closest thing I had to a friend, his face would've met my fist by now.

I told him I didn't want the name, and I meant it. I'd survived thirty-one years without knowing. I could survive thirty-one more, or however long it took before I kicked the bucket.

I returned my attention to Bridget just as a twig snapped nearby, followed by the soft click of a camera shutter.

My head jerked up, and a low growl rumbled from my throat when I spotted a telltale pouf of blond hair peeking from the top of a nearby tombstone.

Fucking paparazzi.

The asshole squeaked and tried to flee when he realized he'd been caught, but I stormed over and grabbed the back of his jacket before he could take more than a few steps.

I saw Bridget stand up out of the corner of my eye, her expression concerned.

"Give me your camera," I said, my calm voice belying my anger. Paparazzi were an inescapable evil when guarding high-profile people, but there was a difference between snapping photos of someone eating and shopping versus snapping photos of them in a private moment.

Bridget was visiting her parents' *graves*, for fuck's sake, and this piece of shit had the nerve to intrude.

"No way," the paparazzo blustered. "This is a free country, and Princess Bridget is a public figure. I can—"

I didn't wait for him to finish his sentence before I yanked the camera from his hand, dropped it on the ground, and smashed it into smithereens with my boot.

I didn't like asking twice.

He howled in protest. "That was a five-thousand-dollar camera!"

"Consider yourself lucky that's all that got broken." I released his jacket and straightened it for him, the movement more a threat than a courtesy. "You have five seconds to get out of my sight before that changes."

The paparazzo was indignant, but he wasn't stupid. Two seconds later, he'd disappeared through the trees, leaving the pieces of his now useless camera behind. A minute after that, I heard an engine turn over and a car peel out of the parking lot.

"I recognize him. He's from the *National Express.*" Bridget came up beside me, looking not at all surprised by the turn of events. "The trashiest of the tabloids. They'll probably run a story about me joining a Satanic ring or something after what you did to his camera."

I snorted. "He deserved it. I can't stand people who don't respect others' privacy."

A small smile flitted across her face, the first she'd given me in days, and the earlier chill abated. "He's paparazzi. It's his job to invade others' privacy."

"Not when people are at the fucking cemetery."

"I'm used to it. Unless I'm in the palace, there's always a chance what I do will end up in the papers." Bridget sounded resigned. "Thank you for taking care of that, even if your method was more...aggressive than I would've advised." A hint of sadness remained in her eyes, and I felt that strange tug in my chest again. Maybe it was because I related to the source of her sadness—the feeling I was all alone in the world, without the two people who were supposed to love me most by my side.

I'd never had that parental love, so despite the hole it left, I didn't understand what I was missing. Bridget *had* experienced it, at least on her father's side, so I imagined the loss was even greater for her.

You're not here to relate to her, asshole. You're here to guard her. That's it. No matter how beautiful or sad she looked, or how much I wanted to erase the melancholy cloaking her.

It wasn't my job to make her feel better.

I stepped back. "You ready? We can stay longer if you want, but you have an event in an hour."

"No, I'm ready. I just wanted to wish my parents a Merry Christmas and catch them up on my life." Bridget tucked a strand of hair behind her ear, looking self-conscious. "It sounds silly, but it's tradition, and I feel like they're listening..." She trailed off. "Like I said, it's silly."

"It's not silly." A tightness formed in my chest and spread until it choked me with memories best left forgotten. "I do the same with my old military buddies." The ones buried in the D.C. area, anyway, though I tried to make it out to the other places when I could.

I was the reason they were dead. The least I could do was pay my respects.

"Do you stay in touch with your friends from the Navy?" Bridget asked as we walked toward the exit.

I kept an eye out for any more paparazzi or ne'er-do-wells, but there was no one else around except for us and ghosts from the past.

"A couple. Not as often as I'd like."

My unit had been my family, but after what happened, it became too hard for the survivors to keep in touch. We reminded each other too much of what we'd lost.

The only person I kept in regular touch with was my old commander from my early days in the Navy.

"What made you leave?" Bridget tucked her hands deeper into her coat pockets, and I resisted the urge to draw her closer so I could share some of my body heat. It was damn cold, and her coat didn't look thick enough to protect her from the wind.

"It got too much. The deployments, the uncertainty, the funerals. Watching the men I served with die right in front of me." The tightness squeezed, and I forced myself to breathe through it before continuing. "It fucked me up, and if I hadn't left when I did..." *I would've lost what was left of myself.* I shook my head. "It's the same story as a lot of vets. I'm no one special."

We reached the car, but when I opened the door for Bridget to get in, she rested her hand on my arm instead.

I stiffened, her touch burning through my clothes more effectively than any chill or flame.

"I'm sorry," she said. "Both for what happened and for prying."

"I got out years ago. If I didn't want to talk about it, I wouldn't. It's not a big deal." I pulled my arm away and opened the car door wider, but the imprint of her touch lingered. "I don't regret my time in the Navy. The guys in my unit were like brothers to me, the closest I ever had to a real family, and I wouldn't give that up for the world. But the frontline stuff? Yeah, I was over that shit."

I'd never shared that with anyone before. Then again, I'd had no one to share it *with* except my old therapist, and I'd had enough issues to work through with her without delving into why I left the military.

"Yet you chose to be a bodyguard after," Bridget noted. "Not exactly a danger-free occupation."

"I have the skills to be a good bodyguard." A lot of former SEALs went the private security route, and Christian may have been a bastard, but he was a persuasive bastard. He'd convinced me to sign on the dotted line less than a day after I returned to U.S. soil. "Don't think I've ever been in as much danger as since you became my client, though."

Her brow scrunched in confusion, and I almost smiled.

Almost.

"My risk of rupturing an artery increased tenfold."

Bridget's confusion cleared, replaced with an odd combination of delight and exasperation. "Glad to see you found your sense of humor, Mr. Larsen. It's a Christmas miracle."

A chuckle escaped my throat, the sound so foreign I barely recognized it as my own, and something in my soul stirred, nudged awake by the reminder other things existed besides the darkness that had haunted me for so long.

Surprise flared in Bridget's eyes before she offered a tentative smile in return, and the *something* lifted its head at the further encouragement.

I shoved it back down.

A laugh was fine. Anything else was not.

"Let's go." I wiped the smile off my face. "Or we'll be late."

BRIDGET

If I could sum up my relationship with Rhys with one song, it would be Katy Perry's "Hot N Cold." One minute, we were fighting and giving each other the cold shoulder. The next, we were laughing and bonding over jokes.

Okay, *bonding* was too strong a word for what had happened in the cemetery parking lot. *Acting like normal human beings* toward each other was more accurate. And Rhys hadn't so much laughed as slipped up with a half chuckle, but maybe that constituted a laugh in his world. I couldn't picture him throwing his head back with mirth any more than I could picture The Rock dancing ballet.

But if there was one thing I'd learned over the past month, it was I needed to take advantage of the ups in our relationship when I could. So, after my planned "surprise" visit to a local high school, where I gave a speech on the importance of kindness and mental health, I brought up a topic I'd been avoiding for the past week.

"I usually stay in Eldorra longer for the holidays, but I'm glad we're heading back to campus earlier this year," I said casually as we settled into our seats at a restaurant by the school.

No answer.

Just when I thought Rhys would ignore the bait, he said, "Spit it out, princess. What do you want?"

There goes the grumpiness again.

A small frown touched my face. I felt like a kid asking permission from a parent when I talked to him, which was ridiculous, but he radiated such authority I sometimes forgot he was my employee and not the other way around.

Well, technically, he was a contractor with the palace, but that was a minor distinction.

"My favorite band is coming to D.C. in January. Ava and I already bought tickets to see them," I said.

"Band name and location."

I told him.

"I'll check it out and let you know." Rhys snapped his menu closed when our server approached. "Burger, medium rare, please. Thank you."

I placed my order and waited for the server to leave before repeating in a tight voice, "I already bought the tickets." *Translation: I'm going whether or not you like it.*

"Refundable ones, I hope." His sharp gaze glided through the restaurant, not missing a single detail about the patrons or room layout.

Aaaand there went the down in our relationship, just like clockwork.

"Your job isn't to run my life. *Stop* acting like an overprotective parent." My frustration mounted. I would rather hate him all the time than have my emotions swing back and forth like a broken gauge. It was exhausting. "How are you still employed? I'm surprised your previous clients haven't complained to your company about your...your..."

Rhys arched an eyebrow while I fumbled for the right words.

"Your overbearing tendencies," I finished lamely. *Dammit.* I needed a bigger arsenal of better insults.

"Because I'm the best. They know it, and so do you," he

said arrogantly. He leaned forward, his eyes darkening. "You think I want to parent you? I don't. If I wanted kids, I'd get myself an office job and shack up in some cookie-cutter suburban home with a picket fence and a dog. I'm in this field of work to save lives, princess. I've taken plenty of 'em, and now —" He stopped abruptly, but his words lingered in the air.

I flashed back to his words from the parking lot. *It got too much. The deployments, the uncertainty, the funerals. Watching men I considered brothers die right in front of me.*

Rhys hadn't gone into detail about what happened when he was in the military, but he didn't need to. I could only imagine.

Guilt and sympathy blossomed in my stomach and curled around my heart.

That was why I vacillated so much in my feelings toward him. I disliked Rhys's attitude and actions, but I didn't dislike *him*, because I understood why he did what he did.

It was a conundrum, and unfortunately, I didn't see a way out of it.

"It only takes one slipup," Rhys finished. "One second of distraction, and you could walk into a minefield and get blown to hell. One lapse of judgment, and you could end up with a bullet in your head." He leaned back, shutters falling over those gunmetal eyes. "So no, I don't give a fuck if you already bought tickets. I'm still gonna check the place out, and if anything looks off, you're not going. End of story."

My mind swirled with a dozen different responses, but the one that came out wasn't the one I'd intended to say at all.

"We're not in a war zone," I said gently. "We don't have to be on guard twenty-four-seven."

Rhys's jaw hardened, and even though he'd gotten out of the Navy years ago, I wondered how long he'd been fighting his own inner battles.

"*Life* is a war zone, princess. The sooner you understand that, the safer you'll be."

While my life wasn't perfect, it was far better than most people's. I knew that. I'd grown up in a bubble, protected from the worst of humanity, and I was incredibly privileged for that reason. But the idea of living life like I was at war with it every day made me indescribably sad.

"There's more to life than trying not to die." I kept my gaze on Rhys as our server brought out our orders and set them on the table. "It's just a concert. I promise I'll be fine."

5

RHYS

I'll be fine, my ass.

Bridget's words, spoken with such confidence a month ago, had come back to bite her, and by extension me, in the proverbial behind. After looking into the concert venue, I'd expressly told her *not* to attend the performance, which took place in some sketchy warehouse that should've been shut down for breaking a thousand and one safety code regulations. The building was one strong gust of wind away from collapsing.

Yet Bridget had gone against my orders and *snuck out* in the middle of the night to attend the damn concert, only to get kidnapped afterward.

That was right. Fucking kidnapped by a mercenary who'd grabbed her and Ava off the street.

It wasn't even the concert that pissed me off. If Bridget had insisted on going, I would've gone with her, because she was the client. I couldn't physically restrain her from doing what she wanted.

No, I was pissed about the fact she'd gone behind my back

and the whole kidnapping incident could've been avoided had she been honest with me.

I glanced in the rearview mirror to reassure myself Bridget was still there. As furious as I was, the sight of her in the backseat, bruised but safe, eased some of the icy terror that had gripped me since I woke up and realized she was gone.

Luckily, I'd had the foresight to plant a secret tracking chip in her phone a few weeks earlier, and it'd led me to Philadelphia, where I found her and Ava tied up and at the mercy of a gunman for hire. The whole situation resulted from a long, sordid saga involving Alex Volkov, Alex's psycho uncle who'd kidnapped Ava as leverage against his nephew, and years of secrets and revenge.

I honestly didn't give a shit about the drama. All I'd cared about was getting Bridget out of there safely, and I had, if only so I could tear her apart with my own hands.

"Ava's staying with us tonight." Bridget smoothed a hand over her friend's hair, her brow knit in a worried frown. "I don't want her to be alone."

Ava lay curled up in her lap, her sobs softer than before but still frequent enough to make me wince. I had no clue what to do around crying people, especially ones whose now ex-boyfriend confessed to lying to her during their entire relationship to get revenge on the man he'd thought had murdered his family. And that was only the CliffsNotes version of what had happened.

It was fucked-up shit, but Alex Volkov had always been a little fucked up in an *I might murder you if I'm in a bad mood* kind of way. At least everyone was alive...except for his uncle and the gunman.

"Fine." The word ricocheted through the car like a bullet.

Bridget flinched, and a small kernel of guilt took root in my stomach. It wasn't enough to drown out my anger, but it was enough to make me feel like an asshole as I pulled up in front of her house. She'd been through hell, and I should let her sleep off the events of the past twenty-hours first before I laid into her.

Keyword: should. But I'd never cared much about what I *should* do. What mattered was what I *needed* to do, and I needed Bridget to understand she couldn't fuck around with my rules. They were there to protect her, dammit, and if anything happened to her...

Fresh terror stabbed at me.

We entered the house, and I waited until Ava retreated to Bridget's room before I jerked my head to my right. "Kitchen. Now."

Bridget wrapped her arms around her chest. Another wave of anger crashed over me at the sight of the raw, reddened skin where the ropes had dug into her wrists.

If the mercenary weren't already dead, I'd carve him up myself, and I would take a longer, sweeter time than Alex had.

She walked into the kitchen and busied herself making a cup of tea, avoiding my gaze the entire time.

"Everything worked out," she said in a small voice. "I'm okay."

A vein pulsed in my temple. "You're okay," I repeated. It came out as a snarl.

We stood five feet from each other. Me in the doorway, my fists clenched at my sides; Bridget by the sink, her hands wrapped around her mug and her eyes huge in her pale face. Her usual cool, regal demeanor had disappeared, stripped bare by the events of the past twenty-four hours, and I detected a slight tremble in her shoulders.

"I made a mistake, but—"

"A mistake?" Fire scorched my veins, searing me from the inside out. "A *mistake* is showing up at the wrong class. A *mistake* is forgetting to lock the door when you leave the house. It's not getting kidnapped and almost killed by a psycho because you snuck out like a high schooler breaking curfew. I'd say that was more than a *mistake*."

My voice rose with each word until I was yelling. I'd never lost my cool with a client before, but Bridget had an uncanny ability to wring every emotion out of me, good and bad.

"It's not like I *wanted* to get kidnapped." Some of the fire returned to Bridget's eyes. "The concert was perfectly safe, despite what you said. It was only after..." She took a deep breath. "They weren't targeting me. They targeted Ava, and I happened to be with her. It could've happened at any time."

The vein in my temple pulsed harder. "No. It *couldn't* have happened anytime." I stalked toward her, my mouth flattening with grim pleasure when I saw her eyes widen in fear. *Good.* She *should* fear me, because I was about to rain hell all over her naive little parade. "Do you want to know why?"

Bridget wisely chose not to answer. For every step I took forward, she took one back until her back pressed against the wall, her white-knuckled hands strangling her mug.

"Because I *would've been there*," I hissed. "I don't give a flying fuck whether you, Ava, or fucking Big Bird was the target. If I'd been there, I would've neutralized the asshole before he ever laid a hand on you." It wasn't arrogance; it was the truth. There was a reason I was Harper Security's most in-demand agent, and it wasn't my personality. "What did I tell you when we first met?"

Bridget didn't respond.

"*What. Did. I. Tell. You?*" I planted my forearm on the wall above her head and my hand by the side of her face, effectively caging her in. We were so close I could smell her perfume— something subtle and intoxicating, like fresh flowers on a summer day—and see the dark ring around her pupils. I'd never seen eyes like that before, so deep and blue it was like staring straight into the depths of the ocean. They were the kind of eyes that lured you in and sucked you under before you knew what was happening.

The fact I noticed those stupid things in the middle of the worst day of my career only pissed me off more.

"Do what you say, when you say it." A hint of defiance tempered her whisper.

"That's right. You didn't, and you almost died." *If I hadn't gotten there when I had...*My blood iced over. Alex had been there, but that crazy fucker was as liable to shoot Bridget as he was to save her. "Do you know what could've—" I stopped mid-sentence. I was yelling again. I clenched my jaw and forced myself to take a deep breath. "I know you think I'm overbearing and paranoid, but I don't say 'no' because I want to torture you, princess. I want to protect you, and if you keep defying me at every turn, you're gonna get yourself and those around you killed. Is that what you want?"

"No." The defiance was still there, but I didn't miss the suspicious sheen in Bridget's eyes or the slight wobble in her chin.

Tough love worked, and she needed a big heap of it.

Still, I softened the harsh edge of my voice when I spoke next.

"You need to trust me. Stop fighting me on everything, and for fuck's sake, *don't* sneak behind my back. Talk to me first next time."

"Every time I try to talk to you, we end up fighting and the conversation goes nowhere." Bridget stared at me, daring me to say otherwise. I didn't. I was used to doing things my way, and my way was usually right. "Trust is a two-way street. You placed a secret chip in my phone—"

"It's a good thing I did, or you'd probably be dead right now," I growled.

She pressed her lips together, and my gaze inadvertently dropped to her mouth. Lush, pink, and capable of more sass than one would expect from a prim and proper princess. Except there was nothing prim and proper about what lay beneath her surface...or about the thoughts running through my mind.

It was the worst possible time for me to be thinking about anything remotely related to sex. She'd gotten kidnapped less than forty-eight hours ago, for Christ's sake. But adrenaline and arousal had always gone hand in hand for me, and if I were honest, there were very few instances when she didn't turn me on. Even when I was pissed at her, I wanted her.

My cock thickened, and my hands clenched into fists once more. I'd guarded the most beautiful women on the planet—movie stars, supermodels, heiresses, many of whom had made it clear they were more than willing to submit to my orders both inside and outside the bedroom—but I'd never taken them up on their offers. Never been tempted to.

Figured the one woman who'd rather see me burn than touch me was the one I ended up lusting after.

"You said I need to trust you. How can I do that if you don't trust me?" Bridget slipped into her negotiation voice, which I recognized from the countless public events I'd accompanied her to.

The voice irked me beyond belief. I'd much rather her snap at me than treat me like some damn stranger she needed to get off her back.

"I propose a compromise. Take out the chip, and I'll do what you say, when you say it, as long as it's security-related." Bridget's gaze burned into mine. "I promise."

Un-freaking-believable. She was in the wrong here, and she was negotiating with *me.*

And I was thinking of saying yes.

"Why should I believe you?" My breath came out in a harsh exhale, and a small shiver rolled through her body. I could see her nipples clearly through the thin black silk of her dress. Hard and pebbled, begging for my touch. Maybe it was because of the chill—the one thick walls and double-glazed windows couldn't quite keep out—but judging by Bridget's flushed cheeks, I wasn't the only one aware of the charged air between us.

My nostrils flared. I was still hard as a rock, and I loathed it. Loathed her, for tempting me this way. Loathed myself, for not having more self-control when it came to her.

"I don't break my promises, Mr. Larsen." Bridget insisted on calling me by my last name the same way I insisted on calling her *princess.* It irritated us both, but neither of us would back down first. *Story of our entire relationship.* "Do we have a deal?"

My jaw ticked in rhythm with my pulse. *One. Two. Three.*

My first instinct was to say *hell no.* The chip was the only reason she was alive right now. But this was the closest we'd ever gotten to a truce, and while I had no problem playing the bad cop, I would much rather work with a cooperative Bridget than breathe down her neck every day.

"Fine," I ground out. "We start with a trial period. Four months. You keep up your end of the bargain, and I back off. If you don't, I will handcuff you to me until you can't even piss in peace. Understand?"

Her lips thinned further, but she didn't argue. "A four-month trial. Fine." She hesitated, then added, "One more thing..."

Disbelief filled my veins. "You've *got* to be kidding me."

Red stained her cheeks. "You can't tell anyone what happened. Especially not the palace."

"You're asking me to lie." I was required to write up every incident with a client and submit it to Christian. The last guy who hadn't...let's just say he regretted his decision. Big time.

"Not lie, omit," Bridget corrected me. "Think about it. If my grandfather finds out what happened, you'll be fired, and your reputation will be trashed."

Appealing to my ego. *Nice try, princess.*

"My reputation can handle it." I raised an eyebrow. "I thought you'd be happy to get rid of me."

The red on her cheeks deepened. "You know what they say. Better the devil you know..."

"Hmm." Aside from the occasional civil interaction, we couldn't stand each other, my hard cock and her hard nipples notwithstanding. Lust was one thing, but if we kept this up, we'd kill each other. Not to mention, I would be breaking all sorts of rules if I kept what happened in Philadelphia secret. I should report it to Christian and let him deal with the palace. He was better at that diplomatic crap, anyway.

But the thought of walking away from Bridget and never seeing her again caused a strange twinge of discomfort. As infuriating as she was, she was one of the more interesting clients I'd had. Smarter, kinder, less spoiled and entitled.

"I don't suppose your request has anything to do with the fact you'll never breathe a second of free air again once the king finds out what happened." My breath tickled her ear, and another shiver rolled through her. "Hmm, princess?"

For someone second in line to the throne, she had quite a bit of leeway in her comings and goings. But if King Edvard found out someone had kidnapped his precious granddaughter, he would have her under lock and key.

Bridget swallowed hard. "Does it matter? We want the

same thing in the end. To maintain the status quo. You keep your reputation; I keep my freedom."

Keep the status quo? *Hardly.*

It would be so easy to give in to the desire roaring through my veins, to wrap her hair around my fist and find out just how much heat she hid beneath that cool exterior. She wanted it as much as I did. I could hear it in her ragged breaths, see it in the way she looked at me, *feel* it in the slight arch of her body against mine.

Apparently, I wasn't the only one riding high on anger and adrenaline.

Think with your big head, Larsen. Not your small one.

I closed my eyes and forced myself to silently count to five. When I opened them again, they clashed with Bridget's.

Gray storms against blue skies.

"You got yourself a deal. But if you break it or go behind my back again..." My voice lowered, dark and full of unspoken threats. "You'll find out the hard way what happens when you bargain with the devil."

6

BRIDGET

TRIAL MONTH ONE

"You're joking." I pulled the black vest out of the package, letting it dangle from my fingers like a dirty piece of laundry.

Rhys sipped his coffee and didn't look up from his newspaper. "I don't joke about safety."

"This is a *bulletproof vest*."

"I'm aware. I bought it."

Inhale. Exhale. "Mr. Larsen, please explain *why* I need a bulletproof vest. Where am I supposed to wear it, class? My next volunteer shift?"

"To protect you against bullets, and sure. If you'd like."

A muscle twitched beneath my eye. It'd been a month since we agreed to our deal, and I got it. I'd messed up. I never should've snuck out with Ava, but she'd been so down about her relationship troubles with Alex and I'd wanted to cheer her up.

Obviously, it had backfired, big time.

The kidnapping incident had thrown a bucket of cold water over my previously rosy outlook on personal safety, and I *was* committed to acting more responsibly. I hated admitting when Rhys was right because he was such an arrogant ass about it most of the time, but he put his life on the line for me every day. However, he also seemed intent on making me renege on the deal by throwing the most outrageous suggestions my way.

Like a freakin' bulletproof vest.

"I bought the vest as a just-in-case item," Rhys said mildly. "Now that you mention it, we should take it for a test spin next time you're in public."

Take out the chip, and I'll do what you say, when you say it, as long as it's security- related. I promise.

I gritted my teeth. Rhys had taken the chip out, and I didn't break my promises.

"Fine." A lightbulb flashed in my head, and a slow smile spread across my face. "I'll put it on now."

He finally raised his head, his face dark with suspicion at how easily I'd capitulated. "Where are we going?"

"Shopping."

If there was one thing Rhys hated, it was accompanying me shopping. It was such a stereotypical male weakness, and I fully intended to exploit it.

My smile widened when his face darkened further.

This is going to be fun.

An hour later, we arrived at the Hazelburg Mall, a four-story mecca of stores I could torture Rhys with. Luckily, it was winter, which meant I could hide most of the vest's bulk beneath a chunky sweater and coat.

According to Rhys, he'd bought a lighter version for me, but the vest was still hot, heavy, and awkward. I almost regretted my shopping revenge plan, but Rhys's ferocious scowl made it all worth it...until catastrophe struck.

I was trying on clothes in our dozenth boutique of the day when I got stuck in a dress. I'd accidentally grabbed the wrong size, and the unforgiving material dug into my ribcage while trapping my arms above my head. I couldn't see, and I could barely move.

"*Shit.*" I rarely cursed, but the situation called for it. One of my lifelong irrational fears was getting stuck in clothing in a store.

"What's wrong?" Rhys demanded from outside the dressing room. "Is everything okay?"

"Yes." I pinched the sides of the dress and tried pulling it up again, to no avail. "I'm fine."

Ten minutes later, I was sweating and panting from exertion and the lack of fresh air, and my arms ached from being held up so long.

Shit, shit, shit.

"What the hell is going on in there?" Rhys's annoyance came through the door, loud and clear. "You're taking too long."

I had no choice. I had to ask for help. "Can you call a sales assistant over? I need their help with a, uh, clothing issue."

There was a long pause. "You're stuck."

Flames of embarrassment licked my skin. "Just call someone over. Please."

"Can't. One employee left for lunch, and the other is six people deep at the register." Figured Rhys would be tracking everyone's movements while he waited for me. "I'll help."

If I could see my reflection, I was sure I'd see a mask of horror staring back at me. "*No.* You can't come in here!"

"Why not?"

"Because I'm..." *Half-naked. Exposed.* "Indecent."

"I've seen half-naked women before, princess. Either let me in so I can get you out of whatever jam you're in, or sit tight for the next hour because that's how long it's gonna take the cashier to get through the weekend crowd. They're moving slower than a turtle on morphine."

The universe hated me. I was sure of it.

"Fine." I forced the word out, the flames of embarrassment burning hotter. "Come in."

The dressing room doors didn't have locks, and a second later, Rhys's presence filled the tiny space. Even if I hadn't heard him enter, I would've felt him. He exuded an intense energy that charged every molecule of air until it vibrated with *him*.

Raw. Masculine. Powerful.

I held my breath as he approached, his boots soft on the linoleum floor. For someone so large, he moved with the grace of a panther.

The dress covered my chest, but my lace panties were on full display, and I tried not to think about how much skin I was showing as Rhys stopped in front of me. He was close enough I could feel the heat radiating from his body and smell his clean, soapy scent.

Tension and silence hummed in equal measure when he gripped the hem of the dress above my head and pulled. It slid up half a centimeter before it stopped again, and I winced when the fabric dug into a fresh section of flesh.

"I'm going to try from the bottom up," Rhys said, his voice detached and controlled.

Bottom up. Meaning he had to put his hands on my bare skin.

"Okay." It came out squeakier than I would've liked.

Every muscle tensed when he rested his palms on the top of my ribcage. He smoothed his thumbs briefly over the chafed area where the dress had dug into my skin before he hooked his fingers beneath the material as much as he could and inched it up.

I couldn't hold my breath anymore.

I finally exhaled, my chest heaving like it was trying to push itself deeper into Rhys's rough, warm touch. The breaths sounded embarrassingly loud in the silence.

Rhys paused. The dress was halfway up my shoulders now, enough to bare my bra-clad chest.

"Calm your breathing, princess, or this ain't gonna work," he said, sounding a touch more strained than he had a minute ago.

Heat scorched my skin, but I wrestled my breathing under control, and he resumed his work.

Another inch...another...and I was *free*.

Fresh air assaulted my nostrils, and I blinked to adjust to the light after being trapped in the dress for the past twenty minutes.

I clutched the material in front of me, my face hot with embarrassment and relief.

"Thank you." I didn't know what else to say.

Rhys stepped back, his jaw like granite. Instead of respond-ing, he picked up the bulletproof vest and T-shirt I'd worn beneath it and crooked his finger. "Come here."

"I can put it on myself."

Again, no response.

I sighed and walked to where he stood. I was too tired to fight, and I didn't resist when he slipped the T-shirt over my head, followed by the vest. I watched him in the mirror while he worked, adjusting the vest and straps until it sat comfortably on my torso. I still held my dress in front of me, angling it so it covered my underwear.

I didn't know why I bothered. Rhys showed as much interest in my half-naked form as he would in a foam mannequin.

A strange needle of irritation pricked at me.

Rhys finished fixing the vest, but before I could step away, his hands closed around my biceps in an iron grip. They were so large they easily encircled my arms.

He locked eyes with me in the mirror and lowered his head until his mouth hovered next to my ear.

My heart skipped a frantic beat, and I clutched the dress tighter in front of me.

"Don't think I don't know what you've been doing all day." Rhys's breath whispered across my skin in a dark warning. "I indulged you this time, princess, but I don't like games. Lucky for you, you passed the test." He slid his hands up my arms until they rested on my vest-clad shoulders, leaving a trail of fire in their wake. "You need to learn how to follow instructions without arguing. I don't care if you think I'm being ridiculous. A second's delay can mean the difference between life and death. I say duck, you duck. I say wear a bulletproof vest to the fucking beach, you wear the vest. Understand?"

My grip strangled the dress. "The vest was a test to see if I would wear it? That is so...*underhanded*." An entire day wasted on a stupid test. Indignation unfurled in my stomach. "I hate when you do stuff like this."

A grim half-smile touched Rhys's lips. "I'd rather you hate me alive than love me dead." He released my shoulders. "Get dressed. We're leaving."

The door shut behind him.

I could finally breathe easy again, but I couldn't stop his words from echoing in my mind.

I'd rather you hate me alive than love me dead.

The problem was, I *didn't* hate him. I hated his rules and restrictions, but I didn't hate *him*.

I wished I did.

It would make my life a lot simpler.

TRIAL MONTH THREE

"I can't go."

"What do you mean you can't go?" Jules's disbelief oozed over the line. "We've been talking about the festival since sophomore year. We have coordinated outfits. Stella rented a car! We might die on the road because she's a terrible driver—"

"I heard that!" Stella yelled in the background.

"—but she's the only one with a license."

"I know." I glared at Rhys, who sat on the couch polishing a knife like a psycho. "A certain bodyguard deemed it unsafe."

My friends and I had planned on attending the Rokbury music festival for years, and now, I had to sit it out.

"So? Come anyway. He works for you, not the other way around."

I wished I could, but we were still in the trial period of our deal, and Rhys's concerns weren't totally off base. Rokbury took place at a campground an hour and a half outside New York City, and while it looked like a blast, something inevitably went wrong every year—a festival goer's tent catching fire, a drunken group fight leading to several hospitalizations, a panic-induced stampede. It was also supposed to storm the weekend of this year's festival, which meant the campground would probably turn into a giant mud pit, but my friends were risking it, anyway.

"Sorry, J. Next time."

Jules sighed. "Tell your man he's hot as hell but a total buzzkill."

"He's not my man. He's my bodyguard." I lowered my voice, but I thought I saw Rhys pause for a millisecond before he resumed polishing his knife.

"Even worse. He's running your life and you're not getting any dick from it."

"*Jules.*"

"You know it's true." Another sigh. "Fine, I get it. We'll miss you, but we'll catch up when we're back."

"Sounds good."

I hung up and sank into the armchair, FOMO—Fear of Missing Out—hitting me hard. I'd bought the festival tickets months ago, before Rhys started working for me, and I'd had to sell them to a random junior in my political theory class.

"I hope you're happy," I said pointedly.

He didn't respond.

Rhys and I had settled into a more functional dynamic over the past three months, but there were still times I wanted to chuck a textbook at him. Like now.

When the day of the festival rolled around the following weekend, however, I woke up to the shock of my life.

I walked into the living room, bleary-eyed, only to find it transformed. The furniture had been pushed to the side, replaced with a pile of boho-printed pillows and cushions on the floor. The coffee table groaned beneath various snacks and drinks, and the Rokbury festival played out in real time on-screen. The pièce de résistance, however, was the indoor tent decorated with string lights, which looked exactly like the ones people set up on the festival grounds.

Rhys sat on the couch, which was now pressed flush against the wall beneath the window, frowning at his phone.

"What..." I rubbed my eyes. Nope, I wasn't dreaming. The tent, the snacks, they were all there. "What is this?"

"Indoor festival," he grunted.

"You put this together." It was a statement of disbelief more than a question.

"Reluctantly, and with help." Rhys glanced up. "Your redheaded friend is a menace."

Of course. That made more sense. My friends must've felt

bad I was missing the festival, so they put together a consolation party, so to speak. But something didn't add up.

"They left last night."

"They dropped everything off beforehand while you were in the shower."

Hmm, plausible. I took long showers.

Appeased and delighted, I grabbed an armful of chips, candy, and soda and crawled into the cushioned tent, where I watched my favorite bands perform their sets on the TV. The sound and picture quality was so good I *almost* felt like I was there.

Admittedly, I was more comfortable than I would've been at the actual festival, but I missed having people to enjoy it with.

An hour in, I poked my head out from the tent, hesitant. "Mr. Larsen. Why don't you join me? There's plenty of food."

He was still sitting on the couch, frowning like a bear who'd woken up on the wrong side of the cave.

"No, thanks."

"Come on." I waved my hand around. "Don't make me party alone. That's just sad."

Rhys's mouth tugged in a small smirk before he unfolded himself from his seat. "Only because you listened about not attending the festival."

This time, I was the one who frowned. "You say it like you're training a dog."

"Most things in life are like training a dog."

"That's not true."

"Show up to work, get paid. Woo a girl, get laid. Study, get good grades. Action and reward. Society runs on it."

I opened my mouth to argue, but he had a point.

"No one uses the word *woo* anymore," I muttered. I hated when he was right.

His smirk deepened a fraction of an inch.

He was too large to fit in the tent with me, so he settled on the floor next to it. Despite my cajoling, he refused to touch the food, leaving me to inhale the snacks on my own.

Another hour later, I'd ingested so much sugar and carbs I felt a little sick, and Rhys looked bored enough to fall asleep.

"I take it you're not a fan of electronic music." I stretched and winced. The last bag of salt and vinegar chips had been a bad idea.

"It sounds like a Mountain Dew commercial gone wrong."

I almost choked on my water. "Fair enough." I wiped my mouth with a napkin, unable to hide my smile. Rhys was so serious I delighted whenever his stony mask cracked. "So, tell me. If you don't like EDM, what do you like?"

"Don't listen to much music."

"A hobby?" I persisted. "You must have a hobby."

He didn't answer, but the brief flash of wariness in his eyes told me all I needed to know.

"You do have one!" I knew so little about Rhys outside his job, I latched onto the morsel of information like a starved animal. "What is it? Let me guess, knitting. No, bird watching. No, cosplay."

I picked the most random, un-Rhys-like hobbies I could think of.

"No."

"Stamp collecting? Yoga? Pokémon—"

"If I tell you, will you shut up?" he said crankily.

I responded with a beatific smile. "I might."

Rhys hesitated for a long moment before saying, "I draw, sometimes."

Of all the things I'd expected him to say, that wasn't even in the top hundred.

"What do you draw?" My tone turned teasing. "I imagine

it's a lot of armored vehicles and security alarms. Maybe a German Shepherd when you're feeling warm and fuzzy."

He snorted. "Except for the Shep, you make me sound boring as shit."

I opened my mouth, and he held up his hand. "Don't think about it."

I closed my mouth, but my smile remained. "How did you get into drawing?"

"My therapist suggested it. Said it would help with my condition. Turns out, I enjoy it." He shrugged. "Therapist is gone, but the drawing stayed."

Another bolt of surprise darted through me, both at the fact he'd had a therapist and that he spoke so freely about it. Most people wouldn't admit to it so easily.

It made sense, though. He'd served in the military for a decade. I imagined he'd lived through his fair share of scarring experiences.

"PTSD?" I asked softly.

Rhys jerked his head in a quick nod. "Complex PTSD." He didn't elaborate, and I didn't press him. It was too personal an issue for me to pry into.

"I'm disappointed," I said, changing the subject since I could *feel* him closing off again. "I'd really hoped you were into cosplay. You would make a good Thor, only with dark hair."

"Second time you've tried to get me to take my shirt off, princess. Careful, or I'll think you're trying to seduce me."

Heat consumed my face. "I'm not trying to get your shirt off. Thor doesn't even—" I stopped when Rhys let out a low chuckle. "You're messing with me."

"When you get riled up, your face looks like a strawberry."

Between the indoor festival setup and the words *your face looks like a strawberry* leaving Rhys's mouth, I was convinced I'd woken up in an alternate dimension.

"I do *not* look like a strawberry," I said with as much dignity as I could muster. "At least I'm not the one who refuses to get surgery."

Rhys's thick, dark brows lowered.

"For your permanent scowl," I clarified. "A good plastic surgeon can help you with that."

My words hung in the air for a second before Rhys did something that shocked me to my core. He laughed.

A *real* laugh, not the half chuckle he'd let slip in Eldorra. His eyes crinkled, deepening the faint, oddly sexy lines around them, and his teeth flashed white against his tanned skin.

The sound slid over me, as rough and textured as I imagined his touch would be.

Not that I had ever imagined what his touch would feel like. It was hypothetical.

"Touché." The remnants of amusement filled the corners of his mouth, transforming him from gorgeous to devastating.

And that was when another catastrophe happened, one far more disturbing than getting stuck in a too-tight dress in a public dressing room.

Something light and velvety brushed against my heart...and *fluttered.* Just once, but it was enough for me to identify it.

A butterfly.

No, no, no.

I loved animals, I truly did, but I could *not* have a butterfly living in my stomach. Not for Rhys Larsen. It needed to die immediately.

"Are you okay?" He gave me a strange look. "You look like you're about to be sick."

"Yes, I'm fine." I refocused on the screen, trying my best *not* to look at him. "I ate too much, too fast. That's all."

But I was so flustered I couldn't focus for the rest of the

afternoon, and when it finally came time for bed, I couldn't sleep a wink.

I could not be attracted to my bodyguard. Not in a way that gave me butterflies.

They'd only fluttered when we first met, but they'd died quickly after Rhys opened his mouth. Why were they returning *now*, when I had a full grasp of how insufferable he was?

Get yourself together, Bridget.

My phone buzzed with an incoming call, and I picked it up, grateful for the distraction.

"Bridge!" Jules bubbled, clearly tipsy. "How are you holding up, babe?"

"I'm in bed." I laughed. "Having fun at the festival?"

"Yessss, but wish you were here. It's not as fun without you."

"Wish I was there, too." I brushed a strand of hair out of my eye. "At least I had the indoor festival. That was a brilliant idea, by the way. Thank you."

"Indoor festival?" Jules sounded confused. "What are you talking about?"

"The setup you planned with Rhys," I prompted. "The tent, the cushions, the food?"

"Maybe I'm drunker than I thought, but you're not making any sense. I didn't plan anything with Rhys."

She sounded sincere, and she had no reason to lie. But if Rhys hadn't planned it with my friends, then...

My heart rate kicked up a notch.

Jules continued talking, but I'd already tuned her out.

The only thing I could focus on was not the one, but the thousand butterflies invading my stomach.

7

BRIDGET

TRIAL MONTH FOUR

By the time graduation rolled around a month later, I'd corralled the butterflies into a cage, but an errant one escaped twice. Once, when I saw Rhys petting Meadow, who'd worn him down with her utter cuteness. Another time when I saw the way his arm muscles flexed as he carried groceries into the house.

It didn't take a lot to get my butterflies going. *Hussies.*

Still, despite the annoying critters living rent-free in my stomach, I tried to act normal around Rhys. I didn't have another option.

"Do I get a medal or a certificate of recognition for my incredible restraint over the past four months?" It just so happened the last day of my trial period coincided with my graduation ceremony, and I couldn't resist teasing Rhys while we waited for Ava to set up the shot on her tripod. She was our unofficial photographer for group photos today.

"No. You get a tracker-free phone." Rhys scanned the quad, his suspicious gaze drilling into suburban dads with beer bellies and WASP-y moms dressed in head-to-toe Tory Burch alike.

"It's been tracker-free this entire time."

"Now it *stays* tracker-free."

Apparently, Rhys had never heard of matching someone's energy. I was trying to be lighthearted, and he was more serious than a heart attack.

Really, Bridget? **This** *is the guy you want to flutter for?*

Before I could come up with a witty response, Ava waved us over for photos, and Rhys lingered behind while I squeezed into the shot with Jules, Stella, Josh, and Ava, who was controlling the camera through an app on her phone.

I'd deal with my inappropriate flutters later. It was my last time on campus with my friends as a student, sort of, and I wanted to enjoy it.

"You stepped on my foot," Jules snapped at Josh.

"Your foot got in my way," Josh snapped back.

"Like I would intentionally put any part of my body in your way—"

"I need to Lysol myself to get your—"

"Stop it!" Stella slashed her hand through the air, startling everyone with her sharp tone. She was usually the most Zen in our group. "Or I'll post the candid and *very* unflattering photos I have of the *both* of you online."

Josh and Jules gasped. "You wouldn't," they said at the same time before glaring at each other.

I stifled a laugh while Ava, who usually played reluctant mediator between her friend and brother, cracked a smile.

Eventually, we wrangled everyone into a respectable group shot, then another, and another, until we took enough pictures to fill a half dozen albums and it was time to say goodbye.

I hugged my friends and tried to swallow the messy ball of emotion in my throat. "I'll miss you guys."

Jules and Stella were staying in D.C. to attend law school and work as an assistant at *D.C. Style* magazine, respectively, but Ava was heading to London for a year-long photography fellowship, and I was moving to New York.

I'd convinced the palace to let me stay in the U.S. as Eldorra's royal ambassador. If an event required a royal Eldorran presence, I was the person for the job. Unfortunately, as much as I wanted to stay in D.C., most of the events took place in New York, so there I would go.

I hugged Ava the hardest and longest. Between her family drama and breakup with Alex, she'd gone through hell the past few months, and she needed extra love.

"You'll adore London," I said. "It'll be a fresh start, and you have the little black book of must-visit spots I gave you."

Ava flashed a small smile. "I'm sure I will. Thanks." She glanced around, and I wondered if she was looking for Alex. No matter what she said, she wasn't over him, and she probably wouldn't be for a while.

I didn't spot him in the crowd, but I wasn't surprised. For a supposed genius, he could be quite the idiot. He'd said and done some hurtful things, but he cared about Ava. He was just either too stubborn or too stupid to act on it.

I made a mental note to pay him a visit before I left for New York. I was tired of waiting for him to pull his head out of his ass.

After one last round of hugs, my friends drifted off with their families until it was just me and Rhys.

My grandfather and Nikolai had wanted to come, but they canceled their trip at the last minute because of some diplomatic crisis with Italy. They were both distraught over missing my graduation, but I'd assured them it was okay.

And it was. I understood the responsibilities that came with the crown and the heir. But it didn't mean I couldn't wallow in a bit of self-pity.

"You ready?" Rhys asked, his tone a shade gentler than usual.

I nodded, tamping down the flicker of loneliness in my stomach as we walked to our car. Graduation, moving cities, saying goodbye to everything I'd loved for the past four years...it was too much change in too short a time.

I was so lost in my thoughts I didn't notice we were heading into the city instead of home until I spotted the Washington Monument glowing in the distance.

"Where are we going?" I straightened in my seat. "You're not dragging me to some warehouse so you can butcher me, are you?"

I couldn't see Rhys's face, but I could *hear* his eye roll. "If I wanted to do that, I would've done so the day after meeting you."

I frowned, more insulted than reassured, but my tart reply died on my lips when he added, "Figured you wouldn't want to stay home and order takeout on graduation night."

I *didn't* want to stay home on graduation night. It seemed so sad, but it seemed sadder to eat dinner by myself in some fancy restaurant.

I had Rhys, but he was paid to be there, and he wasn't exactly a chatty conversationalist. And yet...he knew exactly what I needed without me uttering a word.

Another butterfly escaped in my stomach before I shoved it back into its cage.

"Where are we going, then?" I repeated my question, intrigue edging out my earlier melancholy.

He pulled up in front of a strip mall. There weren't many of those in D.C., but this one contained all the trappings of a suburban outpost, including a Subway, a nail salon, and a restaurant named Walia.

"Best Ethiopian spot in the city." Rhys cut the engine.

My heart tripped. Ethiopian was my favorite cuisine. Of course, Rhys could've chosen it at random without remembering the fact, which I'd let slip one time during a drive home.

"I don't believe you," I said. "Best Ethiopian is on U Street."

It wasn't. One taste of Walia's *injera* sourdough flatbread and *tibs wot* beef half an hour later, and I knew Rhys was right. It *was* the best Ethiopian spot in the city.

"How did I not know about this place?" I demanded, breaking off another piece of *injera* and using it to scoop up the meat. In Ethiopian culture, the bread was an eating utensil as much as it was food.

"It flies under most people's radar. I guarded an Ethiopian VIP for a few months. Only reason I found out about this place."

"You're full of surprises." I chewed my food, thinking. After I swallowed, I said, "Since it's my graduation night, let's play a game. It's called Getting to Know Rhys Larsen."

"Sounds boring." Rhys flicked his eyes around the restaurant. "I already know Rhys Larsen."

"I don't."

He heaved a long-suffering sigh, and I fought the urge to cheer because the sigh meant he was about to cave. It didn't happen often, but when it did, I reveled in it like a kid in a candy store.

"Fine." Rhys sat back and folded his hands over his stomach, the picture of grouchiness. "Only because it's your graduation night."

I smiled.

Bridget: one. Rhys: zero.

For the rest of dinner, I peppered him with questions I'd always wanted to ask, starting with the small stuff.

Favorite food? Baked sweet potatoes.

Favorite color? Black. (Shocker).

Favorite movie? *Reservoir Dogs.*

After I exhausted the basics, I moved on to more personal territory. To my surprise, he answered most of my questions without complaint. The only ones he skirted were those about his family.

Biggest fear? Failure.

Biggest dream? Peace.

Biggest regret? Inaction.

Rhys didn't elaborate on his vague answers, and I didn't push him. He'd already given me more than I'd expected, and if I pushed too hard, he would shut down.

Eventually, I worked up the courage to bring up something that had been needling me for the past few weeks.

The honey wine helped. It made me all warm and buzzy, and it eroded my inhibitions with every sip.

"About the indoor festival you set up for Rokbury..."

Rhys stabbed at a piece of beef, ignoring the table of women ogling him from the corner. "What about it?"

"My friends didn't know what I was talking about when I mentioned it to them." I'd checked with Ava and Stella too, just in case, and they'd both stared at me like I'd grown two heads.

"So?"

I finished my wine, my nerves jumping all over the place. "So, you said my friends helped you with the setup."

Rhys chewed quietly, not answering me.

"Did you..." A strange lump formed in my throat. I blamed it on too much food. "Did you come up with the idea? And set it up all by yourself?"

"It's not a big deal." He continued eating without looking at me.

I'd known it was him since my phone call with Jules, but hearing him confirm it was a whole other matter.

The butterflies in my stomach escaped all at once, and the lump in my throat grew. "It *is* a big deal. It was...very thoughtful. As was tonight. Thank you." I spun my silver ring around my finger. "But I don't understand why you didn't tell me it was your idea, or why you did it all. You don't even like me."

Rhys's brow scrunched. "Who said I didn't like you?"

"*You.*"

"I never said that."

"You implied it. You're always so grumpy and scolding me."

"Only when you don't listen."

I bit back a tart reply. The night was going so well, and I didn't want to ruin it, even if he made me feel like a misbehaving child sometimes.

"I didn't tell you because it was inappropriate," he added gruffly. "You're my client. I should not be...doing those types of things."

My heart crashed against my ribcage. "But you did it, anyway."

Rhys's mouth flattened into a displeased line, like he was angry at his own actions. "Yes."

"Why?"

He finally lifted his eyes to meet mine. "Because I understand what it's like to be alone."

Alone.

The word struck me harder than it should've. I wasn't physically alone—I was surrounded by people all day, every day. But no matter how much I tried to pretend I was a normal college student, I wasn't. I was the Princess of Eldorra. It meant glamour and celebrity, but it also meant bodyguards and round-the-clock protection, bulletproof vests and a life that was planned, not lived.

The other royals I knew, including my brother, were content with living life in a fishbowl. I was the only one clawing at my insides, desperate to escape my own skin.

Alone.

Rhys somehow recognized that inherent truth about me before I did.

"Thoughtful *and* observant." He was observant of his surroundings, but I hadn't expected him to be so observant of *me* he saw parts of me I'd hid from myself. "You really *are* full of surprises."

"Don't tell anyone, or I'll have to kill them."

The tension cracked, and a small, genuine smile blossomed on my lips. "Humorous too. I'm convinced aliens have hijacked your body."

Rhys snorted. "I'd like to see them try."

I didn't ask any more questions after that, and Rhys didn't offer any more answers. We finished our dinner in companionable silence, and after he paid—he'd refused to entertain the idea of splitting the check—we walked off the food in a nearby park.

"You're really letting me walk around here without my vest?" I teased. The bulletproof vest hung in the back of my closet, unused since our trip to the mall.

An image of Rhys's hands on my skin in the dressing room flashed through my mind, and my face heated.

Thank God it's dark out.

"Don't make me regret it." Rhys paused before adding, "You've proven you can handle yourself without me breathing down your neck." He said it almost grudgingly.

I *had* been more careful with my actions in recent months, even without Rhys's explicit instructions, but I hadn't expected him to notice. He'd never said anything about it until now.

A pleasant warmth unfurled in my stomach. "Mr. Larsen, we might not kill each other after all."

His mouth twitched.

We continued walking through the park, where we passed couples making out on the benches, teens huddled by the fountain, and a busker playing his heart out on the guitar.

I wanted to stay in that peaceful moment forever, but dinner, alcohol, and a long day conspired to drive exhaustion into my bones, and I couldn't hold back a small yawn.

Rhys noticed instantly. "Time to go, princess. Let's get you to bed."

Maybe it was because I was delirious from fatigue and the high emotion of the day, or maybe it was because of my recent dry spell with the opposite sex, but a mental image of him "getting me to bed" flashed through my mind, and my entire body flushed.

Because in my imagination, we were doing anything *but* sleeping.

Images of Rhys naked, on top of me, under me, behind me... they all crowded my brain until my thighs clenched and my clothes rasped against my skin. My tongue suddenly felt too thick, the air too thin.

My first sexual fantasy about him, and he was standing less than five feet away, staring right at me.

I was a princess, he was my bodyguard.

I was twenty-two, he was thirty-two.

It was wrong, but I couldn't stop.

Rhys's eyes darkened. Mind reading didn't exist, but I had the eerie sense he could somehow crawl inside my brain and pick out every dirty, forbidden thought I had about him.

I opened my mouth—to say what, I wasn't sure, but I had to say *something* to break the dangerously charged silence.

Before I could utter a word, however, a gunshot ripped through the night, and chaos ensued.

8

BRIDGET/RHYS

BRIDGET

One second, I was standing. The next, I was on the ground, my cheek pressed to the grass while Rhys shielded my body with his, and screams rang out through the park.

It all happened so quickly it took my brain several beats to catch up with my pounding pulse.

Dinner. Park. Gunshots. Screams.

Individual words that made sense on their own, but I couldn't string them together into a coherent thought.

There was another gunshot, followed by more screams.

Above me, Rhys let out a curse so low and harsh I felt it more than I heard it.

"On the count of three, we're running for the tree cover." His steady voice eased some of my nerves. "Got it?"

I nodded. My dinner threatened to make a reappearance, but I forced myself to focus. I couldn't freak out, not when we were in full view of the shooter.

I saw him now. It was so dark I couldn't make out many details except for his hair—longish and curly on top—and his clothes. Sweatshirt, jeans, sneakers. He looked like any of the dozens of guys in my classes at Thayer, and that made him all the more terrifying.

He had his back to us, looking down at something, *someone* —a victim—but he could turn around any second.

Rhys shifted so I could push myself onto my hands and knees, keeping low as I did so. He'd drawn his gun, and the grouchy but thoughtful man from dinner had disappeared, replaced by a stone-cold soldier.

Focused. Determined. Lethal.

For the first time, I glimpsed the man he'd been in the military, and a shiver snaked down my spine. I pitied anyone who had to face him on the battlefield.

Rhys counted down in the same calm voice. "One, two...*three.*"

I didn't think. I ran.

Another gunshot fired behind us, and I flinched and stumbled over a loose rock. Rhys grabbed my arms with firm hands, his body still shielding me from behind, and guided me to the thicket of trees at the edge of the park. We couldn't reach the exit without passing directly by the shooter, where there was no cover at all, so we would have to wait until the police arrived.

They had to be here soon, right? One of the other people in the park must've called them by now.

Rhys pushed me down and behind a large tree.

"Wait here and do *not* move until I give the okay," he ordered. "Most of all, don't let anyone see you."

My heart rate spiked. "Where are you going?"

"Someone has to stop him."

A cold sweat broke out over my body. He couldn't possibly be saying what I thought he was saying.

"It doesn't have to be *you*. The police—"

"It'll be too late by the time they get here." Rhys looked grimmer than I'd ever seen him. *"Don't. Move."*

And he was gone.

I watched in horror as Rhys crossed the wide-open expanse of grass toward the shooter, who had his gun aimed at someone on the ground. A bench blocked my view of who the victim was, but when I crouched lower, I could see beneath the bench, and my horror doubled.

It wasn't one person. It was *two*. A man and, judging by the size of the person next to him, a child.

Now I knew why Rhys had that expression on his face before he left.

Who would target a *child?*

I pressed my fist to my mouth, fighting the urge to throw up. Less than an hour ago, I'd been teasing Rhys over bread and wine and thinking of all the things I still needed to pack before we left for New York. Now, I was hiding behind a tree in a random park, watching my bodyguard run toward possible death.

Rhys was an experienced soldier and guard, but he was still human, and humans died. One minute, they were there. The next, they were gone, leaving behind nothing more than an empty, lifeless shell of the person they used to be.

"Sweetheart, I'm afraid I have bad news." My grandfather's eyes looked bloodshot, and I clutched my stuffed giraffe to my chest, fear spiraling through my body. My grandfather never cried. *"It's your father. There's been an accident."*

I blinked away the memory in time to see the man on the ground turn his head a fraction of an inch. He'd spotted Rhys sneaking up behind the shooter.

Unfortunately, the small motion was enough to tip off the gunman, who spun around and fired a third shot at the same time Rhys discharged his gun.

A cry left my mouth.

Rhys. Shot. Rhys. Shot.

The words cycled through my brain like the world's most horrifying mantra.

The shooter crumpled to the ground. Rhys staggered, but he remained standing.

In the distance, police sirens wailed.

The entire scene, from the first shot to now, had played out in less than ten minutes, but terror had a way of stretching time out until each second contained an eternity.

Dinner felt like years ago. Graduation might as well have happened in another lifetime.

Instinct propelled me to my feet, and I ran toward Rhys, my heart in my throat. *Please be okay.*

When I reached him, he'd disarmed the gunman, who lay bleeding and moaning on the ground. A few feet away, the man the shooter had been targeting also lay bleeding, his face pale beneath the moonlight. The child, a boy who looked about seven or eight, knelt by his side, his eyes huge and terrified as he stared at me and Rhys.

"What the *hell* are you doing?" Rhys bit out when he saw me.

I scanned him frantically for injuries, but he was standing and talking and grumpy as ever, so he couldn't be *too* hurt.

The boy, on the other hand, needed reassuring.

I ignored Rhys's question for now and crouched until I was eye level with the boy.

"It's okay," I said gently. I didn't move any closer, not wanting to spook him further. "We won't hurt you."

He clutched what I assumed was his father's arm tighter. "Is my dad going to die?" he asked in a small voice.

A clog of emotion formed in my throat. He was around my age when my dad died, and—

Stop. This isn't about you. Focus on the moment.

"The doctors will be here soon, and they'll fix him right up." I hoped. The man was fading in and out of consciousness, and blood oozed around him, staining the boy's sneakers.

Technically, the EMTs were coming, not doctors, but I wasn't about to explain the distinction to a traumatized kid. "Doctors" sounded more reassuring.

Rhys knelt next to me. "She's right. The doctors know what they're doing." He spoke in a soothing voice I'd never heard from him before, and something squeezed my chest. Hard. "We'll stay with you until they get here. How does that sound?"

The boy's lower lip wobbled, but he nodded. "Okay."

Before we could say anything else, a bright light shone on us, and a voice blared through the park.

"Police! Put your hands up!"

RHYS

Questions. Medical checkups. More questions, plus a few claps on the back for being a "hero."

The next hour tested my patience as nothing had before... except for the damned woman in front of me.

"I told you to *stay put*. It was a simple instruction, princess," I growled. The sight of her running toward me while the shooter was still out in the open had sent more panic crashing through me than having a gun pointed at my face.

It didn't matter that I'd disarmed the shooter. What if he had a second gun I'd missed?

Terror raked its claws down my spine.

I could handle getting shot. I couldn't handle Bridget getting hurt.

"You were shot, Mr. Larsen." She crossed her arms over her

chest. I sat in the back of an open ambulance while she stood before me, stubborn as ever. "You'd already neutralized the gunman, and I thought you were going to *die*."

Her voice wobbled at the end, and my anger dissipated.

Other than my Navy buddies, I couldn't remember the last time anyone *really* cared about whether I lived or died. But Bridget did, for some unknown reason, and it wasn't just because I was her bodyguard. I saw it in her eyes and heard it in the faint waver of her usually cool, crisp voice.

And I'd be damned if the knowledge didn't hit me harder than a bullet to the chest.

"I'm fine. Bullet grazed me, is all. Didn't even go under the skin." The EMTs had bandaged me up, and I'd be good as new in two or three weeks.

The shooter had been surprised and fired using instinct, not aim. A quick dodge and I'd escaped what would've been a much nastier wound to my shoulder.

The police had hauled him into medical custody. They were still investigating what happened, but from what I'd gathered, the shooter had deliberately targeted the kid's father. Something about a business deal gone wrong and bankruptcy. The shooter had been high as a kite, to the point where he hadn't cared about exacting his revenge in a park full of people.

Thankfully, he'd also been so high he kept rambling about how the kid's father had done him wrong instead of shooting to kill.

The ambulances had taken the kid and his father away a while ago. The father had suffered heavy blood loss, but he'd stabilized and would pull through. The kid was okay too. Traumatized, but alive. I'd made it a point to check on him before they left.

Thank God.

"You were bleeding." Bridget brushed her fingers over the

bandaged wound, her touch searing straight through the gauze into my bones.

I stiffened, and she froze. "Did that hurt?"

"No." Not in the way she'd meant anyway.

But the way she was looking at me, like she was afraid I might disappear if she blinked? It made my heart ache like she'd ripped off a piece of it and kept it for herself.

"Bet this wasn't the way you pictured your graduation night going." I rubbed a hand over my jaw, my mouth twisting into a grimace. "We should've gone straight home after dinner."

I'd used the lame excuse of walking off our food to justify the trip to the park, but in truth, I'd wanted to extend the night because when we woke up, we would go back to what we were. The princess and her bodyguard, a client and her contractor.

It was all we could be, but that hadn't stopped crazy thoughts from infiltrating my mind during dinner. Thoughts like how I could've stayed there with her all night, even though I normally hated answering questions about my life. Thoughts about whether Bridget tasted as sweet as she looked and how much I wanted to strip away her cool demeanor until I reached the fire underneath. Bask in its warmth, let it burn away the rest of the world until we were the only ones left.

Like I said, crazy thoughts. I'd shoved them aside the second they popped up, but they lingered in the back of my mind still, like the lyrics to a catchy song that wouldn't go away.

My grimace deepened.

Bridget shook her head. "No. It was a good night until... well, this." She waved her hand around the park. "If we'd gone home, the kid and his dad might have died."

"Maybe, but I fucked up." It didn't happen often, but I could admit it when it did. "My number one priority as a bodyguard is to protect you, not play savior. I should've gotten you out of here and left it at that, but..." A muscle rolled in my jaw.

Bridget waited patiently for me to finish. Even with her hair mussed and dirt smearing her dress from when I'd pushed her onto the ground, she could've passed for an angel in the fucked-up hell of my life. Blonde hair, ocean eyes, and a glow that had nothing to do with her outer beauty and everything to do with her inner one.

She was too beautiful to be touched by any part of my ugly past, but something compelled me to continue.

"When I was in high school, I knew a kid." The memories unfolded like a blood-stained film, and a familiar spear of guilt stabbed at my gut. "Not a friend, but the closest thing I had to one. We lived a few blocks away from each other, and we'd hang out at his house on the weekend." I'd never invited Travis to my house. I hadn't wanted him to see what it was like living there.

"One day, I went over and saw him getting mugged at gunpoint right in his front yard. His mom was at work, and it was a rough neighborhood, so those things happened. But Travis refused to hand over his watch. It'd been a gift from his old man, who died when he was young. The mugger didn't take kindly to the refusal and shot him right there in broad daylight. No one, including me, did a damn thing about it. Our neighborhood had two rules if you wanted to survive: one, keep your mouth shut, and two, mind your own business."

An acrid taste filled my mouth. I remembered the sight and sound of Travis's body hitting the ground. The blood oozing from his chest, the surprise in his eyes...and the betrayal when he saw me standing there, watching him die. "I went home, threw up, and promised myself I would never be such a coward again."

What's your biggest regret? Inaction.

I'd joined the military to gain a purpose and family I'd

never had. I became a bodyguard to absolve myself of sins I could never cleanse.

Lives saved in exchange for lives taken, directly or indirectly.

What's your biggest fear? Failure.

"It wasn't your fault," Bridget said. "You were a kid too. There was nothing you could've done against an armed attacker. If you'd tried, you might have died too."

There it was. Another hitch on the word *died.*

Bridget looked away, but not before I caught the suspicious sheen in her eyes.

I clenched and unclenched my fists.

Don't do it. But I'd already fucked up multiple times tonight. What was one more?

"Come here, princess." I opened one arm. She stepped into it and buried her face in my non-injured shoulder. It was the most vulnerable we'd been in front of the other since we met, and it chipped away at something inside me.

"It's all right." I patted her awkwardly on the arm. I was shit at comforting people. "It's over. Everyone's fine except for the shithead with the gun. Though I guess tonight was a bad night to leave the bulletproof vest at home."

Her choked laugh vibrated through my body. "Is that a joke, Mr. Larsen?"

"An observation. I don't—"

"Joke," she finished. "I know."

We sat in the back of the ambulance for a while longer, watching the police seal off the crime scene while I tried to tamp down the fierce protectiveness welling in my chest. I was protective of all my clients, but this was different. More visceral.

Part of me wanted to push her far away from me, and

another part wanted to drag her into my arms and keep her as mine.

Except I couldn't.

Bridget was too young, too innocent, and too off-limits, and I'd damn well better not forget that.

9

BRIDGET

SOMETHING CHANGED THE NIGHT OF MY GRADUATION. Perhaps it was the shared trauma, or the fact Rhys had voluntarily opened up to me about his past, but the longstanding antagonism between us transformed into something else— something that kept me awake late at night and drove the butterflies in my stomach nuts.

It wasn't a *crush*, exactly. More like attraction paired with... curiosity? Fascination? Whatever it was, it put me on edge, because on the list of the worst ideas I could have, sneaking out and getting kidnapped was number two. Developing non-platonic feelings for my bodyguard was number one.

Luckily, my schedule in New York kept me so busy I barely had time to breathe, much less indulge in inappropriate fantasies.

Rhys and I moved to Manhattan three days after graduation, and the following summer was a whirlwind of charity board meetings, social functions, and house hunting.

By the time August rolled around, I'd signed the lease on a beautiful Greenwich Village townhouse, worn down two pairs of heels from trekking through the city, and met everyone on the social circuit, some of whom I wished I *hadn't* met.

"It's slipping." Rhys scanned the surrounding crowd.

We were at the opening for a new Upper East Side exhibit celebrating Eldorran artists, which normally wouldn't be a big deal, but the guest list included action movie star Nate Reynolds and the paparazzi were out in full force.

"What?" I said through my smile as I posed for the cameras. The appearances got tiresome after a while. There was only so much smiling, waving, and small talk a girl could stand before she keeled over from boredom, but they were part of my job, so I grinned and bore it. Literally.

"Your smile. It's slipping."

He was right. I hadn't even noticed.

I re-upped the wattage of my smile and tried not to yawn. *God, I can't wait till I'm home.* I still had a luncheon, two interviews, a board meeting for the New York Animal Rescue Foundation, and a couple of errands to run, but after that...PJs and sweet sleep.

I didn't *hate* my job, but I wished I could do something more meaningful than be a walking, talking mannequin.

And so it went. Day after day, month after month of the same thing. Fall turned into winter, then into spring and summer, then fall again.

Rhys stood next to me through it all, stern and grumpy as always, but he'd dialed down the overbearing attitude. For him, anyway. Compared to a normal person, he was still overprotective to the point of neuroticism.

I loved and hated the shift in equal measure. Loved it because I had more freedom, hated it because I could no longer use my irritation as a shield against whatever was crackling between us.

And there *was* a thing. I just wasn't sure whether I was the only one who saw it, or if he did too.

I didn't ask. It was safer that way.

"Do you ever think about doing anything except body-guarding?" I asked on a rare night in. For once, I had no plans other than a date with the TV and ice cream, and I loved it.

It was September, almost two years since Rhys and I first met and over a year since I moved to New York. I'd gone full out with the seasonal decorations, including a fall wreath over the fireplace, earth-toned cushions and blankets, and a mini pumpkin centerpiece for the coffee table.

Rhys and I were watching a screwball comedy that'd popped up in my Netflix recommendations. He sat ramrod straight, fully dressed in his work outfit while I was curled up with my feet on the sofa and a pint of ice cream in my hand.

"Bodyguarding?"

"It's a word," I said. "If it's not, I'm declaring it one by royal decree."

He smirked. "You would. And to answer your question, no, I don't. The day I do is the day I stop 'bodyguarding.'"

I rolled my eyes. "It must be nice to see everything in black and white."

Rhys's gaze lingered on me for a second before he looked away. "Trust me," he said. "Not everything is black and white."

Inexplicably, my heart skipped a beat, but I forced myself not to demand he tell me what he meant. It probably meant nothing. It was a throwaway line.

Instead, I refocused on the movie and concentrated on *not* looking at the man sitting next to me.

It worked. Sort of.

I laughed at something a character said, and I noticed Rhys looking at me out of the corner of my eye.

"It's nice," he said.

"What?"

"Your real smile."

Forget a skipped beat. My heart skipped a whole song.

This time, however, I covered it up by pointing my spoon at him. "That was a compliment."

"If you say so."

"Don't try to play it off." I was proud of how normal I sounded when my insides were doing things that were anything *but* normal. Fluttering, skipping, twisting. My doctor would have a field day. "We've passed a milestone. Rhys Larsen's first compliment to Bridget von Ascheberg, and it only took two years. Mark it down."

Rhys snorted, but humor filled his eyes. "One year and ten months," he said. "If we're counting."

Which he was.

If my heart skipped any more songs, it'd have no playlist left.

Not good. Not good at all.

Whatever I felt toward Rhys, it couldn't develop past what it was now. So, in an effort to rid myself of my increasingly disturbing reactions to my bodyguard, I agreed to go on a date with Louis, the son of the French ambassador to the United Nations, when I ran into him at an event a month after my movie night with Rhys.

Louis showed up for our date at seven o'clock sharp with a bouquet of red flowers and a charming smile, which wilted when he saw the scowling bodyguard standing so close behind me I could feel the heat from his body.

"These are for you." Louis handed me the flowers while keeping a wary eye on Rhys. "You look beautiful."

A low growl rumbled behind me, and Louis noticeably gulped.

"Thank you, they're lovely," I said with a gracious smile. "Let me put them in water and I'll be right back."

My smile dropped when I turned my back to Louis and faced Rhys. "Mr. Larsen, please follow me." Once we entered the kitchen, I hissed, "*Stop* threatening my dates with your gun."

I hadn't needed to see him to know he'd probably pushed his jacket aside just enough to flash his weapon.

Louis wasn't the first guy I'd dated in New York, though the last time I'd gone on a date had been months ago. Rhys kept scaring off my romantic prospects, and half the men in the city were afraid to ask me out for fear he would shoot them.

It hadn't bothered me until now because I hadn't cared for my previous dates, but it was annoying when I was actively trying to move on from whatever weird hold Rhys had on me.

Rhys's glare intensified. "He's wearing shoe lifts. He deserves to be threatened."

I pressed my lips together, but a quick glance at Louis' feet through the kitchen doorway confirmed Rhys's observation. I *thought* he seemed taller. I had nothing against shoe lifts per se, but three inches seemed excessive.

Unfortunately, while I could overlook the shoe lifts, I couldn't overlook the utter lack of chemistry between us.

Louis and I dined at a lovely French restaurant, where I struggled not to fall asleep while he rambled on about his summers in St. Tropez. Rhys sat at the next table with a glower so dark the diners on his other side requested to move tables.

By the time dinner ended, Louis was so flustered by the menacing presence less than three feet away he knocked over his wineglass and nearly caused a server to drop his tray of food.

"It's all right," I said, helping a mortified Louis clean up the mess while the server fussed over the stained linen tablecloth. "It was an accident."

I glared at Rhys, who stared back at me without a hint of remorse.

"Of course." Louis smiled, but the mortification in his eyes remained.

When we finished cleaning up, he left a generous tip for the server and bid me a polite good night. He didn't ask me on a second date.

I wasn't sad about it. I was, however, pissed at a certain gray-eyed pain in my butt.

"You scared Louis half to death," I said when Rhys and I returned home. I couldn't control the anger from seeping into my voice. "Next time, try not to unnerve my date so much he spills his drink all over himself."

"If he scares that easily, he's not worthy of being your date." Rhys had dressed up to adhere to the restaurant's dress code, but the tie and dinner jacket couldn't mask the raw, untamed masculinity rolling off him in potent waves.

"You were armed and glaring at him like he killed your dog. It's hard *not* to be nervous under those conditions." I tossed my keys on the side table and slipped off my heels.

"I don't have a dog."

"It was a metaphor." I unpinned my hair and ran my hand through the waves. "Keep it up and I'll end up like one of those spinsters from historical romance novels. You've scared off every date I've had in the past year."

One thing that hadn't changed after all this time? My refusal to call him anything except Mr. Larsen, and his refusal to call me anything except *princess*.

Rhys's scowl deepened. "I'll stop scaring them off once you get better taste in men. No wonder your love life is in the dumps. Look at the twerps you insist on going out with."

I bristled. My love life was *not* in the dumps. It was close, but it wasn't there yet. "You're one to talk."

He crossed his arms over his chest. "Meaning?"

"Meaning I haven't seen you date anyone since you started working for me." I shrugged off my jacket, and his gaze slid to my bared shoulders for a fraction of a second before returning to my face. "You're hardly qualified to give me dating advice."

"I don't date. Doesn't mean I can't spot worthless idiots when I see 'em."

I paused, startled by his admission. While Rhys was always by my side during the day, he was off duty after I turned in for the night. Sometimes he stayed in, sometimes he didn't. I'd always assumed he was...busy on the nights he didn't.

A strange mixture of relief and disbelief coursed through me. Disbelief, because while Rhys wasn't the most charming guy on the planet, he *was* gorgeous enough for most women to overlook his surly attitude. Relief, because...well, I'd rather not examine that reason too closely.

"You've been celibate for two years?" The question slipped out before I could think it through, and I regretted it instantly.

Rhys arched an eyebrow, his scowl morphing into a smirk. "You asking about my sex life, princess?"

Embarrassment scorched my cheeks, both at my inappropriate question and at hearing the word "sex" leave his mouth. "I did no such thing."

"I may not have attended a fancy college like you, but I can read subtext." Amusement flashed in those gunmetal eyes. "For the record, dating and sex aren't the same thing."

Right. Of course.

Something unpleasant replaced my earlier relief. The idea of him "not dating" someone irked me more than it should've.

"I know that," I said. "I don't date everyone I have sex with, either."

What am I saying? I hadn't had sex in so long I was surprised my vagina hadn't sued me for neglect, but I wanted to...what, prove Rhys wasn't the only one who could have casual sex? Get a rise out of him?

If so, it worked, because his smirk disappeared and his drawl hardened. "And when was the last time you had non-dating sex?"

I lifted my chin, refusing to back down beneath the weight of his steely stare. "That is a highly inappropriate question."

"You asked first," he ground out. "Answer the question, princess."

Breathe. I heard the palace communications secretary Elin's voice in my head, coaching me on how to handle the press. *You can't control what they say, but you **can** control what **you** say. Don't let them see you sweat. Deflect if necessary, take back the power, and guide the conversation where you want it to go. You are the princess. You do not cower in front of anyone.* Elin was scary, but she was good, and I took her advice to heart as I struggled not to rise to Rhys's bait.

One...two...three...

I exhaled and squared my shoulders, looking down my nose at him even though he towered over me by a good seven inches.

"I will not. This is where we end the conversation," I said, my voice cold. *Before it goes any more off the rails.* "Good night, Mr. Larsen."

His eyes called me a coward. Mine told him to mind his business.

The air pulsed with heavy silence during our staredown. It was late, and I was tired, but I'd be damned if I backed down first.

Judging by Rhys's bullish stance, he had the same thought.

We might've stood there forever, glaring at each other, had it not been for the sharp trill of an incoming call. Even then, I waited for my phone to ring three times before I tore my eyes away from Rhys and checked the caller ID.

My annoyance quickly gave way to confusion, then worry, when I saw who was calling. *Nikolai.* My brother and I rarely spoke on the phone, and it was five a.m. in Eldorra. He was a morning person, but he wasn't *that* much of a morning person.

I picked up, aware of Rhys's gaze burning into me.

"Nik, is everything all right?"

Nikolai wouldn't call out of the blue at this hour unless it was an emergency.

"I'm afraid not." Exhaustion weighed down his words. "It's Grandfather."

Panic exploded in my stomach, and I had to hold on to the side table for support as Nikolai explained the situation. *No. Not Grandfather.* He was the only living parental figure I had left, and if I lost him...

Rhys moved toward me, his face now dark with concern, but he halted when I shook my head. The more Nikolai spoke, the more I wanted to throw up.

Fifteen minutes later, I ended the call, numb with shock.

"What happened?" Rhys remained a few feet away, but there was a certain tenseness to his posture, like he was ready to murder whoever had been on the other end of the line for causing me distress.

All thoughts of our stupid argument fled, and the sudden urge to throw myself into his arms and let his strength carry me away gripped me.

But of course, I couldn't do that.

"I—it's my grandfather." I swallowed the tears threatening to spill down my cheeks. Crying would be a horrible breach of etiquette. Royals didn't cry in front of other people. But at that moment, I wasn't a princess. I was just a granddaughter scared to death about losing the man who'd raised her. "He collapsed and was rushed to the hospital, and I..." I raised my eyes to Rhys's, my chest so tight I couldn't breathe. "I don't know if he's going to make it."

10

RHYS

Bridget wanted to leave for Eldorra right away, but I forced her to get some sleep first. We'd had a long day, and while I operated fine on minimal shuteye, Bridget got...cranky.

She insisted she didn't, but she did. I would know. I was often the one on the receiving end of her crankiness. Besides, there wasn't much we could do about the situation at eleven at night.

While she slept or tried to sleep, I packed the necessities, booked a plane using her usual charter company's twenty-four-hour VIP hotline, and crashed for a few hours before I woke up in time to fetch us coffee and breakfast from the closest bodega.

We left the house just as the sun peeked over the horizon and rode to Teterboro Airport in silence. By the time we boarded the charter jet, Bridget was practically vibrating with restless energy.

"Thank you for arranging everything." She fiddled with her necklace and shook her head when the flight attendant offered her a glass of juice. "You didn't have to."

"It's not a big deal. It was just a call." Nothing made me

more uncomfortable than overt gratitude. In an ideal world, people would accept a nice gesture and never mention it again. Made things less awkward all around.

"It wasn't just a call. It was packing and breakfast and... being here, I guess."

"It's my job to be here, princess."

Hurt flashed across her face, and I immediately felt like the world's biggest jackass. *Way to kick someone when they're down, Larsen.*

If I were anyone but me and she were anyone but her, I would try to apologize, but as it stood, I'd probably make things worse. Pretty words weren't my strong suit, especially not with Bridget. Everything came out the wrong way when I talked to her.

I switched subjects. "You look like you could use more sleep."

She winced. "That bad, huh?"

And that's why I need to keep my mouth shut. I rubbed a hand over my face, embarrassed and irritated with myself. "That's not what I meant."

"It's okay. I know I look horrible," Bridget said. "Elin, our communications secretary, would pitch a fit if she saw me like this."

I snorted. "Princess, you couldn't look horrible if you tried."

Even though she looked more tired than usual, with purple smudges beneath her eyes and her skin lacking its usual glow, she still blew other women out of the water.

Bridget's eyebrows shot up. "Was that another compliment, Mr. Larsen? Two in two years. Careful, or I'll think you like me."

"Take it however you want," I drawled. "But I'll like you the day you like me."

Bridget cracked a genuine smile, and I almost smiled back.

Despite my words, we got along fine these days, aside from the occasional argument. Our initial transition had been rough, but we'd learned to adapt and compromise...except when it came to her dates.

Not a single one of those fuckers had been worth her time, and they were lucky I hadn't gouged their eyes out for the way they'd ogled her.

If I hadn't been with her on the dates, they would've tried something for sure, and the thought made my blood boil.

I noticed Bridget's eyes stray to the in-flight phone every few minutes until I finally said, "It's best if it doesn't ring."

Prince Nikolai had promised to call her with any updates. There'd been none so far, but in this situation, no update was a good update.

She sighed. "I know. It's just driving me crazy, not knowing what's going on. I should've been there. I should've moved back after graduation instead of insisting on staying in the U.S." Guilt washed over her face. "What if I never see him again? What if he..."

"Don't think that way. We'll be there soon."

It was a seven-hour flight to Athenberg. A lot could happen in seven hours, but I kept that part to myself.

"He raised us, you know." Bridget stared out the window with a far-off expression. "After my father died, my grandfather stepped in and tried his best to fill the parental role for Nik and me. Even though he's the king and has a ton on his plate, he made time for us whenever he could. He ate breakfast with us every morning he wasn't away traveling, and he attended all our school activities, even the stupid little ones that didn't really matter." A small smile touched her lips. "Once, he rescheduled a meeting with the Japanese prime minister so he could watch me play Sunflower Number Three in my fifth-grade school play. I was a terrible actress, and even my royal status wasn't enough to land me a speaking role."

My lips quirked at the mental image of little Bridget dressed up as a sunflower. "Starting an international incident at age ten. Why am I not surprised?"

She shot me a mock affronted look. "For the record, I was eleven, and the prime minister was quite understanding. He's a grandfather himself." Her smile faded. "I don't know what I'd do if something happened to him," she whispered.

We were no longer talking about the prime minister.

"Things always work themselves out." Not quite true, but I couldn't think of anything else to say.

I really was crap at this whole comforting thing. That was why I was a bodyguard, not a nurse.

"You're right. Of course." Bridget took a deep breath. "I'm sorry. I don't know what's come over me. I don't usually go on like this." She twisted her ring around her finger. "Enough about me. Tell me something about you I don't know."

Translation? *Distract me from the fact my grandfather may or may not be dying.*

"Like what?"

"Like..." She thought about it. "Your favorite pizza topping."

It was a question she hadn't asked during our impromptu Q&A session during her graduation dinner.

"Don't eat pizza." A grin slipped through at the shock on her face. "Kidding. Work on the gullibility, princess."

"In two years, I've never seen you eat one. It's possible," she said defensively.

My grin widened a fraction of an inch. "It's not my favorite food, but I'm a pepperoni guy. Simple is best."

"I can see that." Bridget flicked her eyes over my plain black T-shirt, pants, and boots. Some clients preferred their bodyguards to dress up—suit, tie, earpiece, the whole shebang—but Bridget wanted me to blend in, hence the casual getup.

Her perusal wasn't sexual, but that didn't stop my groin from tightening as her gaze slid from my shoulders to my stomach and thighs. The number of spontaneous boners I'd popped around her was embarrassing considering I was a grown-ass man, not a hormone-riddled schoolboy.

But Bridget was the kind of stunning that came along once in a lifetime, and her personality made things worse, because she actually had one. A *good* one, at that, at least when she wasn't driving me nuts with her hard-headedness.

I took this job thinking she would be spoiled and stuck up like the other princesses I'd guarded, but she turned out to be smart, kind, and down to earth, with just enough fire shining through her cool facade to make me want to strip every layer off her until she was bared to me and me alone.

Bridget's gaze lingered on the region below my belt. My cock swelled further, and I gripped my armrests with white-knuckled hands. This was so messed up. She was worried about her grandfather dying, and I was fantasizing about fucking her ten ways to Sunday in the middle of the goddamn cabin.

I have serious issues. The least of which was a case of blue balls.

"I suggest you stop lookin' at me like that, princess," I said, my voice lethally soft. "Unless you plan on doing something about it."

It was perhaps the most inappropriate thing I'd ever said to her, and way out of the bounds of professionalism, but I was teetering on the edge of sanity.

Despite what I'd implied yesterday, I hadn't touched a woman since I took this job, and I was slowly going crazy because of it. It wasn't like I didn't want to. I went to bars, I flirted, and I got plenty of offers, but I felt nothing every time.

No sparks, no lust, no desire. I would've worried about my boy down there had it not been for my visceral reactions to Bridget.

The only person who made my cock hard these days was my client.

I have the worst fucking luck on the planet.

Bridget jerked her head up, her eyes wide. "I'm not...I wasn't—"

"Ask me another question."

"What?"

"You said you wanted to know more about me. Ask me another question," I said through gritted teeth. *Anything to get my mind off how much I want to hike up that skirt of yours and find out just how wet you are for me.*

Because she was. My long, recent dry spell aside, I had enough experience with the opposite sex to spot the signs of female arousal from a mile away.

Dilated pupils, flushed cheeks, shallow breathing.

Check, check, and fucking check.

"Oh, um." Bridget cleared her throat, looking more flustered than I'd ever seen her. "Tell me...tell me about your family."

Talk about splashing a bucket of cold water over my libido.

I stiffened, my desire draining away as I tried to figure out how to respond.

Of course she wants to know about the one thing I hate discussing.

"Not much to tell," I finally said. "No siblings. Mother died when I was a kid. Never knew my father. Grandparents also gone."

Maybe I should've left the last part out, considering her grandfather's situation, but Bridget didn't appear put off. Instead, her eyes flickered with sympathy. "What happened?"

No need to clarify who she was asking about. *Mother dear-*

est. "Drug overdose," I said curtly. "Cocaine. I was eleven, and I found her when I came home from school. She was sitting in front of the TV, and her favorite talk show was on. There was a half-eaten plate of pasta on the coffee table. I thought she fell asleep—she did that sometimes when she was watching TV—but when I walked over..." I swallowed hard. "Her eyes were wide open. Unseeing. And I knew she was gone."

Bridget sucked in a breath. My story never failed to elicit pity from those who heard it, which was why I hated telling it. I didn't want anyone's pity.

"You know what the funny thing was? I picked up the plate of pasta and washed it like she'd wake up and yell at me if I didn't. Then I did the rest of the dishes in the sink. Turned off the TV. Wiped down the coffee table. Only after all that did I call 911." I let out a humorless laugh while Bridget stared at me with an unbearably soft expression. "She was already dead, but in my mind, she wouldn't *really* be dead till the ambulance showed up and made it official. Kid logic."

Those were the most words I'd spoken about my mother in over two decades.

"I'm so sorry," Bridget said quietly. "Losing a parent is never easy."

She would know better than anyone. She'd lost both her parents, one of whom she'd never met. Just like me, except there was a possibility the one I hadn't met was still alive while hers had died in childbirth.

"Don't feel too sorry for me, princess." I rolled my water glass between my fingers, wishing it contained something stronger. I didn't drink alcohol, but sometimes I wished I did. "My mother was a bitch."

Bridget's eyes widened with shock. Not many people talked about their mother's death, then turned around and called said mother a bitch in the same breath.

If anyone deserved the title, though, Deirdre Larsen did.

"But she was still my mother," I continued. "The only relative I had left. I had no clue who my father was, and even if I did, it was clear he wanted nothing to do with me. So yeah, I was sad about her death, but I wasn't devastated."

Hell, I'd been relieved. It was sick and twisted, but living with my mother had been a nightmare. I'd considered running away multiple times before her overdose, but a misguided sense of loyalty held me back each time.

Deidre may have been an abusive, alcoholic junkie, but I was all she'd had in the world, and she was all I'd had. That counted for something, I supposed.

Bridget leaned forward and squeezed my hand. I tensed as an unexpected jolt of electricity rocketed up my arm, but I kept my face stoic.

"Your father has no idea what he's missing out on." Her voice rang with sincerity, and my chest tightened.

I stared down at the contrast of her soft, warm hand against my rough, calloused one.

Clean versus bloodstained. Innocence versus darkness.

Two worlds that were never meant to touch.

I yanked my hand away and stood abruptly. "I need to go over some paperwork," I said.

It was a lie. I'd finished all the paperwork for a last-minute trip to Eldorra last night, and I felt bad about leaving Bridget alone right now, but I needed to get away from her and regroup.

"Okay." She appeared startled by the sudden change in mood, but she didn't get a chance to say anything else before I walked away and sank into the seat behind her so I didn't have to face her.

My head was all over the place, my cock was hard again, and my professionalism had taken a twenty-story jump out the window.

I scrubbed a hand over my face, silently cursing myself, Christian, her old bodyguard for having a fucking baby and leaving his post, and everything and everyone who'd contributed to the mess I was in. Namely, lusting over someone I shouldn't want and could never have.

I took this job thinking I had one objective, but now it was clear I had two.

The first was to protect Bridget.

The second was to resist her.

11
_____

BRIDGET

RHYS AND I DIDN'T TALK AGAIN ON THE PLANE, BUT HE'D taken my mind off my grandfather's situation enough I crashed after he left. I hadn't slept a wink the night before, and I was out like a light for most of the flight.

When we landed, though, all my nerves came rushing back, and it was all I could do not to snap at the driver to go faster as we sped through downtown toward the hospital. Every second we spent at a red light felt like a second I was losing with my grandfather.

What if I missed seeing him alive by a minute, or two, or three?

A wave of lightheadedness hit me, and I had to close my eyes and force myself to take deep breaths so I didn't drown beneath my anxiety.

When we finally arrived at the hospital, we found Markus, my grandfather's Private Secretary and right-hand man, waiting for us by the secret entrance they used for high-profile patients. I'd spotted the crush of reporters outside the main entrance from the car, and the sight made my anxiety triple.

"His Majesty is fine," Markus said when he saw me. He looked more disheveled than usual, which in Markus's world meant one of his hairs was out of place and there was a small, barely noticeable crease in his shirt. "He woke up just before I came down."

"Oh, thank God." I breathed a sigh of relief. If my grandfather was awake, things couldn't be *too* bad. Right?

We took the elevator to my grandfather's private suite, where I found Nikolai pacing the hall outside with a frown.

"He kicked me out," he said by way of explanation. "He said I was hovering too much."

I cracked a smile. "Typical." If there was one thing Edvard von Ascheberg III hated, it was being fussed over.

"Yeah." Nikolai let out a half-resigned, half-relieved laugh before he swept me into a hug. "It's good to see you, Bridge."

We didn't see or talk to each other often. We lived different lives—Nikolai as crown prince in Eldorra, me as a princess trying her best to pretend she wasn't one in the U.S.—but nothing bonded two people like a shared tragedy.

Then again, if that were true, we should be thick as thieves since our parents' deaths. But things hadn't quite worked out that way.

"It's good to see you too." I squeezed him tight before greeting his girlfriend. "Hi, Sabrina."

"Hi." She gave me a quick hug, her face warm with sympathy.

Sabrina was an American flight attendant Nikolai met during a flight to the U.S. They'd been dating for two years, and their relationship had generated a media firestorm when it first came to light. A prince dating a commoner? Tabloid heaven. Coverage had died down since then, partly because Nikolai and Sabrina kept their relationship under such tight wraps, but their pairing was still very much gossiped about in Athenberg society.

Perhaps that was why I felt such pressure to date someone "appropriate." I didn't want to disappoint my grandfather, too. He'd warmed up to Sabrina, but he'd had a conniption when he first found out about her.

"He's waiting for you inside." Nikolai flashed a lopsided grin. "Just don't hover or he'll kick you out too."

I managed a laugh. "I'll keep that in mind."

"I'll wait here," Rhys said. He usually insisted on following me everywhere, but he seemed to know I needed alone time with my grandfather.

I gave him a grateful smile before I stepped into the hospital room.

Edvard was, as promised, awake and sitting up in bed, but the sight of him in a hospital gown and hooked up to machines brought back an onslaught of memories.

"Daddy, wake up! Please wake up!" I sobbed, trying to break out of Elin's grasp and run to his aside. "Daddy!"

But no matter how loud I screamed or how hard I cried, he remained pale and unmoving. The machine next to his bed let out a flat, steady whine, and everyone in the room was yelling and running around except for my grandfather, who sat with his head lowered and shoulders shaking. They'd forced Nikolai to leave the room earlier, and now they were trying to get me to leave too, but I wouldn't.

Not until Daddy woke up.

"Daddy, please." I'd screamed myself hoarse, and my last plea came out as a whisper.

I didn't understand. He'd been okay a few hours ago. He went out to buy popcorn and candy because the palace kitchen ran out and he said it was silly to ask someone to fetch something he could easily get himself. He said when he got back, we would eat the popcorn and watch Frozen together.

But he never came back.

I overheard the doctors and nurses talking earlier. Something about his car and sudden impact. I didn't know what it all meant, but I knew it wasn't good.

And I knew Daddy was never, ever coming back.

I felt the burn of tears behind my eyes and a familiar tightening in my chest, but I pasted on a smile and tried not to let my worry show.

"Grandpa." I rushed to Edvard's side. I'd called him Grandpa when I was a kid and never grew out of it, but now, I could only say it when we were alone because the address was too "informal" for a king.

"Bridget." He looked pale and tired, but he mustered a weak smile. "You didn't have to fly all the way back here. I'm fine."

"I'll believe it when the doctor tells me so." I squeezed his hand, the gesture as much reassurance for myself as it was for him.

"I'm the king," he harrumphed. "What I say, goes."

"Not for medical matters."

Edvard sighed and grumbled, but he didn't argue. Instead, he asked about New York, and I caught him up on everything I'd been doing since I saw him last Christmas until he got tired and dozed off in the middle of my story about Louis's unfortunate wine spill.

He'd refused to tell me how he ended up in the hospital, but Nikolai and the doctors filled me in. Apparently, my grandfather had a rare, previously undiagnosed heart condition that was usually latent in patients until extreme stress or anxiety triggered it. In such cases, the condition could lead to sudden cardiac arrest and death.

I nearly had cardiac arrest myself when I heard that, but the doctors assured me my grandfather's case had been mild. He'd fainted and had been unconscious for a while, but he didn't need surgery, which was a good thing. However, the condition didn't have a cure and he would need to make major lifestyle changes to reduce his stress levels if he didn't want a more serious incident in the future.

I could only imagine Edvard's response to that. He was a workaholic if there ever was one.

The doctors kept him in the hospital another three days for monitoring. They'd wanted to keep him a week, but he refused. He said it would be bad for public morale, and he needed to get back to work. And when the king wanted something, no one refused him.

After he returned home, Nikolai and I tried our best to convince him to offload some responsibilities to his advisors, but he kept brushing us off.

Three weeks later, we were still at an impasse, and I was at my wits' end.

"He's being stubborn." I couldn't keep the frustration out of my voice as I guided my horse toward the back of the palace grounds. Edvard, sick of both Nikolai and I nagging him to heed the doctor's warnings, had all but kicked us out of the palace for the afternoon. *Get some sun*, he said. *And leave me to stress in peace.* Nikolai and I had not been amused. "He should at least cut back on the late-night calls."

"You know how Grandfather is." Nikolai came up beside me on his own horse, his hair tousled from the wind. "He's more stubborn than you are."

"You, calling *me* stubborn? That's rich," I scoffed. "If I recall correctly, you're the one who went on a hunger strike for three days because Grandfather wouldn't let you skydive with your friends."

Nikolai grinned. "It worked, didn't it? He caved before day three was over." My brother was the spitting image of our father—wheat-colored hair, blue eyes, square jaw—and sometimes, the resemblance was so strong it made my heart hurt. "Besides, that was nothing compared to your *insistence* on living in America. Is our home country really that abhorrent?"

There it is. Nothing like a beautiful fall day with a side of guilt. "You know that's not why."

"Bridget, I can count the number of times you've been home in the past five years on one hand. I don't see any other explanation."

"You know I miss you and Grandfather. It's just...every time I'm home..." I tried to think of the best way to phrase it. "I'm under a microscope. Every single thing I do, wear, and say is dissected. I swear, the tabloids could turn me *breathing* wrong into a story. But in the U.S., no one cares as long as I don't do anything crazy. I can just be normal. Or as normal as someone like me can get."

I can't breathe here, Nik.

"I know it's a lot," Nikolai said, his face softening. "But we were born for this, and you grew up here. You didn't have an issue with the attention before."

Yes, I did. I just never showed it.

"I was young." We came to a stop on our horses, and I stroked my horse's mane, taking comfort in the familiar feel of its silky hair beneath my hand. "People weren't as vicious when I was young, and that was before I went to college and experienced what being a normal girl feels like. It feels...good."

Nikolai stared at me with a strange expression. If I didn't know better, I would've sworn it was guilt, but that made no sense. What could he be guilty about?

"Bridge..."

"What?" My heart pounded faster. His tone, his expression, the tight set of his shoulders. Whatever he had to say, I wouldn't like it.

He looked down. "You're going to hate me for this."

I tightened my grip on my reins. "Just tell me."

"Before I do, I want you to know I didn't plan for this to happen," Nikolai said. "I never expected to meet Sabrina and fall in love with her, nor did I expect this is where we'd be two years later."

Confusion mingled with my apprehension. *What does Sabrina have to do with this?*

"I wanted to tell you earlier," he added. "But then Grandfather got hospitalized and everything was so crazy..." His throat bobbed with a hard swallow. "Bridge, I asked Sabrina to marry me. And she said yes."

Of everything I'd expected him to say, that wasn't it. Not by a long shot.

I didn't know Sabrina well, but I liked her. She was sweet and funny and made my brother happy. That was enough for me. I didn't understand why he would be nervous about telling me. "Nik, that's amazing. Congratulations! Did you tell Grandfather already?"

"Yes." Nikolai was still watching me with a guilty look in his eyes.

My smile faded. "Was he upset? I know he wasn't happy when you started dating because—" I stopped. Icy fingers crawled down my spine as the pieces finally clicked. "Wait," I said slowly. "You can't marry Sabrina. She's not of noble blood."

That was the law talking, not me. Eldorra's Royal Marriages Law stipulated the monarch must marry someone of noble birth. It was archaic but ironclad, and as the future king, Nikolai fell under the law's jurisdiction.

"No," Nikolai said. "She's not."

I stared at him. It was so quiet I could hear the leaves rustle as they fluttered to the ground. "What are you saying?"

Dread ballooned in my stomach, growing and growing until it squeezed all the air from my lungs.

"Bridget, I'm abdicating."

The balloon popped, leaving pieces of dread scattered throughout my body. My heart, my throat, my eyes and fingers and toes. I was so consumed by it I couldn't speak for a good minute.

"No." I blinked, hoping it would wake me up from my nightmare. It didn't. "You're not. You're going to be king. You've been training for it all your life. You can't just throw that away."

"Bridget—"

"Don't." Everything around me blurred, the colors of the leaves and sky and grass blending into one crazy, multicolored hellscape. "Nik, how could you?"

Normally, I could reason my way out of anything, but reason had fled, leaving me with nothing except pure emotion and a sickening sensation in my stomach.

I can't be queen. Icanticanticant.

"You think I *want* to do this?" Nikolai's face tightened. "I know what a big deal it is. I've been agonizing over it for *months,* trying to find loopholes and reasons I should walk away from Sabrina. But you know what Parliament is like. How traditional it is. They would never overturn the law, and I..." He sighed, suddenly looking much older than his twenty-seven years. "I can't walk away from her, Bridge. I love her."

I closed my eyes. Of all the reasons Nikolai could've chosen for abdicating, he'd picked the one I couldn't fault him for.

I'd never been in love, but I'd dreamt of it all my life. To find that grand, sweeping love, the kind worth giving up a kingdom for.

Nikolai had found his. How could I begrudge him something I would myself give up my soul for?

When I opened my eyes again, he was still there, sitting tall and proud on his horse. Looking every inch the king he would never be.

"When?" I asked in a resigned tone.

A smidge of relief softened his expression. He'd probably expected more of a fight, but the stress of the past month had drained all the fight out of me. It wouldn't do any good, anyway. Once my brother set his mind on something, he didn't back down.

Stubbornness ran in our entire family.

"We'll wait until the furor's died down over Grandfather's hospitalization. Maybe another month or two. You know how the news cycle is these days. It'll be old news by then. We'll keep the engagement a secret until then too. Elin's already working on a press statement and plan, and—"

"Wait." I held up one hand. "*Elin* already knows?"

A pink flush stole over Nikolai's cheekbones when he realized his mistake. "I had to—"

"Who else knows?" *Thud. Thud. Thud.* My heart sounded abnormally loud to my ears. I wondered if I had a heart condition too, like my grandfather. I also wondered what would happen if Nikolai abdicated and I died right there in the saddle. "Who else did you tell before me?"

I bit out the words. Each one tasted bitter, coated with betrayal.

"Just Elin, Grandfather, and Markus. I *had* to tell them." Nikolai didn't back down from my glare. "Elin and Markus have to get out in front of this, politically and press-wise. They need time."

A wild laugh emerged from my throat. I'd never made such a feral sound in my life, and my brother flinched at the sound.

"They need time? *I* need time, Nik!" *Freedom. Love. Choice.* Things I'd already had so little of, gone forever. Or they would be after Nikolai officially announced his abdication. "I need the two-and-a-half decades you've already had, preparing you for the throne. I need not to feel like an afterthought in a decision that'll change my entire life. I need…" *I need to get out of here.*

Otherwise, I might do something crazy, like punch my brother in the face.

I'd never punched a person before, but I'd watched enough movies to get the gist.

Instead of finishing my sentence, I urged my horse into a canter, then a full-on gallop. *Breathe. Just breathe.*

"Bridget, wait!"

I ignored Nikolai's shout and spurred the horse faster until the trees whizzed by in a blur.

Bridget, I'm abdicating.

His words echoed in my head, taunting me.

I had never, not once in my life, entertained the possibility Nikolai wouldn't take over the throne. He'd *wanted* to be king. *Everyone* had wanted him to be king. He'd been ready.

Me? I didn't think I'd ever be ready.

When did Nikolai propose to Sabrina? How long had everyone known? Was his planned abdication part of the reason for Grandfather's collapse?

I didn't remember seeing an engagement ring on Sabrina's finger at the hospital, but if they were keeping it under wraps until the announcement, she wouldn't be wearing one.

I was in the dark about something that affected me more than anyone except Nikolai, and I was so consumed by my inner turmoil I didn't notice the low-hanging branch speeding toward me until it was too late.

Pain exploded on my forehead. I fell off my horse and landed on the ground with a hard *thud,* and the last thing I remembered seeing was the storm clouds roll in overhead before darkness swallowed me whole.

12

RHYS

I SENSED TROUBLE BEFORE I EVEN ENTERED THE PALACE'S reception hall, where I heard Prince Nikolai talking in low murmurs. The hairs on the back of my neck prickled, and though I couldn't make out what Bridget's brother was saying, the stressed pitch of his voice set alarms blaring in my head.

My boots squeaked against the reception hall's overly polished marble floors, and Nikolai fell silent. He stood in the middle of the soaring two-story space next to Elin and Viggo, the Deputy Head of Royal Security. I'd memorized every staff member's face and name so I would notice if anyone tried to sneak in by disguising themselves as a palace employee.

I gave the group a curt nod. "Your Highness."

"Mr. Larsen." Nikolai responded with a regal nod of his own. "I trust you're enjoying your day off?"

Since the palace was so heavily guarded, I was off the clock when Bridget was at home, which was most days since her grandfather's hospitalization. It felt strange. I was so used to being by her side twenty-four-seven I...

You do not miss her. I dismissed the ridiculous idea before it became a fully formed thought.

"It's been fine." I'd tried drawing again, but I hadn't gotten much further than a few lines on paper. I ran out of creativity, inspiration—whatever you call it—months ago, and today had been my first time picking up my sketchbook since.

I'd needed something to occupy my hands and mind.

Something that wasn't five-nine with the face of an angel and curves that would fit perfectly beneath my palms.

Oh, for fuck's sake.

I hardened my jaw, determined not to fantasize about my fucking client in front of her brother. Or ever.

"Where's Princess Bridget?" According to her schedule, she was supposed to be horseback riding with Nikolai. But the skies looked ready to pour, so I assumed they'd called it a day early.

Nikolai exchanged glances with Elin and Viggo, and the needle on my trouble radar inched closer to the red zone.

"I'm sure Her Highness is somewhere in the palace," Viggo said. He was a short, heavyset man with a ruddy face and a passing resemblance to a Scandinavian Danny DeVito. "We're looking for her as we speak."

The needle pushed past the red zone into the white-hot emergency zone. "What do you mean, you're looking for her?" My voice remained calm, but alarm and anger bubbled in my stomach. "I thought she was with you, Your Highness."

Elin glared at Viggo. She didn't have to speak for me to hear her scream, *Viggo, you idiot.*

Whatever was happening, I wasn't supposed to know about it.

Nikolai shifted his weight, discomfort sliding across his face. "She was, but we got into an argument and she, ah, took off while we were riding."

"How long ago?" I didn't give a damn if I sounded disrespectful. It was a personal safety issue, and I was Bridget's bodyguard. I had a right to know what happened.

Nikolai's discomfort visibly increased. "An hour ago."

The anger erupted, edging out the alarm by a hair. "An *hour* ago? And no one thought to call me?"

"Watch your tone, Mr. Larsen," Elin admonished. "You're speaking to the Crown Prince."

"I'm aware." Elin could take her glares and shove them up her ass along with the stick permanently residing there. "No one has seen the princess since?"

"A groundskeeper found her horse," Viggo said. "We took it back to—"

"Found her horse." A vein pulsed in my forehead. "Meaning she wasn't riding it and she hadn't returned it to the stables herself." No matter how angry she was, Bridget would never leave an animal behind. Something had happened to her. Panic grated against my insides as I bit out, "Tell me. Have you searched the grounds, or just the palace?"

"Her Highness wouldn't be out there," Viggo blustered. "It's storming! She's inside—"

"Unless she fell off her horse and is unconscious somewhere." Jesus, how the hell had he risen to the deputy security chief position? There were hamsters with more brains than him.

"Bridget is an excellent equestrian, and we have a few people searching outside. She could've run off to one of her hiding places. She used to do that as a kid." Nikolai looked at Viggo. "But Mr. Larsen's right. It doesn't hurt to be extra thorough. Shall we send extra men to check the grounds?"

"If you wish, Your Highness. I'll draw up the quadrants..."

Un-fucking-believable.

I was halfway out the door before Viggo finished his moronic sentence. Too bad the Head of Security, who was actually competent, was on vacation because his deputy was a goddamned idiot. By the time he finished drawing his quadrants, Bridget could be seriously hurt.

"Where are you going?" Elin called after me.

"To do my job."

I picked up my pace, cursing the size of the palace as I sprinted toward the closest door leading outdoors. By the time I hit the grounds, my panic had escalated into full-blown terror. Thunder boomed so loud it rattled the door as I shut it behind me, and it was raining so hard the gardens and fountains blurred in front of me.

The estate was too large for me to search it all by myself, so I had to be strategic. My best bet would be to start at the official horseback riding trail in the southeast corner and go from there, though the rain would've washed away any hoofprints by now.

Luckily, the palace had a fleet of motorized carts to ferry guests around the grounds, and I made it to the riding trail in ten minutes instead of the half hour it would've taken me on foot.

"Come on, princess, where are you?" I muttered, my eyes straining to see past the thick sheet of water slanting through the air.

Images of Bridget lying on the ground, her body twisted and broken, flashed through my mind. My skin turned ice cold, and the wheel slipped against my sweaty palms.

If anything happened to her, I would murder Viggo. Slowly.

I scoured the trails, but twenty minutes later, I still hadn't found her, and I was getting desperate. She *could* be indoors, but my gut told me she wasn't, and my gut was never wrong.

Maybe she was in an area the cart couldn't reach. It wouldn't hurt to check.

I killed the engine and jumped out, ignoring the harsh sting of raindrops on my skin.

"Bridget!" The rain swallowed her name, and I let out a low curse. "Bridget!" I tried again, my boots sinking into the muddy ground as I searched the area near the trail. The rain plastered my shirt and pants to my skin, making it hard to move, but I'd weathered worse than a puny thunderstorm as a SEAL.

I wasn't giving up until I found her.

I was about to move on to a different section of the grounds when I spotted a flash of blonde out of the corner of my eye. My heart tripped, and I froze for half a beat before I sprinted toward her.

Please let it be her.

It was.

I sank onto my knees by her side, my chest hollowing at the paleness of Bridget's face and the large, purplish bruise on her forehead. A small trickle of blood dripped down the side of her face, turning pink when it mingled with the rain. She was unconscious and completely soaked through.

A snarling, protective beast rose in my chest with such ferocity it stunned me.

Viggo was as good as dead. If he hadn't dragged his feet, if someone had fucking *called* me and told me Bridget was missing...

I forced myself to push the anger aside for now. I had more important things to focus on.

I checked her pulse, which was weak but steady. *Thank God.* I quickly scanned the rest of her for signs of injury. Normal breathing, no broken limbs, and no blood except for the cut on her forehead. Her helmet was askew, and dirt smeared her cheeks and clothes.

The beast in my chest snarled again, ready to rip not only Viggo but Nikolai to shreds for not protecting her, or at least being there for her.

He probably couldn't have done anything to prevent Bridget from falling off her horse—judging by her helmet and position on the ground, that must've been what happened—but the beast didn't care. All it knew was she was hurt, and for that, someone had to pay.

Later.

I needed to get her to the doctor first.

I cursed again when I realized I had no cell service. The storm must've knocked it out.

Standard medical advice said I shouldn't move an injured person without professionals present, but I had no choice.

I scooped Bridget up in my arms and carried her to the cart, supporting her neck with one hand. We made it halfway when I heard a low groan.

My heart tripped again. "Princess, you awake?" I kept my voice even, not wanting to panic and scare her.

Bridget let out another groan, her eyes fluttering open. "Mr. Larsen? What are you doing? What happened?" She tried to twist her head to look around, but I stopped her with a firm squeeze on her thigh.

"You're injured. Don't move unless you absolutely have to." We reached the cart, and I set her carefully in the passenger seat before I took the driver's seat and turned on the engine. Relief flooded my veins, so thick it almost choked me.

She was okay. She might have a concussion, judging by the bruise, but she was conscious and talking and *alive.*

"Do you remember what happened?" I wanted to speed back to the palace, which had an in-house doctor, but I forced myself to drive slowly to minimize any bumps and jerky movements.

Bridget touched her forehead with a wince. "I was riding and...there was a branch. I didn't see it until it was too late." She squeezed her eyes shut. "My head hurts, and everything's blurry."

Dammit. Concussion for sure.

My hands strangled the wheel, which I pictured as Viggo's neck. "We'll be at the palace soon. For now, just relax and don't force yourself to talk."

Of course, she didn't listen.

"How did you find me?" Bridget spoke slower than usual, and the faint note of pain in her voice made my stomach lurch.

"I looked." I parked the cart near the back entrance. "You should fire your deputy security chief. He's a moron. If I hadn't found you, he'd still have his people searching the *inside* of the palace like—what?"

"How long did you look for me?" Bridget gave me a strange look, one that made my heart twist in the oddest way.

"Don't remember," I grunted. "Let's get you inside. You're soaked."

"So are you." She stayed in the cart. "Did you...you looked for me in the rain by yourself?"

"Like I said, Viggo is a moron. Inside, princess. You need that cut and bruise looked at. You probably have a concussion."

"I'm okay." But Bridget didn't argue when I slipped my arm around her waist and her arm around my neck, letting her use me as a crutch as we walked inside.

Luckily, the doctor's office wasn't too far from the back entrance, and when she saw the state Bridget was in, she sprang into action.

While she patched Bridget's forehead up and gave her a more thorough check for injuries, I dried off in the bathroom and waited in the hall. I didn't trust myself not to look at Bridget's bruise and cut and not lose my shit.

The sound of rapid footsteps filled the hall, and my lip peeled back in a snarl when I saw Nikolai running toward me, followed by Viggo and Elin. One of the staff must've alerted them when they saw me and Bridget.

Perfect. I needed to let off some steam.

"Is Bridget okay?" the prince asked, his face worried.

"For the most part. The doctor's checking her out now." I waited until Nikolai was inside the doctor's office before I turned my attention to Viggo.

"*You.*" I grabbed the collar of Viggo's shirt and lifted him until his feet dangled in the air. "I *told* you she was outside. Any damn person with common sense would know she was outside, yet you wasted an hour searching *indoors* while Bridget was unconscious in the rain."

"Mr. Larsen!" Elin sounded scandalized. "This is the royal palace, *not* a dive bar where you brawl with other patrons. Put Viggo down."

I ignored her and lowered my voice until only Viggo could hear me. "You better *pray* the princess isn't seriously hurt."

"Are you threatening me?" he sputtered.

"Yes."

"I could fire you."

I bared my teeth in a semblance of a smile. "Try."

The Head of Royal Security oversaw my contract, but Viggo couldn't find a way out of his ass if someone planted neon lights marking the way, much less fire me without his boss's approval.

I released Viggo's collar and set him on the ground when the doctor's door opened.

"Mr. Larsen, Viggo, Elin." If she suspected there'd been a scuffle outside her office, she didn't show it. "I've finished the checkup. Come in."

My anger at Viggo took a backseat to my concern over

Bridget as we crowded into the mini clinic, where Bridget sat on the hospital bed. She didn't look happy to see Nikolai, who stood next to her with a tight expression.

The doctor informed us Bridget did, indeed, have a concussion, but she should recover in ten to fourteen days. She also had a mild wrist sprain and the beginnings of a nasty cold. Nothing life-threatening, but she would be uncomfortable for the next few weeks.

I glared at Viggo, who shrank behind Nikolai like a coward.

I stayed after everyone else left, and the doctor took one look at my face before murmuring an excuse and slipping out the door, leaving me and Bridget alone.

"I'm fine," Bridget said before I could open my mouth. "A few weeks of rest and I'll be good as new."

I crossed my arms over my chest, unconvinced. "What the hell happened? Nikolai said you ran off after you two got in an argument."

Her face shut down. "Sibling squabble. It was nothing."

"Bullshit. You don't run off in anger."

Not to mention, Bridget hadn't spoken to him once while he was in the room, which was telling. She would never ignore her brother unless he'd *really* pissed her off.

"There's a first time for everything," she said.

A frustrated growl rose in my throat. "Dammit, princess, you need to be more careful. If something happened to you, I—" I broke off abruptly, swallowing the rest of my words. *I don't know what I'd do.*

Bridget's face softened. "I'm fine," she repeated. "Don't worry about me."

"Too fuckin' late."

She hesitated, seeming to debate something before she said, "Because it's your job."

The question hung in the air, loaded with a deeper meaning.

My jaw flexed. "Yes," I finally said, my heart doing an odd little twist again. "Because it's my job."

13

BRIDGET

The next few weeks were miserable, not only because I was sick and healing from my injuries, but because the lull in my public schedule gave me plenty of time to freak out about Nikolai's abdication.

I was going to be queen. Maybe not tomorrow or a month from now, but one day, and one day was far too soon.

I lifted my wineglass to my lips and stared up at the night sky. It was three weeks to the day since my conversation with Nikolai.

My concussion had healed, and I'd long since recovered from my cold. I still had to be careful with my wrist, but otherwise, I was up and running again, which meant I had to attend meeting after meeting about how and when to announce the abdication, how to handle the fallout, plans for my permanent move back to Eldorra, and a million other things that made my head spin.

That morning, my family, Markus, and I agreed on an official announcement a month from now. Or rather, everyone else agreed, and I went along with it because I didn't have a choice.

One month. One more month of freedom, and that was it.

I was about to take another drink when the door to the rooftop creaked open. I straightened, my mouth falling open when I saw Rhys step outside. Judging by the way his eyebrows shot up, he was as surprised to see me as I was him.

"What are you doing here?" we asked at the same time.

I huffed out a small laugh. "Mr. Larsen, this is my house. I should be the only one asking that question."

"I didn't think anyone came out here." He took the seat next to me, and I tried not to notice how good he smelled, like soap and something indescribably Rhys. Clean, simple, masculine.

We were on the rooftop of one of the palace's north towers, which could only be accessed via the service hallway near the kitchen. Compared to the palace's actual, terraced rooftop garden, it was nothing, barely big enough for the chairs I'd bribed a staff member to help me bring up. But that was why I liked it. It was my secret haven, the place I escaped to when I needed to think and be away from prying eyes.

I drained the rest of my wine and reached for the bottle at my feet, only to realize it was empty. I rarely drank so much, but I needed something to ease the anxiety following me around like a black cloud these days.

"Just me. Most people don't know about this place," I said. "How did *you* find it?"

"I find everything." Rhys smirked when I scrunched my nose at his arrogance. "I have the palace blueprints, princess. I know every nook and cranny of this place. It's my—"

"Job," I finished. "I know. You don't have to keep saying it."

He'd said the same thing in Dr. Hausen's office. I wasn't sure why it annoyed me so much. Maybe because, for a second, I could've sworn his worry for me went beyond his professional obligations. And maybe, for a second, I could've sworn I wanted it to. I wanted him to care about me as *me*, not as his client.

Rhys's lips quirked before his gaze traveled to my forehead. "How's the bruise?"

"Fading, thank the Lord." It was now a pale yellowish green. Still unsightly, but better than the glaring purple it used to be. "And it doesn't hurt so much anymore."

"Good." He brushed his fingers gently over the bruise, and my breath stuttered. Rhys never touched me unless he had to, but at that moment, he didn't *have* to. Which meant he wanted to. "You gotta be more careful, princess."

"You've said that already."

"I'll keep saying it until you get it in your head."

"Trust me. It's in my head. How can it not be when you keep nagging me?"

Despite my grumbles, I found a strange comfort in his nagging. In a world where everything else was changing, Rhys remained wonderfully, unrelentingly *him,* and I never wanted that to change.

His hand lingered on my forehead for another moment before he dropped it and pulled away, and oxygen returned to my lungs.

"So." Rhys leaned back and laced his fingers behind his head. He didn't look at me as he asked, "Who do you usually bring up here?"

"What?" I cocked my head, confused. I never brought anyone up here.

"Two chairs." He nodded at mine, then the one he was sitting in. "Who's the second one for?" His tone was casual, but a tight current ran beneath it.

"No one. There are two chairs because..." I faltered. "I don't know. I guess I hoped I'd find someone I wanted to bring up here one day." I had silly, romantic notions of me and mystery guy sneaking up here to kiss and laugh and talk all night, but the chances of that were growing slimmer by the minute.

"Hmm." Rhys was silent for a second before he said, "You want me to leave?"

"What?" I sounded like a broken record.

Maybe the hit to my head *had* scrambled my brains because I'd never been this inarticulate.

"Seems like this is your secret spot. Didn't realize I was intruding when I came up here," he said gruffly.

Something warm cascaded through my stomach. "You're not intruding," I said. "Stay. Please. I could use the company."

"Okay."

And that was that.

I couldn't hold back a smile. I didn't think I would enjoy sharing this space with anyone else, but I liked having Rhys here with me. He didn't feel the need to fill the silence with unnecessary small talk, and his presence comforted me, even if he irritated me, too. When he was near, I was safe.

I stretched my legs out and accidentally knocked over the empty wine bottle, which rolled across the floor toward Rhys. I bent to pick it up at the same time he did, and our fingers brushed for a second.

No, not even a second. A millisecond. But it was enough to send electricity sizzling up my arm and down my spine.

I yanked my hand away, my skin hot, as he picked up the bottle and placed it on the other side of his chair, away from both our legs.

Our brief touch felt indecent, like we were doing something we weren't supposed to do. Which was ridiculous. We hadn't even planned it. It was an accident.

You're overthinking.

The clouds shifted, unblocking part of the moon, and light spilled across the tower, illuminating part of Rhys's face. It appeared grimmer than it had a moment ago.

Even so, he was beautiful. Not in a perfect, Greek god sculpture kind of way, but in a pure, unabashedly masculine way. The dark stubble, the small scar slashing through his eyebrow, the gunmetal eyes...

My stomach did a slow roll as I struggled not to focus on how alone we were up here. We could do anything, and no one would know.

No one except us.

"Heard we're leaving next week," Rhys said. I might've imagined it, but I thought he sounded strained, like he, too, was fighting back something he couldn't quite control.

"Yes." I hoped my voice didn't come across as shaky as it did to my own ears. "My grandfather's condition is steady for now, and I need to wrap up my affairs in New York before I move back."

I realized my mistake before the words fully left my mouth.

I hadn't told Rhys about Nikolai's abdication yet, which meant he didn't know about my plans to move back to Athenberg. Permanently.

Rhys stilled. "Move back?" He sounded calm, but the storm brewing in his eyes was anything but. "Here?"

I swallowed hard. "Yes."

"You didn't mention that, princess." Still calm, still dangerous, like the eye of a hurricane. "Seems like an important thing for me to know."

"It's not finalized, but that's the plan. I...want to be closer to my grandfather." That was partly true. He'd recovered nicely from his hospital visit and he had people monitoring him around the clock, but I still worried about him and wanted to be close by should anything happen. However, as crown princess, I was also required to return to Athenberg for my queen training. I was already behind by decades.

Rhys's nostrils flared. "When were you planning to tell me this?"

"Soon," I whispered.

The palace was keeping Nikolai's abdication under tight wraps, and I wasn't supposed to talk about it until closer to the official announcement. I could've told Rhys I was moving back to Eldorra earlier using the excuse I just gave him, but I'd wanted to pretend everything was normal for a while longer.

It was stupid, but my mind had been all over the place lately, and I couldn't make sense of my own actions.

Something flickered in Rhys's eyes. If I didn't know better, I would think he was *hurt*. "Well, now you can finally be rid of me," he said lightly, but his face might as well have been etched from stone. "I'll talk to my boss on Monday, get the paperwork started for the transition."

Transition.

My breath, my heart. Everything stopped. "You're resigning?"

"You don't need me here. You have the Royal Guard. I resign, or the palace releases me from my contract. Same ending."

The thought hadn't crossed my mind, but it made sense. The palace had hired Rhys because they hadn't wanted to pull any Royal Guard members away from their family when I was living in the U.S. Now that I was moving back, they didn't need a contractor.

"But I..." *I **do** need you.*

Rhys and I may not have gotten along in the beginning, but now, I couldn't imagine not having him by my side.

The kidnapping. Graduation. My grandfather's hospitalization. Dozens of trips, hundreds of events, thousands of tiny moments like the time he'd ordered me chicken soup when I was sick or when he'd lent me his jacket after I left mine at home.

He'd been with me through it all.

"So, that's it." I blinked away the ache behind my eyes. "We have one more month and then you'll just...leave."

Rhys's eyes darkened to a near black, and a muscle jumped in his jaw. "Don't worry, princess. Maybe you'll get Booth as your bodyguard again. It'll be like old times for you two."

I was suddenly, irrationally angry. At him, his dismissive tone, the entire situation.

"Maybe I will," I snapped. "I can't wait. He was the best bodyguard I ever had."

It was a low blow, and judging by the way Rhys stiffened, it hit its target.

"Good. Then it's a win-win all around," he said in a cold, controlled voice. He stood and walked to the exit without looking back.

The door slammed behind him, causing me to jump.

The ache behind my eyes intensified until a stray tear slipped down my cheek. I wiped it away angrily.

I had no reason to cry. I'd changed bodyguards plenty of times before, and I was used to people leaving. Rhys hadn't even been with me for that long. Booth had been with me for four years, and I hadn't cried when *he* left.

Another tear fell. I wiped that one away too.

Princesses don't cry. Elin's disapproving voice echoed in my head.

She was right.

I refused to spend my last month of freedom agonizing over Rhys Larsen, of all people. We would return to New York, I would sort my affairs, and I would soak up every minute of my remaining time as a mere princess, not queen to be.

Forget propriety and protocol. If there was ever a time to live my life the way I wanted, it was now.

And if Rhys had a problem with that? Too bad.

14

RHYS

Some people have shitty days or shitty weeks. I'd had a shitty *month.*

Things between me and Bridget had been chilly since she told me she was moving back to Eldorra, and I hated that was how we were spending our last days together.

Our last days together.

My chest clenched at the thought, but I forced myself to ignore it and focus on the task at hand. I was still on the clock. We had a week left in New York. After that, I would accompany her back to Athenberg, where I would stay another week until her new guard fully transitioned into the role.

We didn't know who the new guy would be yet, but I already hated him...though not as much as I hated the guy Bridget was dancing with right now.

We were in the VIP room of Borgia, a fancy nightclub in downtown Manhattan, and Bridget had her arms wrapped around the pretty-boy douche who'd been ogling her all night. I recognized him—Vincent Hauz, an electronics heir and notorious womanizer who spent the majority of his days drinking, partying, and keeping the city's drug dealers flush with cash. He and Bridget had attended a few of the same events in the past.

I'd never wanted to rip his arms off until now.

A person only had to look at his face to know what kind of thoughts were running through his mind, and they had nothing to do with dancing. At least, not the vertical kind.

My blood burned as Bridget laughed at something Vincent said. I was positive he wasn't capable of saying anything witty even if someone threatened to take his inheritance away, but Bridget was also drunk. She'd already downed two cocktails and five shots—I'd counted—and I could spot the alcohol-induced flush on her cheeks from across the room.

She wore a sparkling silver dress that barely covered her bottom and a pair of lethal-looking heels that transformed her from tall to Amazonian. Tousled golden hair, long legs, skin gleaming with a faint sheen of sweat—she was magnificent. And not herself.

Normal Bridget would've never worn a dress like that—not because she couldn't, but because it wasn't her style—but she'd been acting strange since that night on the rooftop. Wilder, less inhibited, and more prone to questionable decisions.

Case in point: Vincent Hauz. She didn't like the guy. She'd said so herself one time, and yet there she was, cozying up to him.

He pulled her closer and slid his hand down her back to cup her ass.

Before I knew what I was doing, I'd shoved my way across the dance floor and clamped my hand on Vincent's shoulder tight enough he flinched and pulled back from Bridget to see who the interloper was.

"Can I help you?" His tone dripped with disdain as he

looked me over, obviously unimpressed by my lack of designer clothes and fancy accessories.

Tough shit. Maybe he'd be more impressed by my fist in his face.

"Yes." I bared my teeth in a semblance of a smile. "Remove your hands from her before I remove them for you."

"And who the fuck are you to tell me what to do?" Vincent sneered.

The man who's about to pummel your face into a pulp.

Before I could respond, Bridget cut in. "No one." She glared at me. "I'm *fine*. Go back to your post."

The hell I will.

If Bridget were anyone but my client, I'd drag her into the bathroom, bend her over, and spank her ass raw for her insolent tone.

Instead, I glared back at her, striving to keep my temper under control.

She wanted to party? Fine. She wanted to give me the cold shoulder? Fine. But over my dead body would she have anything to do with Vincent fucking Hauz. The man must be crawling with STDs.

Vincent's eyes ping-ponged between us before realization dawned. "You're the bodyguard!" He snapped his fingers. "Dude, you should've said so. Don't worry." He wrapped an arm around Bridget's waist and pulled her closer with a leering smile. "I'll take good care of her."

Fuck pummeling his face. I wanted to knock all his teeth out.

Unfortunately, that would cause a scene, and rule number one of bodyguarding, as Bridget called it, was not to cause a scene. So, I did the next best thing. I tightened the grip I still had on his shoulder until I heard a small *crack* above the music.

Vincent yelped and released Bridget, his face awash with pain. "What the *fuck*, man?"

"What did I say about removing your hands from her?" I asked calmly.

"You're insane," he sputtered. "Bridget, who is this guy? Fire him!"

I ignored him and turned to Bridget. "It's time to go, Your Highness." We were attracting attention, which was the last thing I wanted, but fuck if I was going to let this creep take advantage of her. "You have an early morning tomorrow."

She didn't. I was giving her an out—one she didn't take.

"Good idea." Bridget brushed off my warning stare and placed a hand on Vincent's chest. My pulse beat an angry drumbeat beneath my collar. "I'll leave with Vincent. You can take the rest of the night off."

"You heard her." Vincent wrenched himself from my grasp and took a step behind Bridget. *Coward.* "Get outta here. I'll bring her home in the morning." He ran his eyes over Bridget's chest and bare legs, his gaze lecherous.

The man didn't have a single brain cell in his over-inflated head. If he did, he would be running for his life right now.

"Wrong. *This* is what you're going to do." I kept my voice friendly. Conversational. But beneath the polite veneer ran a razor-sharp blade of steel. "You're going to turn around, walk away, and never speak, touch, or so much as look in her direction again. Consider this your first and final warning, Mr. Hauz."

I knew his name. He knew I knew his name. And if he was stupid enough to ignore my warning, I would hunt him down, rip off his balls, and feed them to him.

Vincent's face flushed a mottled purple. "Are you *threatening* me?"

I loomed over him, relishing the fear that skittered through his eyes. "Yes."

"Don't listen to him," Bridget said through gritted teeth. "He doesn't know what he's talking about."

Vincent took another step back, oozing hatred, but the fear in his eyes remained. "Whatever. I'm over this shit." He stormed away and disappeared into the crowd of drunken partygoers.

Bridget spun toward me. "What is your *problem?*"

"My problem is you're acting like a drunk, spoiled brat," I snapped. "You're so shit-faced you have no idea what you're doing."

"I know exactly what I'm doing." She stared up at me, all fire and defiance, and heat curled inside me. I didn't know what it was about her anger that turned me on so much. Maybe it was because it was one of the few times I could see *her* and not the mask she showed the world. "I'm having fun, and I'm leaving with a guy at the end of the night. You can't stop me."

I smiled coldly. "You're right. You are leaving with a guy. Me."

"No, I'm not." Bridget crossed her arms over her chest.

"You have two options." I leaned in close enough to smell her perfume. "You can either walk out of here with me like an adult, or I can throw you over my shoulder and carry you out of here like a child. Which one will it be, princess?"

She wasn't the only one pissed tonight.

I was pissed she'd spent the last half hour letting a weaselly fucker put his hands all over her. I was pissed we were fighting when we had two weeks left together. Most of all, I was pissed at how much I wanted her when I couldn't have her.

If there was one thing her move back to Eldorra made clear, it was that our relationship was a temporary one. It always had been, but it hadn't hit close to home until now.

At the end of the day, she was a princess, and I was the guy they'd hired until they didn't need me anymore.

Crimson stained Bridget's high cheekbones. "You wouldn't dare."

"Try me."

"You forget you're not the boss here, Mr. Larsen."

The temperature of my smile dropped another ten degrees. "You want to test that theory?"

Her lips thinned. For a second, I thought she might stay just to spite me. Then, without saying a word or so much as looking at me, she pushed past me and walked toward the exit, her shoulders stiff. I followed her, my scowl dark enough to make the other clubbers scatter like marbles before me.

We took the first cab we found back to Bridget's townhouse, and it barely stopped before Bridget jumped out and sped walk to the front door. I paid the driver and caught up with her in four strides.

We entered the house, our footsteps echoing on the wood floors. When we reached the second floor, Bridget opened her bedroom door and tried to slam it in my face, but I wedged my arm in the gap before she could do so.

"We need to talk," I said.

"I don't want to talk. You've already ruined my night. Now leave me alone."

"Not until you tell me what the hell's going on." My gaze burned into hers, searching for a hint as to what was going on in that beautiful head of hers. "You've been acting strange for weeks. Something's wrong."

"Nothing's wrong." Bridget gave up trying to bar me from her room and released the door. I pushed it all the way open but remained in the doorway, watching. Waiting. "I'm twenty-three, Mr. Larsen. Twenty-three-year-olds go out and drink and sleep with guys."

A muscle ticked in my jaw. "Not the way you've been doing since we got back to New York."

Not the sleeping with guys part, thank God, but the going out and drinking.

"Maybe I'm tired of living life the way I *should* and want to live life the way I *could.*" Bridget removed her jewelry and placed it on her dresser. "My grandfather almost died. One minute he was standing, the next he collapsed. What's to say the same thing won't happen to me?"

Her words held a ring of truth, but not the full truth. I knew every inflection of her voice, every meaning behind every movement. There was something she wasn't telling me.

"So, you decided you want to spend your potential last moment with Vincent fucking Hauz?" I scoffed.

"You don't even know him."

"I know enough."

"Please." Bridget spun toward me, fury and something infinitely sadder glittering in her eyes. "*Every time* I so much as smile at a man, you bulldoze your way between us like a territorial bear. Why is that, Mr. Larsen? Especially when you told me in no uncertain terms when we first met that you don't get involved in your clients' personal lives."

I didn't answer, but my jaw continued to tick in rhythm with my pulse. *Tick. Tick. Tick.* A bomb waiting to go off and blow up our lives as knew it.

"Maybe..." Bridget's expression turned contemplative as she took a step toward me. *Mistake number one.* "You want to be in their place." She smiled, but the haunted look remained in her eyes. "Do you want me, Mr. Larsen? The princess and the bodyguard. It would make a nice story for your buddies."

Mistake number two.

"You want to stop talking now, Your Highness," I said softly. "And be very, very careful what you do next."

"Why?" Bridget took another step toward me, then another, until she was less than a foot away. "I'm not afraid of you. Everyone else is, but I'm not." She placed her hand on my chest.

Mistake number three.

Her gasp hadn't fully left her throat before I spun her around and bent her over the nearby dresser, one hand gripping her chin and forcing her head back while the other closed around her throat. My cock pressed into her ass, hard and angry.

I'd been on edge all night. Hell, I'd been on edge for two years. The moment Bridget von Ascheberg entered my life, I'd been on a countdown to destruction, and tonight might just be the night everything went to hell.

"You should be, princess. You wanna know why?" I growled. "Because you're right. I do want you. But I don't want to kiss or make love to you. I want to *fuck* you. I want to punish you for mouthing off and letting another man put his hands on you. I want to yank up that tiny fucking dress of yours and pound into you so hard you won't be able to walk for days. I want all those things, even though I can't have them. But if you don't stop looking at me like that..." I tightened my grip on her chin and throat. She stared at me in the mirror, her lips parted and her eyes dark with heat. "I might take them anyway."

They were harsh, bitter words, drenched with equal parts lust and anger. They were meant to scare her off, but Bridget looked anything but scared. She looked *aroused*.

"So, do it," she said. I stilled, my hand flexing around her throat as my cock threatened to punch a hole through my pants. "Fuck me the way you just promised."

15

RHYS

HEARING THE WORD *FUCK* LEAVE BRIDGET'S MOUTH IN that posh, proper voice of hers...

It took every ounce of self-control I had not to do what I'd said I would do. What she'd *asked* me to do.

But even though I wanted nothing more than to throw caution to the wind and say *fuck it,* I'd give her exactly what we both craved, I didn't. Bridget was still drunk. Maybe not as drunk as she'd been half an hour ago, but intoxicated enough to have compromised judgment.

I had no clue if this was her or the alcohol talking. Hell, she'd been ready to go home with Vincent Hauz, and she hated him.

"That wasn't a promise, princess." My fingers dug into her skin.

"It sounded like one to me."

Jesus. Temptation was so close I could almost taste it. All I had to do was reach out and...

What the hell are you thinking, Larsen? my inner conscience snarled. *She's your **client**, not to mention a* *goddamned princess. Get the hell away from her before you do something you regret even more than what you're doing now.*

It didn't matter she was only my client for two more weeks. She was still my client, and we'd already shattered almost every professional boundary tonight.

"This is what I meant," I bit out, unsure who I was more pissed at, her or me. "You're acting like a different person. The Bridget I know wouldn't be asking her bodyguard to fuck her. What the *hell* is going on with you?"

Her face hardened. "I didn't sign up for a heart-to-heart, Mr. Larsen. Either fuck me, or I'll find someone else who will."

She let out a small yelp when I bent her fully over the dresser so her body was at a ninety-degree angle and her cheek pressed against the wood.

I leaned down until I was so close, I heard her every shallow, panting breath. "Do that," I said. "And you'll be responsible for a man's slow, bloody death. Is that what you want, princess?"

Bridget's hands clenched into fists. "You won't touch me, and you won't let anyone else touch me, either. So tell me, what the hell do *you* want, Mr. Larsen?"

You.

My frustration with everything, my whole damn life, reached a boiling point. "I want to know why you've been acting like an impulsive teenager instead of a grown-ass woman!"

Bridget was the most levelheaded person I knew. At least, she had been before her personality transplant.

"Because this is the *last* chance I have!" she yelled. I had never, not once in the two years I'd worked with her, heard her raise her voice, and it shocked me enough I loosened my hold on her and stepped back. Bridget twisted out of my grasp and straightened to face me, her chest heaving with emotion. "I have one week left. One week until…"

Sudden, icy terror gripped me. "Until what?" I demanded, bile rising in my throat. "Are you sick?"

"No." Bridget looked away. "I'm not sick. I'm just getting the one thing most people dream of."

Confusion chased away my brief flash of relief.

"The title of Crown Princess," she clarified. She slumped against the dresser, her face weary. "Before you say it, I know. First-world problems and all that. There are people starving, and I'm complaining about inheriting a throne."

My confusion doubled. "But Prince Nikolai…"

"…Is abdicating. For love." Bridget flashed a humorless smile. "He had the gall to fall in love with a commoner, and for that, he has to give up his birthright. Because the law forbids the monarch of Eldorra to marry anyone not of noble blood."

Of, for fuck's sake. What was this, the seventeenth century? "That's bullshit."

"Yes, but it's bullshit we have to follow. Including me, now that I'm next in line to the throne."

My mouth curled into a small snarl at the thought of her marrying another man. It was irrational, but nothing about my reactions was rational when it came to her. Bridget could wipe away every sense of logic and propriety I had.

She continued, oblivious to my turmoil. "The palace is making the official announcement next week. I'm not supposed to tell anyone until then, which is why I haven't said anything." She swallowed hard. "After the announcement, I'll officially be the heir to the throne, and my life won't be mine anymore. Everything I do and say will reflect the crown, and I can't let my family or country down." She took a deep breath. "That's why I've been going a little…crazy lately. I want to savor being normal for the last time. Relatively speaking."

I was silent as I digested her bombshell.

Bridget, the future Queen of Eldorra. *Holy shit.*

She was right in that most women would kill to trade places with her. But Bridget was the girl who once ran out in the middle of a thunderstorm and danced in the rain. Who spent her free time volunteering at an animal shelter and would rather stay home watching TV and eating ice cream than attend a fancy party.

To her, becoming queen wasn't a dream; it was her worst nightmare.

"It was never supposed to be me. I was the spare." Bridget blinked, her eyes bright with unshed tears. My chest squeezed at the sight. "It was never supposed to be me," she repeated.

I grasped her chin and tilted it until she was looking at me. "You're a lot of things, princess. Stubborn, infuriating, a pain in my ass half the time. But I promise you, you're not a spare anything."

She let out a weak laugh. "That might be the nicest thing you've ever said to me."

"Don't get used to it."

Another small laugh, one that faded as quickly as it had come. "What am I going to do?" Bridget whispered. "I'm not ready. I don't think I'll ever be ready."

"You're Bridget von Ascheberg," I said. "You'll be ready."

Bridget excelled at everything she did, and being queen would be no exception.

"In the meantime..." I hoped I didn't regret what I was about to say. "You're going to live your life the way you want. As long as it doesn't involve Vincent fucking Hauz."

If I ever saw that fucker again, I would break every bone in his body just for touching her and occupying space in her thoughts. He didn't deserve any inch of her.

Bridget brightened a bit. "Does that mean you'll fuck me?"

Definitely still drunk.

I groaned, well aware of the erection that hadn't waned at all this entire time. "No, princess. That's not a good idea."

She frowned. "But it's on my bucket list."

Oh, Jesus. I was almost afraid to ask, but... "You have a bucket list?"

Bridget nodded. "For before I return to Eldorra." She ticked off the items on her fingers. "One, go someplace where no one knows or cares who I am. Two, eat and read and sunbathe all day without having to worry about an event later or waking up early the next day. Three, do an adrenaline rush activity my grandfather will yell at me for, like bungee jumping. And four, have an orgasm I didn't give myself." Her shoulders slumped. "It's been a while."

Fuck. Now the mental image of Bridget giving herself an orgasm would forever be etched in my mind.

I scrubbed a hand over my face. How the *hell* did I get myself into this situation? The night had gone so far off the rails I couldn't see the tracks anymore.

"One is probably off the table," Bridget said. "But you can help me with four."

She was going to achieve something neither my mother nor the military had. She was going to kill me.

"Go to bed," I said in a strained voice. "*Alone.* You're drunk, and it's late."

Bridget stared at my groin, where my obvious arousal tented my pants. "But—"

"No." I needed to get out of there. Stat. "No buts. You'll thank me in the morning."

Before she could protest further, I left and headed straight to my bathroom, where I took the world's longest, coldest shower. It did nothing to slake the heat of my arousal. Neither did fisting my cock until I reached a wholly unsatisfying orgasm.

Only one thing could take the edge off my frustration, and I'd turned it down like an idiot.

I shut off the faucet and dried myself, resigned to a sleepless night.

Meanwhile, the terrible idea that had been brewing in the back of my mind since Bridget told me about her bucket list wouldn't go away. Instead, it sounded more and more like a *good* idea.

It was crazy and possibly dangerous. I had no time to prepare, and it went against all my training and protective instincts.

But I couldn't get Bridget's sad eyes or words out of mind.

I want to savor being normal for the last time.

"I'm going to regret this," I muttered as I stepped out of the bathroom and flipped open my laptop.

It didn't matter.

Because as much as I wanted Bridget safe, I wanted her happy more.

16

BRIDGET

WAS IT POSSIBLE TO DIE OF HUMILIATION?

Forty-eight hours ago, I would've said no, but as I ate breakfast across the table from Rhys, I found myself firmly in the *yes* camp. I would either explode from how red my face was or melt into a puddle of mortification, whichever came first.

"More bacon?" He pushed the plate in my direction.

I shook my head, unable to meet his eye.

I woke up that morning with a pounding headache, throbbing heat between my legs, and a horrifically clear memory of the things I'd done—and said—last night.

Fuck me the way you just promised.

Four, have an orgasm I didn't give myself. It's been a while.

I choked on my toast and broke into a coughing fit.

Rhys's eyebrows rose. "You okay?" He'd been cool and calm all morning, like nothing had happened, and I wasn't sure whether I was relieved or offended.

"Yes," I gasped. I grabbed my water and downed half of it until the coughs subsided.

"You should eat more carbs," he said mildly. "Might help with the hangover."

"How do you know I have a hangover?"

"You had five shots last night, all containing different liquors. It's a safe guess."

His acknowledgment that any part of last night happened only intensified my embarrassment. I wished I could wipe all the events post-Borgia from *both* our minds.

Since I couldn't, I was tempted to play it off and pretend I didn't remember what happened, but I *did* remember, and if I didn't address it, it would haunt me forever.

"Listen. About last night..." I forced myself to look at Rhys. "I was drunk and not thinking clearly, and I said some things I shouldn't have said. I'm sorry if it made you uncomfortable."

Something akin to disappointment flickered across Rhys's face before it disappeared. "So did I," he said. "Call it even."

*I don't want to kiss or make love to you. I want to **fuck** you. I want to punish you for mouthing off and letting another man put his hands on you. I want to yank up that tiny fucking dress of yours and pound into you so hard you won't be able to walk for days.*

A bead of sweat popped out on my brow. I shifted on my stool, trying to ease the throbbing in my clit, but it only made things worse.

I shouldn't have said the things I'd said, but that didn't mean I hadn't meant them. When Rhys had me bent over the dresser with his cock pressed against me...

I gulped down the rest of my water to ease the heat flaming across my skin.

"In that case, the best path forward is to pretend last night didn't happen and never speak of it again."

I really needed more water. And air conditioning. And possibly an ice bath.

"Fine by me." Rhys leaned against the counter and rested one hand on the countertop while sipping coffee from the mug in his other hand. It was a casual, everyday movement that had no business being as hot as it was. "Except for one thing."

Oh, God. "And that would be...?"

"Your bucket list." Those gunmetal eyes drilled into me. "You really want to do all those things before going back to Eldorra?"

Not what I'd expected him to say.

I breathed a sigh of relief before I remembered bucket list number four and blushed all over again. "Yes, but most of it probably isn't possible."

It was more a fantasy list than a bucket list. I knew that when I came up with the items, but a girl could hope.

"What if I told you they were?" Rhys placed his mug in the sink before turning to face me again.

"I'd say you were bullshitting me."

His mouth curled up into a small grin, and tingles raced across my skin. Rhys didn't smile often, but when he did, it was devastating.

"Always nice to hear you curse, princess."

Fuck me the way you just promised.

The memory must've crossed my mind at the same time it did his, because his smile faded and his eyes heated while I sank a little lower in my chair.

"No, I'm not bullshitting you," he said, his voice rougher than it had been a second ago. "I can make your bucket list happen if you want me to."

I wasn't brave enough in the light of day to ask him if that included number four.

"Why would you do that?"

"It's my good deed for the year."

Typical non-answer from Rhys, but intrigue edged out my annoyance.

"Okay, I'll bite," I said. "What do you have in mind?"

"No what, where." Rhys smiled again at my surprise. "We're going to Costa Rica."

17

BRIDGET

Two days later, we landed in Costa Rica like Rhys had promised and drove two hours from the airport to a small town on the Pacific coast.

I stared out the window at the country's lush landscape, my head spinning from how fast everything had moved. I couldn't believe Rhys, Mr. Safety and Security himself, was the one who suggested a last-minute trip, but I wasn't complaining. I hadn't visited Costa Rica before, and four days in a tropical paradise sounded like, well, paradise.

We'd finished packing the townhouse, and I'd turned in my keys that morning. Everything else I needed to do, I could do online. I was, for all intents and purposes, free until we returned to New York.

"This is it." Rhys pulled up in front of a sprawling, two-story villa. "Bucket list number one."

Go someplace where no one knows or cares who I am.

That was definitely the case here. The house was nestled high in the hills and the only residence around. How had Rhys even found this place?

My chest tightened with emotion as we unpacked our suitcases from the back of our rental car and walked toward the entrance. "How did you pull everything together so fast?"

Rhys would never let me go anywhere without doing the proper advance work first, but it had only been forty-eight hours since I told him about my list. For him to have researched the town, booked the charter jet and villa, and handled the millions of details that came with royal travel in such a short time...

"I cheated a bit," he admitted, unlocking the front door. "An old Navy buddy of mine moved down here a couple of years ago and owns this place. He's on vacation right now and let me borrow it for a few days. I visit every year, so I know the town and people well. It's safe. Quiet. Under the radar."

"Exactly what I need," I murmured. The tightness in my chest intensified.

Rhys showed me around the villa. The walls were all glass, offering gorgeous three-hundred-sixty views of the surrounding hills and the Pacific Ocean in the distance. Everything was open, airy, and made of natural stone and wood, and the house's design made it seem like it was flowing into its surroundings instead of dominating them. My favorite feature, however, was the infinity pool on the second-floor terrace. From a certain angle, it looked like it fed straight into the ocean.

Rhys, being Rhys, also walked me through the security setup. Tinted, bulletproof glass all around, state-of-the-art motion sensors, an underground panic room stocked with a year's supply of food. That was all I gathered before I zoned out.

I appreciated the security measures, but I didn't need a detailed breakdown of the make and model of the security cameras. I just wanted to eat and swim.

"Remind me to send your friend a big thank you," I said. "This place is incredible."

"He loves showing it off, usually by letting people stay here," Rhys said dryly. "But I'll tell him."

It was already close to two, so the first thing we did after we finished the tour was change and head into town for lunch. The town was a twenty-minute drive from the villa and, according to Rhys, home to less than a thousand people. Not a single one of them seemed to know or care who I was.

Bucket list number one.

We ate at a small, family-run restaurant whose owner, a round-faced older woman named Luciana, lit up at the sight of Rhys. She smothered him with kisses before embracing me too.

"*Ay, que bonita!*" she exclaimed, looking me over. "*Rhys, es tu novia?*" *How beautiful! Rhys, is she your girlfriend?*

"*No,*" Rhys and I said at the same time. We glanced at each other before he clarified, "*Sólo somos amigos.*" *We're just friends.*

"Oh." Luciana looked disappointed. "One day, you'll bring a girlfriend," she said in English. "Maybe it'll be you." She winked at me before ushering us to a table.

I blamed my blush on the heat.

Instead of ordering off the menu, Rhys told me to trust Luciana's judgment, and I was glad we did exactly that when the food came out twenty minutes later. *Olla de carne, arroz con pollo, platanos maduros*...all so delicious I would beg Luciana for the recipes had I had any kitchen skills beyond scrambling eggs and making coffee.

"This is incredible," I said after swallowing a mouthful of chicken and rice.

"Luci makes the best food in town."

"Yes, but that's not what I meant. I meant *this.*" I gestured at my surroundings. "The trip. The whole thing. You didn't have to do this."

Especially since Rhys was paying for everything out of pocket. I assumed his friend let him borrow the villa for free, but the flight, the car rental...they all cost good money. I'd offered to reimburse him, but he'd responded with such a dark glare I hadn't brought it up again.

"Consider it my goodbye present," Rhys said, not looking up from his plate. "Two years. Figured it was worth a trip."

The chicken that had been so delicious a second earlier turned to ash in my mouth.

Right. I almost forgot. Rhys only had two weeks left as my bodyguard.

I stabbed at my food, my appetite gone. "Do you have a new client already lined up?" I asked casually.

Whoever it was, I already hated them for getting a beginning with Rhys instead of an ending.

Rhys rubbed a hand over the back of his neck. "I'm taking a short break. Maybe I'll come back to Costa Rica, or head to South Africa for a bit."

"Oh." I stabbed harder at my chicken. "Sounds nice."

Great. He'd be playing world traveler while I was attending queen lessons at the palace. Maybe he'd meet some beautiful Costa Rican or South African girl and they'd spend their days surfing and having sex—

Stop it.

"What about you?" Rhys asked, his tone also casual. "Know who your new guard is yet?"

I shook my head. "I asked for Booth, but he's already assigned to someone else."

"Funny. I thought they'd be more accommodating, considering you're the crown princess." Rhys cut his chicken with a little more force than necessary.

"I'm not crown princess yet. Anyway, let's talk about something else." Our conversation was depressing me. "What fun things are there to do around here?"

The answer was, not much. After lunch, Rhys and I walked through town, where I picked up some souvenirs for my friends. We checked out an art gallery featuring local artists, took a cafe break where I had the best coffee I'd ever tasted, and shopped for groceries at the farmer's market.

It was a simple, ordinary day, filled with mundane activities and nothing particularly exciting.

It was perfect.

By the time we returned to the villa, I was ready to pass out, but Rhys stopped me before I could crash. "If you can stay up a while longer, there's something you should see."

Curiosity won out over exhaustion.

"This better be good." I followed him out onto the terrace and sank onto one of the wicker chairs by the pool, where I stifled a yawn. "I get cranky when I don't get enough sleep."

"Trust me, I know." Rhys smirked. "Good of you to admit it though."

I watched as he turned off all the lights, including the outdoor floodlights.

"What are you doing?" He *never* turned off all the lights until right before he went to bed.

He sat down next to me, and I spotted a flash of his teeth in the darkness before he angled his chin up.

"Look up, princess."

I did. And I gasped.

Thousands upon thousands of stars splashed across the sky above us, so numerous and densely packed they resembled a painting more than real life.

The Milky Way, right there in all its sprawling, glittering glory.

It hadn't occurred to me we could see it so clearly here, but it made sense. We were high in the hills, miles away from the nearest big city. There was no one and nothing around except us, the sky, and the night.

"I thought you might like it," Rhys said. "It's not something you see in New York or Athenberg."

"No. It's not." Emotion gripped my chest. "And you were right. I love it. Worth staying past my bedtime and getting cranky for."

His low chuckle settled in my belly and warmed me from the inside out.

We stayed outside for another hour, just staring at the sky and soaking in the beauty.

I liked to think my parents were up there, watching over me.

I wondered if I'd turned out the way they'd hoped, and if they were proud. I wondered what they would say about Nikolai's abdication, and whether my mother knew I was the one who should've died that day in the hospital, not her.

She should've been queen, not me.

At least she and my father were together. They were one of the lucky couples who started off in an arranged marriage and ended up falling in love. My father had never been the same after my mom's death, or so everyone told me. I'd been too young to know the difference.

Sometimes, I wondered if he'd lost control of his car on purpose so he could join her sooner.

I turned my head to look at Rhys. My eyes had adjusted to the dark enough that I could make out the tiny bump in his nose and the firm curve of his lips.

"Have you ever been in love?" I asked, partly because I really wanted to know, and partly because I wanted to pull my thoughts off the morbid path they'd taken.

"Nope."

"Really? Never?"

"Nope," Rhys said again. He cocked an eyebrow. "Surprised?"

"A little. You're old. You should've been in love at least three times by now." He was ten years older than me, which wasn't that old at all, but I liked teasing him when I could.

A deep, rich sound filled the air, and I realized with shock Rhys was *laughing*. The deepest, loudest, realest laugh I'd pulled out of him yet.

It was beautiful.

"One love for every decade," Rhys said when his mirth faded. "By that calculation, you should've been in love twice by now." The intensity of his stare pierced through the darkness. "So tell me, princess. Have you ever been in love?"

"No." I returned my attention to the stars. "But I hope to be one day."

18

BRIDGET

We spent four glorious, perfect days in Costa Rica.

I woke up late, went to bed late, and spent my days eating, sunbathing, and reading a romance novel I'd picked up at the airport. *Bucket list number two.*

On our third day, Rhys drove us two hours to Monteverde for zip lining. He said the company was the best in the area and he'd zip-lined with them several times himself.

Still, his face was taut with tension as I prepared to go down the longest zip line. We'd only done the shorter cables until now, and they were fun, but I was ready for *more*.

The one I was about to get on stretched high above the cloud forest, so long I couldn't see the other end of it. A mixture of excitement and nerves twisted in my stomach.

"Check her again," Rhys said after our guide gave me the thumbs up.

No one bothered arguing. Rhys made the guide triple-check my harness before I went down every line, and arguing was futile.

"If you get stuck, don't panic," Rhys said after the guide okayed me—again. "We'll come get you."

"By 'we'll,' he means me," the guide joked. "But yes, we will come get you. Don't worry, miss."

"I hadn't thought about getting stuck until now, so thank you for that," I said wryly.

Rhys's stern expression didn't budge, but all thoughts of his grumpiness disappeared when I got into position. The guide gave me a push, and I *finally* raced down the line. The wind whipped through my hair, and I couldn't hold back a huge grin.

Ziplining looked scary from the ground, but once I was in the air? It was exhilarating.

I closed my eyes, savoring the wind and the feeling of being *away* from it all. No worries, no responsibilities, just me and nature.

When I made it to the next treetop platform, I was still riding high from the zip line, and I couldn't resist teasing Rhys again when he landed shortly after me.

"See? I'm fine," I said. "You didn't have to pick up pieces of me from the ground."

He did not look amused at all, but I didn't care.

Bucket list number three, check.

For all his overprotectiveness, Rhys *was* more relaxed down here. Not fully relaxed, mind you, but he'd ditched his all-black outfits for shorts and—gasp—*white* T-shirts, and he agreed to most of the activities I wanted to do with minimal complaint, including parasailing and an ATV tour.

The one thing he refused to do, however, was get in the pool with me, and on our last night, I made a last-ditch effort to change his mind.

"I've never heard of a Navy SEAL who doesn't swim." I stepped onto the terrace, where Rhys was drawing in his sketchbook. He hadn't shown me any of his sketches yet, and I hadn't asked. Art was deeply personal, and I didn't want to force him to show me anything if he didn't want to. "Come on. It's our last day, and you haven't taken advantage of this once." I swept my arm at the gleaming pool.

"It's a pool, princess." Rhys didn't look up from his book. "I've been in pools before."

"Prove it."

No answer.

"Fine. I guess I'll swim by myself. Again." I shrugged off my cover-up and let the filmy white material cascade to the floor before I walked past Rhys toward the water.

I may have walked more slowly than normal and added an extra sway to my hips.

I may also have worn my skimpiest, most scandalous bikini. I did, after all, have one more bucket list item to check off.

I'd been drunk when I'd told Rhys about my bucket list, but I was sober now, and I still wanted him to help me fulfill item number four.

I was attracted to him; he was attracted to me. That much was obvious after what happened in my room post-Borgia. He wasn't going to be my bodyguard much longer, and no one would know unless we told them.

One wild, passionate hookup with my sexy bodyguard before I took on the duty of a lifetime. Was that too much to ask?

I waded into the pool and bit back a smile when I felt the heat of Rhys's gaze on my skin, but I didn't turn around until I'd reached the far edge of the water. By the time I looked at him, Rhys's head was bent over his sketchbook again, but his shoulders held a tension that hadn't been there before.

"Are you sure you don't want to join me?" I cajoled. "The water feels amazing."

"I'm good," he said curtly.

I sighed and let it go...for now.

While he sketched, I swam laps around the pool, reveling in the water against my skin and the sunshine on my back.

When I finally came up for a break, it was near sunset, and the warmth of golden hour cast a hazy, dreamlike glow over the surroundings.

"Last chance, Mr. Larsen." I slicked my hair back and blinked the water out of my eyes. "Swim now or forever hold your peace."

It was cheesy, but it made Rhys's lips curve before they flattened into a stern line again. "You gonna stop bugging me if I say no?"

I grinned. "Probably not."

My heart jumped when he closed his book, set it on the table, and stood.

I hadn't expected him to give in.

Rhys walked to the pool, pulling his shirt over his head as he did so, and I lost the ability to breathe.

Broad shoulders, perfectly sculpted muscles, abs one could grate cheese on. Absolute masculine perfection.

My core pulsed as my eyes ate him up. Tattoos swirled across his chest, both biceps, and one side of his ribcage, and a deep V cut arrowed toward what—based on what I'd felt when he'd bent me over my dresser—was a very impressive package.

Rhys entered the water and swam toward me, his big, powerful body slicing through the liquid blue as gracefully as a dolphin.

"There. I'm in the pool." He came up beside me, a lock of damp dark hair falling over his eye, and I resisted the urge to push it out of his face. "Happy?"

"Yes. You should go shirtless more often."

Rhys's eyebrows shot up, and my cheeks flamed before I

quickly amended, "You seem more relaxed that way. Less intimidating."

"Princess, it's my job to be intimidating."

If I never heard the words *it's my job* again, it would be too soon.

"You know what I mean," I grumbled. "You're always so on edge in the city."

He shrugged. "That's what happens when you have C-PTSD."

Complex PTSD. I'd looked it up after he told me he had it. Symptoms included hyper-vigilance, or being constantly on guard for threats. Unlike regular PTSD, which was caused by a singular traumatic event, complex PTSD resulted from long-lasting trauma that continued for months or even years.

My heart squeezed at the thought of what he must've gone through to be diagnosed with the condition. "Does the art help?"

"Kind of." Rhys's face was unreadable. "But I haven't been able to draw anything in months." He jerked his chin toward the table. "I was just messing around. Seeing what I came up with."

"When you do, I want to see it. I love a good security alarm sketch," I joked before I remembered we only had one week left together.

My smile faded.

Rhys watched me closely. "If that's what you want."

I wanted a lot of things, but none of them had to do with art. "Can I tell you something, Mr. Larsen?"

He dipped his head.

"I'm going to miss you."

He went still, so still I thought he didn't hear me. Then, in an uncharacteristically, achingly soft voice, he said, "I'm going to miss you too, princess."

So don't go. There had to be a way he could stay. He wasn't part of the Royal Guard, but he'd been with me for two years. I didn't see why I had to change guards just because I was moving back to Eldorra.

Except for, of course, the fact Rhys would have to move to Eldorra with me. He may have lived with me all this time, but there was a difference between live-in protection in the U.S. and moving to a different country for an indeterminate length of time. Plus, he'd resigned first.

Even if I convinced the palace to extend his contract, would he be willing to accept the offer?

I'd been too afraid to ask in case he said no, but the clock was ticking.

A loud *pop* went off in the distance before I could broach the subject, and Rhys turned sharply to see fireworks explode in the sky.

He relaxed. I didn't, because I finally understood why he'd never taken his shirt off around me before.

His back—his strong, beautiful back—was covered with scars. They crisscrossed his skin in angry, near-white slashes, peppered with a few round marks I was positive were cigarette burn scars.

Judging by the way Rhys's shoulders tensed, he must've realized his mistake, but he didn't hide them again. There was no point. I'd already seen them, and we both knew it.

"What happened?" I whispered.

There was a long silence before he responded. "My mother liked her belt," he said flatly.

I sucked in a breath, and my stomach lurched with nausea. His *mother* did that to him?

"No one said or did anything? Teachers, neighbors?" I couldn't imagine abuse of that level going unnoticed.

Rhys shrugged. "There were plenty of kids in bad home

situations where I came from. Some of them had it a lot worse than me. One kid getting 'disciplined' wasn't going to raise any eyebrows."

I wanted to cry at the thought of young Rhys so alone he was nothing more than a statistic to those who should've looked out for him.

I didn't hate a lot of people, but I suddenly hated everyone who knew or suspected what he'd been going through and didn't do a damn thing about it.

"Why would she do this?" I brushed my fingers over his back, my touch so light it was barely a touch. His muscles bunched beneath my fingers, but he didn't pull away.

"Let me tell you a story," he said. "It's about a beautiful young girl who grew up in a small, shitty town she'd always dreamed of escaping. One day, she met a man who was in town for a few months for business. He was handsome. Charming. He promised he'd take her with him when he left, and she believed him. She fell in love, and they had a passionate affair. But then, she got pregnant. And when she told this man who'd claimed to love her, he grew angry and accused her of trying to trap him. The next day, he was gone. Just like that. No trace of where he went, and it turned out even the name he gave her was fake. She was alone, pregnant, and broke. No friends and parents to help her out. She kept the baby, perhaps out of hope the man would return for them one day, but he never did. She turned to drugs and alcohol for comfort, and she became a different person. Meaner. Harder. She blamed the kid for ruining her chance at happiness, and she took out her anger and frustration on him. Usually with a belt."

As he spoke, his voice so low I could barely hear him, the pieces fell into place one by one. Why Rhys refused to drink, why he rarely talked about his family and childhood, his C-

PTSD...perhaps it was the result of his childhood as much as it had been his military service.

A small part of me empathized with his mother and the pain she must've gone through, but no amount of pain justified taking it out on an innocent child.

"It wasn't the boy's fault," I said. A tear slid down my cheek before I could stop it. "I hope he knows that."

"He knows," Rhys said. He rubbed my tear away with his thumb. "Don't cry for him, princess. He's all right."

For some reason, that made me cry harder. It was the first time I'd cried in front of anyone since my dad died, and I would've been embarrassed had I not been so heartbroken.

"Shhh." He wiped away another tear, his brows drawn into a deep frown. "I shouldn't have told you. It's not the best way to end a vacation."

"No. I'm glad you did." I reached up and covered his hand with mine before he could pull away. "Thank you for sharing it with me. It means a lot."

It was the most Rhys had opened up to me since we met, and I wasn't taking it for granted.

"It's just a story." But his eyes were stormy with emotion.

"There's no such thing as *just* a story. Every story is important. Including yours." *Especially yours.*

I released his hand and swam around to his back, where I brushed my fingers over his skin again before pressing the smallest, gentlest of kisses on one of the scars. "Is this okay?" I whispered.

His muscles bunched further, so tense they trembled beneath my touch, but he responded with a tight nod.

I kissed another scar. Then another.

Everything was silent except for Rhys's ragged breaths and the faint roar of the ocean in the distance.

I'd stopped crying, but my heart still ached for him. For us.

For everything we could never be because we lived in the world we lived in.

But right now, the rest of the world didn't exist, and tomorrow hadn't come yet.

Last chance.

"Kiss me," I said softly.

A shudder rolled through him. "Princess..." The nickname came out low and rough. Pained. "We can't. You're my client."

"Not here." I wrapped my arms around him and placed one hand on his chest, where his heart pumped fast and hard beneath my touch. "Here, I'm just me, and you're just you. Bucket list number four, Mr. Larsen. Remember?"

"You don't know what you're asking me."

"Yes, I do. I'm not drunk like I was the night after Borgia. I know exactly what I'm doing." I held my breath. "The question is, do you?"

I couldn't see his face, but I could practically see the war raging inside him.

He wanted me. I knew he did. But I didn't know whether that was enough.

The water rippled around us. More fireworks exploded in the distance. And still, Rhys didn't answer.

Just when I thought he would shut me down and walk away, he let out a low curse, turned, and yanked me to him, and I only had time to draw a quick breath before his hand fisted my hair and his mouth crashed down on mine.

19

RHYS

Bridget von Ascheberg would be the death of me. I'd known that the moment I'd set eyes on her, and my prediction was playing out in real time as I devoured her.

The death of my self-control, my professionalism, and any sense of self-preservation I had. None of that mattered when I tasted how sweet she was or felt how perfectly her curves fit in my palms, like she was tailor-made for me.

Two years of watching and waiting and wishing. It had all come down to this, and it was even better than I'd imagined.

Bridget's arms wrapped around my neck, her body pliant beneath mine. She tasted like mint and sugar, and at that moment, it became my favorite taste in the world.

I pushed her against the side of the pool and tightened my grip on her hair, my mouth not leaving hers the entire time.

It wasn't a sweet kiss. It was hard, demanding, and possessive, borne out of years of pent-up frustration and tension, but Bridget matched me inch for inch. She tugged on my hair in return, her tongue tangling with mine and her little moans going straight to my cock.

"Is this what you want?" I pinched her nipple through her bikini top. *That fucking bikini.* My eyes nearly fell out when she'd walked past in her get-up earlier, and I was glad she'd never worn it to the beach. If she had, I'd have to kill every fucker who laid eyes on her, and there were other things I'd rather do on vacation...like take my sweet time exploring every inch of her luscious body. "Hmm?"

"Yes." Bridget arched into my touch. "But more. Please."

I groaned. *Definitely the death of me.*

I gave her another hard kiss before I hooked her legs around my waist and carried her out of the pool and up the stairs to her room. For what I had in mind, I needed more than a pool ledge to work with.

I placed her on the bed, soaking in how beautiful she looked. Wet hair, gleaming skin, face flushed with arousal.

I wanted nothing more than to bury myself inside her so deep she'd never forget me, but even in my lust-fueled haze, I knew that wasn't possible.

If we crossed that bridge, I would never let her go, and it would ruin us both. I didn't give a shit about me. I was already ruined.

But Bridget? She deserved more than me.

She deserved the world.

"Bucket list number four. Two rules," I said, my words filled with gravel. "One: if we do this, it stays here. This room, this night. We don't talk about it again. Got it?"

It was harsh, but it had to be said—for both our sakes. Otherwise, I could all too easily lose myself in the fantasy of what could be, and that was more dangerous than any predator or enemy.

Bridget nodded.

"Two: no fucking."

Confusion crossed her face. "But you said—"

"There are other ways to make someone come, princess." I palmed her breast and swept my thumb over her nipple before taking a small step back. "Now be a good girl and take off your bikini for me."

A small shiver rippled through her body, but she knelt on the bed and did as I asked, untying first her bikini top then her bottoms with agonizing slowness.

Jesus Christ. I wasn't a religious man, but if there was ever a time to believe in God, it was now.

Since I couldn't touch her with my hands—not yet—I caressed her with my eyes. Bold and rough, my gaze dragging from her full, firm breasts to the sweet pussy already glistening with her wetness.

"Touch yourself," I ordered. "Let me see what you've been doing all those nights when you're alone in your room."

A deep blush bloomed across her body, turning ivory into rose, and I wanted to trace its path with my tongue. Mark her with my teeth and touch. Proclaim to the world who she belonged to, who she *should* belong to.

Me.

My fists clenched at my sides.

Despite her blush, Bridget didn't take her eyes off me as she caressed her breasts, squeezing and pinching her nipples before one hand slid between her legs.

Soon, she was whimpering with pleasure, her mouth falling open and her breaths turning shallow as she rubbed her clit and fingered her pussy.

Meanwhile, my eyes devoured her the way a lion would tear into a gazelle. Fierce. Ravenous. Destructive.

My cock was so hard it hurt, but I didn't touch it. *Not yet.*

"You thinking of me, princess?" I asked silkily. "Hmm? Are you thinking of how much you want me to pin you to the bed and tongue fuck that sweet little cunt until you come all over my face?"

Bridget whimpered as her fingers worked faster at my filthy words. She was still kneeling, her thighs trembling from her ministrations. "M-maybe."

"It's a yes or no question. *Tell me*," I growled. "Who do you think about when you're finger fucking your tight cunt?"

Bridget shuddered as her head tilted back and her eyes fluttered closed. "You."

"What am I doing to you?"

She moaned.

I stalked to the bed and grasped her chin in one hand, forcing her to meet my gaze again. "What. Am. I. Doing. To. You."

"Fucking me," she gasped. I was close enough to smell her arousal and hear the slick sounds of her fingers sliding in and out of her cunt. "While I'm bent over the dresser, and I can see you behind me in the mirror. Pulling my hair. Taking me from behind. Filling me with your cock."

Fuck. I hadn't come in my pants since I was a freshman in high school, but I was already close to blowing my load.

"You've got a filthy mouth for a princess." I gripped her wrist with my other hand, forcing her to still. Bridget whined in protest, but I didn't break my hold.

I could tell she was about to come, but tonight, all her orgasms belonged to me.

I pushed her down on the bed and pinned her wrists above her head, deftly tying them together with the strings from her bikini top.

"What are you doing?" A mixture of trepidation and anticipation filled Bridget's face.

"Making sure I can take my sweet time with you, princess.

Now lie back and let me check off the last bucket list item for you."

I captured her mouth in another kiss before moving my way down her neck. Collarbones. Shoulders. When I reached her breasts, I licked and sucked on her nipples until she was panting and trying to wriggle out of her makeshift bindings, but the knot was too tight.

One of the most useful skills I learned in the Navy? How to tie a good knot.

I tugged gently on her nipple with my teeth while I pushed one finger inside her, then two, stretching her out.

A groan tore out of my throat. "You're drenched."

"Please." Bridget's skin was hot to the touch. "I need...I need..."

"What do you need?" I kissed my way down her stomach until I reached her pussy. I pushed my fingers deeper inside her before I dragged them out, then thrust them in again. Enough to bring her to the edge, but not enough to tip her over.

"I need to come," she moaned. "Rhys, please."

I stilled. "What did you call me?" I lifted my head, and she stared back at me with lust and something else shining in those gorgeous blue eyes.

"Rhys," she repeated in a whisper.

The sound of my name on her lips may be the most beautiful thing I'd ever heard.

I exhaled a sharp breath before I resumed my ministrations. "You'll come, princess. But not until I say you can."

I lowered my head again and gently scraped my teeth over her clit before I sucked on it. Between that and the finger fucking, she was dripping all down her thighs, and I lapped every drop up like a man starved.

So fucking delicious. I'd never been addicted to anything, but I was addicted to the taste and feel of her pussy.

Bridget ground against my face, her movements frantic and desperate, and her pleading whines grew louder the longer I ate her out.

I finally took pity on her, pressing my thumb against her clit and curling my fingers until they hit the spot that would make her shatter.

"Come," I ordered.

The word barely left my mouth before Bridget arched off the bed with a sharp cry. She came so long and hard it took a good five minutes for her trembles to subside, and the sight of her orgasming was almost enough to make me forget the rule I'd imposed.

No fucking.

I untied her and stroked the faint red marks where the strings had dug into her skin.

Bridget lay in a boneless heap on the bed, but when I moved to get off the bed, she stopped me.

"You're forgetting something." She stared at the obvious bulge in my shorts.

"Trust me, I'm not forgetting anything." It was hard to forget when *it* was so hard it could hammer nails.

"Then let me take care of that for you."

I sucked in a breath when her fingers brushed against me. "That wasn't part of the plan."

"The plan changed." Bridget pulled down my shorts, her eyes widening as she took in my size.

"Bridget..." My protest morphed into a groan when she wrapped her hands around me.

"You said my name." She flicked her tongue over the head of my cock and lapped up the beads of pre-cum before she took me fully in her mouth.

I didn't respond. I couldn't.

Everything had ceased to exist except for her warmth

around my cock, and I was pretty sure heaven itself couldn't feel better than this.

My blood coursed through my veins like liquid fire, and my heart pumped with a mixture of lust and something else I'd rather not name as I tangled my hands in Bridget's hair.

So fucking beautiful.

She tried to fit all of me down her throat, but I was too big or the angle too awkward. She let out a small, muffled sound of frustration, and I rasped out a laugh before I withdrew and repositioned her until she lay on her back again.

"Tell me if it's too much." I slid the tip of my cock across her lips before I nudged it into her mouth. I paused every few inches to let her acclimate to my size until I was finally, blissfully buried all the way down her throat.

Fuck. It wasn't often I had to rely on my old trick of naming baseball rosters in my head, but right now, thoughts of the Washington Nationals were the only thing keeping me from cutting our night short.

Bridget choked and sputtered, her eyes welling with tears, and I pulled out until just the tip remained.

"Too much?"

She shook her head, her eyes dark and eager, and I pushed myself inside her again with a groan.

We worked up to a rhythm—slowly at first, then faster as she got more comfortable. Bridget's sputters gradually eased, replaced with moans that sent tiny vibrations shooting up my cock, and she reached down to finger herself while I pinched and played with her nipples.

"That's it," I growled. "Take every inch down your throat like a good girl."

Sweat beaded on my skin as I drove in and out of her mouth until I couldn't take it anymore. The silky warmth of her mouth, the sight of her playing with herself while her throat bulged around my cock...

My orgasm slammed into me like fireworks and exploded behind my eyes. I pulled out at the last minute and erupted, covering her chest with thick ropes of cum. I came so fucking hard I almost sank to the floor afterward, and that never happened. Ever.

By the time I was finished, Bridget had come again too, and the sounds of our ragged breaths mixed with the heavy scent of sex in the air.

"Wow." She blinked, looking a little shellshocked.

I laughed, my head—both of them—still buzzing from the aftershocks.

"I should be the one saying that." I gave her a quick kiss before I scooped her up from the bed and carried her into the bathroom. "Let's get you cleaned up, princess."

After our shower, during which I couldn't resist fingering her to another orgasm, I replaced the sheets before setting her back down on the bed. Exhaustion and satisfaction lined her face, and for once, she let me fuss over her without complaint as I tucked her beneath the covers and smoothed her hair out of her face.

"Bucket list number four. Don't say I never gave you anything," I teased.

Bridget managed to yawn and laugh at the same time. "Bucket list number four," she murmured sleepily. "It was perfect." She blinked up at me, her blue eyes a little sad. "I wish we could stay here forever."

My chest squeezed. "Me too, princess." I gave her another kiss, the softest of the night, and tried to etch the taste and feel of her in my memory.

After she drifted off, I sat and watched her sleep for a while, feeling like a total creep but unable to look away. Her chest rose and fell with steady breaths, and she had a small smile on her face. She looked more content than she had in weeks, and I wished I had the power to make the moment last forever like she wanted.

If we do this, it stays here. This room, this night. We don't talk about it again.

My rule. One we had to follow because Bridget wasn't just my client. She was the future Queen of Eldorra, and with that came layers of complications and bullshit I hated but couldn't do anything about.

I swept my gaze over her one last time, taking in every detail, before I hardened my expression and left.

Bucket list number four.

No matter what my heart said or wanted, tonight was a fulfillment of her wishes.

That was all it was.

That was all it could be.

20

BRIDGET

I woke up the next morning sore but smiling. I hadn't woken up in such a good mood in ages, and it took me a minute to remember why.

Bits and pieces from last night came back to me, slowly at first, then all at once, and I blushed when I remembered the filthy things I'd said and done in this very room.

But I couldn't stop smiling.

I need to make bucket lists more often.

I lingered in bed for a while, reluctant to break the dreamy haze enveloping me, but we were leaving today for New York and I needed to get up soon.

When I did, I found my travel clothes laid out for me on the dresser, and I realized the rest of the room was spotless. No wayward shoes littering the floor, no bikinis hanging over the chair or makeup scattered over the vanity.

Rhys must've finished packing for me. I'd crashed so hard I hadn't even heard him.

My suspicions were confirmed when I went down to the living room, where I found him waiting next to our luggage.

Gone were the casual T-shirts and board shorts he'd worn the past few days; in their place was his usual all-black outfit.

I felt a small pang in my chest. I missed Vacation Rhys already.

"Good morning, Your Highness," he said without looking up from his phone. "Breakfast is ready in the kitchen. Our flight is at noon, so we should leave in the next forty-five minutes."

My smile faded. *Your Highness.* Not even a *princess.*

We'd agreed to keep what happened last night to last night, but I hadn't expected such a one-eighty so soon. Rhys was almost colder now than when we'd first met.

"Thank you." I was so caught off guard I couldn't think of anything else to say. "For packing and breakfast."

"You're welcome."

My good mood from earlier drained away, but I hid my disappointment as I ate breakfast alone while Rhys checked to make sure everything in the house looked okay before we left.

He saved the kitchen for last, maybe because I was in there.

"Mr. Larsen." It didn't seem right to call him Rhys, given the chill hanging between us.

"Yes?" He opened the now-empty fridge and gave it a cursory scan before closing the door.

"I have a proposition for you."

He tensed, and I couldn't hold back a bitter smile.

"Not that kind of proposition," I said. "And before I say it, I want you to know, it has nothing to do with...recent events." I hoped I wasn't making a fool of myself, but if I was, so be it. If I wanted something, I needed to voice it. Otherwise, I had no one to blame except myself when I was wracked with regrets over what-ifs. "You're a good bodyguard, and I'm already going through enough changes with Nikolai's abdication. I would like someone by my side who I'm comfortable with during the transition."

Rhys was so still he resembled a statue.

"If I put in the request, I think the palace would be amenable to extending your contract until I'm more comfortable in my new role." I took a deep breath. "It would mean you'd have to move to Eldorra temporarily, and I understand if that would be too much. But I wanted to give you the option. In case you wanted to stay."

I hadn't lied when I'd said it had nothing to do with last night. The idea had been brewing for weeks, and I'd kept putting it off. But we were getting down to the wire, and if I didn't speak up now, it would never happen.

Rhys finally blinked. "When do you need an answer by?"

I fought back another wave of disappointment. Of course he needed to think about it. It was a huge commitment. But still, I'd thought...

"Within the next week, before your contract officially ends."

He nodded, his expression neutral. "I'll let you know my answer before the end of the week. Thank you for the opportunity." Rhys left the kitchen, and I stared at the spot where he'd been standing.

That was it.

No smile, no hint as to whether he was happy or surprised or uncomfortable. Just *I'll let you know my answer before the end of the week,* like we were nothing more than professional acquaintances.

I tried eating another bite of toast before I gave up and buried my face in my hands.

Bridget von Ascheberg, what have you done?

RHYS AND I DIDN'T SPEAK DURING OUR LONG CAR RIDE TO the airport or the flight itself. Things between us were so strained I almost wished last night hadn't happened, but I couldn't bring myself to regret it.

The aftermath wasn't pretty, but the moment had been beautiful.

Bucket list number four.

It'd been so much more than a bucket list item, but that would be my secret to keep.

"You don't have to, but...can you join me tomorrow?" I asked as Rhys set my suitcase down in my suite. We'd landed in New York a few hours ago, and we were staying at The Plaza until I left for Eldorra in two days. Nikolai would announce his abdication tomorrow, and I had my press conference after that. The thought made me slightly sick to my stomach. "For the speech."

For the first time that day, Rhys's face softened. "Of course, princess."

It was funny how much I'd hated the nickname at first, but now it made my heart flutter.

Later that night, I tried to sleep, but my mind raced with a million thoughts and worries. Costa Rica, Rhys, whether he would stay on as my bodyguard, the public's reaction to Nikolai's abdication and engagement to Sabrina, my grandfather's health, my debut as crown princess, my move back to Eldorra...

I squeezed my eyes shut. *Breathe. Just breathe.*

Eventually, I fell into a restless sleep, plagued by nightmares of getting crushed beneath a giant crown in front of the palace while everyone pointed and laughed.

The next morning, I woke up earlier than planned to get ready for my press conference and cover the dark circles beneath my eyes with makeup. I skipped breakfast, not trusting myself to hold the food down, but when Rhys showed up at seven o'clock sharp as promised, he insisted on ordering eggs and a smoothie from room service. No coffee. He said it would help with my anxiety, and surprisingly, it did.

Nikolai's speech started at eight, and we watched in silence as my brother—clad in his military dress uniform, his face taut but determined—delivered the words that would change Eldorran history forever.

"...I hereby announce that I am abdicating my title of Crown Prince of Eldorra and removing myself from the royal line of succession. This decision did not come easy..."

The audience's gasps were audible even through the screen, but Nikolai forged on.

Most important decision of my life...

My love for the country...

Succeeded by my sister, Princess Bridget...

I sat stock-still the entire time. I'd known the abdication was coming, but it was surreal to see and hear Nikolai announce it on-screen.

After he ended his speech, the camera switched to a visibly stunned news anchor, but Rhys turned off the TV before I heard what the anchor had to say.

"Do you need a moment?" He radiated such natural confidence and authority it almost soothed frazzled nerves.

Almost.

I had my own press conference coming up soon, and I wanted to throw up.

Yes. Preferably a million moments.

"No." I cleared my throat and repeated in a stronger voice, "No. Let's go."

I checked my hair and clothes one last time before we exited my suite. Everything a royal family member said and wore in public had hidden symbolism, and I'd dressed for battle today in a sleek Chanel suit, heels, and a subtle ruby, gold, and diamond brooch that reflected Eldorra's flag colors.

The message: in control and ready to take over.

The reality: a complete mess.

As Rhys and I took the elevator down to the lobby, a certain numbness set in, making the world around me fuzzy.

Tenth floor...ninth floor...eighth floor...

My stomach sank further with each floor we passed.

When we reached the lobby, the elevator doors swished open, and I saw a thick crowd of reporters clustered around the hotel entrance, held back only by security. Their shouting reached a crescendo when they saw me, and everyone in the lobby turned to stare at the source of the commotion.

Me.

I'd dealt with the press plenty of times in the past, but this was my first encounter with them as crown princess. It shouldn't be any different, but it was.

Everything was different.

My breaths turned shallow. Pinpricks of darkness danced at the edge of vision, and my steps faltered.

"Breathe, princess," Rhys said quietly. Somehow, he always knew. "You are the future queen. Don't let them intimidate you."

Inhale. Exhale.

He was right. I couldn't start my first day in my new role scared and timid. Even if all I wanted was to run to my suite and never come out again, I had responsibilities to fulfill.

I can do this.

I was the future Queen of Eldorra. It was time to act like it.

I took a deep breath, straightened my shoulders, and lifted my chin, ignoring the stares of the other hotel guests as I walked toward the exit and the beginning of my new life.

PART II

21

BRIDGET

Six weeks later

"His Majesty is ready to see you." Markus stepped out of my grandfather's office, his face so pinched he looked like he'd just swallowed a lemon whole.

"Thank you, Markus." I smiled. He didn't smile back. He merely gave a quick nod of courtesy before he spun on his heels and marched down the hall.

I sighed. If I thought my becoming crown princess would improve my relationship with Edvard's closest advisor, I was sadly mistaken. Markus seemed more displeased than ever, maybe because the press coverage after my brother's abdication had...not been great.

Also not great? My nickname: Part-Time Princess. Apparently, the tabloids did not appreciate all the time their future queen had spent away from Eldorra, and they delighted in questioning my commitment to the country and general suitability for the throne every chance they got.

The worst part was, they weren't completely wrong.

"I'll see you tomorrow for the ribbon-cutting," I told

Mikaela, who'd accompanied me to my meeting with Elin earlier regarding image damage control.

"Sounds good." Mikaela snuck a peek at Edvard's half-open door. "Good luck," she whispered.

We didn't know why my grandfather wanted to speak to me, but we knew it wasn't good. He didn't summon me to his office unless it was serious.

"Thanks." I mustered a weak smile.

Mikaela had been my best friend growing up and was currently my right-hand woman during my training to be queen. The daughter of Baron and Baroness Brahe, she knew everything about everyone in Eldorran high society, and I'd recruited her to help me transition back into Athenberg society. I hadn't lived here in so long I was completely out of the loop, which was unacceptable for the future queen.

I hadn't expected her to say yes to such a big task, but to my surprise, she'd agreed.

Mikaela gave my arm a quick squeeze before leaving, and I steeled myself as I entered Edvard's office. It was a huge, mahogany-paneled room with double-height ceilings, windows overlooking the palace gardens, and a desk large enough to nap on.

Edvard's face crinkled into a smile when he saw me. He looked far healthier than he had in the weeks following his collapse, and he hadn't shown any symptoms since the big scare, but I still worried about him. The doctors said his condition was unpredictable, and every day I woke up wondering if that would be the last day I'd see my grandfather alive.

"How's training going?" he asked after I slipped into the seat opposite him.

"It's going well." I slid my hands beneath my thighs to tamp down my nerves. "Though some of the parliamentary sessions are quite..." *Tedious. Snooze worthy. So boring I would rather watch paint dry.* "Verbose."

Nobody liked hearing themselves talk more than a minister who had the floor. It was amazing how little one could say using so many words.

Unfortunately, a monarch's duties included attending parliamentary sessions at least once a week, and my grandfather thought it would be useful for me to get acquainted with the process now.

Ever since I returned to Eldorra, my days had been jam-packed with meetings, events, and "queen lessons" from the moment I woke up to the moment I went to sleep. I didn't mind, though. It kept my mind off Rhys.

Dammit. My chest squeezed, and I forced myself to push aside all thoughts of my old bodyguard.

Edvard's chuckle brought me back to the present. "A diplomatic way of putting it. Parliament is a different beast than what you're used to, but it *is* an essential part of government, and as Queen, you'll need a good relationship with them... which brings me to why I asked you here today." He paused, then said, "Actually, there are three things I wanted to discuss, starting with Andreas."

Confusion mingled with my wariness. "My cousin Andreas?"

"Yes." A small grimace crossed Edvard's face. "He'll be staying in the palace for a few months. He's due to arrive on Tuesday."

"*What?*" I quickly composed myself, but not before my grandfather frowned at the breach of propriety. "Why is he coming here?" I asked in a calmer voice, though I was anything but calm. "He has his own house in the city."

Andreas, the son of my grandfather's late brother Prince Alfred, was—how should I put this tactfully—a complete and utter ass. If entitlement, misogyny, and general asshole-ness could walk and talk, they would come in the form of one Andreas von Ascheberg.

Luckily, he'd moved to London for university and stayed there. I hadn't seen him in years, and I didn't miss him one bit.

Except now, he was not only returning to Eldorra but staying in the palace with us.

Kill me now.

"He would like to return to Eldorra permanently," Edvard said carefully. "Become more involved in politics. As for why he's staying here, he said he would like to reconnect with you since you haven't seen each other in so long."

I didn't believe that excuse for a second. Andreas and I had never gotten along, and the thought of him anywhere near politics made me want to run for the hills.

Unlike most constitutional monarchies, where the royal family stayed politically neutral, Eldorra welcomed royal participation in politics on a limited basis. I wished it didn't if it meant Andreas would have a hand in anything that might affect people's lives.

"Why now?" I asked. "I thought he was busy living the party life in London."

Andreas had always talked a big game, bragging about his grades and subtly hinting at what a good king he would make—sometimes to Nikolai's face, back when Nikolai had been first in line to the throne—but that was all it'd been. Talk. The closest he'd gotten to actually taking part in politics was majoring in it.

Edvard raised one thick, gray brow. "He's next in line for the throne after you."

I stared at him. He couldn't be implying what I thought he was implying.

Since my mother had been an only child and I didn't have

any children, Andreas was indeed second in the line of succession now that Nikolai had abdicated. I tried to picture him as king and shuddered.

"I'll be frank," Edvard said. "Andreas has hinted at certain...ambitions regarding the crown, and he does not believe a woman is up for the job."

Oh, how I wished Andreas was in the room right now so I could tell him where to shove his ambitions. "Perhaps he should tell Queen Elizabeth that the next time we visit Buckingham Palace," I said coolly.

"You know I disagree with him. But Eldorra is not Britain or Denmark. The country is more...traditional, and I'm afraid many members of Parliament secretly hold the same sentiment as Andreas."

I curled my fingers around the edge of my chair. "It's a good thing Parliament doesn't appoint the monarch then."

I may not *want* to rule, but I wouldn't stand for anyone telling me I *couldn't* rule because of my gender. Never mind the fact the monarchy was merely symbolic. We were the face of the nation, and there was no way in hell I'd let someone like Andreas represent us.

Edvard hesitated. "That's the other reason I wanted to speak with you. Parliament may not appoint the monarch, but there is the matter of the Royal Marriages Law."

A tight coil of dread formed in my stomach. The Royal Marriages Law, enacted in 1732, was the archaic law requiring monarchs to marry someone of noble blood. It was the reason Nikolai abdicated, and I'd avoided thinking about it as much as possible because it meant my chances of marrying for love were slim to none.

It wasn't simply a matter of finding a nobleman I liked. Potential marriage partners were chosen for maximum political gain, and I wasn't naïve enough to hope for a love match.

"I don't have to marry yet." I fought to keep the tremble out of my voice. "I have time—"

"I wish that were true." Edvard's face creased with a mixture of guilt and trepidation. "But my condition is unpredictable. I could collapse again any minute, and the next time, I might not be so lucky. Now that Nikolai has abdicated, there's even more pressure to ensure you're ready for the throne as soon as possible. That includes finding an acceptable husband."

Marriage technically wasn't a requirement for the monarch, but Eldorra hadn't had an unmarried ruler in...well, ever.

Bile rose in my throat, both at the possibility I might lose my grandfather at any minute and at the prospect of living out the rest of my life with a man I didn't love.

"I'm sorry, dear, but it's the truth," Edvard said gently. "I wish I could shield you from the harsh truths of life the way I used to, but you're going to be queen one day, and the time for sugarcoating is over. You are the last person in our direct line of succession, the only one who stands between Andreas and the crown"—we shuddered in unison—"and marriage to a respectable aristocrat, ideally within the next year, is the only way to ensure the throne and the country remains in good hands."

I dropped my head, resignation filling me. I could abdicate the way Nikolai had, but I wouldn't. As much as I resented him for putting me in this position, he'd done it for love. If I did it, it would be out of pure selfishness.

Besides, the country wouldn't survive *two* abdications so close to each other. We would be the laughingstock of the world, and I would never tarnish our family name or the crown by passing it on to Andreas.

"How am I supposed to find a husband so soon? My

schedule is already so full I hardly have time to sleep, much less date."

My grandfather's eyes crinkled, and he suddenly looked more like a mischievous youth than a king who'd ruled for decades. "Leave that to me. I have an idea, but before we get into it, there's one last thing we need to discuss. Your bodyguard."

The word *bodyguard* made my heart twist. "What about him?"

I was still getting used to my new bodyguard, Elias. He was fine. Nice, competent, polite.

But he wasn't Rhys.

Rhys, who'd rejected my offer to extend his contract.

Rhys, who'd walked away a month ago without looking back.

Rhys, who'd given me the most perfect four days of my life and acted like it had meant nothing to him afterward.

Maybe it hadn't. Maybe I'd imagined the connection we had, and he was busy living his best life in Costa Rica or South Africa right now.

Bucket list number four.

A familiar burn spread through my chest and behind my eyes before I set my jaw and composed myself.

Princesses don't cry. Especially not over a man.

"We received a rather unusual call from Harper Security," Edvard said.

Harper Security. The agency Rhys worked for.

"Is Rh—Mr. Larsen okay?" My pulse quickened with terror. Was he hurt? *Dead?*

I couldn't think of any other reason his employer would call, considering he was no longer contracted with the palace.

"He's fine." Edvard gave me a strange look. "However, they had an odd request. We normally wouldn't entertain such an idea, but Christian Harper has a considerable amount of influence. He's not someone you say no to lightly, even if you're the king, and he asked for a favor of sorts on behalf of Mr. Larsen."

I was growing more confused by the minute. "What's the favor?"

"He wants to rejoin your personal security detail."

If I hadn't been sitting, I would've fallen over in shock, and that was before Edvard added, "Permanently."

22

RHYS

"THAT MAKES US EVEN."

I stuck my phone between my ear and shoulder so I could grab my suitcase out of the overhead bin. "I told you already that it does."

"I want to make sure it sinks in." Christian's drawl seeped over the line, its smooth, lazy veneer hiding the razor blades beneath the surface. It reflected the man behind the voice, a debonair charmer who could kill you with one hand and a smile on his face.

Many a person had failed to look beyond the smile until it was too late.

It was what made Christian so dangerous and such an effective CEO of the world's most elite private security agency.

"I didn't realize you'd become so attached to the princess," he added.

My jaw flexed at the insinuation, and I nearly bowled over an older man wearing an unfortunate mud brown jacket in my haste to get off the plane. "I didn't become *attached*. She's the least annoying client I've had, and I'm sick of rotating between random pop stars and spoiled heiresses every few months. It's a practical decision."

In truth, I knew I'd fucked up less than twenty-four hours after I turned down her offer to extend my contract. I'd been on the plane back to D.C., and I would've forced the pilot to turn back if doing so wouldn't have landed me on the no-fly list and resulted in a very unpleasant detention courtesy of the U.S. government.

But Christian didn't need to know that.

"So you move to Eldorra, the country you hate most." It wasn't a question, and he sounded less than convinced. "Makes sense."

"I don't hate Eldorra." The country came with a lot of baggage for me, but I had nothing against the actual place. It was a me problem, not a them problem...for the most part.

The woman walking next to me in an I Heart Eldorra T-shirt stared at me, and I glared back until she blushed and hurried past.

"If you say so." A note of warning crept into Christian's voice. "I agreed to your request because I trust you, but don't do anything stupid, Larsen. Princess Bridget is a client. The future queen of Eldorra, at that."

"No shit, Sherlock." Christian was technically my boss, but I'd never been good at kissing ass, not even when I was in the military. It'd gotten me into my fair share of trouble. "And you didn't do this because you trust me. You did it because I spent the past month dealing with *your* mess."

If I hadn't, I would've taken the next plane back to Eldorra after I landed in D.C.

Then again, if I hadn't, Christian might not have agreed to pull his many strings for me. He didn't do anything purely out of the good of his heart.

"Either way, remember why you're there," he said calmly.

"You are to protect Princess Bridget from bodily harm. That's it."

"I'm aware." I exited the airport and was immediately hit with a blast of frigid air. Winter in Eldorra was cold as shit, but I'd survived colder in the Navy. The wind barely fazed me. "Gotta go."

I hung up without another word and took my place in the taxi line.

What had Bridget's reaction been when she found out I was returning? Happy? Angry? Indifferent? She hadn't refused my request to be reinstated as her bodyguard, which was a good sign, but I also wasn't sure the palace gave her a choice.

Whatever it was, I'd deal with it. I just wanted to see her again.

I'd left because I thought it was the right thing to do. We'd agreed what happened in Costa Rica would stay in Costa Rica, and I'd tried my best to distance myself afterward. To give us both a fighting chance. Because if we stayed near each other, we would end up in a place that could destroy her.

Bridget was a princess, and she deserved a prince. I wasn't that. Not even close.

But it only took a day away from her for me to realize I didn't give a damn. I couldn't act on my feelings, but I also couldn't stay away, so here I was. Being by her side without actually *being* with her would be a special form of torture, but it was better than not being near her at all. The past six weeks were evidence of that.

"You dropped this."

My muscles coiled, and I did a quick five-second assessment of the stranger who came up behind me.

He looked to be in his early to mid-thirties. Sandy hair, expensive coat, and the soft hands—both in full view—of someone who'd never done more taxing physical labor than lifting a pen.

Nevertheless, I kept my guard up. He wasn't a physical threat, but that didn't mean he couldn't be a threat in other ways. Plus, I didn't take well to random people approaching me.

"That's not mine." I flicked my eyes to the cracked black leather wallet in his hand.

"No?" He frowned. "I thought I saw it fall out of your pocket, but it's so crowded. I must've seen wrong." He examined me, his hazel eyes piercing. "American?"

I responded with a curt nod. I hated small talk, and something about the man unsettled me. My guard inched up further.

"I thought so." The man spoke perfect English, but he had the same faint Eldorran accent as Bridget. "Are you here on vacation? Not many Americans come in the winter."

"Work."

"Ah, I came back for work too, in a manner of speaking. I'm Andreas." He held out his free hand, but I didn't move.

I didn't shake random strangers' hands, especially not at the airport.

If Andreas was fazed by my rudeness, he didn't show it.

He slid his hand into his pocket and smiled, but it didn't quite reach his eyes. "Enjoy your stay. Maybe I'll see you around."

To some, it might've sounded friendly or even like a come-on. To me, it sounded vaguely like a threat.

"Maybe." I hoped not. I didn't know the guy, but I knew I didn't trust him.

I reached the head of the taxi line, and I didn't spare Andreas another glance as I tossed my suitcase in the trunk and gave the driver the palace's address.

It took almost an hour to reach the sprawling complex

thanks to traffic, and my body tightened with anticipation when the familiar gold gates came into view.

Finally.

It'd only been six weeks, but it felt like six years.

It was true what people said about not knowing what you had until it was gone.

After the entrance guard cleared me, I checked in with Malthe, the head security chief, then with Silas, the head of the royal household, who informed me I would stay in the palace's guesthouse. He showed me to the stone cottage, located fifteen minutes from the main building, and rambled on about household rules and protocol until I interrupted him.

"Is Her Highness here?" I stayed at the guesthouse every time I came to Eldorra, and I didn't need to listen to the whole song and dance again.

Silas heaved a deep sigh. "Yes, Her Highness is in the palace with Lady Mikaela."

"Where?"

"The second-floor drawing room. She's not expecting you until tomorrow," he added pointedly.

"Thank you. I can take it from here." Translation: *Go away.*

He let out another huge sigh before leaving.

After he left, I took a quick shower, changed, and headed back to the palace. It took a full half hour for me to reach the drawing room, and my steps slowed when I heard Bridget's silvery laugh through the doors.

God, I'd missed her laugh. I'd missed everything about her.

I pushed open the doors and stepped inside, my eyes immediately zeroing in on Bridget.

Golden hair. Creamy skin. Grace and sunshine, clad in her favorite yellow dress, which she always wore when she wanted to look professional but relaxed.

She stood in front of a giant whiteboard with what looked

like dozens of tiny headshots taped to it. Her friend Mikaela was waving her hands around and speaking animatedly until she noticed me.

"Rhys!" she exclaimed. She was a petite brunette with a head of curly hair, freckles, and an unnervingly perky personality. "Bridget told me you were coming back. It's so good to see you again!"

I tipped my head in greeting. "Lady Mikaela."

Bridget turned. Our eyes met, and the breath stole from my lungs. For six weeks, I'd only had the memory of her to cling to, and seeing her in person again was almost overwhelming.

"Mr. Larsen." Her tone was cool and professional, but a faint tremor ran beneath it.

"Your Highness."

We stared at each other, our chests rising and falling in sync. Even from halfway across the room, I could see the pulse fluttering at the base of her throat. The tiny beauty mark beneath her left ear. The way her dress hugged her hips like a lover's caress.

I never thought I'd be jealous of a dress, but here we were.

"You're just in time." Mikaela's voice shattered the spell. "We need a third opinion. Bridget and I can't agree."

"On what?" I kept my eyes on Bridget, who remained frozen where she stood.

"What should rank higher when it comes to a romantic partner, intelligence or a sense of humor?"

Bridget's shoulders stiffened, and I finally dragged my gaze away from her to Mikaela. "Rank?"

"We're ranking the guests for Bridget's birthday ball," Mikaela explained. "Well, I am. She refuses. But there's going to be so many men there, and she can't dance with them all. We need to narrow it down. There's one dance slot left, and I'm torn between Lord Rafe and Prince Hans." She tapped her pen against her chin. "Then again, Prince Hans is a *prince,* so maybe he doesn't need a sense of humor."

My warmth at seeing Bridget again vanished.

"What," I said, my voice a full two octaves lower than normal, "are you talking about?"

"Bridget's birthday ball." Mikaela beamed. "It's doubling as a matchmaking event. We're going to find her a husband!"

23

BRIDGET

I wanted to die.

If the floor opened up and swallowed me whole, I'd be the happiest person on earth. Or under earth, as the case would be.

Sadly, I remained in the drawing room with a whiteboard covered with pictures of European bachelors, a stone-faced Rhys, and an oblivious Mikaela.

"It's the event of the season," she continued. "The timing is rushed, but Elin's team is working on it around the clock and invites went out this morning. Dozens of people already RSVP'd yes." She let out a dreamy sigh. "All those handsome men, all dressed up in one room. I could simply die."

Yes, the big idea my grandfather had alluded to the other day in his office was a thinly veiled matchmaking gala. I'd protested, horrified at the thought of spending an entire evening—my *birthday*, no less—making small talk and dancing with over-inflated egos disguised as humans.

I'd been overruled.

Apparently, my twenty-fourth birthday was a good excuse to invite every eligible bachelor in Europe to the party, *and* it was coming up in a few weeks, which made for perfect timing, even if it was, as Mikaela had said, rushed.

"I didn't realize you were looking for a husband, Your Highness," Rhys said so coldly goosebumps erupted on my arms.

The current of electricity running between us froze, turning to ice.

At the same time, indignation kindled in my stomach. He had no right to be angry. *He* was the one who'd left and insisted on keeping things between us professional after Costa Rica. He couldn't possibly think he could waltz in here again after six weeks because he changed his mind and expect me to have put my life on hold for him.

"It's a politics and public image thing," Mikaela said before I could answer. "Anyway, what were we talking about? Right." She snapped her fingers. "Lord Rafe and Prince Hans. Never mind about that. Prince Hans ranks higher, of course." She moved his headshot to the *yes* side of the board.

"I'll leave you to it then, Your Highness. I was just checking in." Rhys's face shut down, and frustration stabbed at me, joining the cocktail of emotions coursing through my veins— excitement and giddiness at seeing him again, annoyance at his hypocrisy, lingering anger over his initial departure, and a smidge of guilt, even though we weren't dating, we'd never dated, and I was free to dance with every man in Athenberg if I wanted.

If we do this, it stays here. This room, this night. We don't talk about it again.

That was *his* rule, so why did I feel guilty at all?

"Mr. Larsen—"

"I'll see you tomorrow, Your Highness."

Rhys left.

Before I knew what I was doing, I followed him out the door, my spine hardening with determination.

I would *not* get drawn into an endless cycle of what-ifs again. I had enough to worry about. If Rhys had a problem, he could tell me to my face.

"Where are you going?" Mikaela called after me. "We still need to figure out the dance order!"

"Ladies' room," I said over my shoulder. "I trust you. Order them how you wish."

I quickened my steps and caught up with Rhys around the corner. "Mr. Larsen."

This time, he stopped but didn't turn around.

"The ball was my grandfather's idea. Not mine." I didn't owe him an explanation, but I felt compelled to give one anyway.

"It's your birthday, princess. You can do whatever you want."

I set my jaw even as my stomach fluttered at the word *princess*. "So, you're okay with me dancing with other men all night?"

Rhys finally turned, those inscrutable gray eyes flickering. "Why wouldn't I be? It sounds like the perfect solution. You'll find a nice prince, marry, and rule happily ever after." A mocking inflection colored his words. "The life of a princess, exactly as it should be."

Something inside me snapped, just like that.

I was *angry*. Angry at Nikolai for abdicating and running off to California with Sabrina afterward so they could "take some time" for themselves. Angry at not having control over my life. And most of all, angry at Rhys for turning our reunion into something ugly after we'd been apart for *six weeks*.

"You're right," I said. "It *is* the perfect solution. I can't wait.

Maybe I'll do more than dance. Maybe I'll find someone to kiss and take up to—"

Two seconds later, I found myself pinned to the wall. Rhys's eyes weren't flickering anymore. They had darkened, turning gray into near-black thunderclouds like the kind drenched the city in springtime. "Not a good idea to finish that sentence, princess," he said softly.

I'd provoked him on purpose, but I had to fight a shiver at the danger rolling off him.

"Take your hands off me, Mr. Larsen. We're not in the U.S. anymore, and you're overstepping your boundaries."

Rhys moved in closer, and I struggled to focus when I was so consumed by *him*. By his scent, his breath on my skin. By memories of lingering looks and stolen laughs and sunsets in a pool halfway across the world.

"Fuck my boundaries." Every word came out slow and deliberate, like he wanted to etch them into my skin.

"What a first day back on the job. It's just like old times." I pressed my back tighter against the wall, trying to escape the searing heat from Rhys's body. "Why are you here, Mr. Larsen? You were perfectly happy to walk away when I asked you to stay."

"If you think I was anything close to happy these past six weeks," he said grimly, "You couldn't be more wrong."

"You were happy enough to stay away for that long." I tried and failed to hide the note of hurt in my voice.

Rhys's face softened a smidge. "Trust me, princess. If I had a choice, I would've been back far sooner than that."

The velvety tips of butterfly wings brushed my heart.

Stop it. Stay strong.

"Which brings me back to my question," I said. "Why are you here?"

A muscle jumped in his jaw. He hadn't shaved that day, and thicker stubble peppered his face than I was used to.

I curled my hands into loose fists, resisting the urge to run them over the short black hairs on his cheek and the scar on his eyebrow. Just so I could reassure myself he was actually there.

Angry and infuriating, but *there*.

"Because I—"

"Am I interrupting something?"

Rhys moved off me so fast it took me a few seconds to process what happened. Once I did, and I saw who had interrupted us, my stomach sank.

Because standing at the end of the hall, wearing a half curious, half smirking expression, was none other than my cousin Andreas.

"I was on my way to my room when I heard something and came to investigate," he drawled. "Apologies if I...intruded."

Rhys spoke up before I could. "What the hell are you doing here?"

"I'm Bridget's cousin." Andreas smiled. "I guess I *will* see you around after all. Small world."

My head whipped between them. "You know each other?" How was that possible?

"We met at the airport," Andreas said casually. "I thought he dropped his wallet but, alas, I was mistaken. We had a nice little chat, though I never caught your name." He directed the last part at Rhys, who waited a few beats before answering.

"Rhys Larsen."

"Mr. Larsen is my bodyguard," I said. "He was...helping me get something out of my eye."

Secretly, I kicked myself for being so careless. We were in a side hallway of a quieter part of the palace, but there were eyes and ears everywhere. I should've known better than to get into it with Rhys where anyone could pass by and overhear.

Judging from Rhys's expression, he thought the same thing.

"Really? How considerate of him." Andreas didn't sound convinced, and I didn't like the way he was sizing us up.

I drew myself up to my full height and stared him down. I wouldn't let him intimidate me. Not in my own home.

"You mentioned you were on your way to your room," I said pointedly. "Don't let us stop you."

"First time we've seen each other in years, and this is the greeting I get." Andreas sighed, pulling off his gloves with deliberate slowness before slipping them in his pocket. "You're different now that you're crown princess, dear cousin."

"You're right," I said. "I *am* different. I'm your future queen."

Andreas's smile slipped, and I saw Rhys smirk out of the corner of my eye.

"I'm glad you made it here safely." I extended a small olive branch, if only because I had no desire to engage in overt hostilities with my cousin for the next month or however long he planned on staying here. "But I have a meeting I need to return to. We can chat later."

By later, I meant never, hopefully.

"Of course." Andreas tipped his head and cast one last glance at me and Rhys before disappearing down the hall.

I waited a good two minutes before I allowed myself to relax.

"Your cousin seems like a shithead," Rhys said.

I laughed, and the mood between us finally lightened.

"Not seems. He *is*. But he's also family, so we're stuck with him." I twisted my ring around my finger, trying to find a tactful way to bring us back to our earlier conversation. "About what happened before Andreas interrupted..."

"I came back because I wanted to come back," Rhys said. "And..." He paused, like he was debating whether to say what he was about to say. "I didn't want you to be alone while you're dealing with all this shit." He gestured toward our lavish surroundings.

Alone.

It was the second time he'd said it. First on my graduation night, and now. He was right both times.

I'd tried and failed to name the empty, gnawing feeling that'd haunted me since Rhys left. The one that crept up on me when I lay in bed at night and tried to think of something I looked forward to the next day. The one that washed through me at the oddest moments, like when I was in the middle of an event or pretending to laugh along with everyone else.

Now, I had a name for it.

Loneliness.

"Well." I smiled, trying to hide how much his words had affected me. "It's nice to have you back, Mr. Larsen. At least, when you're not acting like a grade-A you-know-what."

He chuckled. "It's nice to be back, princess."

This was the reunion I'd wanted. I didn't like Andreas, but at least he'd broken the ice between me and Rhys.

"So, where do we go from here?" No matter what we said, he wasn't just my bodyguard, and deep down, we both knew it.

"We go wherever you go," Rhys said. "I keep you safe. The end."

"You make it sound so simple." *When reality is so complicated.* Between Costa Rica, his departure, and his reappearance right when pressure to find a "suitable" husband bore down on me, I felt like a bug stuck in a web of secrets and responsibilities I couldn't free myself from.

"It is simple." Rhys spoke with such quiet confidence it resonated in my bones. "I made a mistake when I left, and I'm fixing it."

"Just like that."

"Just like that." The corner of his mouth tipped up. "Though I imagine you'll make it as difficult for me as possible."

I let out a soft laugh. "When have things ever been easy for us?"

But even though I was still upset with Rhys for leaving in the first place, I realized something. The empty, gnawing feeling had disappeared.

24

BRIDGET

"Might I say, you look absolutely beautiful tonight, Your Highness," Edwin, the Count of Falser, said as he guided me across the dance floor.

"Thank you. You look quite handsome yourself." With his sandy-colored hair and athletic build, Edwin wasn't hard on the eyes, but I couldn't summon much enthusiasm beyond my bland compliment.

After weeks of frenzied planning, the night of my big ball was finally here, and I couldn't be more underwhelmed. My dance partners had all been duds so far, and I hadn't had a chance to so much as breathe since I arrived. It'd been dance after dance, small talk after small talk. I hadn't eaten anything other than the two strawberries I snuck from the dessert table between dances, and my heels felt like razor blades strapped to my feet.

Edwin puffed out his chest. "I *do* put a lot of effort into my appearance," he said in a poor attempt at a humble tone. "Athenberg's top tailor customized my tuxedo, and Eirik—recently named by *Vogue* as Europe's top hairstylist—comes to my house every two weeks for maintenance. I also built a new gym in my house. Maybe you'll see it one day." He shot me a cocky smile. "I don't want to brag, but I believe it'll match anything you have in the palace. Top-of-the-line cardio machines, DISKUS dumbbell sets made of Grade 303 non-reactive stainless steel..."

My eyes glazed over. *Dear God.* I would rather listen to my last dance partner analyze Athenberg's traffic patterns during rush hour.

My dance with Edwin thankfully ended before he could expound further on his gym equipment, and I soon found myself in the arms of my next suitor.

"So." I smiled gaily at Alfred, the son of the Earl of Tremark. He was a few inches shorter than me, and I had a direct view of his balding spot. I tried not to let it deter me. I didn't want to be one of those shallow people who only cared about looks, but it would be easier *not* to focus on his looks if he gave me something else to work with. He hadn't looked me in the eye once since we started dancing. "I hear you're quite the, er, bird connoisseur."

Alfred had built an aviary on his estate, and according to Mikaela, one of his birds famously pooped on Lord Ashworth's head during the Earl's annual spring ball.

Alfred mumbled a reply.

"I'm sorry, I didn't catch that," I said politely.

Another mumble, accompanied by a crimson flush that spread all the way to his bald spot.

I did us both a favor and stopped talking. I wondered who'd forced him to attend tonight and who was having a worse time —him or me.

I stifled a yawn and looked around the ballroom, searching for something interesting to hold my attention. My grandfather held court with a few ministers in the corner. Mikaela hovered near the dessert table, flirting with a guest I didn't recognize, and Andreas snaked through the crowd, looking like, well, a snake.

I wished my friends were here. I'd video chatted with Ava, Jules, and Stella earlier that day, and I missed them so much it hurt. I would much rather spend my birthday eating ice cream and watching cheesy rom coms than dancing my feet off with people I didn't even like.

I need a break. Just a small one. Just so I could breathe.

"Apologies," I said so abruptly a surprised Alfred stumbled and nearly knocked the tray out of a passing server's hand. "I'm...not feeling well. Would you mind if I cut our dance short? I'm terribly sorry."

"Oh, not at all, Your Highness," he said, his words finally audible and filled with relief. "I hope you feel better soon."

"Thank you." I snuck a peek at Elin. She had her back turned as she chatted with the society columnist covering the party, and I slipped out of the ballroom before she saw me.

I hurried down the hall until I reached the restroom tucked into a quiet alcove, half-shielded by a giant bronze bust of King Frederick I.

I locked the door, sat on the toilet seat, and kicked off my shoes with a sigh of relief. My dress poufed around me in a cloud of pale blue silk and tulle. It was a gorgeous creation, as were my strappy silver heels and the diamond necklace resting against my collarbone, but all I wanted was to change into my pajamas and crawl into bed.

"Two more hours," I said. Or maybe it was three. It couldn't be more than three. I must've already danced with every man in the room, and I was no closer to a husband than I'd been at the beginning of the night.

I closed my eyes and rested my head in my hands. *Don't think about it.*

If I started thinking—about how the entire nation was watching me and how one of the men in the ballroom was likely my future husband—I would spiral. And if I started thinking about one particular man, gruff and scarred with eyes that could melt steel and hands that could melt *me*, I would end up on a path that could only lead to ruin.

I'd avoided looking at Rhys all night, but I knew he was there, dressed in a dark suit and earpiece and oozing such raw masculinity several female guests fluttered around him instead of the princes who were usually hot commodities at such parties.

We hadn't had any time alone since that day outside the drawing room, but that was probably a good thing. I didn't trust myself around him.

I stayed in the bathroom for another few minutes before I forced myself to leave. Otherwise, Elin would hunt me down and drag me back like I was an errant child.

I slipped my shoes back on with a small wince, opened the door—and walked straight into a wall.

A six-foot-five, unsmiling wall.

"Dear Lord!" My hand flew to my chest, where my heart beat triple time. "You scared me."

"Sorry." Rhys didn't sound sorry.

"What are you doing here?"

"You left the party. I'm your bodyguard." He raised an eyebrow. "Put two and two together."

Classic Rhys. If there was a rude way to answer a question, he'd find it.

"Fine. Well, I'm ready to return to the party, so if you'll excuse me..." I sidestepped him, but he grabbed my arm before I could go any further.

Time stopped and narrowed to where his large hand encircled my wrist. His natural tan contrasted with my winter pale skin, and his fingers were rough and callused, unlike the smooth, soft hands of the lords and princes I'd danced with all night. A knee-weakening desire to feel them slide over my skin, branding me as his, overtook me.

Bucket list number four.

My breathing sounded shallow in the tiny, intimate alcove. It wasn't right, the power this man had over me, but I was help-less in the face of my heart, hormones, and the indomitable force that was Rhys Larsen.

After what felt like an eternity, but in reality was only a few seconds, Rhys spoke. "I didn't get a chance to say this earli-er," he said. "But happy birthday, princess."

Thump, thump, thump, went my heart. "Thank you."

He didn't let go of my wrist, and I didn't ask him to.

The air between us thickened with unspoken words.

I wondered if we would've worked in a different life, a different world. One in which I was just a woman and he was just a man, unburdened by the rules and expectations of others.

And I hated myself for wondering those things because Rhys had never given me any indication he was interested in me beyond physical attraction and professional obligation.

None, except for the fleeting moments when he looked at me like I was his whole world, and he never wanted to blink.

"How are you enjoying the ball?"

I might've imagined it, but I thought I felt his thumb rub the soft skin of my wrist.

Thump. Thump. Thump.

"It's fine." I was too distracted by what might or might not be happening to my wrist to come up with a better answer.

"Just fine?" *There it was.* Another thumb rub. I could've sworn it. "You spent quite a bit of time with the Earl of Falser."

"How do you know which one the earl is?"

"Princess, I know every man who even *thinks* about

touching you. Much less one who you danced with. Twice,"
Rhys added, the word lethally soft.

It should've frightened me, but instead, my skin tingled and
my thighs clenched.

What is wrong with me?

"That's quite a talent." I'd only danced with Edwin twice
because he'd insisted, and I was too tired to argue.

Rhys's smile didn't quite reach his eyes. "So. The Earl of
Falser. Is he the one?"

"No." I shook my head. "Not unless I want to spend the
rest of my life hearing about his clothes and gym equipment."

Rhys pressed his thumb against my pounding pulse.
"Good."

The way he said it made it sound like the earl had escaped
death by a hair's breadth.

"I should return to the dance," I said, even though that was
the last thing I wanted. "Elin must be going crazy."

"*Going?*"

I laughed my first real laugh of the night. "You're terrible."

"But not wrong."

This was the Rhys I'd missed. The dry humor, the glimpses
of his hidden softness. This was the real Rhys.

"How does twenty-four feel?" he asked as we walked back
to the ballroom.

"Like twenty-three, except hungrier and more tired. How
does thirty-four feel?" He'd turned thirty-four during the weeks
we'd been apart. I'd thought about calling him on his birthday
but chickened out at the last minute.

"Like thirty-three, except stronger and smarter."

A grin touched his mouth at my half-amused, half-annoyed
huff.

When we returned to the ball, we found Elin waiting for us
at the entrance with her arms crossed over her chest.

"Good. You found her," she said without looking at Rhys. "Your Highness, where have you been?"

"I had to use the ladies' room." It was only half a lie.

"For forty minutes? You missed your dance with Prince Demetrios, who just left." Elin sighed. "Never mind. There are more potential suitors here. Go, quickly. The night is almost over."

Thank God for that.

I resumed my dances. Elin watched me like a hawk, and I was too terrified to look in Rhys's direction lest something show on my face that I didn't want her to see.

"Am I that boring?"

"I'm sorry?" I dragged my attention back to my current partner Steffan, the son of the Duke of Holstein.

"You keep looking over my shoulder. Either there's something fascinating happening behind me, or my in-depth analysis of the palace's architectural style isn't as scintillating as I thought."

A blush warmed my cheeks. "My apologies." None of my previous dance partners had picked up on my wandering attention, and I'd assumed he wouldn't either. "That was terribly rude of me."

"No apologies necessary, Your Highness." Steffan's eyes crinkled in a good-natured smile. "I must admit, I could've come up with a better conversation topic than the history of neoclassicism. That's what happens when I'm nervous. I spout all sorts of useless facts."

I laughed. "There are worse ways to deal with nerves, I suppose."

My skin suddenly burned, and I stumbled for a second before I caught myself.

"Are you all right?" Steffan asked, looking concerned.

I nodded, forcing myself not to look at Rhys, but I could *feel* the heat of his stare on my back.

Focus on Steffan. He was the most enjoyable dance partner I'd had all night, and he checked every box for an eligible Prince Consort: funny, charming, and handsome, not to mention the bluest of blue bloods.

I liked him. I just didn't like him *romantically*.

"It seems our time has come to an end," Steffan said when the music wound down. The night was finally over. "But perhaps we could go out sometime, just the two of us? The new skating rink on Nyhausen is quite nice, and they serve the best hot chocolate in the city."

A date.

I wanted to say no because I didn't want to lead him on, but that was the whole point of the ball—to find a husband, and I couldn't get a husband without dating first.

"That sounds lovely," I said.

Steffan grinned. "Excellent. I'll call you later and we'll set up the details."

"It's a plan."

I left to give my closing speech thanking everyone for attending, and after the guests filtered out one by one, I hurried out of the ballroom, eager to leave before Elin could get a hold of me.

I made it halfway to the exit before someone blocked my path.

"Your Highness."

I stifled a groan. "Lord Erhall."

The Speaker of Parliament stared down his nose at me. He was a tall, spindly man with graying hair and eyes like a reptile's, cold and predatory. He was also one of the most powerful people in the country, hence why he received an invite despite not being in the eligible bachelor age range.

"His Majesty and I missed you at yesterday's meeting," he said. "We discussed the new proposed tax reform legislation, which I'm sure you would have contributed greatly to."

I didn't miss the mocking undertone. I sometimes attended the weekly meetings my grandfather had with the Speaker, and Erhall had insinuated multiple times he thought I had no business being there.

He was one of the Parliament members Edvard had referred to when he'd said there were people who didn't want to see a woman on the throne.

"Indeed," I said coolly. "You've been trying to pass similar legislation for years, have you not, Mr. Speaker? It *does* seem it could benefit from new ideas."

Erhall's mouth tightened, but his voice was deceptively light when he responded. "I hope you enjoyed the ball, Your Highness. Husband hunting is surely a top priority for a princess."

Everyone knew the true purpose of the ball, but no one was stupid or untactful enough to voice it out aloud...except for Erhall, who wielded enough power he could get away with insulting the crown princess at her own party. There were even rumors he might be the next Prime Minister when he inevitably ran for the office.

I resisted the urge to slap him. That would play right into his game. No one would be happier than Erhall if my public image took a hit, which it would if I was caught attacking the Speaker of Parliament on my birthday.

"Let me be frank, Your Highness." Erhall smoothed his tie. "You are a lovely young woman, but being the monarch of Eldorra requires more than a pretty face. You have to understand the politics, the dynamics, the serious *issues* at hand. Your brother was trained for it, but you haven't even lived in Eldorra for the past few years. Don't you think it would be best if you handed the responsibilities of the crown to someone more suited to the role?"

"Who might that be?" My voice dripped poisonous honey. "Someone male, I presume."

It was unbelievable we were having this conversation, but no one had ever accused Parliament of moving forward with the times.

Erhall smiled, wise enough not to give a direct answer. "Whoever you think best, Your Highness."

"Let me be clear, Mr. Speaker." My face was hot and blotchy from humiliation, but I pushed past it. I wouldn't give him the satisfaction of seeing he'd gotten under my skin. "I have no intention of abdicating, stepping aside, or handing my responsibilities to anyone else." *No matter how much I want to.* "One day, I'll sit on the throne, and you'll have to answer to me —*if* you are still in power then." Erhall's face darkened at my not-so-subtle dig. "Therefore, it's best for everyone involved if we have a civil relationship." I paused, then added, "On that note, I suggest monitoring your tone when speaking with me or any member of the royal family. You are a guest here. That's it."

"You—" Erhall took a step toward me, then blanched and quickly stepped back.

Rhys came up beside me, his face expressionless but his eyes darker than a thundercloud. "Is he bothering you, Your Highness?"

Erhall glared at him but wisely kept his mouth shut.

"No. The Speaker was just leaving." I flashed a polite smile. "Weren't you, Mr. Speaker?"

The Speaker's lips thinned. He gave me a tight nod and a curt "Your Highness" before spinning on his heel and marching away.

"What did he say to you?" Menace rolled off Rhys in

palpable waves, and I was certain he would hunt Erhall down and snap his neck if I gave the okay.

"Nothing worth repeating. Really," I repeated when Rhys continued glaring at the spot where Erhall had stood. "Forget about him."

"He was about to grab you."

"He wouldn't have." I wasn't sure what Erhall had planned to do before Rhys showed up, but he was too savvy to lose his cool in public. "Please, drop it. I just want to sleep. It's been a long night."

I didn't want to waste more energy on Erhall. He wasn't worth it.

Rhys complied, though he didn't look happy about it. Then again, he rarely looked happy.

He escorted me to my room, and when we arrived at my door, he pulled something out of his suit pocket.

"Your birthday present," he said gruffly, handing me a rolled-up sheet of paper tied with a ribbon. "Nothing fancy, but I had it and thought you might like it."

My breath caught. "You didn't have to get me anything."

We never bought each other birthday presents. The most we did was buy each other a meal, and even then, we pretended it was for something other than the other's birthday.

"It's not a big deal." Rhys watched, shoulders tense, while I carefully untied the ribbon and unrolled the paper.

Once I saw what was on it, I gasped.

It was me.

A drawing of me, to be exact, in a pool surrounded by hills with the ocean in the distance. Head tipped back, smile on my face, looking freer and happier than I ever remembered feeling. The curve of my lips, the sparkle in my eyes, even the tiny mole beneath my ear...

He'd captured it all in exquisite, painstaking detail, and

looking at me through his eyes, I believed I was the most beautiful woman in the world.

"It's not jewelry or anything like that," Rhys said. "Keep it if you want or toss it. I don't care."

"Toss it?" I clutched the drawing to my chest. "Are you kidding? Rhys, this is beautiful."

My words hung in the air, and we realized at the same time I'd called him by his name again. My first time doing so since Costa Rica.

But it felt right because, at that moment, he *wasn't* Mr. Larsen. He was Rhys.

And Rhys had given me the best gift I'd ever received. He was right—it *wasn't* a fancy purse or diamond jewelry, but I would much rather have one sketch from him than a hundred Tiffany diamonds.

Anyone could buy a diamond. No one except him could've drawn me the way he did, and it didn't escape my notice this was the first time he'd ever shared his art with me.

"It's all right." He shrugged.

"It's not all right, it's *beautiful*," I repeated. "Seriously, thank you. I'll treasure this forever."

I never thought I'd see the day, but Rhys blushed. Actually *blushed*.

I watched in fascination as the red spread across his neck and cheeks, and the desire to trace its path with my tongue gripped me.

But of course, I couldn't do that.

I could tell he wanted to say something else, but whatever it was, he thought better of it. "It's no security alarm, but I can save that for Christmas," he said with a lopsided smile.

I grinned, giddy from the combination of his gift and his joke. There was nothing I loved better than seeing the normally serious Rhys joke around. "I'll hold you to that."

"Good night, princess."

"Good night, Mr. Larsen."

That night, I lay in bed and stared at Rhys's drawing in the moonlight filtering through the curtains. I wished I was that girl again. Not yet crown princess, soaking up the sun in a remote town where no one could find me. But I wasn't.

Perhaps I loved Rhys's drawing so much not only because he was the artist, but because it immortalized a version of myself I could never be again.

I gently rolled the sketch up and tucked it into a safe corner of my bedside drawer.

Part-Time Princess.

Being the monarch of Eldorra requires more than a pretty face.

Let me be clear, Mr. Speaker. I have no intention of abdicating, stepping aside, or handing my responsibilities to anyone else.

Until now, I'd been a passive participant in my own life, letting others make my decisions, the press run roughshod over me, and the likes of Erhall condescend to me.

Not anymore. It was time to take matters into my own hands.

The game of Eldorran politics was a battlefield, and this was war.

25

RHYS

SOMEONE ONCE SAID HELL WAS OTHER PEOPLE.

They were right.

Specifically, hell was *watching* other people swan around an ice rink, drinking hot chocolate and making googly eyes at each other like they were in the middle of a goddamn Hallmark movie.

It wasn't even Christmas season, for fuck's sake. It was worse.

It was Valentine's Day.

A muscle flexed in my jaw as Bridget's laughter floated over, joined by Steffan's deeper laugh, and the urge to murder someone—someone male with blond hair and a name that began with S—intensified.

What was so fucking hilarious, anyway?

I couldn't imagine anything being that funny, least of all something Steffan the Saint said.

Bridget and Steffan shouldn't even *be* on a date right now. It was only four days after her birthday ball. Who the hell went on a date with someone they met four days ago? There should be background checks. Red tape. Twenty-four-seven surveillance to make sure Steffan wasn't secretly a psycho killer or adulterer.

Princesses shouldn't go on a date until there was at least a year's worth of data to comb through, in my opinion. Five years, to be on the safe side.

Unfortunately, my opinion meant jack shit to the royal family, which was how I found myself at Athenberg's biggest ice-skating rink, watching Bridget smile up at Steffan like he'd cured world hunger.

He said something that made her laugh again, and his grin widened. He brushed a stray strand of hair out of her face, and my hand twitched toward my gun. Maybe I would've pulled it, had reporters not packed the rink, snapping pictures of Bridget and Steffan, recording on their cameras, and live-tweeting the date like it was an Olympic event.

"They make such a cute couple," the reporter next to me, a curvy brunette in a bright pink suit that hurt my eyes, cooed. "Don't you think so?"

"No."

She blinked, clearly surprised by my curt response. "Why not? Do you have something against his lordship?"

I could practically see her salivating at the prospect of a juicy story.

"I'm staff," I said. "I have no opinions about my employer's personal life."

"Everyone has opinions." The reporter smiled, reminding me of a shark circling in the water. "I'm Jas." She held out her hand. I didn't take it, but that didn't deter her. "If you think of an opinion...or anything else..." A suggestive note crept into her voice. "Give me a call."

She pulled a business card out of her purse and tucked it into my hand. I almost let it fall to the floor, but I wasn't *that* much of an asshole, so I merely pocketed it without looking at it.

Jas's cameraman said something to her in German, and she turned away to answer him.

Good. I couldn't stand nosy people or small talk. Besides, I was busy—busy trying not to kill Steffan.

I'd run a background check on him before today's date, and on paper, he was fucking perfect. The son of the Duke of Holstein, one of the most powerful men in Eldorra, he was an accomplished equestrian who spoke six languages fluently and graduated top of his class from Harvard and Oxford, where he studied political science and economics. He had a well-established record of philanthropy and his last relationship with an Eldorran heiress ended on amicable terms after two years. Based on my interactions with him so far, he seemed friendly and genuine.

I hated him.

Not because he grew up in a life of privilege, but because he could freely touch Bridget in public. He could take her ice skating, make her laugh, and brush her hair out of her eye, and no one would blink an eye.

Meanwhile, all I could do was stand there and watch, because women like Bridget weren't meant for men like me.

"You'll never amount to anything, you little piece of shit," Mama *slurred, her eyes mean and hateful as she glared at me.* *"Look atcha. Useless and scrawny. I should've gotten rid of you when I had the chance."*

I stayed quiet. The last time I talked back, she beat me so hard with her belt I'd bled through my shirt and couldn't sleep on my back for weeks. I'd learned the best way to handle her bad moods was to hope she eventually forgot I was there. That usually happened after she was halfway through whatever bottle she was drinking.

"If it wasn't for you, I'd be out of this stinkin' town by now."

Resentment poured off her in waves. Mama stood by the table, wearing her faded pink robe and chain-smoking a cigarette. Her cheeks were pale and sunken, and even though she was only in her late twenties, she could pass for her forties.

I tucked my hands beneath my arms and tried to shrink into myself while she continued to rant. It was Friday night. I hated Friday nights because it meant I had an entire weekend of just Mama and me.

"Waste of space...nothing like your father...are you listening to me, you piece of shit?"

I stared at the cracks in the floor until they blurred together. One day, I would get out of here. Somehow, some way.

"I said, are you listening to me?" Mama grabbed my shoulders and shook me so hard my teeth rattled. "Look at me when I'm talking to you, boy!" She backhanded me so hard I stumbled, the pain making my ears ring.

My body twisted, and I saw it coming, but I didn't have time to brace myself before the corner of the dining table smashed into my head and everything went black.

I blinked, and the smell of old spaghetti sauce and vodka faded, replaced by that of fresh ice and Jas's overpowering perfume.

Bridget and Steffan skated over, and the cameras went crazy.

Click. Click. Click.

"...for a while," Steffan said. "But I would love to take you out again when I return."

"Are you going somewhere?" I asked.

It was inappropriate for me to butt into their conversation, but I didn't give a fuck.

Steffan cast a startled glance in my direction. "Yes. My mother fell and broke her hip yesterday. She's fine, but she's recovering at our house in Preoria. She's quite lonely with my father here in session for Parliament, so I'll be staying with her until she feels better."

He answered with full graciousness, which only annoyed me more. The harder he was to hate, the more I hated him.

"How sad," I said.

Steffan paused, clearly unsure how to read my tone.

"Hopefully, she recovers soon." Bridget shot me a look of mild rebuke. "Now, about that hot chocolate..."

She guided him toward the hot chocolate stand at the other end of the rink while I fumed.

Taking a permanent position as Bridget's bodyguard meant I'd have to deal with seeing her date other people. I knew that, and that would be my cross to bear.

I just hadn't expected it to happen so soon.

She'd dated in New York, but that had been different. She hadn't liked any of those guys, and she hadn't planned on *marrying* one of them.

Acid gnawed at my gut.

Thankfully, the date ended soon after, and I whisked her into the car before Steffan could pull any first date kiss bullshit.

"Initial recovery for a broken hip takes one to four months," I said as we drove back to the palace. "Too bad for his lordship. What shitty timing."

Even fate didn't think it was a good pairing. If it did, it wouldn't have pulled Steffan away so soon after he met Bridget.

I'd never believed in fate, but I might have to send her a big, fat thank you card later. I might even toss in some chocolates and flowers.

Bridget didn't take the bait. "Actually, it's perfect timing," she said. "I'll be away from Athenberg for a few weeks as well."

I eyed her in the rearview mirror. That was fucking news to me.

"It's not confirmed yet, so don't give me that look," she said. "I've proposed going on a goodwill tour around the country. Meet with locals and small businesses, find out what's on their minds and what issues they're facing. I've gotten a lot of criticism for not being in touch with what's happening in Eldorra, and, well, they're right."

"That's a great idea." I turned onto King's Drive.

"You think so?" A note of relief tempered the uncertainty in Bridget's voice.

"I'm no expert on politics, but it sounds right to me."

Bridget may not want to be queen, but that didn't mean she wouldn't make a great one. Most people thought the most important quality in a leader was strength, but it was compassion. Strength meant jack shit when you didn't use it for the right reasons.

Luckily for her and for Eldorra, she had both in spades.

"The king still has to approve it," she said after we parked and walked to the palace entrance. "But I don't anticipate him saying no."

"You mean your grandfather." Royals did things differently, but it weirded me out how formal they were with each other sometimes.

Bridget flashed a quick smile as we entered the grand front hall. "In most cases, yes. But in matters like this, he's my king."

"Speaking of the king..."

We both stiffened at the new voice.

"...He wants to see you." Andreas swaggered into view, and irritation curled through me. I didn't know what it was about him that bugged me so much, but Bridget didn't like him, and that was good enough for me. "How was the date? Did you get a marriage proposal yet?"

"You need to find a new hobby if you're that invested in my love life," Bridget said evenly.

"Thank you, but I have plenty of hobbies to keep me occupied. For instance, I just came from a meeting with His Majesty and Lord Erhall on the tax reform legislation." Andreas smiled at Bridget's surprise, which she quickly covered up. "As you may know, I'm interested in taking up politics, and the Speaker was kind enough to let me shadow him for a few weeks. See how it all works."

"Like an intern," Bridget said.

Andreas's smile sharpened. "One who's learning quite a lot." He slid his glance toward me. "Mr. Larsen, good to see you again."

Wish I could say the same. "Your Highness." I loathed addressing him with the same title as Bridget. He didn't deserve it.

"His Majesty is waiting for you in his office," Andreas told Bridget. "He wants to see you. Alone. Now, if you'll excuse me, I have some pressing matters that require my attention. Though none as exciting as a date at an ice-skating rink, I'm sure."

It took all my self-control not to knock all his teeth out.

"Say the word, and I can make it look like an accident," I said after Andreas was out of earshot.

Bridget shook her head. "Ignore him. He's been a satanic little turd since we were children, and he thrives on the attention."

A startled laugh rose in my throat. "Tell me the words 'satanic little turd' didn't just leave your mouth, princess."

She responded with a sly smile. "I've called him worse in my head."

That's my girl.

It was nice to see glimpses of the real Bridget shine through, even when she was weighed down with all the royal bullshit.

While she met with the king, I returned to the guesthouse,

though I supposed it was my actual house now that I was working here permanently.

I'd just entered my room when my phone rang. "Yeah."

"Hello to you, too," Christian drawled. "People have no phone manners these days. It's such a shame."

"Get to the point, Harper." I placed him on speaker and yanked my shirt over my head. I was about to toss it in the laundry basket when I paused. Looked around.

I couldn't put my finger on it, but something was off.

"Always the charmer." There was a short pause before Christian said, "Magda's gone."

I froze. "What do you mean, gone?"

I'd spent a month guarding Magda at Christian's request until another hand-selected guard finished his contract with his previous client and took over. It was why I couldn't return to Eldorra earlier.

"I mean, gone. Rocco woke up this morning, and she'd disappeared. No tripped alarms, nothing."

"You can't find her?"

Christian could find anyone and anything with even the smallest digital footprint. His computer skills were legendary.

His voice chilled. "I can and I will."

I suddenly felt sorry for anyone who had a hand in Magda's disappearance. But they deserved what was coming to them if they were stupid enough to cross Christian Harper.

"What do you need me to do?"

"Nothing. I'll take care of it. Just thought you should know." Christian's drawl returned. Even when he was furious, as I imagined he must be over getting one-upped, he could act like everything was just dandy...before he gutted the offending party like a fish. "How goes it with the princess?"

"Fine."

"Heard she went on a date today."

A vein pulsed in my forehead. First Andreas, now him. Why did every person insist on bringing that up? "I was there. But thank you for the breaking news."

The bastard laughed.

I hung up, cutting him off. It was turning into a habit, but if he had a problem with it, he could tell me to my face.

Then again, Christian had bigger problems on his hands if Magda was missing.

I looked around my room again, trying to pinpoint the source of my earlier nagging feeling. The windows were closed and locked from the inside, all my belongings were where they should be, and nothing was physically amiss.

But my gut was never wrong, and something told me someone had been in here recently...someone who shouldn't be.

26

BRIDGET

My grandfather wanted to know how my date with Steffan went.

That was right. The reason the king summoned me to his office immediately after I returned to the palace was so I could give him a detailed breakdown of my first date with the future Duke of Holstein—and potential future Prince Consort. He did also apologize for not including me in the "emergency" tax reform meeting, which Erhall called at the last minute. I was convinced Erhall did so knowing I wouldn't be able to attend because of my date with Steffan, but I couldn't prove it.

Edvard, meanwhile, was convinced Steffan was *the one.* Based on what, I wasn't sure, but I imagined Steffan's title, photogenic looks, and diplomatic demeanor had something to do with it.

My grandfather wasn't the only one. The press and public went *wild* for the photos of us at the ice-skating rink, and everyone was already buzzing about our "burgeoning relationship" even though I'd spoken to Steffan twice in my life.

Still, Elin insisted I capitalize on the attention with another date. It would be a "private" one with no reporters—to give the illusion of intimacy—but would later "leak" to the press. I agreed, if only because she was right. The Part-Time Princess headlines had disappeared, replaced by breathless speculation over the new "love" in my life.

If only they knew.

On paper, Steffan would make the perfect husband. He was good-looking, intelligent, kind, and funny, and he was by far the best option out of the so-called eligible bachelors who'd attended my birthday ball.

There was only one problem: no chemistry.

None. Zip. Nada.

I had as much romantic interest in Steffan as I did the succulent plant in my room.

"It's because you haven't kissed him yet," Mikaela said when I told her about my dilemma. "At least kiss the man. You can tell everything based on one kiss."

She may be right.

So, at the end of my second date with Steffan, I worked up the nerve to kiss him, even though it seemed far too soon. But he was leaving for Preoria tomorrow, and I *needed* to know if this would go anywhere. I couldn't spend weeks wondering.

"I must admit, I was surprised you wanted to meet again so soon after our first date." He gave me a shy smile. "Pleasantly surprised, that is."

We walked through the Royal Botanic Gardens' large, heated greenhouse. Lush flowers bloomed around every corner, scenting the air with their sweet perfume, and strings of lights twinkled overhead like tiny stars. It was as romantic a setting as one could hope for, and I tried to focus on Steffan instead of the scowling bodyguard shadowing our every move.

If looks could kill, Rhys would've put Steffan six feet in the ground by now.

That was another reason I was hesitant to kiss Steffan. It seemed...wrong to do that in front of Rhys.

God, I wished I'd thought this through beforehand.

"I had fun," I said when I realized I hadn't responded yet. "Thanks for agreeing even though I'm sure you're busy preparing for your trip tomorrow."

"Of course."

Steffan smiled.

I smiled.

My palms slicked with sweat.

Just do it. One tiny kiss. You have nothing to feel guilty about. You and Rhys aren't dating.

"I'm not sure why, but I have the strangest desire to give a rundown of all the fun facts I know about flowers," Steffan said. "Did you know tulips were worth more than gold in seventeenth-century Holland? Literally."

That's what happens when I'm nervous. I start spouting all sorts of useless facts.

A subtle hint from Steffan he wanted a kiss too. He had no reason to be nervous otherwise.

I discreetly wiped my palms on my skirt. *Don't look at Rhys.* If I did, I would never go through with it.

"That's fascinating." I winced when I realized that was the sort of answer someone gave when they found the subject anything *but* interesting. "Truly."

Steffan laughed. "I'm afraid there's only one way to stop me from boring you death with my floral knowledge, Your Highness," he said somberly.

"What's that?" I asked, distracted by the sensation of Rhys's gaze burning a hole in my side.

"This." Before I could react, Steffan's lips were on mine, and even though I knew the kiss was coming, I was still so stunned I could only stand there.

He tasted faintly of mint, and his lips were soft as they brushed against mine. It was a nice, sweet kiss, the kind cameras zoomed in on in movies and most women swooned over.

Unfortunately, I wasn't one of them. I might as well be kissing my pillow.

Disappointment crashed into me. I'd hoped a kiss would change things, but it only confirmed what I already knew. Steffan, for all his wonderful traits, wasn't for me.

Maybe I was naïve for thinking I could find a fiancé to whom I was attracted to *and* whose company I enjoyed, but I was only in my twenties. No matter how much everyone tried to rush me, I wasn't ready to give up on my hope for love yet.

I finally gathered enough of my wits to pull back, but before I could, a loud crash shattered the silence in the greenhouse.

Steffan and I jumped apart, and my eyes fell on Rhys, who stood next to a broken pot of lilies.

"My hand slipped." His voice held not an ounce of apology.

That was, for lack of a better term, utter crap. Rhys didn't slip. He may be larger than the average person, but he moved with the lethal grace of a panther.

That was what he reminded me of right now—a panther preparing to pounce on unwitting prey. Taut face, coiled muscles, and eyes trained with laser intensity on Steffan, who shifted with discomfort beneath his stare.

"*Attention all guests, the gardens are closing in fifteen minutes.*" The announcement blared over the PA system, savings from the most awkward moment of my life. "*Please make your way to the exits. The gardens are closing in fifteen minutes. Visitors in the gift shop, please finalize your purchases.*"

"I guess that's our cue." Steffan held out his arm with a

smile, though he kept a wary eye on Rhys. "Shall we, Your Highness?"

We'd booked the greenhouse for ourselves, though the rest of the gardens remained open to the public. We could probably stay longer if we wanted, but I had no desire to drag out the night.

I took Steffan's arm and walked to the exit, where we said goodbye with a stilted half-hug, half-kiss on the cheek and promises to meet up again when he returned to Athenberg.

Rhys and I didn't speak until we reached our car.

"You're paying for the flowerpot," I said.

"I'll take care of it."

The parking lot was empty except for a handful of cars in the distance, and tension rolled between us, so thick I could practically taste it.

"I know he fits the image of Prince Charming, but you might want to keep looking." Rhys unlocked the car doors. "I've seen you kiss a cat with more passion."

"Is that why you knocked over the lilies?"

"My. Hand. Slipped," he bit out.

Maybe it was the wine I'd had at dinner, or the stress was getting to me. Whatever it was, I couldn't help it—I burst into laughter. Wild, hysterical laughter that left me gasping for breath and clutching my stomach right there in the middle of the parking lot.

"What the hell is so funny?" Rhys's grumpy tone only made me laugh harder.

"You. Me. Us." I wiped tears of mirth from my eyes. "You're an ex-Navy SEAL and I'm royalty, and we're in such denial we might as well apply for Egyptian citizenship."

He didn't crack a smile at my admittedly lame attempt at a joke.

"I don't know what you're talking about."

"Stop it." I was tired of fighting. "I asked you before, and I'm asking you again. Why did you come back, Mr. Larsen? The real answer this time."

"I gave you the real answer."

"The *other* real answer."

Rhys's jaw clenched. "I don't know what you want me to say, princess."

"I want you to say the truth."

I knew my truth. I needed to hear his.

My truth? There was only one man who'd ever given me butterflies with a kiss. One man whose touch set me on fire and made me believe in all the fantastical things I'd dreamed about since I was a child.

Love, passion, desire.

"Truth?"

Rhys took a step toward me, the hard steel in his eyes giving way to turbulent thunderstorms.

I took an instinctive step back until my back hit the side of our SUV. There was another car next to us, and the two vehicles formed a makeshift cocoon that crackled with electricity as he planted his hands on either side of my head.

"The *truth*, princess, is I came back knowing this was what I signed up for. To see you every day and not be able to touch you. Kiss you. *Claim* you." Rhys's breath was hot against my skin as he lowered one hand and slid it up my thigh. It seared through the thick layers of my skirt and tights until my pussy clenched and my nipples tightened into hard points. "I came back despite knowing the torture I'd have to go through because I can't stay away from you. Even when you're not there, you're everywhere. In my head, in my lungs, in my fucking soul. And I'm trying very hard not to lose my shit right now, sweetheart, because all I want is to cut off that fucker's head and serve it on a platter for daring to touch you. Then bend you over the hood and spank your ass raw for letting him." He cupped me between my legs and squeezed. I whimpered with a mixture of pain and pleasure. "So don't. Push. Me."

A thousand emotions ran through my veins, turning me lightheaded with arousal and danger.

Because what Rhys just said was dangerous. What we were doing, *feeling*, was dangerous.

But I couldn't bring myself to care.

"Rhys, I—"

The blare of a car alarm sliced through the still night air, followed by a burst of laughter in the distance. I blinked, some of the haze clearing from my head, yet I didn't move.

Rhys pushed himself off me with a hard smile. "There's your truth, princess. Happy?"

I tried again. "Rhys—"

"Get in the car."

I did as he asked. I wasn't stupid enough to push him right now.

"We need to talk about this," I said once we were on the road.

"I'm done talking."

From my seat in the back, I could see the muscles in his neck corded with anger, and he gripped the steering wheel so tight his knuckles popped.

He was right. There would be no more talking tonight.

I stared out the window at the passing lights of Athenberg. If I thought my life was complicated before, it was nothing compared to the mess I found myself in now.

27

BRIDGET

Two weeks after my date with Steffan, I left for my goodwill tour with Mikaela, Rhys, another bodyguard named Elliott, the palace photographer Alfred, Alfred's assistant Luna, and Henrik, a reporter from the *Eldorra Herald*.

Everyone loved my idea, including my grandfather, and the palace had worked around the clock to put together the perfect itinerary on short notice. We hit all the country's most important regions, including the manufacturing hub of Northern Kurtland and the oil and energy center of Hesbjerg. I felt like I was campaigning for an office I'd already won, somewhat undeservingly, thanks to genetic lottery.

But I had to do it. After years of living abroad, I needed to reconnect with the people of Eldorra. Understand the way they lived, what problems kept them up at night, and what they wanted that was within my power to give. In practice, the prime minister and Parliament ruled the country, but the royal family, as an institution, wielded considerably more power in Eldorra than in other countries. It boasted an eighty-nine percent approval rating—far higher than any politician—and the monarch's opinions held a lot of sway.

If I were to be a good queen, I needed to get back in touch with the people. It didn't matter that I didn't want the crown. It would be mine one day regardless.

"It's just us and a handful of staff," Ida, the owner of the dairy farm we were visiting, said. "Our farm is on the smaller side, but we do the best we can."

"It looks like you're doing a lovely job." I walked through the barn. It was smaller than the others we'd visited, but it was well-kept, and the cows looked healthy. However, I noticed half of the stalls were empty. "Are the other cows with the farmhands?"

Behind us, Alfred's camera clicked and whirred. The Part-Time Princess headlines, which were already fading thanks to my dates with Steffan, had all but disappeared during the tour, replaced with pictures of me touring factories and reading to schoolchildren.

I would've done the tour even if no one covered it, though. I *enjoyed* meeting with locals, far more than I did another tedious gala.

"No." Ida shook her head. "The dairy industry isn't doing so well. Milk prices have gone down over the years, and a lot of farms in the area have shut down. We had to sell some of our cows for extra cash. Plus, there isn't enough demand for milk to justify keeping so many of them around."

Despite her words, sadness flitted across her face. The farm had belonged to her family for generations, and I could only imagine how difficult it must be to see it shrink year after year.

"Have you contacted your minister about the issue?"

According to my briefing materials, the drop in milk prices resulted from a trade fight between Eldorra and a few other countries in Europe. Trade and tariff policies fell under Parliament's purview.

Ida shrugged, looking resigned. "We used to write to our officials, but we only got form responses, so we stopped. No one listens to us anyway."

I frowned. The whole point of Parliament was to represent constituents' concerns. What were they doing if not their job?

"You can write to me," I said on impulse. "All of your friends and neighbors can write to me. If you have an issue you want addressed, write or email me and I'll bring it up with Parliament. I can't guarantee legislation, but I can at least make sure your voices are heard."

Elin coughed, and Henrik the reporter scribbled furiously in his notepad.

Ida blinked. "Oh, I couldn't possibly—"

"I insist," I said firmly. "Elin, can you please share the mailing and email addresses with Ida before we leave? Actually, please share them with everyone we've met so far."

Elin rubbed her temple. "Yes, Your Highness."

She waited until we returned to the inn that night before laying into me.

"Princess Bridget, the point of this tour is to create *goodwill*," she said. "Not make things more complicated with Parliament. Do you really want random people writing to you about the smallest problem?"

"They're not random people, they're Eldorrans." I sat in the common room with Rhys while Elin stood by the fireplace, her hands on her hips. Henrik, Alfred, Luna, and Elliott had already retired to their rooms. "I'm not changing policy. I'm merely helping people get their voices heard. No," I said when Elin opened her mouth. "I'm not arguing about this. It's been a long day, and we have an early morning tomorrow."

Her mouth pinched, but she conceded with a reluctant, "Yes, Your Highness."

She was a master at choosing which battles to fight, and apparently, this one wasn't worth fighting.

She disappeared up the stairs, leaving me alone with Rhys.

He sat in the corner, staring at the flames in the hearth with a brooding expression. Whatever was bothering him, it wasn't us and what happened in the parking lot of the Royal Botanic Gardens. It was something else. He'd been moodier than usual since the trip started.

"Penny for your thoughts," I said. We'd barely talked the entire trip, unless *good morning* and *good night* counted as talking.

Rhys finally looked at me. The firelight flickered over his face, casting dancing shadows over his strong jaw and chiseled cheekbones

"You seem happy," he said. "Far happier than I've seen you at those fancy parties you go to in Athenberg."

He noticed. Of course he had. He was the most observant man I'd ever met.

"I love it," I admitted. "Meeting people, hearing their concerns, having something concrete to contribute at my next meeting with the Speaker. I feel like I can finally do something meaningful. Like I have a purpose in life."

That was one thing that had bugged me so much about being a princess. Yes, the monarchy was symbolic, but I didn't want to spend my life just smiling for the cameras and giving lifestyle interviews. I wanted something *more.*

But maybe I'd been thinking about my role all wrong. Maybe, instead of conforming to what being the crown princess had always meant, I could shape it into what I wanted it to be.

A small smile touched Rhys's lips. "I always knew you would make a great queen."

"I'm not queen yet."

"You don't need a crown to be queen, princess."

The words slid over my skin, leaving a trail of tingles in their wake. I let myself soak them in for a minute before I changed the subject, painfully aware of who and what we were.

No tingles allowed.

"Are you enjoying the trip?" I asked. "It's nice to be out of the city."

His smile faded. "It's fine."

"Just fine?" Perhaps I was biased, but Eldorra was beautiful, and we'd visited some of the country's most stunning regions.

He lifted those broad shoulders in a half shrug. "I'm not the biggest fan of Eldorra. Almost didn't take this job so I wouldn't have to visit."

"Oh." I tried not to take offense. I failed. "Why not?"

Eldorra was like Switzerland or Australia. Not everyone loved it, but no one hated it.

The silence stretched for several long beats before Rhys replied.

"My father was Eldorran," he said, his voice flat and emotionless. "He promised my mother he would bring her here and they'd live happily ever after. She never quite gave up on that dream, even after he left and it became clear he wasn't coming back. She kept talking about Eldorra, how she was going to leave our shit town and move here. She had postcards and magazine articles about the place all over the house. That was all I heard growing up. Eldorra, Eldorra, Eldorra. She loved the fantasy of the country more than she did me, and I grew to hate it. It became a symbol of everything wrong with my childhood. Still, I might've gotten over my hang-up eventually, but..."

Rhys's hand clenched and unclenched around his knee. "One of my last deployments was a joint mission. Both the U.S. and Eldorra had agents who'd been caught by the terrorist group they were tracking, and we were supposed to retrieve them. For diplomatic reasons, we had to keep our mission under wraps, which meant no air support. We were deep in hostile territory, outnumbered and outgunned. Our biggest advantage was the element of surprise."

Cold foreboding trickled down my back.

"The night of the mission, one of the Eldorran soldiers—a brash, hotheaded type—strayed from the plan. We'd clashed from the beginning, and he hated we were using my plan instead of his." Rhys's expression was bleak. "Instead of waiting for my signal like we agreed upon, he fired when he saw one of the group leaders leave the compound. The one in charge of torturing the prisoners, according to our intel. It was a high-profile kill...but it hadn't been our priority, and it gave away our location. Everything went to shit after that. We were swarmed, and out of the eight men in my squad, three survived. The agents didn't make it out alive, either. It was a total fucking bloodbath."

His words tripped something in my memory. A unit of Eldorran soldiers had all been wiped out in a joint mission gone wrong a few years ago. It had received nonstop news coverage for a week, and I bet it was the same mission Rhys was talking about.

Horror and sympathy gripped my chest. "I'm so sorry."

I should be loyal to Eldorra, and I *was*, but loyalty didn't mean blindness. Everyone messed up, and in Rhys's case, the soldier's mistake had cost him the lives of those he loved.

"Don't be. It's not your fault." Rhys rubbed a hand over his face. "It happened years ago, and yeah, it added to my huge fucking hang-ups about Eldorra, but what's past is past. Can't do a damn thing about it now."

We fell silent again, each lost in our own thoughts, before I worked up the courage to ask, "Why did you take the job as my bodyguard then? If you knew it meant having to visit Eldorra."

Rhys's expression relaxed into a smirk. "You got a real pretty face." His smirk widened at my exasperated huff. "I don't know. Guess it felt right at the time."

"We always end up where we're meant to be," I said softly.

His eyes lingered on mine. "Maybe."

He hated Eldorra, yet he'd not only taken the job but moved here permanently. For me.

"Well." I forced a smile, hardly able to hear myself over the roar of my heart. "I should turn in for the night. Early morning tomorrow."

Rhys rose when I did. "I'll walk you to your room."

The soft creak of the wooden stairs beneath our feet mingled with the sounds of our breaths—mine shallow, Rhys's deep and even.

Did he feel it, the electric current running between us? Or was it only in my imagination?

Perhaps not, because when we arrived at my room, I didn't open the door, and he didn't leave.

Goosebumps peppered my flesh, either from Rhys's proximity or from the air-conditioning blasting through the hall.

Even when you're not there, you're everywhere. In my head, in my lungs, in my fucking soul.

His confession from the parking lot echoed in my head. We hadn't talked about that night since, but maybe we didn't need words.

Rhys's eyes dipped to my breasts. I followed his gaze and noticed for the first time just how thin my blouse was. I wore a lace bra, but my nipples were so hard they showed clearly through the two layers of flimsy material.

I should leave, but Rhys's molten gaze pinned me in place, erasing my earlier chill and leaving a deep, fiery ache in its wake.

"You know what you said earlier? About how we always end up where we're meant to be?" He grazed his hand over the side of my neck, and my heart thudded so hard against my ribcage I half expected it to leap out of my chest and into his arms.

I couldn't bring myself to speak, but I managed a small nod.

The heaviness of the air caressed me like a bold lover's touch, and I *knew*, deep in my gut, I stood on a dangerous precipice. The slightest movement from me, and I would fall.

The question was whether I wanted to save myself, or if the pleasure would be worth the eventual pain.

"Perhaps..." Rhys's touch skimmed down my neck and over the curve of my shoulder. I shivered, my skin blossoming with a thousand more goosebumps. "I was always meant to find my way to you."

Oh, God.

Every ounce of oxygen disappeared from my lungs.

"You should go into your room, princess." His voice was full of gravel, dark and rough. "Go into your room and lock the door."

I shook my head. "I don't want to."

Whatever was happening, it was different from Costa Rica. We didn't have a bucket list or excuses to fall back on. It was just him and me, making a choice that had been a long time coming.

Rhys groaned, and with that one sound, I knew he'd made his choice.

Breathe. Even when there was no oxygen, no air, nothing but him. *Breathe.*

He dipped his head, but instead of kissing my mouth, he kissed the hollow of my throat. It was so soft it was more a whisper of breath than a kiss, but it was enough to make my knees weaken.

I was a lightning rod, and Rhys was the strike that lit me up from the inside out.

I closed my eyes and stifled a moan as he dragged his mouth up my neck, inch by inch. Just as the lazy possessiveness of his touch lulled me into a semi-stupor, he yanked me toward him with one hand and sank his teeth into the curve between my neck and shoulder. Hard. Almost as hard as the thick arousal pressing against my stomach and causing my core to throb with need. Rhys's other hand clamped over my mouth, muffling my surprised yelp.

"Tell me." His voice lowered. "What would your boyfriend think about this?"

Boyfriend? It took a minute before it clicked. *Steffan.*

We'd gone on two dates. Hardly enough to be considered my boyfriend, no matter what the press said.

But I had a feeling that argument wouldn't hold sway with Rhys, who loosened his hand enough for me to gasp out, "Steffan's not my boyfriend."

The air thickened with danger.

"I don't like hearing his name on your lips." Lethally soft words, each one delivered with the precision of a guided missile. "But you went on dates with him. You kissed him." Rhys's voice darkened further, and he pressed me further against the wall while wrapping one hand around my throat. "Did you do that to bait me, princess? Hmm?"

"N-no." I was soaking wet. The darkness of the hall, the roughness of Rhys's voice, it all went straight to the heat pulsing between my legs. "I had to date someone after the ball. And I didn't think you cared."

"I care about everything you do. Even when I shouldn't." Rhys's grip tightened on my throat. "One last chance, princess. Tell me to stop."

"No."

I was all too aware that Elin, Mikaela, and the rest of the group slumbered behind the doors on either side of us. It would only take one late-night bathroom break, one light sleeper to hear us and blow the situation to hell.

But somehow, the danger only intensified the thrill running through my veins. Whatever this was between us, it had been building since the moment Rhys stepped out of his car outside my house at Thayer, and I couldn't stop it even if I wanted to.

Rhys hissed out a breath and released my throat, only to curl his hand around the back of my neck. He yanked me to him again, crushing my mouth to his, and my world imploded.

Tongues, teeth, hands. We devoured each other like the world would end and this was our last chance to *feel* something. Perhaps it was. But I wouldn't think about that now, not when our bodies pressed so tight against each other we might as well be one, and I was falling, falling into an abyss I never wanted to get out of.

Mikaela had been right. You could tell everything from a kiss.

I tugged on Rhys's hair, desperate for *more*. More of his touch, his taste, his scent. I wanted to fill every inch of my soul with this man.

He drew my bottom lip between his teeth and tugged. I gasped, so aroused I could feel my wetness slicking my thighs.

"Quiet," he rasped. "Or someone will hear." He swept his palm up my inner thigh to my core and let out a low groan when he discovered how wet I was. "You're killing me, princess."

He rubbed his thumb over my clit through my drenched panties, and I fought back a moan as I arched into his hand. He slid my panties to the side, and—

A bed creaked behind the door next to mine.

Rhys and I froze in unison, our breathing harsh.

We'd gotten so wrapped up in what we were doing we'd forgotten all about the people sleeping just a few feet away.

We heard another creak, followed by the shuffle of someone getting out of bed. Henrik, if the direction of the sound was any indication.

Rhys cursed under his breath and pulled his hand away. It was the smart thing to do, but I still wanted to weep at the loss of contact.

He opened the door to my room behind me and gently pushed me inside. "Tomorrow night. Gazebo," he said in a low voice. "We'll go together."

There was a gazebo behind an abandoned farm, about a fifteen-minute walk from our inn. We'd passed by it on our way into town.

"And princess...don't bother wearing any underwear."

The throbbing between my legs intensified.

Rhys closed my door right as Henrik's opened. Their voices filtered through wood as I tiptoed to my bed and climbed in, my head spinning from the events of the past hour.

Would the pleasure be worth the eventual pain?

I only had to listen to the frantic beats of my heart to know the answer.

28

RHYS

I'd tried to resist. I really had.

Perhaps I would've succeeded had Bridget been beautiful and nothing else. Beauty, on its own, meant nothing to me. My mother had been beautiful, until she wasn't—and I don't mean physically.

But that was the problem. Bridget wasn't beautiful and nothing else. She was everything. Warmth, strength, compassion, humor. I saw it in the way she laughed, in her empathy as she listened to people's problems and her composure as they railed to her about everything they thought was wrong with the country.

I'd known she was more than a pretty face long before this trip, but something inside me snapped last night. Maybe it was the way she'd looked at me, like she thought I was everything too when I was nothing, or maybe it was the knowledge she could be ripped away from me at any moment. She could get engaged next week and I would lose even the possibility of her forever.

Whatever it was, it erased every bit of remaining self-control I had. Costa Rica had been a crack, but this? This was full-on obliteration.

The grass rustled as Bridget and I made our way through the fields toward the gazebo. We'd snuck out after everyone had gone to sleep, and even though it was late, the moon shone bright enough we didn't need the lights from our phones to guide the way.

Was what we were doing—what we were about to do—a bad idea? Fuck yes. Ours was a story destined for a tragic ending, but when you were already on a train headed off the cliff, all you could do was hold on tight and make every second count.

We stayed silent until we reached the gazebo, where she walked to the middle and took it all in. Besides the chipped paint, it'd withstood the test of time surprisingly well.

"No one comes here?" she asked.

"Not a soul." I'd done my research. The town had a small population, but it sprawled across vast acres of farms. The inn was the nearest inhabited building, and everyone there was asleep. I'd made sure of that before I texted Bridget to meet me in the lobby.

"Good." Her response came out slightly breathless.

Southern Eldorra was far warmer than Athenberg, and we could get away with not wearing jackets even at night. I'd donned my usual uniform of T-shirt, combat pants, and boots, while Bridget wore a purple dress that swirled around her thighs.

I drank her in, not missing a single detail. The wisps of hair curling around her face, the nervous anticipation in her eyes, the way her chest rose and fell in time with my own uneven breaths.

Part of me wanted to march over, hike up her skirt, and fuck her right then and there. Another part of me wanted to savor the moment—the last wild, beating seconds before we destroyed whatever was left of our boundaries.

I was a rule follower by nature. It was how I'd survived most of my life. But for Bridget, I would break every rule in the book.

It only took six weeks of being apart from her and another six of fucking agony for me to accept the truth, but now that I had, there was no going back.

"So." Bridget tucked a strand of hair behind her ear, her hand trembling. "Now that we're here, what do you have planned, Mr. Larsen?"

I smiled, slow and wicked, and a small, visible shiver rippled through her body.

"I have lots of plans for you, princess, and every single one ends with my fingers, tongue, or cock inside your sweet little cunt."

I didn't waste time beating around the bush. This had been two years in the making, ever since I stepped onto her driveway and saw her staring back at me with those big, blue eyes.

Bridget von Ascheberg was mine and mine alone. It didn't matter that she wasn't mine to take. I was taking her anyway, and if I could tattoo myself onto her skin, bury myself into her heart, and etch myself onto her soul, I would.

Her eyes widened, but before she could respond, I closed the distance between us and grasped her chin with my hand.

"But first, I want to make one thing clear. From this point on, you're mine. No other man touches you. If they do..." My fingers dug into her skin. "I know seventy-nine ways to kill a man, and I can make seventy of them look like an accident. Understand?"

She nodded, her chest rising and falling more rapidly than usual.

"I mean it, princess."

"I understand." *Definitely breathless.*

"Good." I swiped my thumb over her bottom lip. "I want to hear you say it. Who do you belong to?"

"You," she whispered. I could smell her arousal already, sweet and heady, and I couldn't hold back any longer.

"That's right," I growled. "Me."

I grabbed the back of her neck, pulled her close, and crushed my lips to hers. She wrapped her arms around my neck, her body warm and pliant against mine as I plundered her mouth. She tasted like mint and strawberries, and I wanted more. *Needed* more.

My heart was a loud drum in my chest, beating in time with the throbbing in my cock. All of my senses sharpened to near-painful clarity—the taste of her on my tongue, the feel of her skin beneath my hands, the smell of her perfume and the sounds of her little whimpers as she clung to me like we were drowning and I was her last lifeline.

I backed Bridget up against one of the wooden beams, shoved her dress up around her hips, and parted her thighs with my knee. I reached between her legs and hummed in approval when I found her slick and bare for me.

"No underwear. Good girl," I purred. "Because if you'd disobeyed my order..." I nipped her bottom lip and thrust a finger into her tight, wet heat, smiling when I heard her gasp. "I'd have to punish you."

Her hips bucked up when I pushed another finger inside her. I worked them in and out, slowly at first, then speeding up until I was knuckles deep inside her and the filthy sounds of my fingers fucking in and out of her mingled with her moans.

Bridget's eyes were half-closed, her mouth half-open. Her head fell back against the beam, exposing the slender length of her throat, and her entire body trembled as she neared orgasm.

I slowed my pace at the last minute, earning myself a frustrated groan.

"Please." She clutched at my arms, her nails digging tiny crescents into my skin.

"Please what?" I thrust my fingers into her again, hard, until her body bowed and she let out a tiny yelp. "Please what?" I repeated.

Sweat beaded my skin, and my cock strained at my pants, so hard it could pound nails. I was fucking dying, desperate to get inside her, but I could also watch her like this all night. No fake smiles, no inhibitions, just pleasure and wild abandonment as her pussy convulsed around my fingers and coated them with her juices.

So fucking beautiful. So fucking *mine*.

"Fuck me," she gasped. Her nails dug harder into my biceps until a tiny bead of blood welled on my skin. "Please fuck me."

"Such a dirty mouth for a princess." I worked my cock out of my pants and slid on a condom using my free hand before I yanked my fingers out, lifted her up, and hooked her legs around my waist. "You know there's no going back after this."

"I know." Bridget's eyes were wide and trusting and glazed with lust.

My chest clenched. I didn't deserve her, but fuck it, I was beyond caring.

No one ever said I was a good man, anyway.

I positioned the tip of my cock at her entrance and waited for a heartbeat before I slammed into her with one forceful thrust. She was so wet I slid in almost frictionlessly, but I could still feel her pussy stretching and struggling to accommodate my size.

Bridget cried out, her walls clamping around me like a vise, and I let out a string of curses.

Hot. Wet. Tight. *So tight.*

"You're killing me," I groaned. I dropped my forehead to hers and closed my eyes, picturing the unsexiest things I could think of—broccoli, dentures—until I mustered enough control to continue.

I slid my cock out until just the tip remained, then slammed forward again. And again. And again.

I set up a fast, deep, brutal rhythm, making her take every inch of me until my balls slapped against her skin and her moans became screams.

"Shh. You'll wake people up, princess." I pushed the neckline of her dress down. Her breasts bounced with each thrust, her nipples pebbled with arousal, and the sight almost set me off.

I gritted my teeth. *Not yet.*

I lowered my head and licked and sucked on her nipples while I savagely fucked in and out of her tight, clenching pussy.

By that point, I was more animal than man, driven by nothing more than a primal need to bury myself into her as deep as I could and claim her so completely we would never get each other out from under our skin.

Thunder boomed in the distance, muffling the sounds of my groans and Bridget's squeals.

Dimly, I realized it was about to rain and we didn't have an umbrella or anything to cover us once we left the gazebo, but I'd worry about that later. Right now, the only thing that mattered was us.

"*Rhys.* Oh, God," Bridget sobbed. "I can't...I need—"

"What do you need?" I grazed my teeth over her nipple. "You need to come? Hmm?"

"Y-yes." It came out as a half plea, half moan.

She was wrecked. Her hair a mess, her face streaked with tears, her skin slick with sweat and hot with arousal.

I lifted my head and dragged my mouth up her neck until I reached her ear, where I whispered, "Come for me, princess."

I pinched her nipple and fucked into her with the hardest thrust yet, and she exploded, her mouth falling open in a soundless scream while her cunt strangled my cock.

Thunder boomed again, closer this time.

I held Bridget's limp, shaking body up against the beam until she caught her breath. Once she did, I set her on the floor, turned her around, and bent her over.

I hadn't come yet—the old trick of reciting baseball rosters still worked—and my body vibrated with barely controlled tension.

"Again?" she panted as I slid my cock along her slick folds.

"Sweetheart, I wouldn't be doing my job if you didn't come on my cock at least three times tonight."

The storm broke right as I pushed into her, and rain lashed sideways at us as I fucked her against the wooden beam. Lightning ripped through the sky, illuminating the pale curve of Bridget's shoulder as she clung to the railing for dear life. She'd turned her head sideways so her cheek pressed against the wood, and I could see her mouth fall open as she struggled to catch her breath between my thrusts.

I wrapped her hair around my fist and used it as leverage to make her take me deeper.

"This is for all the times you didn't listen." I squeezed her ass before delivering a sharp slap that made her yelp. "This is for Borgia." *Slap.* "And this is for the gardens." *Slap.*

My pent-up frustration over the years bloomed across her skin in pink, and a dark chuckle rose in my throat when Bridget bucked harder against me with each slap.

"You like that?" I pulled her head back by her hair until she was looking up at me with tear-filled eyes. "You like getting your ass slapped while I pound that tight royal pussy with my hard cock?"

"*Yes.*" The word broke into a moan, and her knees buckled.

I hissed out a breath. God, she was fucking perfect. In every way.

I wrapped one arm below her waist, holding her up, and bent over her until my chest pressed against her back. I covered most of her body with mine, shielding her from the splashes of rain as I buried myself so deep inside her I didn't think I would ever get out.

I didn't want to. This right here, this was all I wanted.

Bridget. Just Bridget.

"Oh, God, *Rhys!*"

The sound of my name on her lips as she shattered around me again finally did me in.

I came right after her with a loud groan, my orgasm ripping through me with the force of a hurricane. I swore I lost my hearing for a second there, but when I came back to my senses, everything seemed amplified. The smell of the rain and earth mingled with sex and sweat, the sound of the water pattering against the wood, the coolness of the droplets on my overheated skin.

Bridget trembled beneath me, and I lifted her up and placed her deeper into the gazebo, away from the rain.

"You okay, princess?" My breaths finally eased into something resembling normal as I slid the straps of her dress back onto her shoulders and smoothed her hair out of her face before giving her a soft kiss.

I wasn't a sweet, lovey type of guy in any area of my life, but perhaps I'd been too rough with her. If I had my way, we would've done this in a proper room with a proper bed, but the walls were paper thin at the inn.

Bridget nodded, still shaking somewhat. "Wow."

I chuckled. "I'll take that as a good thing." I kept an arm around her, still holding her up. A fierce protectiveness washed over me as she pressed her face into my chest.

God, this woman. She had no idea the things I would do for her.

We stayed in the gazebo until the rain stopped, which thankfully didn't take long. I would've been happy to stay there forever, but I wanted to make sure Bridget had time to shower and grab some shuteye before our morning call time.

"You don't have to carry me. I can walk again." Bridget laughed as I scooped her up in my arms and set off back to the inn. "I don't know about tomorrow, though. I have a feeling I'm going to be sore."

"Ground's wet and it's dark," I said. A cloud had drifted over the moon, and I had to walk slowly to make sure I didn't step in anything I didn't want to step in. "Better if I carry you, sweetheart."

She didn't respond, but she tightened her arms around my neck and pressed a soft kiss to my jaw that made my heart twist in the strangest way.

Then again, nothing about my life had been normal since Bridget von Ascheberg came into it.

29

BRIDGET

AFTER OUR NIGHT IN THE GAZEBO, RHYS AND I DIDN'T GET any more time alone during the tour. But when we returned to Athenberg a few days later, we managed to sneak in trysts despite my packed schedule.

The guesthouse at midnight, after everyone had gone to sleep. The supply closet on the third floor of the staff quarters during lunch hour. My favorite rooftop above the kitchen. No place was off-limits.

It was risky, dangerous, and out of character for both of us, given how practical we usually were, but we couldn't have stopped if we wanted to. We'd waited too long and needed it too much.

It was a crazy ride that would eventually have to end, and while we never talked about the future, we'd come to a silent agreement to enjoy every second we could.

But, as much as I wanted to spend all my days and nights with Rhys, I had other responsibilities, and three weeks after my return to Athenberg, I found myself in my grandfather's office, waiting for Erhall to finish speaking so I could present my agenda items.

"Let me guess. You have another *citizen* issue you'd like to bring up. Your Highness," Erhall added tightly, no doubt remembering my grandfather was also in the room.

I responded with a serene smile. "Yes. That is what we do, isn't it? Help the citizens of Eldorra?"

Erhall, Edvard, Andreas, and I sat around Edvard's desk for the king's weekly meeting with the Speaker. It was my third such meeting since I returned from my goodwill tour, which had been a smash success. Henrik ran a glowing profile of me in the *Eldorran Herald,* and my public approval rating shot sky high, nearly rivaling that of my grandfather's.

I personally didn't care much about ratings, but it was one of the most powerful weapons in my arsenal since I didn't hold any actual political power. I also took great pleasure in the fact Erhall's rating was nearly twenty points lower than mine.

"Of course." Erhall smoothed down his tie, looking like he'd just sucked on a lemon. "What would you like to discuss?"

I'd built on my impulsive decision at Ida's farm and created an official Citizen Letters program by which Eldorrans could write or email me with their concerns, and I acknowledged every one. The most important ones, I brought to Erhall's attention during the weekly meetings. He probably wouldn't do anything about the majority of them, but I had to try.

"It's about the roads in Rykhauver..." I launched into my presentation, ignoring Andreas's smirk. I hated that he was there, but he was still "shadowing" Erhall, and since he was second in line to the throne, no one objected to him joining the meetings.

It didn't matter. He would never be King, not if I had anything to say about it—and, as crown princess, I had plenty to say.

"I'll look into the issue," Erhall said. Code for *I'm going to pretend this conversation never happened after I leave this room.* "Now, Your Majesty, about the tax reform..."

Edvard cast a sympathetic glance in my direction. He refrained from fighting my battles for me because it wouldn't look good if I ran to him for help every time Erhall was a jerk, but I—

Oh God. I nearly jumped out of my seat.

Erhall paused and gave me a strange look before resuming his speech.

I pressed my thighs together beneath the table as the silent but powerful vibrations resumed between my legs.

I'm going to kill him.

Rhys had ordered me to wear a vibrator all day and I, like an idiot, had agreed. It'd sounded hot, and Rhys had a minute-by-minute breakdown of my day. He'd kept the vibrator off during my meetings, so why—

My eyes fell on the grandfather clock in the corner.

Dammit. We were running over. Fifteen minutes over, to be exact. Rhys probably thought I was out by now.

A bead of sweat formed on my forehead as I tried not to moan, squirm, or do anything that might give me away.

"Are you alright? You look...flushed." Andreas raised his eyebrows, his eyes sharp as he stared at me.

"Yes." I forced a smile. "Perfectly all right."

"You don't look so well," Edvard said, sounding concerned.

Dear God, every minute they spent asking about me was another minute the meeting dragged on. It needed to end, soon, before I came in the middle of a discussion about freaking tax legislation.

"It's just a little hot in here. Please, don't stop on my account," I managed.

The vibrations ratcheted up a notch, and my nails dug into my skin so hard it left little grooves in my palms.

Edvard looked unconvinced, but he and Erhall resumed their conversation while Andreas watched me with narrowed eyes.

Normally, I would give him an icy stare right back, but I couldn't concentrate on anything except the throbbing of my clit and the rasp of my nipples against my bra.

Thankfully, the meeting ended soon after. I bid Edvard a hasty goodbye, gave Erhall a curt nod, and ignored Andreas completely before exiting as normally as I could. I didn't want to raise their suspicions any further by running from the room, even if I was a hair's breadth away from orgasming.

The instant I was in the hall, the vibrations ceased.

Of course they did.

I smoothed a hand over the front of my skirt and managed to walk semi-normally to my office, where Rhys waited for me.

My heart leaped when I saw him leaning against my desk. Eyes dark, arms crossed over his chest, his pose casual and arrogant.

"That was cruel." I pinned him with a stern stare even as my clit throbbed again—not from the vibrator, but from the sight of him. The stubble, the tattoos, the way he looked at me like I was the only person in the world...*Stop. Focus.* "I was in a meeting."

"It was supposed to end half an hour ago."

"It ran over."

"Clearly." Rhys's eyes lit up with a wicked gleam. "Come here, princess."

I shook my head, even though I was so turned on the faintest gust of air against my skin caused my breath to quicken. It was the principle of the matter. "No."

"That wasn't a request."

My nipples hardened into aching points at his authoritative tone, and I folded my arms over my chest to hide them. "You can't tell me what to do."

"Come. Here." His voice dropped to a dangerously soft decibel. "Before I bend you over my lap and spank you so hard you won't be able to sit for days."

My core clenched at the mental image, and I almost refused so he could do exactly that. But after hours of teasing, I couldn't wait anymore, and I walked forward on shaky legs until I stood in front of him.

"There. That wasn't so hard." Rhys grabbed the back of my neck and pulled me toward him. "Remember. In public, you're my princess, but in private, you're my whore." His other hand reached down and pinched my swollen clit until I squealed, and the beginning tremors of an orgasm rocked through me. "You'll do what I say, when I say it, and you'll take my cock however I want. Won't you?"

Oh God. Another rush of moisture flooded between my legs.

"Yes," I breathed.

The word hadn't fully left my mouth before he swallowed it with a hard, knee-buckling kiss, and any vestiges of resistance crumbled.

I wrapped my arms around his neck, reveling in the taste and feel of him. We'd been insatiable since the night in the gazebo, and I still couldn't get enough.

The sneaking around, the late-night trysts and loaded glances in rooms full of people...it could all crash down around us at any second. But for once in my life, I didn't care.

I'd never felt more alive.

"How was your day, sweetheart?" Rhys breathed against my lips, his tone gentling from moments ago.

"Good. *Frustrating*," I said pointedly before I, too, softened my voice. "I missed you."

I hadn't seen him since breakfast.

His eyes crinkled into a beautiful smile, and my heart soared so high I thought I might float off the ground.

If I could have any three things in the world, it would be world peace, my parents back, and Rhys's smiles forever.

"I missed you too." He gave me a softer, lingering kiss before he slid his hand up my inner thigh again and a low groan escaped his throat. "You are soaked." His tone returned to the hard, commanding one I was used to. "Bend over and lift your skirt."

I obeyed, the prospect of having him inside me soon making my fingers shake as I bent over the desk and yanked my skirt over my hips.

"Take off your underwear."

I slipped my hand into the waistband of my panties and shimmied them down until they pooled around my ankles.

Heat rose on my cheeks when I realized Rhys now had an unimpeded view of my vibrator and the mess it'd left behind— my panties completely drenched, my thighs slick with my juices.

Still, I was turned on enough to brush past my embarrassment.

I gripped the edge of the desk, my body taut with anticipation, but there was only silence. No words, no touch.

I twisted my head in confusion.

Rhys stood behind me, his eyes ravenous as he soaked me in. Between his hungry stare and my current position, I felt like a sacrificial lamb waiting for a lion to pounce and devour me.

"Spread your legs wider. Let me see that pretty pussy dripping for me."

Heat scalded me from head to toe, but I did as he asked.

"So beautiful." He palmed my ass with both hands and squeezed. "What would the good citizens of Eldorra say if they could see you now, hmm? Their prim and proper princess bent over and spread wide, waiting for a hard cock to fuck her."

Was it possible to come from words alone? Because I was this close to doing so.

"Not just any cock," I panted. "Yours. Now are you going to keep talking, or are you actually going to fuck me?"

Rhys laughed. He made quick work of his belt and pants, and my mouth dried. I would never get over how huge he was. Thick, long, and hard, the head already dripping pre-cum.

"That's right." He pulled the vibrator out and positioned the tip of his cock at my entrance. "Mine. *Only* mine. And don't you forget it, princess."

He drove into me with one deep thrust, and my initial yelp turned into a series of whimpering moans as he pounded me from behind. They mingled with his grunts, the creaking of the desk as it shook beneath the force of his fucking, and the sound of flesh slapping against flesh. A delicious, filthy symphony that muddled my thoughts until all I could focus on was the feel of him thrusting in and out of me—

"Bridget? Are you in there?"

Mikaela.

It took a few seconds for her voice to penetrate my sex-drenched fog, but once it did, my eyes flew open and I tried to stand up, only for Rhys to push me down again.

"Not done with you yet, princess." He thrust into me again and clapped a hand over my mouth to muffle my moan.

"Rhys, she's *right outside*," I hissed when he loosened his hold enough for me to speak. I desperately wanted to come, but my stomach churned at the prospect of being caught.

I could've pretended I wasn't there, but Mikaela and I had a scheduled meeting I'd completely forgotten about until now.

"The door's locked."

"She could hear us."

We spoke only loud enough for the other to hear, but to my paranoid ears, we might as well be shouting.

"Then you better keep quiet, hmm?" Rhys's hot breath slid over my skin as he reached around to pinch my nipples. Another jolt of lust rocketed through me.

"Bridget." Mikaela sounded impatient now. "The door's locked. Is everything okay?"

"Y-yes. I'm"—Rhys slammed into me with a particularly brutal thrust—"coming!"

My last word devolved into a gasp as my orgasm crashed over me in a tidal wave.

I buried my face in my arms and bit down to stifle my screams.

Rhys's breathing changed, and a second later he came with a quiet grunt before sliding out of me.

We didn't have the luxury of basking in post-coital bliss, and the aftershocks of my orgasm were still rippling through me as we cleaned ourselves up.

"One minute!" I called out for Mikaela's benefit.

I glared at Rhys, who'd fixed himself up in record time and looked like he was trying not to laugh. "This isn't funny."

"Nice double entendre there at the end," he said with a smirk.

I'm coming.

I flushed as I finished straightening my clothes and hair. A quick glance in the mirror told me I still looked a bit disheveled, but I could blame that on running around the palace all day.

"I almost miss the days when you were an overbearing, overprotective ass."

"Then you'll be pleased to hear I'm still an overbearing, overprotective ass. And princess." Rhys's voice stopped me when I was halfway to the door. "You're forgetting something."

My face flamed when he held up the vibrator.

"You are *trying* to get us into trouble." I snatched the vibrator from him and wrapped it hastily with a tissue before shoving it inside a desk drawer. I'd deal with it later.

"It's Mikaela. She doesn't notice anything that doesn't have to do with parties and society gossip. You could shove an elephant in front of her and she probably wouldn't notice. You think I would've done that had it been Markus or Elin at the door?"

Okay, Mikaela wasn't the most observant person on the planet, but Rhys was exaggerating. In this case, though, I hoped he was right.

I opened the door and finally let my annoyed-looking friend in.

"What took so long?" she grumbled. "I have to meet my mother—" She stopped when she saw Rhys. "Oh, hey, Rhys. What are you doing here?"

He was technically off duty when I was in the palace, and I scrambled to think of a plausible excuse.

"We were going over security plans," I improvised. "For Nik's wedding. Some of it is, uh, confidential. Which is why I took so long to answer."

Nikolai and Sabrina were still in California, but they were getting married in Athenberg and preparations were in full swing.

Mikaela frowned. "Just the two of you? I thought the Royal Guard was handling that."

"*Personal* security plans," I amended quickly.

"Oh." The confusion in Mikaela's eyes cleared. "Is now still a good time to meet? I can come back if not."

"Now works," I said, even though all I wanted was to

shower and take a nap. I was just grateful she didn't ask any more questions about why it took me so long to unlock the door. My excuse would've unraveled faster than a cheap sweater under any scrutiny.

"I'll see you later, Your Highness. Lady Mikaela." Rhys inclined his head and left, but not before shooting me a wink.

I bit back a smile.

"It's too bad," Mikaela said, her eyes lingering on his backside a tad longer than I would've liked before the door shut behind him.

"What is?" I absentmindedly shuffled some papers on my desk and tried to push aside the mental images of what I'd been doing on that exact spot ten minutes ago.

"That Rhys is a bodyguard." Mikaela returned her attention to me and plopped into the chair opposite mine. "He is *so* gorgeous. I don't know how you see him every day without drooling. If he weren't a commoner..." She fanned herself. "I would be all over that."

My entire body stiffened, for multiple reasons.

"Just because he doesn't have a title doesn't mean he's less than anyone who does have one."

I should've gone along with what she said because Lord knows I didn't want to encourage any attraction she had toward Rhys, but I hated the implication aristocrats were better just because they were lucky enough to be born into a titled family.

Mikaela blinked in surprise at my sharp tone. "Of course not," she said. "But you understand the social dynamics, Bridge. Getting involved with the staff is so tacky. And I'm the daughter of a baron." An unusual note of bitterness punctuated the last sentence. "My social standing isn't high enough to survive *that* kind of scandal."

The aristocracy had a strict hierarchy, and barons and baronesses sat at the bottom. I suspected that was part of the reason Mikaela worked so hard at networking and staying on top of society gossip—to overcome her perceived lower status, even though her family was still wealthier than the average Eldorran.

"Like I said, too bad, but at least I can look at him." Mikaela brightened again. "You're so lucky to have a hot bodyguard. Or not, since you can't hook up with him."

She laughed, and I forced myself to join.

"Of course not," I said. "That would be crazy."

30

RHYS

I was addicted.

Me, the man who'd avoided most addictive substances all his life—drugs, smoking, alcohol, even sugar, to an extent—had found the one thing I couldn't resist.

Strength, resilience, and light, wrapped up in five feet nine inches of creamy skin and cool composure that hid a heart of fire underneath.

But fuck, if she was an addiction, I never wanted to be cured.

"Are you going to paint me like one of your French girls?" Bridget teased, stretching her arms over her head.

My cock jumped with interest at the sight of her draped over the couch, naked, though let's be honest, there were very few things Bridget did that *didn't* interest my cock.

She had a rare day off after her morning meetings, and we'd spent the entire afternoon in a hotel room on the outskirts of Athenberg. If anyone asked, Bridget was taking a spa day, but in reality, all we'd done was fuck, eat, and fuck some more. It was the closest we'd ever gotten, and that we *could* get, to a real date.

"Careful with teasing me, princess, unless you want a wart on your portrait," I threatened.

She grinned, and the sight hit me like a punch in the gut.

I would never tire of her smiles. Her *real* smiles, not the ones she showed the public. I'd seen Bridget naked, in fancy gowns, and in lingerie, but she was never more beautiful than when she was herself, stripped of all the pretenses her title forced her to wear.

"You wouldn't." She rolled over and propped her chin on her hands, which rested on the arm of the couch. "You're way too much of a perfectionist about your art."

"We'll see about that." But she was right. I *was* a perfectionist about my art, and the piece I was working on might be my favorite so far aside from the one of her in Costa Rica, which had finally broken my artist's block. "Hmm, let's see. I'll add a third nipple here...a hairy wart there..."

"Stop!" Bridget laughed. "If you're going to give me warts, at least put them somewhere inconspicuous."

"All right. On your belly button it is."

This time, I was the one who laughed when she tossed a throw pillow at me. "Years of grumpiness, and you suddenly have jokes."

"I've always had jokes. I just never told them." I shaded in her hair. It spilled down her back, following the graceful curve of her neck and shoulder. Her lips parted in a small smile, and her eyes sparkled with mischief. I did my best to make the charcoal sketch realistic, though nothing compared to the real thing.

We fell into a comfortable silence—me sketching, Bridget watching me with a soft, slumberous expression.

I was more relaxed than I'd been in a long time, despite still being on high alert about someone possibly snooping through my guesthouse. I'd upgraded the security system and added hidden cameras that fed directly to a feed I could access on my phone. Nothing out of the ordinary had happened yet, so it was a wait-and-see game.

For now, I'd enjoy one of the rare moments Bridget and I could spend together without worrying about someone catching us.

"Do you ever show your art to anyone?" she asked after a while. Sunset crept closer, and the golden late afternoon light bathed her in an otherworldly glow.

"I show it to you."

"Besides me."

"Nope." Not even Christian had seen my sketches, though he knew they existed. Ditto with my old therapist.

Bridget lifted her head, her lips parting in surprise. "So I'm..."

"The first person I showed? Yeah." I focused on finishing my sketch, but I felt the weight of her stare on my face.

"Mr. Larsen."

"Yes?" I drawled, picking up on the sensual note in her voice.

"Come here."

"You ordering me around?"

Bridget flashed another grin. "Maybe. I'm in trouble and I need your help."

I set down my pencil with a sigh. "You're not in trouble. You *are* trouble."

I strode over to the couch, and she squealed when I picked her up and set her in my lap. My cock nestled against her pussy, with only the material of my briefs separating us. "I'm here. Now what?"

"Now..." She pushed herself up on her knees so she could pull down my briefs. "You help me out. I'm a little tense."

I hissed out a breath when she sank onto my cock. "You're insatiable." For someone so regal in public, Bridget was a firecracker in the bedroom. Or living room, or shower, or kitchen counter.

Her grin widened. "You love it."

My chuckle morphed into a groan as she settled into an exquisite rhythm. "Yeah, princess. I do." I watched her, taking almost as much pleasure in the flushed arousal on her face as I did in the sensation of her pussy gripping me.

Half an hour later, after we were both breathless and sated, I curled an arm around her as we lay on the couch. That was my favorite type of moment with Bridget—the peaceful ones where we could just be together. We got so few of those.

"How did you get this?" She brushed her fingers over the scar on my eyebrow. "You never told me about this one."

"Hit it on a table." I stroked Bridget's arm absentmindedly. "My mother flew into one of her rages and backhanded me. I fell. I was lucky I didn't hit my eye, or you'd be fucking a pirate impersonator."

Bridget didn't smile at my failed attempt at a joke. Instead, she brushed her fingers over the scar again before pressing her lips to it in a soft kiss, the way she had for the scars on my back in Costa Rica.

I closed my eyes, my chest heavy and tight.

I'd talked about my mother more with Bridget than I had anyone else, including my old therapist. It wasn't so hard anymore, but Bridget had a way of making even the hardest things for me easy.

Relax. Talk. Laugh. Simple things that made me feel almost human again.

"Do you ever think about finding your father?" she asked. "For closure."

"Thought about it? Yeah. Acted on it? No." If I wanted, I

could track my father down tomorrow. Christian had told me more than once it would take little more than a few presses of a button for him to dig up that information for me, but I wasn't interested. "I have no interest in meeting him. If I did, I'd probably get arrested for murder."

My father was a piece of shit, and as far as I was concerned, he didn't exist. Any man who could leave a woman high and dry like that didn't deserve recognition.

Even if all I wanted was a family, I would rather eat nails than waste energy seeking him out.

"It's crazy how much our parents shape our lives," Bridget said. "With their choices, their memories, their legacies."

A shadow of sadness passed through her eyes, and I knew she was thinking about her own parents. One gone at child-birth, the other passing just a few years later, and she'd had to grieve, as a child, with millions of eyes watching her.

I remembered seeing a photo of her walking behind her father's casket as a kid, her face scrunched in an obvious attempt to hold back tears, and thinking that even though I had a shitty home situation, at least I could cry at my parent's funeral.

"I think part of the reason I'm so scared about being queen is I'm afraid of not living up to my mother's legacy. Of disappointing her somehow." Bridget stared at the ceiling, her expression pensive. "I never met her, but I read and watched every interview I could get my hands on. The home videos, the stories from the staff and my family...she was the perfect princess and daughter and mother. She would've made a great queen. Better than me. But I killed her." Her voice caught, and somehow, I knew that was the first time she'd ever voiced those words.

A deep ache pierced my heart, and it only grew when I saw the unshed tears in her eyes.

I straightened and cupped her face in my hands. "Bridget, you did not kill your mother," I said fiercely. "Do you understand? You were a baby. You are not guilty just because you were born."

"They didn't plan for me." A tear slipped down her cheek. "I was an accidental pregnancy. If it weren't for me, she'd still be alive, and she would be queen, and things would just be better for everybody."

Fuck. Something cracked in my chest, hard enough it would've alarmed me had I not already been so torn up over Bridget. There were very few things in the world I couldn't withstand, but Bridget crying was one of them.

"Not for me," I said. "Not for your friends, family, or any of the people whose lives you've touched. Your mother made a choice to have you, and no one blames you for what happened to her. It was a medical situation that could've happened to anybody. It had nothing to do with you."

"I know." Her voice cracked.

I gripped her tighter, desperate for her to understand. I didn't know why it was so important. I just knew it was. "Do you remember what you told me during the tour? We always end up where we're meant to be, and you were always meant to be here." *With me.*

Bridget let out a half-laugh, half-sob. "Mr. Larsen, I do believe that's the most words you've ever said to me in one sitting."

"I'm sure that's not true. If it is, I expect a royal medal."

She laughed again and wiped her eyes. "I'm sorry. I don't usually break down like this. I don't know what's gotten into me."

"No need to apologize." I rubbed a remaining tear away with my thumb. "Just tell me you understand."

"Yeah," she whispered. "I think I do."

I kissed the top of her head, my heart still aching. If only she could see herself the way I saw her.

Beautiful, smart, strong. Perfect in every way that mattered.

By the time we left our suite, the sun had dipped below the horizon and Bridget had regained her cool composure, though a hint of vulnerability remained in her eyes.

We walked in silence toward the elevator, once again the princess and her bodyguard. But when we turned the corner, she stopped so suddenly I almost ran straight into her.

My senses snapped into high alert as I scanned the area for visible threats.

No weapons. No paparazzi.

But what I saw was almost worse.

"Bridget." Steffan's eyes widened with a mixture of surprise and alarm. "What are you doing here?"

31

BRIDGET

"Steffan." My heart thumped with panic, even though I wasn't doing anything wrong. Not at that second, anyway. "I didn't know you were back in town."

"I—uh, yes," he stuttered, looking uncharacteristically flustered. "It was a last-minute decision. I wasn't supposed to be back until next week, but I had an emergency in the city and I needed to get back straight away. I was going to call you tomorrow after everything settled." His eyes slid to his left, and I realized he wasn't alone.

A petite, pretty woman with curly dark hair stood next to him, her face red and her arms wrapped tight around her waist.

"Your Highness." She dipped into a small curtsy, her lips fixed in a strained smile.

"This is Malin." Steffan's discomfort visibly increased. "She gave me a ride back to the city."

"Didn't realize future dukes needed to hitch rides." A blade of suspicion sharpened Rhys's otherwise even tone.

The playful, gentle Rhys from earlier in the afternoon had

disappeared, replaced by the stoic, composed bodyguard I knew so well.

"She was coming back to the city anyway, so it made sense." Steffan's eyes flicked between me and Rhys.

Something didn't add up. If he had an emergency in the city, why was he at a hotel on the outskirts of Athenberg this late at night?

Then again, I of all people wasn't going to question why he was here.

The four of us stood in the hall, each eyeing the others warily. The elevator pinged in the distance, and the air conditioning hummed with anxiety. The tension was so thick I could slice through it with a fingernail.

"The hotel isn't in the city," Rhys said. He hadn't moved a single inch since we ran into Steffan and Malin.

Malin looked at the ground while Steffan ran a hand through his hair. "I had a dinner meeting at the restaurant. And Malin was, uh, kind enough to wait while I finished. What are you doing here?"

He addressed the last part to me, and I realized I hadn't answered him the first time he asked. "I took a spa day. We were just leaving."

I avoided looking at Rhys, afraid the movement would somehow give away what we'd really been doing all afternoon.

What does a head turn mean in Eldorran? Oh, just that I fucked my bodyguard in a dozen different positions over the course of six hours.

"Of course. I didn't mean to hold you up." Steffan stepped aside so I could pass, but before I could, Malin spoke up.

"Steffan, wasn't there something you wanted to ask Her Highness?" She fixed her eyes on Steffan, whose lips thinned as he stared back at her. Some unspoken communication passed between them before he turned to me.

"This wasn't how I wanted to do it," he said with a hint of apology. "But since we're here, I *did* have something to ask you. Please forgive me if I'm being presumptive, but, ah, would you like to be my date to Prince Nikolai's wedding?"

Rhys finally moved, his body shifting closer to mine and his hand sliding toward the gun at his waistband.

"I..." Of all the things I'd expected Steffan to ask, that hadn't been one of them. We'd exchanged a few polite texts after our date at the Royal Botanic Gardens, but we hadn't spoken in weeks and, to be honest, he hadn't crossed my mind again until now.

I also suspected he and Malin had a more complicated relationship than he let on, perhaps even a romantic one. He clearly hadn't wanted to ask me out, and she was staring at the floor again with a frown.

But if they were together, why would she push him to go on a date with me?

"I was going to ask when I called you tomorrow," Steffan added. He smiled, and I glimpsed the old friendly, relaxed Steffan again. "We'd mentioned meeting up after I returned, and since the wedding is coming up, I thought you might like to go together. Unless you already have a date..."

Nikolai and Sabrina's wedding was in a month, and they were due back this weekend for the final preparations. I was a bridesmaid along with Sabrina's sister and best friend from the U.S.

"I don't." I was expected to, but I hadn't even thought about it. I'd been too wrapped up in the Citizen Letters program, training, and Rhys.

I hesitated, debating, before I finally answered, "I would be happy to be your date. Thank you for asking."

Rhys stiffened further next to me.

"Excellent." Steffan cleared his throat. "Let's hash the details out later, shall we? I'm looking forward to it."

"Me, too."

"You'd make a lovely couple." There was something in Malin's voice. A hint of warning, maybe? Or animosity mixed with sadness. I couldn't pinpoint it, but whatever it was, it made Steffan flinch.

"Thank you." It took all my training not to inject a question mark at the end. What was I supposed to say to something like that?

Another awkward silence fell before I finally excused myself and left Steffan and Malin standing in the hall, glaring at each other.

Rhys waited until we were in the elevator before he said, "They're fucking."

The thought had crossed my mind, but it didn't make sense. "You don't know that."

"Trust me. I can tell when people are fucking, and they are."

We stepped out of the elevator and into the lobby. "If they are, why did she encourage him to ask me out?"

"I don't know. Maybe they're into group play." Rhys didn't look at me.

He was pissed. He didn't say it, but I could *feel* it, and I didn't have to guess what he was angry about.

"I had to say yes to the date," I said after we got in the car. "Everyone expects me to bring someone to Nik's wedding."

Edvard and Elin had not forgotten about my husband search and kept bringing it up at every turn, but there wasn't much they could do with Steffan gone. Now that he was back...

More complications. Less time with Rhys.

Frustration curled in my stomach.

"I see," Rhys said in a neutral tone, but there was nothing

neutral about the danger emanating from him like heat off sunbaked asphalt.

I hated that I couldn't bring Rhys as my date and that we had to hide and sneak around, even though the only thing keeping us apart was a stupid accident of birth. It was the twenty-first century, but we might as well be living in the eighteenth.

The frustration sharpened and stabbed at my insides.

How did we go from our glorious, dreamy afternoon together to *this* so fast?

"You're still expected to marry soon." Rhys made a right turn, his hands so tight on the wheel his knuckles turned white.

"Yes," I said quietly.

The past few weeks had been our version of a honeymoon, one in which we could be together without worrying about the thunderclouds in the distance. But the storm had arrived, and it was about to rain all over our parade.

I was the crown princess, and he was my bodyguard.

No matter how much it felt like forever, we would eventually have to part ways...unless I did something drastic.

Something no one had ever done before.

Like repeal the Royal Marriages Law.

32

BRIDGET

PROBLEM: I COULDN'T REPEAL THE LAW ON MY OWN. I
needed backup, and I had limited options. I didn't want to tell
Rhys until I had a more concrete plan, and I certainly couldn't
tell my family or any of the palace handlers. My friends in D.C.
were too far away and removed from Eldorran politics to help.

There was only one person left I could trust.

"You want to *what?*" Mikaela's mouth hung open as she
stared at me like I'd sprouted a second head. "Bridget, the
Royal Marriages Law is almost as old as the country itself. It's
impossible to overturn, especially with those fuddy-duddies in
Parliament."

"It's not impossible, it's improbable," I corrected. "There's a
difference. And improbable things can become probable with
the right strategy."

"Okay. What's the strategy?"

"I don't know yet."

She groaned. "Bridge, this is crazy. Why are you going to all
the trouble to overturn the law? I thought everything was going
well with Steffan. I mean, he was gone for a while, but he's

back and as delicious as ever. *And* he's your date to Nikolai's wedding." She sipped her tea and set it on the table. "Am I missing something?"

I bit my lip. Should I spill the beans about Rhys? I trusted Mikaela, but I didn't quite trust her reaction to the news, given what she'd said in my office about dating the staff.

"The law is archaic," I said. "It's not just for me. It's for all the kings and queens after me. If it wasn't for the law, Nikolai would still be crown prince *and* happily engaged to Sabrina."

"Okay, but laws can't be repealed unless the Speaker brings the motion to the floor *and* a three-fourths majority of Parliament votes in favor," Mikaela pointed out. "When was the last time they repealed a law?"

Fifteen years ago, when they repealed a law prohibiting speed limits of higher than fifty-five miles per hour throughout the country.

The odds weren't in my favor.

"I'll figure it out." Erhall would be difficult, but I would think of a way to persuade him. "Will you help?"

"You're crazy. This is crazy."

But for all her grumbling, Mikaela reluctantly agreed, and for the next week, I threw all my energy into creating a workable plan. I analyzed every repealed law in Eldorran history—there weren't many—and studied the different ministers in Parliament, dividing them up based on how likely they were to pass the motion. I hadn't figured out a strategy for Erhall yet, so I left him for last.

However, it wasn't until my next check-in with Elin that something clicked. Something so simple I felt like an idiot for not thinking of it before.

"His Majesty is delighted you're attending Prince Nikolai's wedding with Steffan," Elin said with an approving nod. "Coverage has been positive with the goodwill tour and wedding, but we want to keep the momentum going. Plus, we want to make sure everything is in place for when you eventually take the crown. Nothing says stability like a good marriage with a good, solid consort, and Lord knows we need some stability after the abdication."

"I don't see how marriage affects the ability to rule," I said, stifling a yawn. I stayed up late last night doing research, and I was paying the price today.

"It affects public opinion, Your Highness," Elin said in a tone that suggested I should know this already. "No one is immune to public opinion. Not even the royal family."

I froze. "What did you just say?"

She raised a questioning brow. "No one is immune to public opinion, not even the royal family."

A lightbulb went off in my head, and I almost jumped out of my chair in excitement. "Elin, you're a genius," I breathed. "An absolute genius. You deserve a raise immediately."

"Excellent. Please tell His Majesty the next time you speak with him." She checked her watch. "That's all I have for today unless—"

"No." I was already up and halfway to the door. "This was a lovely meeting. I'll see you next week."

I practically ran into the hall.

"Your Highness, please remember, princesses don't run!" Elin called after me.

I ignored her. The ideas rushed in so fast I couldn't keep up. Some were more devious than others, but at least one had to work. It *had* to.

Parliamentary elections were coming up in the fall, and I was still riding high from the goodwill tour. If I could get the public to back a repeal—

I slammed into a brick wall.

"Whoa. Where are you off to in such a hurry?" Rhys's

amused voice cut through the chatter in my brain as he gripped my arms and steadied me.

I smiled, my heart skipping at the sight of him. "What are you doing here?"

We didn't have a meetup scheduled, but schedules were overrated, anyway.

"Thought I'd explore. See if anything interesting is happening, or if any princesses need protecting." His mouth formed a small, teasing grin.

"Hmm." I adopted a thoughtful expression. "I don't know about protecting, but I can think of a few things that might interest you."

There was no one else in the hall, even so, we kept our voices low. Intimate.

Heat turned Rhys's eyes into molten silver. "Yeah? Like what?"

"Like a tour of the throne room." I slowly walked backward until I reached the door leading into the ceremonial space, and we cast a quick look around before slipping inside.

I'd planned to brainstorm ways I could get the public to support a repeal, but that could wait. I hadn't seen Rhys all day.

"So, this is a throne room." Rhys looked around the lavish space. With its massive crystal chandeliers, thick crimson carpet and wall coverings, and gold trim, it was the most over-the-top room in the palace, but we only used it for the occasional knighting ceremony or official function. No one came in here unless they had to. "Looks exactly the way I pictured a throne room would look."

"Don't act like you haven't studied every inch of every room in the palace already."

Rhys gave me a slow smile, and my stomach flipped. "You think you know me so well."

"I do."

"Hmm." He walked closer to me until we were mere inches apart. "Then do you know what I'm going to do right now?"

I held my breath. "What?"

He leaned down and whispered, "I'm going to sit you on that nice little throne over there and eat your pretty cunt out until you beg me to stop."

I gasped out a laugh as he picked me up and tossed me over his shoulder with the ease of someone picking up a rag doll. "You can't! No one sits on the throne except the monarch."

Rhys set me down on the gold and velvet chair.

"It's going to be yours one day. Might as well get used to it," he said. "How does it feel?"

"I..." I looked around. The room seemed different from this vantage point. Bigger, more intimidating. "Strange. And scary. But...not as scary as I thought."

In my mind, the throne was so large I'd never grow into it, but now that I was actually sitting in it? It seemed manageable.

"Because you're ready for it." Rhys said it like it wasn't even a question. "You're a fucking queen, and don't let anyone tell you otherwise. Including yourself."

My mouth tipped up while my heart melted into a puddle. "If you ever give up on the bodyguard gig, you could make a killing as a motivational speaker."

He chuckled. "Not motivation, just the truth. The throne suits you. Now..." He knelt before me and spread my thighs. "How can I serve you, Your Highness?"

Heat consumed my body as he pulled my underwear down.

"Rhys," I hissed, my pulse racing with a mix of lust and anxiety. "Someone will catch us."

The odds were slim, but they weren't zero.

His wolfish smile caused my toes to curl. "Then we better make it worth it. Hmm, princess?"

I didn't get a chance to respond before he draped my legs

over his shoulders, dipped his head between my thighs, and all
my protests crumbled into ash.

Rhys devoured me with the hunger of a man lost in the
desert, sucking on my clit and thrusting his tongue inside me
until my vision went hazy. I writhed and whimpered, sliding
halfway off the throne until my legs on his shoulders and his
crushing grip on my hips were the only things keeping me from
collapsing.

Too much. Not enough. Everywhere. More.

I couldn't think straight.

My moans echoed in the room, bouncing off the tapestries
and portraits of previous kings and queens, all of whom glared
at me disapprovingly while my bodyguard tongue fucked me
into oblivion on the throne.

He sucked hard on my clit, and I yelped at the overload of
sensation. I tried to pull away, but Rhys's hands clamped
around my thighs like iron bands, forcing me to hold still until
my body convulsed and came apart.

Before I could gather myself back together, he was up and
inside me, his big body shielding me from sight should anyone
walk in and his cock driving into me forcefully enough to send
the chair inching back with each thrust.

So wrong. This was so wrong, but I couldn't bring myself to
care as Rhys grabbed my ankles and placed my legs on his
shoulders again, bending me nearly in half.

"Now this is how a queen should be treated," he said, his
eyes dark and ravenous as they dropped from my face to where
his cock pumped in and out of me. "Don't you agree?"

"Mmph ungh." I moaned something unintelligible, unable
to speak. To *think*.

I was pure sensation, fire inside and out, and the last
coherent thought I had before another volcano erupted and
melted me into nothing was, *sometimes, it's good to be queen.*

33

RHYS

OUR TRYST IN THE THRONE ROOM WAS THE LAST BIT OF alone time Bridget and I had before her brother and future sister-in-law arrived, and she got swept up in a flurry of pre-wedding obligations. I thought normal weddings were tedious, but royal weddings were off the charts.

On the bright side, it meant Bridget didn't have time to see Steffan, either. The fucker was back in town, and the thought of seeing them on another date made my blood burn.

I've gone off the rails. Hell, I'd gone off the entire fucking track. I'd never so much as gone on a third date with a woman in the past. None had interested me enough. And now I was thinking of killing over one.

Bridget had my head well and truly fucked.

"Get it together," I muttered, slamming a jar of tomato sauce on the counter. "It's one day."

Except it wasn't only one day because eventually, she would have to marry someone noble. Someone blue-blooded. Someone not me.

Fury and pain rippled through me, and I forced myself to

focus on the task at hand before I spiraled too far down that path. It wouldn't end well for me or anything in the kitchen.

I'd just turned on the stove when someone knocked on the door. Bridget was at some pre-wedding night thing with the rest of the bridesmaids, so it couldn't be her. Who else would visit at this time of night?

I turned the stove off again and checked the security camera.

You gotta be shitting me.

I exited the kitchen, crossed the living room, and opened the front door. "What the hell are you doing here?"

Andreas raised his eyebrows. "I'm getting offended by the rude greetings you and Bridget insist on giving me. Perhaps she can get away with it, but I am a prince, and you are not." There was an odd note in his voice when he said that, but it disappeared so quickly I wondered if I'd imagined it.

"You show up at my door unannounced, you get whatever greeting I want to give." My smile contained more threat than humor. "Be glad you're not staring down the barrel of my gun."

Andreas clucked in disappointment. "And to think, I came here to help."

"I doubt that."

"Contrary to what Bridget may have told you, I'm not a bad guy. I want what's best for my family and country." He straightened the cuffs of his shirt. "For example, I find it quite admirable, how Nikolai abdicated for true love. At the end of the day, he's the one who has to live his life, and he chose happiness. Good for him."

Impatience spiraled through me. "Do you have a point, or do you just like hearing yourself talk?"

"I do enjoy hearing myself talk," Andreas said. "Usually because I speak the truth. But Nikolai's wedding made me wonder...which would Bridget choose if she had the choice? Her heart or her country?"

My hand closed around the doorknob. I was *this* close to slamming the door in his face, prince or not. "She's not abdicating. Whatever scheme you have in mind, it's not gonna work."

"You might be right, in which case I feel sorry for my cousin. Stuck in a marriage of political convenience for the rest of her life." Sympathy crossed Andreas's face, but it didn't fool me. "She's a romantic, even if she tries to hide it. Grand love and all that. Sadly, that's not always in the cards for the heir to the throne." He paused. "Then again, Steffan Holstein could very well be an exception. They make a good-looking couple, don't you think?"

A muscle pulsed in my jaw.

"Like I said, I look out for my family and country." Andreas's eyes flickered. "I want everyone to be happy, and while Steffan seems like perfectly adequate consort material, Bridget would be far happier if she abdicated."

"So you can be king," I said flatly.

He shrugged. "She never wanted to be queen, anyway. Why not pass the throne to me?"

"You know, this all sounds like a personal problem. For you," I said coldly. "Don't understand why you're telling me all this."

Andreas's smile made my guard shoot straight up. "An American contractor who moved to another country so he can be the princess's permanent bodyguard? I think you do." He turned, but before he left, he added, "Thank you for indulging me, Mr. Larsen. It's been quite an enlightening conversation."

Bridget was right. He *was* a satanic little turd, not to mention a dangerous one. If he didn't know about Bridget and me, he at least suspected I had feelings for her.

I shut the door with a slam.

Was Andreas the one who'd snooped through the guest-house? I couldn't think of a good reason why he'd do that unless he'd hoped to find something incriminating about Bridget, in which case he was shit out of luck.

What was the penalty for punching a prince in the face? Whatever it was, it might be worth it.

My phone rang, and I answered it without glancing at the caller ID. "What?" I barked. It was probably Christian again, calling to throw me deeper into a shitty mood.

"Did I catch you at a bad time?" Bridget's amused voice flowed over the line.

My muscles relaxed, and I blew out a breath. "Thought you were someone else, princess." I leaned against the wall. "Aren't you supposed to be at the bridesmaid thing?"

"Yes. I snuck into the bathroom. I can't talk for long, but the wedding's tomorrow and..." Bridget's voice lowered. "I miss you."

We saw each other every day, but I knew what she meant. I missed the moments that belonged only to us.

"I miss you too, princess." I smiled a real smile this time. "Any chance I can convince you to sneak out the bathroom window so we can end the night with a bang? So to speak."

She snorted out a laugh, which she cut off halfway with a gasp.

I broke into a laugh of my own. "Did you just snort?"

"No."

"Not very princess-like of you."

"I did *not* snort." I could practically see her face glowing red on the other end of the line. She was so fucking adorable. "Anyway, I can't sneak out the window. We're on the third floor."

"Third floor's not that high."

Bridget huffed. "Easy for you to say. You're not the one at

risk of dying."

"Trust me, princess. I would rather end my own life than ask you to do anything that might hurt you."

I hadn't meant to say those words. They just fell out, like they'd been there all along and were waiting for the right moment to make themselves known.

Funny thing was, I wasn't upset or embarrassed, even though they came too close to a confession for comfort. They just felt right.

Everything with Bridget felt right.

"I know," she said, so soft and warm she might as well be right there next to me, caressing me. "I trust you."

A charged silence stretched over the line, filled with other, unspoken words waiting for their moment, and my heart thudded like it was warning me not to screw up.

"We've come a long way, haven't we?" I drawled, finally breaking the tension before I did—or said—something I would regret. Something neither of us was ready to acknowledge. "From fighting like cats and dogs to fucking like—"

"Rhys."

"What? You let me eat you out on the throne but I can't say the word *fucking?*"

"You're impossible." Amusement softened her admonishing tone. "I—" I heard a knock in the background, followed by muffled voices. Bridget must've covered the phone with her hand. "Sorry, that was Sabrina," she said, her voice clearer. "I have to go, but I'll see you tomorrow." Her voice softened further. "Good night, Mr. Larsen."

"Good night, princess."

I waited until she hung up before I ended the call.

I stood there for a long while, my mind filled with images of a certain blonde as I stared around my royal guesthouse in Eldorra and wondered how the hell I got where I was.

34

BRIDGET

"Is everything okay?" Sabrina asked after I exited the bathroom. She'd knocked to check on me, and I realized I'd been gone for almost half an hour.

"Yes. I just had to deal with some last-minute prep for an event next week," I said, ashamed of how easily the lie rolled off my tongue. "Apologies."

"No need to apologize." Sabrina gestured to her sister and best friend, who'd passed out on the couch while *The Devil Wears Prada* played on-screen. "At least you're awake."

I let out a small laugh. "We *should* go to sleep soon. You have a big day tomorrow."

"You're probably right. I can't believe it's almost here." Sabrina fiddled with her engagement ring, looking overwhelmed and a little lost. "It feels surreal. I wanted a small wedding, but..."

"You got a three-ring circus?" I sank onto the couch next to her. "Welcome to the royal life. Even if Nik abdicated, he's still a royal by blood, and everything he does is a reflection of the crown."

"I know. I just hope I don't embarrass myself." Sabrina gave me a nervous smile before her expression grew serious. "Bridget, I know we don't know each other that well, but I wanted to thank you for agreeing to be part of my bridal party. Truly. It means a lot to me."

"Of course. You're going to be my sister-in-law."

When Nikolai first told me about his abdication, I resented her. It wasn't something I was proud of, but it was true. If he hadn't met Sabrina, he'd still be Crown Prince, and I'd be living my life in New York.

But as I stared at her now, I realized I wouldn't go back to my life in the U.S. even if I could. It had been an illusion of freedom, nothing else. I'd been trapped in the same day in, day out monotony of fake smiles and mind-numbing events. Being crown princess came with more rules and a smaller cage, but it also came with more purpose, and that was the one thing that'd always been missing in my life.

Somehow, somewhere along the way, I'd grown into my new role. It would take a while before I was fully comfortable with it, but I was getting there.

"Yes. Good ones, I hope." Sabrina squeezed my hand. "I love Nikolai, and I'd be lying if I said I'm not happy he abdicated. But I also know what a huge burden it placed on you, and for that, I'm sorry."

"No apologies needed. You did nothing wrong except fall in love."

I knew that. I'd always known that. But it wasn't until I said it at that moment that any lingering resentment I had toward Nikolai and Sabrina faded away.

It wasn't their fault. There were no wrong choices. If Nikolai had chosen the throne over Sabrina, it would've been devastating for him, but it would've been understandable. If he'd chosen Sabrina, as he had, that was understandable too.

Love or country. An impossible choice when the future of a nation rests on your shoulders.

The only thing at fault was the system that forced him to choose.

"My brother adores you," I added. Nikolai and I weren't super close, but I knew him well enough to spot the difference. He changed into a different person when he was around Sabrina, a happier one, and I would never begrudge him that.

Sabrina's face lit up, erasing some of the earlier stress. "It still feels like a dream sometimes," she admitted. "To meet someone who sees me for who I am, faults and all, and loves me regardless." She squeezed my hand again, her eyes wise beyond her twenty-five years. "I hope you find that kind of love one day, too. Whether it's with Steffan or someone else."

Trust me, princess. I would rather end my own life than ask you to do anything that might hurt you.

I forced a smile. "One day."

But later that night, as I stared at the ceiling and thought about Rhys, Steffan, and my less-than-certain efforts to repeal the Royal Marriages Law, I couldn't help but wonder if there was only room for one happy ending in this kingdom...and if it wasn't already too late for mine.

35

RHYS

As expected, Prince Nikolai and Sabrina's wedding was a madhouse. Half the city's roads were closed, helicopters buzzed overhead capturing aerial footage of the procession, and thousands of people crowded the streets, eager for a glimpse of the fairytale unfolding in real life. Press flew in from all over the world, breathlessly covering every detail from the length of Sabrina's wedding dress train to the star-studded guest list. The only reporters allowed inside the actual ceremony were those from Eldorra's national newspaper and broadcaster, who'd received exclusive first coverage rights, but that didn't stop the others from fighting for the best view outside the church.

Bridget spent the day running around doing whatever bridesmaids did. While they got ready in the bridal suite, I kept watch in the hall with Sabrina's bodyguard Joseph, who was also an American contractor since Nikolai had given up his rights to the Royal Guard when he abdicated.

While Joseph rambled on about the exploits of his previous client—unprofessional as hell, but I wasn't the man's boss—I monitored the surroundings. There was all sorts of potential for a big day like today to go wrong.

Luckily, all seemed quiet, and before long, the door opened and Sabrina stepped out, beaming in her fancy white gown and veil. The bridesmaids filed out after her, with Bridget rounding up the rear.

She wore the same pale green dress as the other bridesmaids, but she glowed in a way no one else could. My eyes lingered on the shadow of her cleavage and the way the dress hugged her hips before I dragged them up to her face, where my breath got stuck in my throat.

Half the time, I couldn't believe she was real.

Bridget flashed me a secretive smile as she passed by, her gaze sweeping over my suit and tie with appreciation. "You clean up nice, Mr. Larsen," she murmured.

"So do you." I fell into step behind her and lowered my voice until it was barely audible. "Can't wait to tear that dress off you later, princess."

She didn't respond, but I saw enough of her profile to spot the rosy glow on her cheeks.

I grinned, but my good mood didn't last long, because when we entered the wedding hall, the first person I saw was Steffan fucking Holstein sitting in one of the front pews. Shiny shoes, hair coiffed, and eyes fixed on Bridget.

I was convinced he was fucking the woman we saw him with at the hotel, but if he didn't stop looking at Bridget like that, I was going to rip his tongue out and choke him to death with it.

I forced myself to focus on the ceremony and not the violent thoughts swarming through my head. It hadn't been included in Elin's instructions, but I assumed murdering a high-ranking guest in the middle of a royal wedding was frowned upon.

Bridget took her place at the altar while I remained in the side shadows, drinking her in. She stood on the side facing me, and as Nikolai and Sabrina recited their vows, she caught my eye and gave me another one of her little smiles, the kind so subtle one would miss it unless they were attuned to her every micro expression.

My shoulders relaxed, and my mouth tipped up in its own ghost of a smile.

A moment just for us, stolen beneath the noses of hundreds of people in Athenberg's grandest church.

After the ceremony ended, everyone drove to the palace's ballroom for the grand first reception. The second, more intimate evening reception took place at Tolose House, Nikolai and Sabrina's new residence, which was located only a ten-minute walk from the palace. Only two hundred of the family's closest friends and relatives received invites, no press allowed.

It was where the guests really let loose...and where I had to watch Bridget and Steffan dance together. One of his hands rested on her lower back, and she smiled at something he said.

Jealousy clawed at me, sharp and ruthless.

"They make a nice-looking couple," Joseph said, following my gaze. "The princess and the duke. Fairytale shit." He shook his head and chuckled. "Too bad she'd never go for an average Joe like you or me, huh? I would fuck—"

"Be careful what you say next." Lethal quiet razored my words. "Or it'll be the last thing you say."

Steffan may be untouchable, but Joseph? I could tear him apart and use his bones to pick my teeth.

He must've known it too, because he fell silent and moved an inch away from me. "It was a joke," he muttered. "Take your job a bit too seriously, don't you?"

"Show some respect. That's the crown princess." *And you're not worthy of scraping the dirt off her shoes.*

How the hell had Sabrina ended up with Joseph as her bodyguard? The man had the social tact of a brick, and that was coming from me, someone who couldn't—and wouldn't—kiss ass if someone glued my lips to one.

Joseph was smart enough not to talk again. He stood a few feet away with a surly expression, but I didn't give a crap if he was offended. I had other things to worry about.

The song changed, but Steffan and Bridget remained on the dance floor. I knew she was staying out of social obligation, but it didn't suck any less to see them together, especially since Joseph was right. They *did* make a well-matched couple. Bridget, angelic and regal. Steffan, clean-cut and debonair in his fancy tuxedo.

Then there was me, tattooed and scarred, haunted by the things I'd done and the blood on my hands.

By all accounts, Steffan was the better, and easier, option for Bridget. Her grandfather, the palace, the press...they were all salivating for a Princess and the Duke love story.

I didn't give a flying fuck.

Bridget was mine.

She wasn't mine to take, but I was taking her anyway. Her laughs, her fears, her joy and her pain. Every inch of her body and beat of her heart. All mine.

And I'd had enough of watching her in another man's arms.

I left my post and stalked across the dance floor, ignoring Joseph's noise of protest. I was breaking every rule of protocol, but it was late and most guests were already too drunk to pay attention to me. I was an employee, beneath most of their notice, and in that instance, it worked in my favor.

"Your Highness." A dark edge bled through my otherwise even voice. "Sorry to interrupt, but Jules called. There's an emergency."

I was holding Bridget's phone while she danced, so the excuse made sense.

Alarm crossed her face. "Oh, no. It must be serious. She never calls for emergencies." She glanced at Steffan. "Would you mind terribly if I—"

"Of course not," he said. There was no trace of the awkward, uncomfortable Steffan from the hotel. "I understand. Please, take the call. I'll be here."

I bet you will. Maybe I could bribe a server to slip something into his drink. Not enough to kill him, but enough to incapacitate him for the rest of the night.

I handed Bridget her phone to keep up the ruse as we exited the reception room, but I said, "Jules didn't call."

"What?" Her brow knit in confusion. "Then why did you—"

"He was getting too close." I clenched my teeth so hard my jaw hurt.

A beat passed before Bridget's face cleared. She glanced around before whispering, "You know I had to dance with him."

"You danced with him *twice.*"

"Rhys, he's technically my date."

It was the wrong thing to say, and judging by the way Bridget winced, she knew it.

I stopped in front of what I knew was the library from my pre-wedding advance work. "Get in," I said curtly.

A hard swallow disturbed the delicate lines of Bridget's throat, but she obeyed without argument.

I followed her inside and locked the door behind us with a soft click. The room wasn't fully furnished yet, and it was empty save for a rug, a table, and a large mirror. The lights were off, but there was enough moonlight streaming through the curtains for me to spot Bridget's wary expression.

"I told you, I had to bring him," she said. "Everyone expected me to bring a date, and it would've been weird if I only danced with him once."

"Stop saying the word 'date.'" It came out soft and dangerous enough she shivered.

I walked to the table by the window and leaned against it while watching Bridget through dark, hooded eyes.

Possessiveness and anger gripped me—not at her, but at our situation and a world where we were forced to sneak around like criminals. I hated having to hide her, *us*. I wanted the world to know she was mine and mine alone. I wanted to tattoo myself into her skin and sink into her so fucking deep she could never get me out.

"Take off your dress," I said.

"Rhys—"

"Take. It. Off."

I heard Bridget's breath hitch from across the room, but she didn't argue again. Instead, she reached behind her and did as I asked, keeping her eyes on mine the entire time.

Other than our harsh breaths, the soft metallic slide of the zipper was the only sound breaking the silence.

I remained still, my muscles coiled with tension.

I couldn't claim her the way I wanted outside these walls, but right here, right now, when it was just the two of us?

I was going to take her until we were both utterly ruined.

36

BRIDGET

My dress pooled around my ankles, leaving me in only my lace bra and thong. Trembles wracked me—from anticipation or the slight chill in the air, I wasn't sure. Probably a mixture of both.

Rhys was silhouetted against the moonlight so I couldn't see his face, but I could *feel* the heat of his gaze as it raked over me. Dark and possessive like a lover's touch, leaving a trail of delicious goosebumps in its wake.

I wet my lips, dying to touch him, but knowing it was in my best interest not to move until he told me to.

"Bra. Off."

Two seconds later, white lace joined green silk on the floor.

I reached down to shimmy out of my underwear, but a low growl halted my movements.

"I didn't tell you to do that." Rhys's eyes lingered on my breasts, and my nipples, already so hard they could cut glass, pebbled further. "Keep your underwear, gloves, and heels on," he said, still in that deceptively soft tone. "And crawl to me."

My breath gusted out in shock even as my core spasmed at the order.

I'd never crawled for anyone in my life—while I was all but naked, no less. Even if I wasn't the future queen, it would be degrading. Humiliating. Depraved.

And I'd never been more turned on.

I sank to my hands and knees, shivering again at the feel of the cool wood floor against my bare skin.

And I began to crawl.

The room wasn't that big, but the anticipation made it seem endless. Halfway across, I glimpsed myself in the full-length mirror mounted on the wall, and my skin burned at the sight.

I still wore the elegant elbow-length gloves that came with my bridesmaid outfit, but when paired with only my heels and thong, they looked obscene.

My breathing grew choppier. I was so wet my thighs slid against each other, and by the time I reached Rhys, I was dripping all down my legs.

I stopped at his feet and looked up. I could see him more clearly now, but his expression remained unreadable except for the fire blazing in his eyes.

"Good girl." He fisted my hair with one hand and used the other to unbuckle his pants. His cock sprung out, thick and hard, the swollen head dripping with pre-cum.

God, I needed to taste him. No one had ever turned me on as much as he did. Every word, every touch, every glance. I wanted it all.

I stared at him with pleading eyes.

Rhys hadn't finished nodding before I took him in my mouth, savoring his groans and the way he pulled my hair as I eagerly licked and sucked.

"What would your people say if they could see you now, princess?" he grunted, pushing his cock deeper until it hit the back of my throat. I spluttered, my eyes watering from the sheer size of him. "Crawling and choking on your bodyguard's cock?"

I moaned out an unintelligible response. My hand drifted between my legs, but I didn't make contact before he yanked me up and captured my mouth in a hard, punishing kiss.

He was still angry about Steffan. I could taste it on his tongue, feel it in the roughness of his hands as he squeezed my ass.

"You're more than just a bodyguard to me." I needed him to understand that, even amid our lust-drenched haze.

"Yeah, I can get you off, too," Rhys said caustically. "Bet none of the lily-livered aristocrats out there can fuck you the way you need."

I didn't take the bait. "It's more than that."

It was the closest I'd come to voicing what was in my heart.

Something vulnerable flickered in Rhys's eyes, and his touch gentled for a second before his face hardened again. He spun me around and bent me over the table, pressing his body against mine until every inch of him melded into every inch of me.

He lowered his mouth to my ear and tangled one of his hands with mine. "I want you to know something, princess," he said, his voice a hoarse rasp against my skin. "There's not much in the world I want to claim as mine. I've seen and done too much shit in my life to believe in forever. But you..." He grasped my chin with his free hand. "You belong to me. I don't give a fuck what the law or anyone else says. *You are mine.* Understand?"

"Yes." I squeezed his hand, my heart and body aching for completely different reasons.

Rhys exhaled a harsh, shuddering breath and pulled back. I was about to protest before he roughly parted my thighs and yanked my underwear down.

The ball of anticipation in my stomach coiled tighter.

"There's something else you should know." He dragged two fingers through my wetness before shoving them in my mouth, forcing me to taste my juices. An unbidden moan slipped out at the unfamiliar tang on my tongue. "I don't like it when other people touch what's mine. Especially when it's a *date* who's not me."

I knew I'd been in trouble the minute I said that.

"But maybe you need a lesson to drive that point home." Rhys rubbed his thumb over my swollen clit before his palm landed where his thumb had been. My body jerked, and a yelp of surprise and pain tore from my throat, but Rhys's fingers in my mouth muffled the sound.

His palm landed on my pussy again with a loud slap. And again. And again.

I was shaking, my eyes filled with tears as razor-sharp sensation spiked through me. My entire world had narrowed to the pulsing heat between my legs and the man who doled out pain and pleasure in equal measure.

"Who does your pussy belong to?" Rhys removed his fingers from my mouth and squeezed my breast.

"You," I gasped, clutching the edge of the table so hard my knuckles turned white.

"Say it again." Hard. Demanding. Authoritative.

"You! My pussy belongs to you." My voice broke in a sob as he delivered another stinging slap to my clit.

"That's right. It belongs to me, and don't you ever forget it." *Slap.*

I let out a keening wail, trying to scrabble away and push back harder against him at the same time. I couldn't tell whether I loved or hated what was happening, only that I was dripping and burning and every scrape of my nipples against the wooden table sent another jolt of heat straight to my throbbing clit.

"Are you going to dance with your *date* again?" Rhys's voice sounded remarkably even, if tightly controlled.

I shook my head, the tears sliding down my cheeks.

"Good." *Slap.* "You are so wet, princess." *Slap.* "You should see how pretty and swollen your clit looks right now. Like it's begging for me to spank it harder." *SLAP.*

It was too much. The words, the brutal, filthy punishment, the fact we were doing this just around the corner and down the hall from my family and friends.

I exploded. Hard. Long. Violent. Ears buzzing, knees buckling, showers of lights bursting behind my eyes. I would've fallen to the floor had Rhys not held me up while the strongest orgasm of my life tore through me like an electric storm, and I had to drop my head and bury my face in my arm to stifle my screams.

I was still riding out the waves of my mind-shattering release when I felt Rhys's tongue gently stroke my clit, licking and soothing until the burn faded.

Just as I gathered myself together, he stood and slowly pushed his cock inside of me. He withdrew equally slowly, until just the tip remained inside, and paused. I inhaled, but my first real breath of the night broke into a squeal when he suddenly slammed into me with a vicious thrust. His fist in my hair kept me in place as he bottomed out with each downward stroke, and the contrast between the gentleness of his entry and the savage fury with which he now fucked me scrambled my senses to the point where I could only hold on to the table for dear life.

In and out. Harder and faster each time until the tingles at the base of my spine came back to life, and I crashed over the edge again.

"Oh, God, *Rhys.*"

"That's it, princess." He pressed a kiss to my shoulder, his movements growing jerkier. He was about to come, too. "Such a good girl. Come for me."

I did, endlessly and unashamedly, breaking into a million pieces around him.

And as Rhys, too, came with a loud groan, I wondered if he knew he owned every one of those pieces—not just of my body, but also my heart.

37

BRIDGET

RHYS AND I NEVER MADE IT BACK TO THE RECEPTION. By the time he finished with me, there was no way I could've fixed myself up enough to face other people, so we slipped out a side door and snuck back to the palace. By some miracle, no one saw us.

It was horrible form for a bridesmaid to leave early without a word, but the party had already been winding down by the time we excused ourselves, and most people had been too drunk to notice my absence, anyway.

I did, however, feel awful about leaving Steffan high and dry. I called him the next morning and apologized profusely, claiming my friend's emergency took longer than expected. He was, as expected, gracious about it. He hadn't been as jumpy during the reception as he'd been at the hotel, but he'd been distracted, and I suspected he might've been relieved by my abrupt departure.

"Where did you go?" Mikaela asked after I wrapped up my call. We were in my room, brainstorming ways to get Erhall to bring the repeal motion for the Royal Marriages Law to the floor. "You disappeared halfway through the reception."

"One of my college friends called with an emergency." I avoided her gaze as I studied Erhall's parliamentary voting record.

"Really?" She sounded doubtful. "Even though you're in different countries?"

"She needed advice on a personal issue."

Another lie. They were piling up, one after another, and soon I wouldn't be able to dig myself out.

I turned the page with more force than necessary.

"Okay." A hint of doubt remained, but Mikaela didn't press the issue. "I only ask because your cousin was looking for you."

I froze. "Andreas? He was looking for me at the reception?"

"Yeah, he said he had something important to tell you."

My heart rate kicked into overdrive. *You're overreacting.* I'd thought Andreas had already left. I'd heard him say goodbye to Nikolai and Sabrina long before Rhys and I exited. Had I heard wrong, or had he returned for some reason? Did he see me and Rhys leave? Even if he had, he couldn't have known what we were doing...unless he followed us. But if Andreas *did* know, he would've thrown it in my face the minute he could, and an entire day had already passed.

My head spun as I ran through every possible scenario.

"Did you tell him where I was?"

"No," Mikaela said slowly. "I didn't know where you were. Remember?"

"Right. Sorry." I pressed my fingers to my temple, trying to sort through my thoughts. "My brain is fried right now. Can we pick this up later?"

"Sure. I have a dinner reservation soon anyway." Worry slid across her features as she packed her bag and slung the strap over her shoulder. "Are you sure nothing else is the matter? You've been acting weird for weeks."

"Yes, I'm just stressed. I need a vacation." I forced a laugh. "I'll talk to you later. Enjoy dinner."

After Mikaela left, I set my notes on Erhall aside and answered that week's letters from citizens instead. The mail volume, both physical and electronic, had grown so much I'd had to bring on assistants, but I still liked to reply personally when I could. Besides, it was a good distraction from my worries over Andreas.

I was reading too much into one throwaway comment from Mikaela. Andreas could've been looking for me for any number of reasons, and he had a skewed idea of what was important. He'd probably wanted to complain about being seated at the wrong table for the reception or something.

I'd made it halfway through the pile of letters when my laptop pinged with a new email notification. I almost ignored it, but something compelled me to click into it, and my suspicion spiked when I saw the sender's email message—a random string of numbers and letters hosted by a domain I'd never heard of— and the one-line message.

Not careful enough, Your Highness.

I stared at the MP4 file attached to the email. No name, no hint as to what it contained.

Not opening strange files from unknown senders was Computer Security 101, but this was an email only my close circle had. I had a separate one for public correspondence.

Then again, it wasn't difficult to find an email, even a private one.

My curiosity outweighed my reservations, and I clicked on the file.

Forgive me, computer security gods.

The video popped up and auto-played. It was so dark and

grainy it took me a minute to figure out what was happening, but when I did, all the blood drained from my face.

I clutched the edge of my desk and stared in horror at the clip of me and Rhys in Nikolai's library. Even with no sound, it was damning—me bent over the table, him gripping my hair and pounding into me from behind.

It was dark enough we would've been unrecognizable had I not turned my head halfway through the video. Rhys's face never showed on camera, but his hair, height, and build made his identity a foregone conclusion, and it wouldn't take much editing to clean up the quality and brighten it enough that anyone who watched would know exactly who was doing what.

I'm going to be sick.

My skin felt hot and clammy, and a strange buzzing filled my ears as question after question raced through my head.

Where did the video come from? Who could have gotten their hands on it so quickly? Who knew where to look?

Judging by the angle, the camera had been inside the room, even though Nikolai and Sabrina had been adamant about not having security cameras in their private quarters. Someone must've planted it there. Were they hoping to catch Nikolai and Sabrina doing something and caught Rhys and me instead? But why would've they have planted a camera in an unfinished library, of all places? Why not the bedrooms or office?

Most importantly of all...what did the sender want?

38

BRIDGET

I was a mess of nerves for the rest of the week. I tried to hide it, but everyone noticed—Rhys, Mikaela, my family. I blamed it on stress, but I wasn't sure anyone believed me.

I didn't tell anyone about the video. Not yet. The sender hadn't contacted me since, and my replies to their email all bounced. I convinced Nikolai and Sabrina's security team to sweep their house for bugs as a "preventative measure," but they didn't find anything, not even in the library.

It should've made me feel better, but it only put me more on edge. Whoever the sender was, they could move in and out of one of the city's most highly guarded buildings without being detected, and that wasn't good. At all.

My top suspect was Andreas, but he wasn't the type to hold back. If he had a damning video of me and Rhys, he would hold it over my head. Taunt me with it. Probably blackmail me. He wouldn't send it once and not follow up again for almost a week.

He'd looked for me at the reception—I still didn't know

what for, as I hadn't seen him since the wedding and he hadn't contacted me—but that was while Rhys and I were in the library.

If it *wasn't* Andreas, who could it be? And when would the other shoe drop?

Because there was another shoe. I was sure of it.

"Something's bothering you," Rhys said on our way back to the palace from a charity shop ribbon-cutting ceremony. "Don't tell me it's stress. It's not."

I mustered a weak smile. "You think you know everything."

I *should* tell Rhys. He'd know what to do. But a small, stupid, selfish part of me was afraid of what telling him would do to us. If he found out someone knew about us, would he withdraw and break things off?

If I didn't tell him, though, the video could blow up in our faces, and I'd lose him anyway.

My head ached with indecision.

"I know everything about you." Rhys's words rolled over me, deep and confident.

Just tell him. Get it over with like ripping off a Band-Aid. Otherwise, the secret would hang over my head for God knew how long, like a guillotine waiting to strike.

Before I could broach the subject, however, the car stopped. I'd been so caught up in my thoughts I hadn't realized we were heading away from the palace instead of toward it.

Rhys had parked on the side of the road, next to a forest on the outskirts of Athenberg. I'd camped there once with Nikolai in high school—under strict supervision, of course—but I hadn't been back since.

"Trust me," he said when he noticed my confusion, which only increased as he led me through the forest. A clear trail snaked between the trees, so other people must've taken the shortcut, even though the forest had a main entrance with a gift

shortcut, even though the forest had a main entrance with a gift shop and parking lot.

"Where are we going?" I whispered, not wanting to break the reverent hush blanketing the trees.

"You'll see."

Cryptic as always.

I sighed, equally annoyed and intrigued.

Part of me wanted to tell him about the video *now*, but I couldn't very well ruin the mood before I saw the surprise, could I?

Excuses, excuses, my conscience whispered.

I ignored it.

When we arrived at our destination, though, I couldn't hold back a small gasp. "Rhys..."

We stood in a clearing, empty of everything except for a large, beautiful gazebo. I didn't even know the forest had a gazebo.

My heart pinched at the clear callback to our first time together.

"If we get caught, pull rank." Rhys held out his hand. I took it and followed him inside the wooden structure. "We're pretty far from the main trail though, so we should be fine."

"How did you find this place? You're like the Gazebo Whisperer."

He laughed. "I planned on hiking here sometime and studied the trail maps. The gazebo isn't a secret. Most people are just too lazy to come all the way out here."

"Why..." I trailed off again when he fiddled with something on his phone and soft music filled the air.

"We never got to dance at the wedding," he said simply.

"You don't like it when I dance," I half-joked, trying to hide the emotion welling in my chest.

What happened in the library during Nikolai's reception would forever be etched in my mind.

"I love it when you dance. But only with me." He placed his free hand on the small of my back.

"You don't dance."

"Only with you."

The burn intensified. "Careful, Mr. Larsen, or I'll think you actually like me."

His mouth curled into a grin. "Baby, we're way beyond like."

The butterflies in my stomach exploded, and a sweet, golden warmth filled my veins.

For the first time in days, I smiled.

I stepped into Rhys's embrace, and we swayed to the music while I buried my face in his chest and inhaled his clean, comforting scent.

Our dances would always be ours. Secret, private...forbidden.

Part of me cherished the moments that belonged to us alone, but part of me wished we didn't have to hide. We weren't a dirty secret. We were the most beautiful thing in my life, and I wanted to share it with the world the way all beautiful things deserved to be shared.

"Where'd you go, princess?" He skimmed his knuckles down my back, and I smiled through the ache in my heart.

He knew me so well.

"I'm right here." I tilted my face up and kissed him. We took it slow and sweet, exploring each other with the leisure of people who had all the time in the world.

Except we didn't.

The kiss, the music, the gazebo...it was the perfect moment. But, like all moments, it couldn't last.

Eventually, it would end, and so would we.

"Bridget, wake up!"

The next morning, loud pounding roused me from my sleep.

I groaned, my body resisting movement even as my heart involuntarily galloped at the sheer panic in Mikaela's voice.

"Bridget!" More pounding.

"One moment!" I forced myself out of bed and threw on a dressing gown before I opened the door, taking in Mikaela's wide eyes and nervous expression. Her skin was paler than usual, making her freckles stand out like a dark constellation across her nose and cheeks.

She lived only a few minutes from the palace, but she wouldn't be here so early unless it was an emergency.

"What is it?"

Was it the video?

My stomach lurched. God, I should've told Rhys yesterday, but I hadn't wanted to destroy our time at the gazebo, and then...then...

Oh, who was I kidding? I had plenty of time to tell him afterward. I'd just chickened out like a coward, and now, the chickens were coming home to roost.

Breathe. Stay calm. You don't know what's actually happening yet.

"It's..." Mikaela hesitated. "Bridge, turn on *The Daily Tea*."

The Daily Tea was a celebrity news and entertainment media company that included the country's most-read magazine and one of its most-watched television stations. Some considered it trashy, but it had a huge audience.

Mikaela followed me to the sitting room, where I picked up the remote with shaky hands and turned on the TV.

"...reports Princess Bridget is in a relationship with her

bodyguard, an American contractor named Rhys Larsen." The *Daily Tea* host's voice trembled with excitement. "Larsen has been by her side since her senior year at the prestigious Thayer University in the U.S., and suspicions about their relationship have abounded for years..."

For years? That was, for lack of better words, utter bull crap. Rhys and I hadn't even *liked* each other years ago.

I watched, disbelief searing through me, as candid pictures of us flashed on-screen with the host's voiceover commentary. Us walking down the street with Rhys's hand on my lower back —to steer me around a puddle when I wasn't looking, if I remembered correctly. Rhys helping me out of the car at a charity gala while our eyes locked onto each other. Me standing a little too close to him at an outdoor event a few months ago, but only because it was freezing and I needed the body warmth.

All innocent moments that, framed in a certain way and captured at a certain second, made them look like more than they were.

Then the more damning photos surfaced. Rhys glaring at Steffan during our ice-skating date, looking for all the world like a jealous boyfriend. Him pressing me against the car in the parking lot of the Royal Botanic Gardens. Us leaving the hotel where we'd spent that one glorious afternoon, our heads bent close together.

How the *hell* had someone captured those pictures? Other than the ice rink, we hadn't spotted any paparazzi following us. Then again, we'd been distracted—horribly so.

On the bright side, there was no mention of the sex tape. If *The Daily Tea* had gotten their hands on it, it would be the only thing they talked about.

"Is this true?" Mikaela asked, her eyes huge. "Tell me it's not true."

"They're just pictures," I deflected.

I breathed a little easier. Only a little, because it was still a huge mess, but it was fixable. They didn't have the video. "We can—"

"BRIDGET!"

Mikaela and I exchanged wide-eyed glances as my grandfather's bellow thundered down the hall.

Uh-oh.

AN HOUR LATER, I SAT IN MY GRANDFATHER'S OFFICE WITH Elin, Markus, and Nikolai, who'd insisted on joining the emergency meeting. Mikaela had been politely but firmly dismissed. I wasn't sure where Rhys was, but it would only be a matter of time before he was roped into the conversation.

"Your Highness, you must tell us the truth. It's the only way we can help you fix this." Whenever Elin was pissed, her left eye would twitch, and right now, it was twitching hard enough to pop a blood vessel. "Is there any truth to the allegations?"

I'd reached a fork in the road.

I could either lie and drag out the charade, or I could tell the truth and let the chips fall where they may.

If I did the latter, Rhys would be fired, but he was probably already on the chopping block whether or not the allegations were true. He was too high profile now, and people would gossip regardless. The palace couldn't afford that kind of distraction.

But if I lied, I could at least buy us some time. Not a lot, but some, and that was better than nothing.

"Bridge, you can trust us," Nikolai said gently. "We're here to help you."

Not really, I wanted to say. *You're here to help the crown and its reputation.*

Perhaps that was unfair, but it was true to varying extents. They didn't care about me, Bridget. They cared about the princess, the crown, and our image.

My grandfather and brother loved me, but when it came down to it, they would choose what was good for the royal family as an institution over what was good for me.

I didn't fault them for it. It was what they had to do, but it meant I couldn't trust them with my best interests.

The only person who had ever seen me and put me first was Rhys.

I looked around the room. There was my grandfather, whose expression remained neutral even as anger and worry flickered in his eyes. Markus, tight-faced and tight-lipped, who was no doubt fantasizing about wringing my neck. Elin, who for once wasn't looking at her phone but was instead staring at me with bated breath. And finally, Nikolai, by far the most sympathetic of the bunch, though wariness creased his brow.

Then I thought about Rhys. His rough hands and rough voice, and the way he held me. Kissed me. Looked at me, like he never wanted to blink.

Baby, we're way beyond like.

I took a deep breath, steeled myself, and took a fork in the road.

"The allegations are true," I said. "All of them."

I heard a sharp intake of breath all around. Markus pinched his temple while Elin flew into action, her fingers moving over her phone fast enough to start a Category Four hurricane.

Disappointment carved deep grooves into Edvard's face. "Mr. Larsen's employment is terminated, effective immediately," he said, his tone sharper than I'd ever heard it. "You will end the relationship and never see or speak to him again."

He spoke not as my grandfather, but as my king.

My nails dug into my thighs. "No."

Another sharp intake of breath from everyone present.

Edvard straightened, the remaining neutrality in his face giving way to anger. I'd never disobeyed him, not when it came to the big things. I loved and respected him, and I hated disappointing him.

But I was sick and tired of other people dictating how I should live and who I should be with. While I would never have the freedom of a normal person, one who hadn't been born into this life, I had to draw the line somewhere. How was I supposed to rule a country if I couldn't even rule my own life?

"I can't stop you from firing Rhys," I said. "But I'm not ending my relationship with him."

"Oh, for fuck's sake." It was the first time I'd ever heard Markus curse. "Your Highness, he is—*was*—your bodyguard. He is a commoner. You are first in line to the throne, and the law dictates—"

"I know what the law dictates. I have a plan."

Well, half a plan, but if I rounded up, it was a full plan. I knew what I needed to do, I just needed to figure out *how* to do it. There were a handful of ministers I was certain would support a repeal of the Royal Marriages Law, but the others needed overwhelming public support for political cover.

However, if I brought up the issue now, with the allegations floating around, I might as well wave a sign screaming *It's true! I'm in a relationship with my bodyguard!*

Edvard's face reddened while Markus glared at me.

"How?" My grandfather's adviser looked like he wanted to chuck one of the thousand-page law tomes lining the walls at me. "If you think Parliament will overturn the law, trust me, they won't. We went over this with Prince Nikolai. For them to even consider it, the Speaker has to introduce the motion, and Lord Erhall has made it *very* clear he would never do so."

"Elections are coming up," I said. "If I could—"

A loud thud interrupted me.

For a second, I thought Markus had finally cracked and thrown something in his anger. Then I heard Nikolai's alarmed shout and realized, with ice-cold horror, that the sound wasn't of something hitting the ground.

It was of *someone*—my grandfather, who had collapsed out of his chair and onto the floor.

39

RHYS

"*...REPORTS THE KING IS IN STABLE CONDITION AFTER HIS heart attack four days ago. The palace asks the public to please respect the royal family's privacy at this difficult time, while well-wishers have left thousands of cards and flowers outside the palace...*"

The news anchor's voice droned from the TV in the corner as I stared down at the guard in front of me.

"Let me be clear," I said, my calm voice belying the fury churning inside me. "I'm going to see Princess Bridget today, one way or another. Don't make this the hard way."

The guard drew himself up to his full height, which was still a good six inches shorter than me. "Are you threatening me?"

I smiled, and he gulped. "Yes."

"Now you listen. I'm a Royal Guard—"

"I don't. Give. A. Shit." I enunciated slowly and carefully in case he was too dumb to notice I was *this* close to shoving a syringe in his throat if he didn't get out of my way.

We stood outside the king's private wing of the hospital.

It'd been four days since the allegations about Bridget's and my relationship broke and the king suffered a heart attack.

Four days of not seeing her, talking to her, or knowing whether she was okay.

Four days of fucking hell.

The palace had terminated my contract the same day the allegations came out, citing concerns over my ability to do my job due to my "increased media profile."

I didn't care as much about the termination, which I'd expected, as I did not seeing Bridget before security escorted me off the grounds. She hadn't answered my calls or texts since that day, and I needed to know she was okay before I lost my mind. Hell, I was already halfway there.

"You're not her bodyguard anymore," the guard said. "Only family and approved staff are allowed inside. How did you get in here, anyway?"

While part of me appreciated him standing his ground since he was right, I *wasn't* allowed in, a much larger part was fast running out of patience.

"Not your concern. What you *should* be concerned about is stepping aside before you have to explain to the Head of Royal Security how you ended up with a broken nose."

In truth, I'd had to disguise myself like a fucking pop star hiding from the press to get past the paparazzi camped outside the hospital. News of Bridget and me had taken a backseat to the king's hospitalization, but my face had been splashed all over Eldorran TV, and I couldn't risk someone spotting me.

Things at the hospital were so crazy I snuck up to the VIP floor and the king's private suite without detection. It didn't say much about hospital or royal security, even if I could evade guards and cameras better than the average person.

The guard opened his mouth, but before he could spew more bullshit, the door swung open. My heart soared for a second at the flash of blonde hair, only to crash back to earth when I saw Elin's frown.

"Mr. Larsen," she said. "I thought I heard your voice." She nodded at the guard. "I'll take it from here."

Relief spread across his face, and I made a noise of disgust. I'd trained eighteen-year-old Navy recruits with more balls than him.

Elin opened the door wider, and I wasted no time in pushing past the guard and into the king's wing. I didn't see Bridget, but she could be in any of the half dozen rooms. The place was bigger than most people's houses.

"I assume you're here to see Princess Bridget." Elin crossed her arms over her chest, perfectly put together as always with her bun, suit, and heels. Not a hair out of place or a wrinkle on her clothing.

I dipped my chin. "Where is she?"

"The king's room. Third door on the left."

Suspicion unfurled in my stomach. *This is too easy.* "Just like that?"

Elin gave me a hard smile. "You're already here, Mr. Larsen, and it's safe to assume you won't leave until you see her. I don't engage in futile exercises, so please." She gestured down the hall. "Go ahead."

My suspicion ramped up another notch, but fuck it, I wouldn't look a gift horse in the mouth.

I walked to the king's room and stopped in front of the door, my breath knotting in my throat when I saw Bridget through the small window.

She sat next to her grandfather's bed, holding his hand and looking smaller and more vulnerable than I'd ever seen her. Even from a distance, I spotted the paleness of her face and the redness of her eyes.

Something grabbed my heart and twisted. Hard.

I opened the door and stepped inside. "Hey, princess." I kept my voice soft, not wanting to disturb the hushed quiet or wake up the king. Sunlight streamed through the windows on either side of the hospital bed, adding a touch of cheer to the somber mood, but there was no avoiding the beeping monitors, or the tubes stuck to Edvard's chest.

Bridget's shoulders stiffened, and a few beats passed before she faced me. "Rhys. What are you doing here?"

"I came to see you."

Something felt off. Maybe it was the way she avoided my eyes or the tightness of her expression, but she'd gone through hell the past few days. I couldn't expect her to throw herself into my arms with a big smile. "How's your grandfather?"

"Better. Weak, but stable." She squeezed his hand. "They're keeping him here a few more days, but they said he could be discharged next week."

"That's good. Can't be too bad if they're letting him leave."

Bridget nodded, still avoiding my gaze, and unease rippled down my spine. "Let's talk in another room. He just fell asleep."

She gave her grandfather's hand another squeeze before we stepped into the hall. Elin was gone, and only the smell of antiseptic and faint beeps from the monitor on the other side of the door disturbed the air.

"Here." Bridget led me to a room two doors down. "This is where I've been sleeping."

My eyes swept over the space. It had a pullout couch, a kitchenette, and a bathroom. A thick blanket draped over the back of the couch, and a half-empty bottle of Coke sat on the table next to a pile of magazines.

I pictured Bridget sleeping here alone, night after night, waiting to hear if her grandfather's condition had worsened, and a needle of pain jammed into my heart.

I wanted to sweep her up in my arms and hold her tight, but a strange distance stretched between us, giving me pause. She stood only a few feet away, yet it might as well be miles.

"I'm sorry I haven't answered your calls or texts," she said, fiddling with the blanket. "It's been a crazy couple of days. The palace is trying to figure out how the press got their hands on those photos of us, and between that and my grandfather's hospitalization—"

"I get it." We could deal with all that later. "And you? How are you doing?"

"About as well as you'd expect." She finally looked at me, her eyes tired and missing their usual sparkle, and the needle of pain pierced deeper. "Nik and I have been staying here overnight, but he went home to take care of some paperwork. He and Sabrina are postponing their honeymoon until Grandfather's better." She let out a weak laugh. "What a wedding present, huh?"

Yeah, it sucked, but I didn't give a crap about Nikolai and Sabrina. I only cared about one person in the world, and she was hurting.

"Come here, princess." I opened my arms.

Bridget hesitated for a beat before she finally closed the distance between us and buried her face in my chest, her shoulders shaking.

"Shh, it's okay." I kissed the top of her head and stroked her hair, a heaviness sinking into my bones at the sound of her soft sniffles. I'd weathered artillery fire, nighttime missions in subarctic temperatures, and more broken bones and near-fatal injuries than I could count, but Bridget crying came closer to breaking me than all those things combined.

"No, it's not. I almost killed him." Bridget's voice was muffled, but her pain shone through loud and clear. "He had a heart attack because of *me*."

I tightened my hold, her pain seeping through my skin until it became my own. "That's not true."

"It is. You weren't there. You don't know..." She pulled back, her nose red and her eyes glassy. "We were having an emergency meeting about the news of...you and me. I confessed the allegations were true, and when he told me to end things with you, I refused. I was arguing with Markus about it when he collapsed." She blinked, her lashes glittering with unshed tears. "It was me, Rhys. Don't tell me it wasn't my fault, because it was."

A deep fissure split my heart in half. Bridget already blamed herself for her mother's death. To add the guilt from her grandfather's heart attack on top of that...

"It's not," I said firmly. "Your grandfather has an underlying condition. Anything could've set it off."

"Yes, and this time it was me. He was supposed to cut back on his stress, and I gave him a year's worth in one day." Bridget's laugh sounded hollow as she stepped all the way out of my embrace and wrapped her arms around her waist. "What a great granddaughter I am."

"Bridget..." I reached for her again, but she shook her head, her eyes fixed on the floor.

"I can't do this anymore."

Everything fell silent. My heartbeat, my pulse, the hum of the fridge and the ticking of the clock on the wall.

Could I still be alive if my heart wasn't beating?

"Do what anymore?" My voice sounded strange in the vacuum Bridget's words created. Lower, more guttural, like an animal ensnared in a trap of its own making.

It was a stupid question.

I knew the answer. We both knew. A part of me had been expecting this moment since our kiss in a dark hallway a lifetime ago, but still, I hoped.

Bridget blinked, those beautiful blue eyes shimmering with heartache before they hardened, and my hope died a swift, fiery death.

"This. Us." She gestured between us. "Whatever we had. It has to end."

40

BRIDGET

Don't look at him.

If I looked at him, I would lose it, and I was already half out of my mind. The stress, guilt, and exhaustion of the past four days had seeped into my bones, turning me into a walking zombie.

But I couldn't help myself. I looked.

And my heart promptly splintered into even more pieces than it already had.

Rhys stared at me, so still he could've passed for a statue had it not been for the pain flickering in his eyes.

"Had?" That calm, even tone never boded well.

"It was fun while it lasted." The words tasted bitter on my tongue, like poison pills of lies I fed myself to get through the next hour and possibly the rest of my life. "But people know. Everyone's watching us. We can't continue whatever...this is."

"Fun." Still in that dangerously calm voice.

"Rhys." I wrapped my arms tighter around myself. The hospital staff had set the temperature to a comfortable seventy-three degrees, but my skin felt like ice beneath my palms. "Please don't make this any harder than it has to be."

Please let my heart break in peace.

"The hell I won't." His gray eyes had darkened to a near black, and a vein throbbed in his temple. "Tell me something, princess. Are you doing this because you want to, or because you feel like you have to?"

"I don't *feel* like I have to. I *do* have to!" Frustration seared through me, sharp and hot. Didn't he get it? "It's only a matter of time before the press confirms the allegations. Elin and Markus and my family already know. What do you think is going to happen once it's all out in the open?"

"Your Majesty!"

"Grandfather!"

Nikolai, Markus, and Elin rushed to Edvard's side while I stood there, unable to move.

I should join them. Make sure he was okay.

*But **of course** he wasn't okay. He'd just collapsed... because of me and what I said. Because I thought, for one second, I could have a semblance of control over my life.*

If he died, the last conversation we had would have been an argument.

"You will end the relationship and never see Mr. Larsen again."

"No."

Something inside me shriveled into a husk.

"Bridget..."

The sound of my name, deep and raw, scraped against my willpower, leaving dents in something that had never been strong to begin with. Not when it came to him.

I closed my eyes, trying to find the cool, unshakable version of myself I presented to the public. The one who'd smiled through hours of standing and waving while my feet bled through my heels. The one who'd walked behind my father's casket and held back tears until I crumpled into a ball in the bathroom during the wake.

But I couldn't. I'd never been able to hide who I truly was from Rhys.

I heard him walk toward me. Smelled that clean, masculine scent that had become my comfort scent over the years because it meant he was near and I was safe. Felt him rub away a tear I hadn't even noticed had escaped with his thumb.

Don't look at him. Don't look at him.

"Princess, look at me."

I shook my head and squeezed my eyes shut tighter. My emotions formed a tight knot in my throat, making it near impossible to breathe.

"Bridget." Firmer this time, more commanding. "Look at me."

I resisted for another minute, but the need to save myself from further heartache paled compared to my need to soak in every last bit of Rhys Larsen I could.

I looked at him.

Gray thunderstorms stared back at me, crackling with turmoil.

"The mess with the pictures, we'll figure it out." He grasped my chin and rubbed his thumb over my bottom lip, his expression fierce. "I told you, you're mine, and I'm not letting you go. I don't care if the entire Eldorran military tries to drag me away."

I wished it were that easy and I could sink into his faith, letting it sweep me away.

But our problems went way beyond the pictures now.

"You don't get it. There *is no* happily ever after for us." We weren't a fairytale. We were a forbidden love letter, tucked into the back of a drawer and retrieved only in the darkness of night.

We were the chapter of bliss before the climax hit and every-thing crumbled into ash. We were a story that was always meant to end. "This is it."

My mother died giving birth to me.

My father died on his way back from buying something *I'd* asked him to get.

My grandfather almost died because I'd refused to give up the one thing that ever made me happy.

That was what I got for being selfish, for wanting some-thing for *me*. Future queens didn't live for themselves, they lived for their country. That was the price of power.

No matter how much I tried to change reality, it remained the truth, and it was time I grew up and faced it.

Rhys's grip on my chin tightened. "I don't need a happily ever after. I need to be by your side. I need you happy and healthy and safe. Goddammit Bridget, I need *you*. In any way I can have you." His voice broke for the first time in all my years with him, and my heart cracked in response. "If you think I'm leaving you to deal with this bullshit alone, you don't know me at all."

Trouble was, I *did* know him, and I knew the one thing that would make him snap, but I couldn't bring myself to say it right now.

One last selfish thing.

"Kiss me," I whispered.

Rhys didn't question the sudden shift in my tone. Instead, he curled his hand around the back of my neck and crushed his lips to mine. Deep, hard, and possessive, like nothing had changed between us.

He always knew what I needed without me saying it.

I drank up every drop of him I could. His taste, his touch, his scent...I wished I could bottle it all up so I had something to keep me warm in the nights and years to come.

Rhys picked me up and carried me to the couch, where he pulled my skirt up and my panties down and sank into me with exquisite, deliberate slowness. Stretching me. Filling me. Breaking me into a thousand pieces and putting me back together, over and over again.

Even if my heart ached, my body responded to him the way it always had: eager, willing, and desperate for more.

Rhys palmed my breast and swiped his thumb over my nipple, playing with the sensitized nub until a fresh wave of heat crested in my stomach. All the while he pumped into me, the slow, leisurely slides of his cock hitting a spot that made me see stars.

"Rhys, *please.*"

"What do you want, princess?" He pinched my nipple, the sudden roughness of the action causing my mouth to fall open with a gasp.

You. Forever.

Since I couldn't say that, I settled for a panted, "Faster. Harder."

He lowered his head and replaced his hand with his mouth, swirling and licking while he picked up the pace. My nails dug into his back, and just as I teetered over the precipice, he slowed down again.

I nearly screamed with frustration.

Faster. Slower. Faster. Slower.

Rhys seemed to intuit the precise second I was about to come, and he varied his speed, edging me until I was a dripping, whimpering mess. Finally, after what felt like an eternity, he groaned and slammed into me, his mouth claiming mine in a bruising kiss as he fucked into me so hard the couch inched across the floor with a squeak.

Lights exploded behind my eyes. I arched up, my cry swallowed by his kiss as another orgasm tore through me and left me drained.

Rhys came right after me with a silent shudder, and we sank into each other's arms, our heavy breaths mingling as one.

I loved sex with him, but I loved the quiet moments afterward even more.

"Again." I wrapped my limbs around him, not ready to break free of our cocoon yet. *Just a little more time.*

"Insatiable," he whispered, running the tip of his nose up my neck and along my jawline.

I smiled at the reminder of our afternoon at the hotel. Our last truly happy time together before everything went to hell.

"You love it," I said.

"Yeah princess, I do."

We spent the next hour like that, climbing high and crashing down together.

It was perfect, as were all our stolen moments together. We fucked hard and fast and made love sweet and slow. We pretended this was our life, not just a snapshot in time, and I pretended like my heart still beat in my chest when the pieces lay scattered at our feet.

"There's no other way, Your Highness." Elin's eyes flickered with sympathy for a second before it vanished and her expression hardened again. "It has to be done."

"No." I shook my head, denial digging its claws deep into my skin. "It's too soon. He's fine. The doctors said—"

"The doctors said he'll recover...this time. The fact is, His Majesty was hospitalized twice in one year. We can't risk a third hospitalization."

"We can cut back on his workload," I said desperately. "Have his aides handle the more strenuous paperwork and meetings. He can still be king."

Elin glanced at Markus, who stood in the corner looking grimmer than I'd ever seen him.

"We'd discussed this with His Majesty after his first hospitalization," he said. "He expressly said that if he collapses a second time, he would step down."

I vaguely remembered my grandfather saying something like that in the weeks after his first collapse, but I'd been so focused on Nikolai's abdication the implications of it had gone right over my head.

"I realize this is perhaps not the best time to discuss this," Elin said with another flicker of sympathy. "But His Majesty's condition is stable, and we need to start preparations right away."

"Preparations." *Something terrible took root in my stomach and spread. It seeped into my chest, my neck, my arms and my legs, numbing me from inside out.*

Elin and Markus exchanged glances again.

"Yes," Elin said. "Preparations for your coronation as queen."

I'd thought I had more time, both with Rhys and to convince Parliament to repeal the Royal Marriages Law, but I didn't. Time was up.

"Do you remember Costa Rica?" Rhys's lips brushed against mine as he spoke. He lay on top of me, his powerful body swallowing me up, but he'd propped a forearm on the couch so he didn't crush me with his weight.

"How could I forget?" It was one of the happiest memories of my life.

"You asked me if I'd ever been in love. I said no." He pressed a soft kiss to my mouth. "Ask me again, princess."

My lungs constricted. *Breathe.*

But that was hard when everything hurt to the point where

I couldn't remember what it felt like *not* to hurt. My heart, my head, my soul.

"I can't." I forced myself to push Rhys away.

My skin immediately chilled at the absence of his heat, and small shivers wracked me as I got off the couch and walked to the bathroom. I cleaned myself and straightened my clothes with shaky hands while his gaze burned a hole in my back through the open door.

"Why not?"

"Because." *Tell him. Just tell him.* "I'm going to be queen."

"We already knew that."

"You don't understand." I washed my hands and returned to the room, where I finally looked at him again. Tension lined his face and notched a deep groove between his brows. "I don't mean someday. I mean I'm going to be queen in nine months."

Rhys froze.

"That's not all." I could barely speak past the lump in my throat. "Because of the Royal Marriages Law, I have to—"

"Don't say it." His voice was so quiet I almost didn't hear him.

"I *have* to marry or at least get engaged before my coronation." There would already be backlash against me taking the throne so soon. *You need all the political goodwill you can get,* Markus had said. I hated it, but he was right. "I—"

"Don't. Fucking. Say it."

"I'm marrying Steffan. He already agreed."

It wasn't a marriage of love. It was a political contract. Nothing more, nothing less. Markus had reached out to the Holsteins yesterday and made them sign an NDA before making the proposition. They'd agreed a few hours later. It'd all happened so quickly it made my head spin.

Just like that, I had a fiancé, at least in theory. Per the agreement, Steffan would officially propose next month, after the furor over my grandfather's hospitalization died down. As a bonus, the engagement would drive the allegations about me and Rhys out of the headlines, as Elin had not so subtly pointed out.

Rhys unfolded himself from the couch. He'd already fixed his clothes. All black. Black shirt, black pants, black boots, black expression.

"The fuck you are."

"Rhys, it's done."

"No," he said flatly. "What did I tell you in the gazebo, princess? I said from that point on, no other man touches you, and I meant it. You sure as fuck aren't marrying someone else. We have nine months. We will figure. It. Out."

I wanted to agree. I wanted to be selfish and steal more time with him, but that wouldn't be fair to either of us.

I'd already had Rhys for three years. It was time to let him go.

No more being selfish.

"What if I *want* to marry someone else?"

Rhys's nostrils flared. "Don't lie to me. You barely know Steffan. You went on *three* fucking dates with the guy."

"Royal marriage isn't about knowing someone. It's about suitability, and the fact is, he's suitable and you're not." I hoped Rhys didn't notice the wobble in my voice. "Plus, Steffan and I have the rest of our lives to get to know each other."

A shudder rippled through his body, and hurt slashed across his face, so raw and visceral it cut through my soul.

"I'm the crown princess, and I need to act like one," I said, hating myself more with every second. "In *all* areas of my life. I can't be with a bodyguard. I..." Tears clogged my throat, but I pushed past them. "I'm meant to be with a duke. We both know that."

Rhys flinched. One tiny movement, but it would haunt me forever.

"So we're over. Just like that." It came out low and dangerous, edged with pain.

No, not just like that. You'll never know how much my heart is breaking right now.

"I'm sorry," I whispered.

I wished I could tell him I'd never been happier than when I was with him.

I wished I could tell him it wasn't about the throne or power, and that if I could, I would give up a kingdom for him.

But *I'm sorry* were the only words I was allowed to say.

The emotion wiped clean from Rhys's eyes until I was staring at steel walls, harder and more guarded even than when we'd first met.

"No, Your Highness," he said. "*I'm* sorry."

He walked out.

One minute, he was there. The next, he was gone.

I crumpled, my knees giving out beneath me as I sank onto the floor and hot tears scalded my cheeks and dripped off my chin. My chest heaved so hard I couldn't draw enough oxygen into my lungs, and I was sure I would die right there on the hospital floor, just a few feet away from the best doctors and nurses in the country. But even they wouldn't be able to fix what I'd just broken.

"You have to move."

"I beg your pardon?"

"Your house. It's a security nightmare. I don't know who signed off on this location, but you have to move."

"Have you ever been in love?"

"No. But I hope to be one day."

"Good night, princess."

"Good night, Mr. Larsen."

Snippets of memories crowded my brain, and I pressed my face into the blanket draped over the couch, muffling my sobs.

"Your Highness?" Elin's voice floated through the door, followed by a knock. "Can I come in?"

No. I would be happy if I never talked to you again.

But I had responsibilities to fulfill, and an engagement to plan.

I forced my sobs to slow until they tapered off.

Deep, controlled breaths. Head tilted up. Tensed muscles. It was a trick I'd learned that had come in handy quite a few times over the years.

"One moment," I said after I got myself under control. I pushed myself off the floor and splashed water on my face before fixing my hair and clothes. I opened the door, my spine stiff. "What is it?"

If Elin noticed any lingering redness around my eyes or nose, she didn't mention it. "I saw Mr. Larsen leave."

My chin wobbled for a split second before I pressed my lips together. "Yes."

"So, it's done." She regarded me with a searching look.

I responded with a short nod.

"Good. It's the right thing to do, Your Highness," she said in a far gentler tone than I was used to. "You'll see. Now." She snapped back to her usual brisk self. "Shall we go over the plans for Lord Holstein's proposal?"

"Sure," I said hollowly. "Let's go over the plans for the proposal."

41

RHYS

My first taste of alcohol burned. So did the second. By the time I made it through half the bottle of whiskey, however, it'd stopped burning and started numbing, which was the best I could've hoped for.

In the two days since Bridget ended things, I'd spiraled. Hard. I hadn't left my hotel room since I returned from the hospital–partly because I had nowhere to go and partly because I had zero interest in dealing with the paparazzi. I had enough problems without getting charged with assault.

I lifted the bottle to my lips as I watched *The Daily Tea*. The hospital discharged Edvard yesterday, and now that the king was no longer in mortal danger, the press had dived back into breathless speculation about me and Bridget.

If they only knew.

The whiskey seared down my throat and pooled in my stomach.

I should turn the show off because half the shit they came up with was utter crap—like their claims Bridget and I had an orgy with a certain pop star couple in the south of France—but as masochistic as it was, their video clips of her were the only way I could get my fix.

I wasn't addicted to alcohol, not yet, but I was addicted to Bridget, and now that I no longer had her, I was going through withdrawal.

Clammy skin, nausea, difficulties sleeping. Oh, yeah, and a giant fucking hole the size of Alaska in my chest. *That* wasn't listed on the Addicts Anonymous website.

I can't be with a bodyguard. I'm meant to be with a duke.

Days later, and the memory still cut deeper than a serrated hunting knife. Bridget hadn't meant it. I knew that. The words were cruel, and she was anything but cruel. But they mirrored my doubts—about how I wasn't good enough and how she deserved better—too much for them not to affect me.

I hit the bottom of the bottle. I tossed it aside in disgust, hating myself for sinking so low I'd turned to alcohol and hating myself even more for leaving things the way I had with Bridget.

I'd walked out on her in the heat of the moment, when the anger and hurt had overridden everything else, and I'd regretted it before I even hit the lobby.

She'd done what she thought she had to, and it fucking broke my heart, but it wasn't her fault.

As if on cue, the camera cut to a shot of Bridget exiting the hospital with the king and her brother. She was elegant and polished, as always, but her smile looked empty as she waved to the press. Sad and lonely, two things I never, ever wanted her to be.

My chest burned, and it wasn't from the whiskey. At the same time, something hardened within me: determination.

Bridget wasn't happy. I wasn't happy. And it was about damn time I did something about it.

I didn't give a fuck what the law said. She wasn't marrying

Steffan. I'd visit every minister in Parliament and force them to rewrite the law if I had to.

Someone knocked. "Housekeeping."

My spine turned rigid at the familiar voice.

Two seconds later, I threw open the door with a scowl. "What the *fuck* are you doing here?"

Christian arched an eyebrow. "Is that the proper way to greet your boss?"

"Fuck you."

He laughed, but the sound lacked humor. "Charming as always. Now let me in so we can clean up your mess."

I gritted my teeth and stepped aside, already regretting this day, this week, and my whole damn life.

He walked in, his gaze skimming over my half-unpacked suitcase and the remains of my room service dinner on the coffee table before resting on the empty whiskey bottle. Surprise flashed across his face before he covered it up.

"Well, this is sad," he said. "You're at the nicest hotel in Athenberg and you couldn't spring for the filet mignon?"

On the surface, Christian looked like the stereotypical charming, good-natured playboy he portrayed himself to be. Even though he was thirty-one, he could've passed for his mid to late twenties, and he used it to his advantage. People looked at his pretty-boy face and tailored Italian suits and underestimated him. They didn't realize he was a wolf in expensive clothing until it was too late.

"What are you doing here, Harper?" I repeated.

I knew, of course. He'd chewed me out on the phone last week after the news about me and Bridget broke, but I hadn't expected him to fly here so soon with Magda still missing.

I should've known better, which proved just how fucked in the head I was about Bridget. I couldn't think straight. All I could think about was where she was, who she was with, and how she was doing.

It didn't matter that she'd ripped my heart out the other day. If anyone hurt my princess in any way—physically, mentally, or emotionally—there would be hell to pay.

"Take a wild guess." Christian leaned against the counter, the picture of insouciance, but his hard gaze belied his casual pose. "Your client, Larsen. A *future queen*."

"They're tabloid rumors, and she's not my client anymore." *I need another drink.*

I understood now why people turned to alcohol for comfort now. It filled a part of ourselves we'd lost, or at least it gave the illusion of doing so.

"You forget. I know when you're lying." Christian's voice dropped several decibels. His anger burned cold, not hot, and it was when he got quiet that people ran and ducked for cover. "Even if I didn't, you think I didn't look into the situation myself? What you did is a fireable offense."

"So fire me." I had enough money saved up to tide me over for a nice long while, and the prospect of playing bodyguard to anyone but Bridget held zero appeal for me.

The thought crystallized and took root.

"Actually, you know what? I quit."

Christian stared at me. "Just like that."

"Just like that." My mouth flattened into a grim line. "I fucked up, and I'm sorry. But I'm done with the bodyguard game."

He tapped his fingers on the dresser. Watching. Thinking. "I assume things with the princess are over, considering the whispers I'm hearing about her, Steffan Holstein, and an upcoming engagement."

A low growl rumbled from my throat, but he ignored it.

"Why are you still here, Larsen? Living like a hermit and

drinking." His lip curled with distaste. Christian owned one of the most extensive and expensive rare alcohol collections in the U.S. He had nothing against drinking, but I assumed he took offense at the way I did it. "You don't drink."

"Apparently, I do."

"It's time to leave. I say this not as your boss, but as your friend. This..." He gestured around the room. "...is pathetic. Not to mention, your visa expires soon. There's no use in dragging out the inevitable."

I was in Eldorra on a special visa thanks to my previous employment with the palace, but it expired at the end of the month now that I was no longer working for them.

"You're not my boss anymore," I said coldly. "I'll leave when I want."

"Jesus Christ, what happened to you? Use your head, Larsen," Christian snapped. "The one on your shoulders, not between your legs. Or is her royal pussy that good—"

A snarl ripped out of my chest. He didn't get the rest of his sentence out before I crossed the room in two long strides and slammed him against the wall.

"Talk about her like that again, and I'll feed you your teeth."

Christian looked unfazed even though he was two seconds away from getting his face pounded in. "It's never bothered you before. And careful with the suit. I just got it custom made."

"You've done a lot for me over the years." Danger thickened the air, so potent I could almost taste it. I'd been spoiling for a fight, and he might just give it to me. "But if you don't watch what you say, this is the end of our friendship."

He assessed me with sharp eyes. "Well, well." A hint of surprised amusement colored his tone. "I never thought I'd see the day. Rhys Larsen in love."

In love.

I'd never been in love. Never wanted to be in love. Hell, I didn't even know what love *was*. It was always something I'd heard about, not experienced, until I met a woman who cracked my ironclad defenses like no one had before. Someone who loved the rain and animals and Rocky Road ice cream on quiet nights. Someone who saw all my scars and ugliness and still found me worthy, and somehow, someway, she'd filled the cracks in a soul I never thought would be whole again.

I might not know what love was, but I knew I was in love with Bridget von Ascheberg, to the point where even I—the man who was so good at denying himself anything good in life —couldn't deny it.

The realization hit me like a bullet in the chest, and I loosened my hold on Christian.

"No denial," he observed. He shook his head. "I have nothing against love, other than the fact I find it tedious, boring, and utterly unnecessary. People in love are the most insufferable on the planet." He glanced at a piece of lint on his suit with disdain before brushing it off. "But if that's what you want, go for it. Just not with the princess."

"My personal life is none of your business."

His gaze turned pitying, and I wanted to punch him all over again. It was a decent summary of our fucked-up friendship. One of us wanted to kill the other at any given time. It'd been that way since we met in Tangier, where I'd saved him from a slow, torturous death at the hands of a warlord he'd pissed off.

Sometimes, like now, I wished I'd left him to the warlord's mercy.

"Leave Eldorra. Now. Before things get even more out of control," Christian said. "No matter how many detours you take, your story only has one ending. Cut it off before you're in too deep and you can't get out."

Too late. I was already in too deep.

"Get out," I said.

"You think I'm being heartless, but I'm trying to help you. Consider it my repayment for Tangier."

"Get. Out."

"You really want to do this." It wasn't a question.

"Let me worry about what I'm going to do."

Christian sighed. "If you insist on continuing down this road, I have something that might be of interest. I did a little digging after those *heartwarming* photos of you and the princess surfaced." He reached into his jacket pocket and pulled out a small envelope. "You want to look at this. Soon."

I didn't take it. "What the hell is it?"

Never trust a Christian Harper bearing gifts. That should be everyone's motto in life.

But nothing could've prepared me for what he said next.

"The identity of your father." He paused. "And your brother."

42

RHYS

It was funny how one moment could change your life.

One moment, my mother was alive, then she wasn't.

One moment, my squad mates were alive, and the next everything got blown to hell. Literally.

One moment, I knew my place in the world, only for it to get turned upside down with the simple unfolding of a paper.

Last night had been a mind fuck in every way, and I was still debating the soundness of my decision to pay my brother a visit as I stared at the townhouse in front of me. There wasn't as much security as I'd expected, though the townhouse was in one of the safest neighborhoods in northern Athenberg.

Until now, the only brothers I had were the ones in my SEAL unit. The idea of having a *real* brother? It kind of fucked me up, to be honest.

I walked to the front door and knocked, my skin crawling with anticipation.

Christian had left that morning. His had been the quickest

trip in the history of international trips, but he had a mess on his hands in the U.S. so I couldn't blame him.

It was just like him to drop a bombshell then leave, though.

My brother answered on the second knock. If he was surprised to see me standing on his doorstep unannounced on a Thursday afternoon, he didn't show it.

"Hello, Mr. Larsen."

"Hello, brother." I didn't bother beating around the bush.

Andreas's smile disappeared. He regarded me for a long moment before he opened the door wider and stepped aside.

I walked in, my shoes squeaking on the shiny marble floor. Other than a few touches of white, everything in the house was gray. Light gray walls, gray furniture, gray rugs. It was like step-ping into an expensive rain cloud.

Andreas led me to the kitchen, where he poured two cups of tea and handed me one.

I didn't take it. I hadn't come for tea.

"You knew." I got straight to the point.

He appeared put out by my refusal and placed the extra mug on the counter with a frown. "Yes."

"Why the fuck didn't you say anything?"

"Why do you think, Mr. Larsen? The world thinks I'm a prince. I *am* a prince. Do you really think I'd jeopardize that to claim kinship with an American bodyguard who, I might mention, has been quite rude to me in every interaction we've had?"

I stared Andreas down. "How did you find out?"

When Christian handed me the paper with my father's and brother's names, I'd almost thrown it out. I knew in my gut opening it would lead to trouble. But in the end, I couldn't resist.

Two names.

Andreas von Ascheberg, my half-brother.

Arthur Erhall, my father.

Our father.

I was related to the two people I despised most in Eldorra. Go figure.

Andreas was silent for a long while. "When I found out Nikolai was abdicating, I was...worried. About Bridget. She'd never cared much for the throne, and I didn't think she even liked Eldorra that much. She certainly spent enough time away from it to give that impression. I thought she wasn't suited for the role of queen."

Barbed wire dug into my heart at the sound of Bridget's name.

Blonde hair. Sparkling eyes. A smile that could light up even my cold, dead soul.

It'd only been three days, and I already missed her so goddamned much I would've cut off my right arm for the chance to glimpse her in person, but she'd been locked up tight at the palace since she left the hospital. Probably busy planning her engagement to Steffan.

Acid seeped into my veins, and I forced myself to focus on what Andreas was saying instead of spiraling again.

"I realize you don't have a high opinion of me, but I do want what's best for the country. Eldorra is my home, and it deserves a good ruler."

I bristled at the implied insult. "Bridget would make a damn good ruler."

"Yes, well, you're biased, aren't you?" Andreas drawled. "I had someone dig into what she'd been doing during her time in New York. Figure out where her head was at. They mentioned you two seemed...close. Closer than the average bodyguard and client."

"Bullshit. I would've noticed a tail."

"You were distracted, and it wasn't one. It was multiple."

Andreas laughed at my dark expression. How the *fuck* had I missed a tail? "Don't feel too bad. They weren't there to hurt her. Just gather information. I was curious about you, the body-guard who seemed to have my cousin so enamored, so I had my people dig into *your* background, including your parentage." His smile hardened. "Imagine my surprise when I found out we had the same father. Small world."

His tone remained light, but the tenseness of his jaw suggested he wasn't as unbothered as he wanted me to think.

The story was plausible, except for me missing the tail. I *had* been distracted, but I didn't think I'd been *that* distracted.

My mind flashed back to my uncharacteristic confrontation with Vincent in Borgia, the last-minute trip to Costa Rica, and the thousands of tiny things pre-Bridget me would've never done.

I do not become personally involved in my clients' lives. I am here to safeguard you from physical harm. That is all. I am not here to be your friend, confidant, or anything else. This ensures my judgment remains uncompromised.

I scrubbed a hand over my face. *Fuck.*

"Say that's true. Want to explain to me how you're a prince when your father is a mere lord?"

Erhall. Of all the people, it had to be Erhall.

Bile rose in my throat at the reminder we were related.

Andreas's eyes shuttered. "My mother had an affair with Erhall. My father—my real father, even if he wasn't my biolog-ical one—didn't know until she told him before she died. Six years ago, cancer. I guess she wanted to go with a clear conscience. My father didn't tell me until before *he* died, three years ago." He barked out a short laugh. "At least my family can take secrets with them to their graves. Literally."

"Does Erhall know?"

"No," Andreas said a little too sharply. "And he won't. My

father was the one who raised me, not Erhall. My father..." A shadow flickered across his face and disappeared. "He was a good man, and he loved me enough to treat me like his own son even after he found out I wasn't. Erhall, on the other hand, is a sniveling weasel."

I snorted. At least we agreed on something.

Andreas's smirk returned as he took another sip of tea. "Here's a secret for you. I don't want the throne. Never did. I'd step up if I had to, of course, but I would much rather have someone else fill that role—as long as they're capable. The throne is the most powerful seat but also the smallest cage in the palace."

"That's utter crap," I growled. "You've made your intentions clear multiple times. The meetings with the king and Speaker, the 'helpful' visit to my guesthouse the night before Nikolai's wedding. Remember those?"

"Bridget needed a push," he said coolly. "I wanted to see if she'd fight for the crown. But I also came back because..." He hesitated for a brief second. "I wanted to give Erhall a chance. See if we could connect somehow. That's why I asked to shadow him during his meetings, more so than me wanting to be king. As for the guesthouse, I was trying to help *you*. I'm not an idiot, Mr. Larsen. Or should I call you Rhys, now that we both know we're brothers?"

I glared at him, and he chuckled.

"Mr. Larsen it is," he said. "I knew something was going on with you and Bridget long before the news broke. I didn't have confirmation, but I could see it in the way you looked at each other. It's a tough choice, love or country. Nikolai made his. Bridget, well, I guess she made hers, too. But before she agreed to marry Steffan"—the acid in my veins thickened and pooled in my stomach—"you two had a shot. Thought I'd give you a little nudge. You *are* my brother, and she *is* my cousin. Two of the few family members I have left. Consider it my good deed for the year."

"What charity," I said, my sarcasm evident. "You should be sainted."

"Laugh all you want, but I was willing to push you two together because you were so clearly in love, even if it meant I had to take up the mantle should Bridget abdicate. Is that not a sacrifice?"

It *was* a sacrifice. But I wasn't admitting that to Andreas.

My head pounded with the volume of new information rushing in. There was every chance Andreas was bullshitting me, but my gut told me he wasn't.

"I almost told her about our father, you know. At Nikolai's wedding reception. It doesn't help much with the Royal Marriages Law, since it requires the monarch to marry someone of *legitimate* noble birth. You were born out of wedlock and never acknowledged by Erhall as his son—he doesn't even know you *are* his son—so you don't qualify." Andreas finished his tea and set it in the sink. "But she disappeared from the reception and before I could talk to her, *The Daily Tea* allegations broke." He shrugged. "*C'est la vie.*"

Dammit. I'd hoped, now that I knew I was the son of a lord...

"If it doesn't help with the law, why would you tell her?" I demanded.

"Because I have an idea of how it might help in a roundabout way." Andreas smiled. "It might even help you get Bridget back if you work fast enough. Holstein's scheduled to propose next month. I'm willing to help you..."

"But?" There was always a *but* in these kinds of games.

"But you stop treating me like an enemy and as...perhaps not a brother, but a friendly acquaintance. We are, after all, the only direct family left besides our lovely father." Something flickered across Andreas's face before it disappeared.

"That's it." Suspicion curled in my stomach. It seemed too easy.

"That's it. Take it or leave it."

Something occurred to me. "Before I answer, I want to know. Did you ever snoop around my guesthouse when I wasn't there?"

He gave me an odd look. "No."

"The truth."

Andreas drew himself up to his full height, looking affronted. "I am a prince. I do not snoop around *guesthouses*..." the word dripped with disdain, "...like a common thief."

I pressed my lips together. He was telling the truth.

But if he wasn't the culprit, who was?

I supposed it didn't matter anymore, considering I no longer lived there, but the mystery rankled.

I did, however, have more important things to focus on.

I didn't trust Andreas. He may be honest today, and he may not want to steal the crown from Bridget, but that didn't mean he would be honest always.

Unfortunately, I was running out of both time and options.

I hope I don't regret this.

"Your idea," I said. "I'm listening."

43

BRIDGET

THE PALACE ASSIGNED BOOTH AS MY BODYGUARD AGAIN.
I'd been in a terrible mood since Rhys left, and the palace
handlers assumed it would help if someone I knew and liked
replaced him.

Booth took the role after Edvard left the hospital two weeks
ago, and while no one could replace Rhys, it was nice to see
Booth's smiling face again.

"Just like old times, huh, Your Highness?" he said as we
waited for Elin and Steffan in my office. I usually didn't have a
guard in the palace, but meetings with external guests were an
exception.

I forced a smile. "Yes."

Booth hesitated, then added, "A lot has changed over the
years. I'm no Mr. Larsen, but I'll try my best."

A fierce ache gripped my chest at Rhys's name. "I know.
I'm glad to have you back. Truly."

And yet, thoughts of dark hair and gunmetal eyes, scars and
hard-won smiles still consumed me.

There was a time when I would've given anything to have Booth as my bodyguard again. In the immediate weeks after his departure, I'd cursed him every day for leaving me alone with Rhys.

Insufferable, domineering, arrogant Rhys, who refused to let me walk on the outside of sidewalks and treated every visit to a bar like a mission into a war zone. Who scowled more than he laughed and argued more than he talked.

Rhys, who'd planned a last-minute trip for me so I could fulfill my bucket list, even though it must've gone against his every instinct as a bodyguard, and who kissed me like the world was ending and I was his last chance at salvation.

The ache intensified and spread to my throat, my eyes, my soul.

He was everywhere. In the chair where we'd kissed, the desk where we'd fucked, the painting where we'd laughed over how the artist had drawn one of the subject's eyebrows a little higher and more crooked than the other, giving her a permanent expression of surprise.

Even if I left the office, he would still be there, haunting me.

The door opened, and I curled my hand around my knee to steady myself as Elin and Steffan walked in.

"Thank you for coming," I said as Steffan took the seat opposite me. It was my first time seeing him in person since he'd agreed to the engagement.

He gave me a smile that looked almost as forced as mine felt. "Of course, Your Highness. We are going to be engaged, after all."

The way he said it, I wondered if I hadn't been the only one forced into this arrangement. He'd seemed eager enough on our first two dates, but he'd been distant and distracted since he returned from Preoria.

My mind flashed back to the tension I'd picked up on between him and Malin.

An awkward silence fell before Elin cleared her throat and pulled out her pen and notebook. "Excellent. Shall we start the meeting then, Your Highness? Top of the agenda is the timing and venue for the proposals. Lord Holstein will propose in three weeks at the Royal Botanic Gardens. It'll be a good call-back to your second date. We'll tell the press you've been in regular correspondence while he was in Preoria so it doesn't seem like the proposal came out of nowhere..."

The meeting dragged on. Elin's voice blurred into a running stream of noise, and Steffan sat straight-backed in his chair with a glassy look in his eyes. I felt like I was attending a business merger negotiation, which I was, in a way.

Just the fairytale girls dream of.

"...your honeymoon," Elin said. "Thoughts?"

Her expectant gaze yanked me out of the place I'd mentally escaped to while she droned on about media interviews and outfit options for the proposal.

I blinked. "Excuse me?"

"We need to decide on a honeymoon location," she repeated. "Paris is classic, if cliche. The Maldives are popular but getting too trendy. We could choose somewhere more unique, maybe in Central or South America. Brazil, Belize, Costa Rica..."

"No!"

Everyone jumped at my uncharacteristic shout. Booth's eyes grew round, and Elin's brow creased with disapproval. Only Steffan's expression remained neutral.

"No, not Costa Rica," I repeated more calmly, my heart pounding. "Anywhere but there."

I would rather honeymoon in Antarctica wearing nothing but a bikini.

Costa Rica belonged to me and Rhys. No one else.

Bucket list number four.

Have you ever been in love?

No. But I hope to be one day.

Look up, princess.

A now-familiar burn pulsed behind my eyes, and I forced myself to breathe through it until it passed.

"It's too soon to talk about the honeymoon anyway." My voice sounded far away, like that of one speaking in a dream. "We're not officially engaged yet."

"We want to iron out the details as soon as possible. Planning a royal marriage *and* coronation in the same year is no small feat," Elin said. "The press will want to know."

"Let's get through the proposal first." My tone brooked no opposition. "The press can wait."

She sighed, her mouth so pinched I worried it would freeze that way. "Yes, Your Highness."

After an hour, the meeting finally ended, and Elin rushed off to another meeting with my grandfather. Edvard had been doing well after his hospitalization, but we hadn't discussed Rhys or what happened in his office before his heart attack yet.

I had no issues with that. I wasn't ready for those discussions.

Meanwhile, Steffan remained in his chair. His fingers tapped out a rhythm on his thighs, and the glassy look in his eyes gave way to something more somber. "May I speak with you, Your Highness? Alone?" He glanced at Booth, who looked at me.

I nodded, and Booth slipped out of the room.

Once the door shut, I said, "You can call me Bridget. It would be odd if we were engaged and you still called me Your Highness."

"Apologies. Force of habit, Your—Bridget." Discomfort

crossed his face before he said, "I hope this doesn't make things too awkward, but I wanted to speak with you regarding, er, Mr. Larsen."

Every muscle tightened. If there was one person I wanted to discuss Rhys with less than my grandfather, it was my future fiancé.

"I won't ask you whether the, uh, news is true," Steffan added hastily. He knew it was. Rhys's glower throughout our first date, the cracked flowerpot at the Royal Botanic Gardens, the day he ran into us at the hotel...I could see the pieces clicking together in his head. "It's not my business what you did before our...engagement, and I know I'm not your first choice for a husband."

Guilt warmed my cheeks. If we married, I wouldn't be the only one trapped in a loveless union. "Steffan—"

"No, it's fine." He shook his head. "This is the life we were born into. My parents married for political convenience, and so did yours."

True. But my parents had loved each other. They'd been lucky, until they hadn't.

"You don't love me, and I don't expect you to. We...well, we've only spoken a few times, haven't we? But I enjoy your company, and I'll try my best to be a good consort. Perhaps this isn't the fairytale love you may have dreamed of, but we could have a good life together. Our families, at least, will be happy." Other than the twinge of bitterness coloring his last sentence, Steffan sounded like he was reciting from a teleprompter.

I studied him while he stared at the desk, his face taut and his hands gripping his knees with white-knuckled hands.

I more than recognized that expression and stance. These days, I *lived* them.

"Is it Malin?"

Steffan's head jerked up, his expression resembling that of a deer in headlights. "Pardon?"

"The woman you're in love with," I said. "Is it Malin?"

Steffan's throat flexed with a hard swallow. "It doesn't matter."

Three words. One confirmation of something we both already knew.

Neither of us wanted this. Our hearts belonged to other people, and if we married, it would be comfortable. Pleasant. Second best.

But it wouldn't be love. It would never be love.

"I think it matters quite a lot," I said gently.

Steffan released a long breath. "When I met you at your birthday ball, I had every intention of pursuing you," he said. "You are lovely, but then in Preoria...she was my mother's aide while she was recovering. It was only us in the house besides my mother, and slowly, without me even realizing it..."

"You fell in love," I finished.

He cracked a small smile. "Neither of us expected it. We couldn't stand each other at first. But yes, I fell in love." The smile faded. "My father found out and threatened not only to cut me off if I didn't end the relationship, but to ensure Malin never worked again in Eldorra. He doesn't bluff. Not when a relationship with the royal family is at stake." Steffan rubbed a hand over his face. "Apologies, Your H—Bridget. I realize this is extremely inappropriate for me to share, considering our arrangement."

"It's all right. I understand." More than most people would.

"I had a feeling you might."

I brought up something that had been nagging me since our hotel encounter. "If you were together, why did she push you to ask me out?"

Sadness flickered in his eyes. "The hotel was our last time

together," he said. "My father had returned to Preoria and dismissed her as my mother's aide, so we had to go somewhere where we wouldn't...where we could be alone. She knew about you and what my father expected of me. It was her way of letting us go."

I tried to imagine myself pushing another woman into Rhys's arms and recoiled at the thought.

I barely knew Malin, but I hurt for her.

"I'm sorry."

"Me too."

Silence lapsed for a beat before Steffan cleared his throat and straightened. "But I do enjoy your company, Bridget. We shall make a suitable match."

A sad smile curved my lips. "Yes, we shall. Thank you, Steffan."

I stayed in my office after he left, staring at the letters on my desk, the royal seal, and the calendar mounted on my wall.

Three weeks until my proposal.

Six months until my wedding.

Nine months until my coronation.

I could picture it all already. The dress, the church, the Coronation Oath, the heavy weight of the crown on my head.

I squeezed my eyes shut. The walls pressed in from all sides, and the roar of blood pounded in my ears, blocking out every other sound.

I'd grown accustomed to the idea of being queen. Part of me was actually excited to take the role and bring it into the twenty-first century. The monarchy had so many outdated customs that no longer made sense.

But I hadn't expected it to happen so soon, nor had I expected it to happen without Rhys by my side, even if it was only as my bodyguard.

Stern and steady, grumpy and protective. My rock and anchor in the storm.

Breathe, princess. You are the future queen. Don't let them intimidate you.

I wondered if Rhys had left Eldorra yet, and if he'd remember us ten, twenty, thirty years from now.

I wondered if, when he saw me on TV or in a magazine, he would think about Costa Rica and storms in a gazebo and lazy afternoons in a hotel room, or if he'd flip past with nothing more than a spark of nostalgia.

I wondered if I would haunt him as much as he haunted me.

"I wish you were here," I whispered.

My wish bounced off the walls and drifted through the room, lingering, before it finally faded into nothing.

Hours later, I was still in my office when my grandfather showed up.

"Bridget, I'd like to speak with you."

I looked up from my pile of citizen letters, my eyes bleary. I'd been working since my meeting with Elin and Steffan, and I'd dismissed Booth long ago.

Work was the only thing keeping me going, but I hadn't realized how late it'd gotten. The late afternoon sun slanted through the windows and cast long shadows on the floor, and my stomach rumbled with anger. I hadn't eaten since my yogurt and apple—I checked the clock—seven hours ago.

Edvard stood in the doorway, his face tired but his color markedly better than it had been a few days ago.

"Grandfather!" I jumped out of my seat. "You shouldn't be up so late."

"It's not even dinnertime yet," he grumbled, walking in and sitting across from me.

"The doctors said you need rest."

"Yes, and I've had enough the past two weeks to last me a lifetime." His chin jutted out at a stubborn angle, and I sighed. There was no arguing with him when he was like this.

If there was one thing Edvard hated, it was idle hands. He'd cut back on work as the doctors had instructed, but since his duties as king had prevented him from picking up any hobbies over the years, he was going out of his mind with boredom—a fact he never failed to mention whenever he saw me or Nikolai.

"Citizen Letters program?" He examined the documents on my desk.

"Yes, I'm finishing up this week's batch." I didn't mention the backlog of emails in the official inbox. Even with two assistants helping me, we were swamped. It turned out the citizens of Eldorra had a lot to say.

I was over the moon about the program's success, but we needed to hire more staff soon. Professionalize it instead of treating it as a side project.

"There are a few items I'd like to bring up at the next Speaker's meeting," I said. "I imagine Erhall will be thrilled."

"Erhall hasn't been thrilled since he was first elected Speaker ten years ago." Edvard steepled his fingers beneath his chin and studied me. "You're doing well. Holding your ground, even when he tries to undermine you. You've really come into your own these past few months."

I swallowed hard. "Thank you. But I'm no you."

"Of course not, but you shouldn't try to be. None of us should strive to be anyone except ourselves, and you are no less than me or anyone else." Edvard's expression gentled. "I know it's overwhelming, the prospect of becoming queen. Did you know, I was a wreck for months before my coronation?"

"Really?" I couldn't imagine my proud, regal grandfather being nervous about anything.

"Yes." He chuckled. "The night before the ceremony, I threw up in the Dowager Queen's favorite potted plant. You should've heard her scream when she discovered the, ah, gift I left."

A small laugh bubbled in my throat at the mental image his words created. My great-grandmother had died before I was born, but I'd heard she'd been a force to be reckoned with.

"The point is, it's normal to feel that way, but I have faith in you." Edvard tapped the royal seal on my desk. "Your coronation is coming sooner than any of us expected, but you will be a good queen. I don't doubt that for a second."

"I haven't even finished my training," I said. "Nik trained all his life to take over, and I've only been at it for a few months. What if I mess things up?"

Cold inched down my spine, and I pressed my hand against my knee again to keep it from bouncing.

"No one expects you to be perfect, even if it may seem that way," Edvard said. "I admit, there's less leeway for a king or queen to make mistakes, but you *can* make them, as long as you learn from them. Being a leader is not about technical knowledge. It is about *you,* as a person. Your compassion, your strength, your empathy. You have all that in spades. Besides..." His eyes crinkled into a smile. "There's no better way to learn than on the job."

"With millions of people watching."

"It's a job for those who thrive under pressure," he acknowledged.

My laugh sounded rusty after a week of non-use.

"Do you really think I can do it?" Uncertainty gnawed at me, and I tried not to think of what my mother would've done in my place. How much more gracefully she would've handled all this.

"I know it. You're already taking charge in the Speaker's meetings, going head-to-head with Erhall, and the people love you." Edvard radiated such confidence it reminded me of Rhys, who had never once doubted my ability to do anything.

You don't need a crown to be queen, princess.

God, I missed him. More than I thought I could ever miss someone.

"I'm always here if you want to talk about anything pertaining to the Crown, but that's not why I came today." Edvard examined me, his eyes incisive despite his recent hospitalization. "I want to talk about *you*, Bridget. Not the princess."

Wariness crept into my veins. "What about me?"

"You are deeply unhappy, my dear. You have been since I left the hospital." A wry smile quirked his lips. "For my own sake, I'll assume it's not because you're devastated I made it out alive. But it just so happens the time frame coincides with a certain upcoming proposal and the departure of a certain bodyguard."

The desk blurred before I blinked and my vision cleared. "I'm fine. You were right. It was time to end things, and Steffan would make a fine consort."

"Don't lie to me." Edvard's voice deepened with regal authority, and I flinched. "You are my granddaughter. I know when you are lying, and I know when you're miserable. Right now, you're both."

I wisely chose not to reply.

"I was—and still am—quite upset about your relationship with Mr. Larsen. It was reckless, and the press is still having a field day over it. But..." He heaved a sigh, filled with sadness and sympathy. "You are, first and foremost, my granddaughter. I want you to be happy above all else. I thought what you had was a casual affair but judging by the way you've been walking around like a heartbroken zombie, I assume that wasn't the case."

I pinched myself beneath the desk to make sure I wasn't dreaming. The sharp sting confirmed the phrase "heartbroken zombie" really had left my grandfather's mouth.

But as out of character as the phrase was, he wasn't wrong.

"It doesn't matter," I said, echoing Steffan's sentiment earlier that day. "It's too late. I was trying to repeal the Royal Marriages Law before it became an issue, but there's not enough time."

"Nine months, if I remember correctly."

"Three weeks till the proposal," I pointed out.

"Hmm." The sound came out loaded with meaning.

He couldn't be saying what I thought he was saying. "Grandpa, you *wanted* me to break up with Rhys. You've been pushing me to marry Steffan all this time and..." A messy ball of emotion tangled in my throat. "You had a heart attack when I refused."

Horror drenched his expression. "Is that what you think?" Edvard straightened, his eyes suddenly fierce. "Bridget, it wasn't because of you or any one thing. It was because of an accumulation of stress. If anything, it was my fault for not listening to you and Nikolai." He grimaced. "I should've cut back on my workload, and I didn't. My heart attack was unfortunate timing, but it was *not* your fault. Do you understand?"

I nodded, the ball of emotion expanding until it filled my nose and ears. My chest felt too tight, my skin too hot, then too cold.

"I don't blame you for what happened. Not one bit," he said. "And by royal decree, I order you to stop blaming yourself."

I cracked a small smile at the same time a hot tear scalded my cheek.

"Oh, sweetheart." Edvard let out another, heavier sigh. "Come here."

He opened his arms, and I walked around the desk and hugged him, breathing in his familiar, comforting scent of leather and Creed cologne. Some of the tightness I'd carried around since his heart attack eased.

I hadn't realized how much I'd needed his implicit forgiveness until now.

"You are my granddaughter, and I want you to be happy." Edvard squeezed me tight. "We can't break the law, but you're a smart girl, and you have nine months. Do what you have to do. Do you understand what I'm saying?"

"I think so," I whispered.

"Good." He pulled back and kissed me on the forehead. "Think like a queen. And remember, the best rulers are those who can wield both the carrot and the stick in equal measure."

The best rulers are those who can wield both the carrot and the stick in equal measure.

Edvard's words lingered long after he'd left and the late afternoon sun morphed into the cool blues of twilight.

I picked up my phone, my mind racing with the implications of what I wanted to do.

I had one card left up my sleeve, but I hadn't entertained the notion until now because it was manipulative, underhanded, and went completely against my morals.

It wasn't a carrot *or* a stick. It was the equivalent of a nuclear bomb.

But while I had nine months in theory, I respected Steffan too much to humiliate him by breaking up with him after his proposal should I succeed in repealing the Royal Marriages

Law. I also couldn't *not* go through with the proposal without a good reason. It would send the palace into a tailspin.

So, I had three weeks to get Erhall, who despised me, to bring forward a motion he'd gone on record as being against *and* convince three-fourths of Parliament to overturn one of the nation's oldest laws.

The nuclear bomb was my only feasible option.

I scrolled through my contacts list until I reached the name I was looking for. I hesitated, my thumb hovering over the screen.

Did I really want to do this? Would I be able to live with myself?

This is the life we were born into.

We have nine months. We will figure. It. Out.

Baby, we're way beyond like.

I dialed the number. He answered on the first ring.

"I'm calling in my favor." I skipped the greeting and got straight to the point. If anyone appreciated efficiency, it was him.

"I was expecting your call." I could practically see Alex Volkov's smile over the phone, icy and humorless. "What can I do for you, Your Highness?"

44

BRIDGET

I'd lost my mind, asking Alex for help. He might be dating Ava, and he might be less...sociopathic since they'd gotten back together last year, but I still trusted the man as far as I could throw him.

Yet for all his faults, he truly loved Ava, and he owed me for kicking his ass into gear before I left for New York. If I hadn't, he'd still be moping over her and terrorizing everyone around him.

Our call four days ago had been short and succinct. I told him what I wanted, and he confirmed he could get it. I didn't doubt his ability to pull through, because this was Alex we were talking about, but he hadn't given me a delivery date and I'd been on pins and needles since.

"Your Highness." Booth spoke at a lower volume than usual, and his body vibrated with nervous energy as we walked to my room. We'd just returned from an event at the National Opera House, and I'd been so distracted by thoughts of my plan I hadn't questioned why Booth was accompanying me to my suite when he usually bid me goodbye at the palace entrance.

"Yes?" I arched an eyebrow at Booth's furtive glances around the empty hall. He was a good bodyguard, but he would make a terrible spy.

"Read it when you're alone." He slipped a piece of paper into my hands, his words almost inaudible.

I frowned. "What—"

A maid turned the corner, and Booth stepped back so fast he nearly crashed into the porcelain vase on a nearby side table.

"Well," he said, his voice now so loud I flinched. "If that's all, Your Highness, I'll be going." He dropped to a whisper again. "Don't tell anyone else about it."

He waved and speed-walked down the hall until he disappeared around the same corner the maid had rounded.

My frown deepened.

What in the world? It wasn't like Booth to be so cryptic, but I did as he asked and waited until I shut the door behind me before I unfolded the paper. Booth wasn't a secret notes type of person. What had—

Time stopped. My blood rushed to my face, and my stomach swooped at the familiar, messy scrawl before me.

9 p.m. tonight, princess. Two chairs.

No name, but I didn't need one.

Rhys was still in Eldorra.

A whoosh of relief darted through me, followed by anxiety and a twinge of panic. We hadn't talked since the hospital, and we hadn't exactly ended things on a good note. Why was he reaching out now, two-and-a-half weeks later? How had he convinced Booth to sneak me a note? What—

"Bridget!"

For a second, I thought the call of my name came from

outside my room, but then I looked up and saw the petite brunette standing in my suite.

Another, wholly different kind of disbelief flooded me.

"Ava? What are you doing here?" I hastily shoved Rhys's note into my pocket, where it seared through the silk and into my skin.

Her face broke into a wide smile. "Surprise! I'm here to see you, of course. And I'm not alone."

On cue, Jules swanned into the sitting room dressed in a familiar-looking green coat. "Good afternoon, Your Highness," she sang.

I cocked my head. "Is that my coat?"

"Yes," she said with zero shame. "I love it. It makes my hair pop." The emerald color did, indeed, make her red hair pop. "Your closet is *everything*. I need an in-depth tour later."

"You already had an in-depth tour, courtesy of yourself." Stella came up behind her, clad in a sleek white dress that made her olive skin glow. As the fashion blogger in our group, her closet rivaled mine, though her clothing choices were more casual. "You spent half an hour examining her shoe collection."

"It's called research," Jules said. "I'm going to be a lawyer. Power heels are essential for stomping all over the opposition."

I let out a soft laugh as I hugged my friends, my shock gradually morphing into excitement. I hadn't seen them in person since I moved back to Eldorra, and I hadn't realized how much I'd missed our face-to-face chats until now.

However, I held off on greeting the last person in the group with a hug.

"Alex." I nodded at Ava's boyfriend, which seemed too tame a word to describe him. Boyfriends were sweet and kind. Alex, with his cold eyes and colder demeanor, was anything but, though his expression did warm a degree when he looked at Ava.

"Bridget."

Neither of us gave any sign we'd interacted beyond these types of group settings. I felt bad hiding my call from Ava, but the less she knew about what we were up to, the better. Plausible deniability mattered.

"We saw what happened on the news, with your grandfather and Rhys." Ava's brow knit with concern. "We would've come sooner, but Jules had to wrap up her internship and I couldn't take time off until now. How are you holding up?"

"I'm all right. My grandfather's a lot better." I purposely didn't mention Rhys.

"I *knew* something was going on with you and your hottie bodyguard. I'm never wrong," Jules joked before she, too, turned serious. "Do you need anything from us, babe? Maybe some paparazzi ass you need kicked? A decoy while you sneak off to a midnight rendezvous with your lover? I can dye my hair blonde."

"J, you're like three inches shorter than her," Stella said.

Jules lifted one shoulder. "Minor issue. Nothing heels won't solve."

I laughed again, even as Rhys's note burned a hole in my pocket. *9 p.m. Two chairs.* "How did you guys get in here?"

"We worked with Nikolai on the surprise," Jules said. "Too bad he's taken. Your brother's hot."

"We're here for the weekend," Stella added, brushing a stray curl out of her face. With her green eyes, tanned skin, and leggy grace, she was the most gorgeous person I'd ever met, and while she was fully aware of the effect her looks had on others —especially men—she never flaunted it. "I wish we could stay longer, but we can't take that much time off from work."

"It's okay. I'm just glad you're here." The knot of loneliness in my stomach loosened an inch. As much as I wanted to reread Rhys's note over and over again until I memorized every swoop and curve of the letters, I also wanted to hang out with my friends. It had been far too long. "Tell me. What did I miss?"

Since I didn't have any meetings for the rest of the day, I spent the afternoon catching up with my friends while Alex took a series of business calls. I told them about my training, goodwill tour, and birthday ball. They told me about their jobs, their dating fails, and their road trip to Shenandoah National Park.

Eventually, we passed the light topics and reached the elephant in the room.

"You and Rhys." Ava squeezed my hand. "What happened?"

I hesitated, debating how much to tell them before I settled on a brief, sanitized version of the story, starting with when I learned about Nikolai's abdication and ending with our breakup in the hospital. I recounted everything without breaking down, which I considered a major win.

Once I finished, my friends gaped at me, their expressions ranging from shock to sadness to sympathy.

"Holy shit," Jules said. "Your life is a Hallmark movie."

"Not exactly." Hallmark movies had happy endings, and mine was still up in the air.

"Is there anything we can do?" Sympathy creased Stella's face. For once, she wasn't on her phone, which was a major feat, since she practically lived on the internet.

I shook my head. "I'll figure it out."

If Alex comes through. I glanced at where he stood by the window, speaking rapid-fire Russian into his phone.

"It'll work out, babe." Jules radiated confidence. "It always does. If it doesn't, declare martial law and *tell* them you're keeping your crown *and* hot bodyguard. What are they going to do, guillotine you?"

My lips inched up into a smile. I could always count on

Jules to come up with the most outrageous ideas. "It doesn't work like that, and they might."

"Fuck 'em. I'd like to see them try. If they do, Alex will take care of it. Right, Alex?" Jules's voice took on a teasing, singsong quality.

Alex ignored her.

"Stop provoking him," Ava said. "I can't always save you."

"I'm not provoking him. It's a compliment. Your man can get anything done." When Ava turned away, Jules leaned in and whispered, "He's totally whipped. Watch." She raised her voice to a panicked level. "Oh my God! Ava, are you bleeding?"

Alex's head snapped up. Less than five seconds later, he ended his call and crossed the room to a confused-looking Ava, whose hand froze halfway to the scones on the table.

"I'm fine," Ava said as Alex searched her for injuries. She glared at Jules. "What did I just say?"

"I can't help it." Jules's eyes sparkled with mischief. "It's so much fun. It's like playing with a windup toy."

"Until the toy comes alive and kills you," Stella murmured loud enough for everyone to hear.

Alex stared at Jules with displeasure scrawled all over his face. His features were so perfect it was a little unnerving, like seeing a carefully sculpted statue come to life. Some people were into that, but I preferred men with a little more grit. Give me scars and a nose that was slightly crooked from being broken too many times over perfection.

"Pray you and Ava stay friends forever," Alex said, icy enough to elicit a rash of goosebumps on my arms.

Jules didn't appear fazed by the implied threat. "First of all, Ava and I *will* be friends forever. Second of all, bring it on, Volkov."

Ava sighed. "Do you see what you left me in D.C. with?" she muttered to me.

I made a sympathetic noise.

My friends stayed for another hour before they left for dinner. I declined their invitation to join, saying I had some official business to take care of before tomorrow, but I promised to give them a palace tour in the morning.

I snuck a peek at the clock.

Three more hours until nine p.m.

Nerves cascaded through my stomach. What would I say once I saw Rhys? What would *he* say? I didn't want to tell him about my plan until I was sure I had the pieces in place, and he might not approve, anyway. My methods weren't aboveboard by any means.

"I'll be right out." Alex kissed Ava on the forehead. "I'm going to use the restroom first."

After everyone filed out, I turned to Alex and crossed my arms over my chest. "It took you long enough. And you could've given me a heads up you were coming."

"I run a Fortune 500 company. I do have other business to attend to besides your personal life." He straightened his shirt sleeve. "You might also want to look up the definition of 'surprise.' Ava insisted."

I sighed, not wanting to get into a drawn-out argument with him. "Fine. Do you have what I need?"

Alex reached into his pocket and retrieved a USB drive. "Information on all one hundred eighty members of Eldorra's Parliament, as requested." *Information*, AKA blackmail material. "Once I hand this over to you, my debt is paid."

"I understand."

He studied me for a long moment before he dropped the drive into my outstretched hand.

My fingers closed around the tiny gadget while my heart skittered like a frightened rabbit. *I can't believe I'm doing this. I* wasn't a blackmailer. But I needed leverage, fast, and this was the only way I could think to get it.

I hoped I wouldn't have to resort to using the information. However, with the clock ticking down and my private appeals to ministers politely but firmly rebuffed, I might need to.

"I have to say, I'm impressed," Alex drawled. "I didn't think you had it in you. Maybe you'll make a good queen after all."

Of *course* he thought good leadership rested on manipulation and deceit. His favorite philosopher was probably Machiavelli.

"Alex," I said. "Don't take this the wrong way, but you are a complete dick."

"One of the nicer things people have said about me." He checked his watch. "I would say thank you, but I don't care. I trust you can take it from here?" He nodded at the USB drive.

"Yes." Something occurred to me. I shouldn't ask because I had a feeling I wouldn't like the answer, but... "You have a blackmail file on me too, don't you?"

Though I hadn't done much in my life that was blackmail-worthy except for my relationship with Rhys when it'd been a secret...and what I was doing now.

The irony.

Alex's lips curved a centimeter. "Information is power."

"If anything leaks, Ava will never forgive you."

It was the only threat that worked against him.

I didn't think he would reveal anything, but one never knew with Alex Volkov.

His expression chilled. "That concludes our business, Your Highness." He paused at the door. "I suggest looking at Arthur Erhall's family file first. There's some information there you'll find *very* interesting."

He disappeared into the hall, leaving me with nothing but a flash drive and a sick feeling in my stomach.

Drawing Alex into the situation had been a horrible idea, but it was too late for regrets.

I retrieved my burner laptop and plugged the USB in. I didn't trust him enough to plug anything he gave me into my personal computer.

I pulled up Erhall's file. Finances. Past relationships. Family. Political deals and scandals that had been covered up. I was tempted to dive into the last one, but I clicked on the family file first, as Alex had suggested.

At first, it looked normal, just a rundown of Erhall's lineage and information about his ex-wife, who'd died in a plane crash years ago. Then my eyes snagged on the word *children* and the two names listed beneath it.

My hand flew to my mouth.

Oh my God.

45

RHYS

She wasn't coming.

I stood on the rooftop of the palace's northernmost tower, my jaw tight as I watched the minutes tick by on my watch.

Six minutes past nine. Seven. Eight.

Bridget was always punctual unless she had a meeting that ran over, and she didn't have any meetings that late at night.

Tick. Tick. Tick.

Uncertainty coiled in my stomach. It'd been a gamble, reaching out to Booth and sneaking into the palace, but I'd been desperate to see her.

I'd known there was a chance Bridget, stubborn as she was, wouldn't show up. But I also knew *her*. No matter what she said, she'd wanted to let me go as much as I wanted to leave her, and I was banking on the fact the past two weeks had been hell for her as much as it had been for me.

Part of me hoped it hadn't, because the thought of her hurting in any way made me want to want to burn the palace to the fucking ground. But another, selfish part hoped I'd haunted her as she had me. That every breath was a struggle to draw enough oxygen into her lungs, and every mention of my name caused a sharp needle of pain to pierce her chest.

Because hurt meant she still cared.

"Come on, princess." I stared at the red metal door and willed her to walk through it. "Don't let me down."

Twelve minutes past nine. Thirteen.

The rhythm in my jaw pulsed in time with my heartbeats.

Fuck it. If tonight didn't work, I'd try again until I succeeded. I'd fought and won impossible battles all my life, and the one for Bridget was the most important one of all.

If she couldn't or wouldn't fight for us—because of her guilt, her duty, her family, or any other reason—I'd fight enough for us both.

Fourteen minutes past nine. Fifteen.

Dammit princess, where are you?

Either Bridget hadn't received the note, or she'd chosen not to come.

Booth had texted saying he'd given her the note, and I trusted him. I wouldn't have reached out to him otherwise. If what he said was true, then...

Pain lanced through me, but I forced myself to push it aside. I'd wait all night if I had to, in case she changed her mind, and if—

The door banged open and, suddenly, she was there. Out of breath, cheeks flushed, hair fluttering across her face from the wind.

My pulse ratcheted up several notches in the space of a millisecond.

I straightened, air filling my lungs as I finally came alive again.

Bridget remained in the doorway, one hand on the door-knob, her lips parted and her chest heaving.

The moonlight splashed across the roof, turning her golden

hair silver and illuminating the slender curves of her body. The wind carried a faint hint of her lush jasmine scent toward me, and her green dress fluttered around her thighs, baring her shoulders and the long, smooth expanse of her legs.

I loved that dress. She knew I loved that dress. And something inside me unclenched for the first time in weeks.

"Hi," she breathed. Her grip tightened on the doorknob like she was trying to steady herself.

My mouth curved. "Hi, princess."

The space between us hummed, so taut with anticipation and unspoken words it was a living, breathing thing that pulled us closer together. No more of the distance I'd felt in the hospital. She was in my skin, my soul, the very air I breathed.

Everything I'd gone through the past two weeks to get here had been worth it.

"Apologies for being late. I ran into Markus and got roped into a conversation about the coronation." Bridget brushed her hair out of her face, and I detected a small tremble in her hand. "It turns out the archbishop—"

"Come here, baby."

I didn't give a fuck about Markus or the archbishop. I needed her. Only her.

She froze at my low command, roughened by weeks of longing. For a second, I thought she'd turn tail and run, which might be smart, considering the pent-up fire raging through me. But then she ran *toward* me, her hair streaming behind her in the wind.

I caught her easily while our mouths crashed against each other. Tongues dueling. Teeth scraping. Hands roaming over every inch of flesh we could access.

Two weeks might as well have been two years, based on the way we devoured each other.

I cupped her ass and nipped her bottom lip in punishment

for forcing us to waste all the time we could've spent together. For thinking anything she said could make me give her up when she was the only thing I'd ever wanted.

Even if I did stupid shit like walk out in the heat of the moment, I'd always find my way back to her.

"I'm sorry," Bridget whispered, her voice thick with emotion. "For what I said at the hospital. I don't want to marry Steffan, and I don't—"

"I know." I skimmed my palm over her back, over heated flesh flowing into cool silk, and another small shiver rippled through her. "I'm sorry for walking out."

Regret twisted my insides. Our separation had been as much my fault as hers. I should've stayed. Fought harder.

Then again, she'd needed the space to sort through her thoughts. Her grandfather's heart attack had been fresh in her mind, and there'd been no changing her mind that day.

"I thought you weren't coming." My hand lingered on the small of her back. "Remind me to kill Markus the next time I see him."

She released a small laugh. "Done." Bridget tipped her chin up until her eyes met mine. "I..." She appeared to think better of what she'd been about to say. "How did you get in here? If anyone saw you..."

"They didn't. Navy SEAL, remember?" I drawled. "I can evade a few palace guards."

She rolled her eyes, and my mouth twitched at the familiar sight of her amused exasperation. Fuck, I'd missed her. This. *Us*.

"And Booth?"

"Nearly scared the guy to death when I showed up at his house, but I can be pretty persuasive." It'd taken less convincing than I thought. According to Booth, Bridget had been in a funk since the hospital, and he'd hoped seeing me would help. He wasn't stupid—he'd guessed Bridget and I really did have something going on.

Booth could lose his job if someone found out he was smuggling notes from me to Bridget, but he'd taken the risk anyway.

I owed that man a nice, cold beer and a steak dinner in the future.

"I hadn't expected you to reach out after what happened," Bridget said. "I thought you were upset with me. I thought..." Her throat flexed with a hard swallow. "You might've left."

"I did. Had to leave the country to get a new visa," I clarified when her eyebrows shot up. "Six months as a tourist." I flashed a crooked smile. "Guess I have to get an 'I Love Eldorra' T-shirt now."

The tiniest of smiles crossed her lips. "So, you're staying for six months?" She sounded both relieved and sad.

Six months was a long time and nowhere long enough.

"No, princess. I'm staying for as long as you're here."

Bridget's eyes flared with delight before her muscles tensed again. "How...why..."

"Let me figure out the how. As for the why..." I pressed her tighter to me. "I'm not leaving *you*. If you're in Eldorra, I'm in Eldorra. If you're in Antarctica, the Sahara, or the middle of the fucking ocean, I'm there. I'm as much yours as you are mine, princess, and a *law* isn't keeping me away. I don't care what a piece of paper says. I'll burn down the entire fucking Parliament if I have to."

A thousand emotions passed over her face. "Rhys..."

"I'm serious."

"I know you are. And something must be wrong with me because I've never been more touched by the prospect of arson." Her quick smile faded. "But there's something I need to tell you. Several things, in fact."

Wariness filled me at her tone. "Okay."

"It's funny you mentioned burning down Parliament. I have an idea...not *physically* burning it down," she added hastily when my eyebrows rose. "But a way to repeal the law before Steffan proposes."

The beast in my chest snarled at his name. Andreas's plan didn't solve the short-term problem of Bridget and Steffan's engagement—and it *would* be a short-term problem—but I'd deal with it myself. No way in hell would Bridget wear another man's ring on her finger.

"I don't know if I can go through with it, though." A touch of vulnerability entered her eyes. "It's not exactly aboveboard."

"What is it?"

Pink tinged Bridget's cheeks before she straightened and said, "Blackmail the ministers into opening the motion and voting for a repeal."

Wait one fucking second. "Repeat that."

She did. "Like I said, it's not the most aboveboard strategy, but—"

A strangled noise emerged from my throat, cutting her off.

Her brow knit into a frown. "What?"

"Have you been talking to Andreas?" If she hadn't, it was too ironic for words.

Her frown deepened. "No. Why would I talk to Andreas about this? He wants to steal the crown."

Not exactly. Andreas and I had spent a fair amount of time together hashing out the plan, and while I still trusted him only as far as I could throw him, I knew he didn't want the crown. He enjoyed his carefree lifestyle as a prince without responsibilities too much.

"Because he has a similar idea, though his only applies to Erhall, not all of Parliament." My mouth tipped up. "You always were an overachiever."

"Why are you talking to..." Bridget's eyes widened. "You

know."

My surprise mirrored hers. How did she...then it hit me. Her blackmail on Erhall. It must've included information about me and Andreas.

But before I said anything, I wanted to make sure we were on the same page. I'd been working up to the reveal about my parentage; I didn't want to just drop the bombshell on her in case I assumed wrong. "I know about Andreas." I watched her carefully. "That he's..."

A tense silence vibrated between us.

"Your brother."

"My brother."

We spoke at the same time, and there it was. My secret, out in the open.

After thirty-four years of no family except my mother, who'd barely counted as family, it was strange to think I had a brother.

"So, it's true." Bridget released a long breath, the vestiges of shock lingering on her face. "How did you find out?"

"Christian did some digging and told me. I confronted Andreas." I filled her in on what happened at his townhouse, as well as Andreas's plan to blackmail Erhall with the information about me being his son. Erhall couldn't afford a scandal ahead of elections, and a long-lost love child fell squarely under "scandal."

"I'm a little terrified I came up with the same idea as my cousin." I could see the gears spinning in Bridget's mind as she digested the information. "How do you know we can trust him?"

"I don't, but we have leverage. He doesn't want anyone to find out Erhall is his father, or..."

"...he could lose his royal status," Bridget finished. "A fate worse than death in his eyes."

"Yeah."

The whole situation was so fucked. I hated playing mind games, and we were trapped in the most twisted web of games and one-upmanship possible. I also didn't love the idea of blackmail, but if that's what I had to do, I'd do it.

Bridget examined me, those beautiful blue eyes sympathetic. "It must've been a shock, learning about Erhall and Andreas. I know you have mixed feelings about your father."

That was one way to put it. Another way was I despised him even more now that I knew his identity.

"He's not my father." Erhall was, at best, a sperm donor. "But I don't want to talk about him right now. Let's focus on your plan."

I had a lot of shit to sort out when it came to Erhall, but I could do that later.

Bridget picked up on my cue and changed the subject.

"Okay. So." She lifted her chin. "We're really doing this. Blackmailing the Speaker of Parliament."

Despite her bravado, a note of nervousness ran beneath her words, and the fierce need to protect her—from the world, from her own doubts and insecurities—consumed me.

I wished she could see herself as I saw her. Fucking perfect.

I framed her face with my hands. "If we do it, we do it together. You and me against the world, princess."

Her smile sent warmth crashing against my ribcage. "I wouldn't have anyone else by my side, Mr. Larsen." She took a deep breath. "We might need the information to push Erhall, but I want to try something before we resort to doing the same with Parliament. All this time, I've been treating the tabloids as my enemy, but maybe they can be an ally."

She explained her plan. It was easier than blackmailing one hundred eighty of Eldorra's most powerful, but it was also a major gamble.

"You sure?" I asked after she finished. "It's a big risk."

Bridget had the most to lose if it didn't pan out.

"Yes. I can't believe I didn't think of it earlier." She paused. "Actually, I can. I was scared of what people would say and that it would lessen my legitimacy as a ruler. But I'm tired of being afraid. With great risk comes great reward, right?"

A small smile touched my lips. "Absolutely."

Bridget was, after all, my greatest risk *and* my greatest reward.

She lifted one hand and tangled her fingers with mine. "I missed you."

The mood shifted, transitioning from the brisk practicality of our plan to something softer and achingly vulnerable.

"I'm right here. I'm not leaving." I swept my thumb over her bottom lip. "I take care of what's mine, and you've been mine since the moment I saw you outside your poorly secured house at Thayer. Until I fixed it, of course."

A smile tugged at her mouth. "You couldn't stand me back then."

"Doesn't matter. You were still mine." I curled my hand around the back of her neck while keeping my thumb on her lip. "Mine to fight with. Mine to protect. Mine to fuck." My voice dropped. "Mine to love."

Bridget sucked in an audible breath.

"In Costa Rica, you asked if I'd ever been in love. I said no." I lowered my head until our foreheads touched and her lips were scant inches from mine. "Ask me again."

It was the same request I'd made at the hospital, but this time, Bridget didn't break our gaze as she asked, "Have you ever been in love, Mr. Larsen?"

"Only once." I slid my hand up from her neck to the back of her head, cupping it. "And you, princess. Have you ever been in love?"

"Only once," she whispered.

I exhaled sharply her words sank into my soul, filling cracks I hadn't known existed.

Until Bridget, I'd never loved or been loved, and I finally understood what the fuss was about. It was better than any bulletproof armor or oblivion I found at the bottom of the bottle during my short-lived affair with alcohol.

Alcohol was for numbing, and I didn't want to be numb. I wanted to feel every goddamn thing with her.

I pulled Bridget close until our bodies pressed flush against each other. "Damn right," I said fiercely. "Only once. First and last. Don't forget that, princess."

I fisted her hair and tugged her head back, my mouth pressing hot and insistent against hers while I maneuvered us to a chair.

There were nights when I took my time, savoring every inch of her body before I gave us what we both wanted, and there were nights like this, when our desperate need to just *be* together overrode everything else.

"Rhys..." She gasped as I pushed her skirt up around her hips and ripped her panties off, too impatient to shimmy them down when she was sitting. I tossed the torn silk on the floor and pushed her legs wider with my knee.

"I love when you say my name." I sank into her, swallowing her small cry with my kiss and pushing deeper until I was buried to the hilt.

We had to muffle our moans so they didn't carry on the wind, and somehow that only heightened the intensity of the moment, like we were containing all our emotions in this small bubble where we were the only ones who existed.

"Harder, *please*." Bridget arched into me, her nails digging grooves into my skin, her warm skin contrasting against the chill of the night air on my back.

I held onto the back of the chair for better leverage and gave her what she asked for, a groan ripping from my throat when she buried her face in my chest to muffle her scream. "You feel so good, princess."

My blood ran white-hot as I slammed into her again and again, my muscles flexing from the effort. She was slick and tight, her breath hot against my skin as she clenched and shattered around me with a wordless cry.

My orgasm followed soon after, racing through me with such intensity it took me twice as long to recover than usual.

When the aftershocks finally subsided, I pushed myself up on my arms so I didn't crush Bridget with my weight, but she wrapped her legs around my waist, keeping me close.

"Round two?" I brushed a strand of hair out of her face. She looked sleepy and lazy and content, and it still boggled my mind she was real.

Not only real but here, with me.

She let out a soft laugh. "You're insatiable," she said, turning the word I'd used for her against me.

"When it comes to you?" I kissed her jaw. "Always."

Bridget's eyes turned liquid beneath the moonlight, and her hold on me tightened. "I love you."

Another breath rushed out of me.

"I love you too," I said, my voice gruff with long-buried emotion.

I kissed her again.

Her mouth against mine, her limbs wrapped around my body, our breaths and heartbeats mingling until they were one...I'd lived in hell my whole life, and it wasn't until now I glimpsed what heaven felt like.

But as our kiss deepened and I sank into her once again, I realized I was wrong.

Bridget felt better than heaven. She felt like home.

46

BRIDGET

AFTER MY NIGHT WITH RHYS, I KICKED MY PLAN INTO high gear and prayed it worked. I didn't feel *too* bad about pressuring Erhall, but it wasn't smart to alienate all of Parliament. I didn't believe in ruling through fear.

That was how I found myself standing in front of three dozen journalists on Sunday, three days after my rendezvous with Rhys. We were gathered on the palace's north lawn, and behind the press gaggle, spectators pressed against metal barricades, eager for an in-person glimpse of a royal.

My friends had left that morning. I'd filled them in on my plans, but I'd waited until they were on the plane back to the U.S. before holding the press conference. I didn't want them to have to deal with the craziness that was about to ensue. They hadn't been happy—they'd wanted to be here for moral support, but this was something I had to do on my own.

"Good afternoon." My voice echoed across the grounds, and the noise quieted. "Thank you for coming on such short notice. I realize it's a Sunday, and there are likely other places you'd rather be right now, like brunch or your bed"—a small ripple of startled laughter. They weren't used to members of the royal family speaking so informally—"so I appreciate your attendance. But before I take questions, I would like to say a few words about why I brought you here."

I looked around at the expectant faces staring back at me. *Thump. Thump. Thump.* Despite my pounding heart, I was strangely calm. It was like I'd expended so much energy worrying about it beforehand I had none left for the moment itself.

Rhys was right. This was a huge risk, and Elin nearly had a coronary when she found out about the last-minute press conference, but I was done playing it safe.

If I wanted something, I had to fight for it, even if meant the possibility of crashing and burning in front of the entire world.

If I wasn't brave enough to stand up for what I wanted, I had no hope of standing up for what the people needed.

"I am a proud citizen of Eldorra. I love this country and the people in it, and I'm honored to serve as your princess. I also hope that when the time comes, I will be a queen *you* can be proud of." *Breathe. You can do this.* "However, I'm aware there have been concerns about my desire and suitability to serve since I became crown princess. Those concerns haven't been entirely unfounded."

A wave of murmurs greeted my statement, but I pushed forward.

"I think I can speak for everyone here when I say none of us could have predicted the events that have led me to where I am today—nine months out from my coronation as the queen of this great country." I took a deep breath. "When I first found out about my brother Prince Nikolai's plans for abdication, I was scared. Scared of taking on a role I'd never expected to have, scared I wouldn't live up to the title and fail my family, my country. But fear is no reason to stay still, and thankfully, I have a wonderful team to guide me through the intricacies required of such an important role. Earlier this year, I spent three weeks earlier traveling around the country, meeting and getting to know citizens just like you. How they lived, what concerns kept them up at night..."

I continued my speech, talking about not only the tour but the Citizen Letters program and the agenda items I brought before Parliament before I hit the most important part of my speech. "I've come to realize being queen is not just about representing the country as it is. It's about moving the nation forward and keeping the traditions that make Eldorra such a unique, wonderful place while shedding the ones that hold it back. That is true of the reforms I've helped push through Parliament. It is also true of traditions binding the Crown to outdated norms and expectations...such as the Royal Marriages Law. Which brings me to my next point."

More murmurs, louder this time.

I took another, deeper breath. *Here we go.*

"As you may know, information came to light last month about an alleged relationship between myself and my former bodyguard, Rhys Larsen. Those allegations were officially denied. But I am here today to tell you they are true."

The murmurs exploded into a roar. The reporters jumped from their seats, shouting and thrusting their microphones at me. Behind them, the crowd went wild

Camera flashes. Shouts. A million phones raised in the air, aimed at me.

My heart rate slowed and roared in my ears.

I tried not to picture Elin's or my family's reactions. They must be freaking out. I'd refused to tell them what I would say beforehand, and I'd insisted they stay in the palace for the event.

Today was all on me.

I raised my voice to speak above the din. "I am also here today to tell you I am *still* in a relationship with Mr. Larsen."

Pandemonium.

It was so loud I couldn't hear myself think, but my speech was over. It was time to turn it over to the reporters—one in particular.

"Yes." I gestured at Jas, the reporter from *The Daily Tea.*

"Your Highness." The crowd quieted to hear her question. "What about the Royal Marriages Law? You will be crowned as queen in less than nine months, and the law requires you to marry someone of noble birth before the ceremony," Jas said, just as we'd agreed upon.

It was amazing what the promise of the first exclusive interview with the Queen of Eldorra could accomplish.

I smiled. "Thank you, Jas. You bring up a good point. But while the Royal Marriages Law requires the monarch to marry a noble, it does *not* require them to be married before the coronation. That being said, I believe it is time we rethink the law. It was created in the eighteenth century, when Eldorra needed the alliances secured through royal marriage to survive as a nation, but it is no longer the eighteenth century. Europe is no longer at war. And I believe it is long past time to repeal the Royal Marriages Law."

"You would need the Speaker to bring the motion to the floor and at least three-fourths of Parliament to pass a repeal," Jas said, right on cue. "This issue came up during the abdication of former Crown Prince Nikolai. There weren't enough votes."

"That is true." I paused, forcing the crowd to wait for what I had to say next. *Keep them in suspense.* Elin's voice echoed in my head. We didn't agree on everything, but she knew what she was doing when it came to the press. "What happened with my brother was a tragedy. He would've made a wonderful king, but he had to choose between love and country, and he chose love. I think that's something all of us can relate to. While we, as a royal family, strive to represent the country and serve the citizens of Eldorra the best we can, we are also human. We love, and we grieve..." My voice caught as my parents' faces flashed through my mind. "And sometimes, we have to make impossible decisions. But neither my brother nor anyone standing here should *have* to make that choice. Whether or not the monarch marries a noble has *no* bearing on their ability to serve. The Royal Marriages Law is a relic from a time that no longer exists, and I appeal to Parliament to reconsider their stance on the issue."

That was what my words said, but my real appeal—the whole point of my speech—was directed to the public. Address their concerns about me from the start, connect with them emotionally via my confession about being scared to take on my role, remind them of the good I'd done and my experience with Parliament, and explain the logic of why the law needed to be repealed.

Ethos and logos.

I'd meant every word, but I'd also spent hours strategically crafting the speech. If I wanted to succeed as queen, I needed not only to play the game but dominate it, and public opinion meant everything when I had no real political power.

Of course, there was one important part of the press conference left.

Pathos.

"You keep mentioning the choice between love and country," Jas said. "Does that mean you are in love with Mr. Larsen?"

The crowd held its breath. The entire country, it seemed, held its breath.

In the distance, a car honked, and a bird swooped overhead,

its wings flapping against the clear blue sky. Neither disturbed the heavy hush blanketing the lawn.

I waited for one beat. Two. Then, with a small smile, I said, "Yes. I am. That is all. Thank you to everyone for coming today."

I left the podium to a frenzy of shouts and cheers.

My legs shook, and my heart thundered as I walked to the back of the palace. *I did it.* I couldn't believe it.

But I couldn't celebrate just yet. I had one thing left on my to-do list.

I stepped into the marble-floored breezeway by the palace's side entrance. Rhys waited in the shadows of the columns, his gray eyes burning with a molten flame. "You did good, princess."

I stepped into his embrace, my pulse hammering in my throat. "It's not over yet." I wrapped my arms around his neck and whispered, "Kiss me like the world's watching."

His slow smile dripped through me like rich, smooth honey. "Gladly, Your Highness."

Rhys's mouth descended on mine, and I heard the soft, telltale click of a camera shutter from the nearby bushes.

"Think they got it?" His lips brushed against mine as he spoke.

"Definitely."

He grinned and kissed me again. Deeper this time, more insistent, and I pressed against him, letting his touch and taste sweep me away.

The first kiss was for the world. This one was for us.

47

RHYS

1 WEEK LATER

"Your Highness!" Erhall's assistant jumped up from her desk, her eyes wide. "I'm so sorry. I don't know what happened, but we don't have you on the calendar. There must've been a mix-up—"

"It's all right," Bridget said with a gracious smile. "I didn't make an appointment, but we would like to speak with the Speaker. Is he available?"

"Oh, um." The flustered-looking woman rifled through her papers before she shook her head. "Yes, of course. Please, follow me."

She led us through the Speaker's chambers toward his office. The thick blue carpet muffled the sounds of our footsteps, and my muscles knotted with tension.

We're really doing this.

I wasn't scared of Erhall, but this would be my first time seeing him since I found out he was my father. Biologically, anyway. He hadn't done jack shit to earn the honor the title deserved.

Erhall's assistant knocked on his door. No answer. She knocked again.

"What? I told you not to disturb me!" he barked.

The woman flinched. "Mr. Speaker, Her Highness Princess Bridget is here to see you. And, um, Mr. Larsen." She cast a quick, awed glance in my direction.

I fought a grimace.

After the past week, everyone in Eldorra—hell, everyone in the *world*—knew my face and name. They'd taken over headlines from Tokyo to New York, and the footage from Bridget's press conference, as well as the "candid" photos and videos of us kissing afterward, had played on repeat on every news channel.

The press spun the story as a reverse fairytale about a princess and her bodyguard, and the commentators ran with it, penning entire articles and op-eds about love, duty, and tradition.

The public ate it up. According to Bridget, Parliament had been inundated with calls about repealing the law, and the hashtag #LoveOverCountry had been trending all week on social media.

Love was the most universal emotion. Not everyone experienced it, but they all wanted it—even those who said they didn't—and Bridget's press conference had tapped into that core need. She wasn't just a royal anymore. She was a human and, more importantly, relatable to every person out there who couldn't be with the person they wanted for whatever reason.

There was nothing more powerful than power people could relate to.

Bridget's plan had worked better than we could've hoped, but it was disconcerting seeing my face all over the newsstands and having people stop and stare wherever I went.

But I'd agreed to the plan knowing it would destroy any

semblance of privacy I had left, and if stepping out of the shadows and into the spotlight was what it took for us to be together, I'd do an interview with every goddamned magazine out there.

Bridget, Erhall's assistant, and I waited for the Speaker's response to Bridget's visit.

I heard the slam of a desk drawer followed by several beats of silence before the door swung open, revealing an irritated-looking Erhall.

The knots in my muscles doubled. *My father.* I didn't know what I'd expected. Maybe a tug in my stomach at the sight of the man who was technically one half of me, or the loathing that had simmered beneath the surface for over three decades, waiting for the day when I could unleash it in a hail of fists and blood and curses.

Instead, I felt nothing. Nothing except a vague distaste for Erhall's overly coiffed, gel-slick hair and anger at the tight, bordering-on-disrespectful smile he gave Bridget.

"Your Highness. Please, come in." His tone indicated he was less than pleased by the surprise, and he didn't acknowledge me as we stepped into his large, oak-paneled office.

Bridget and I took the seats across from him. The office reflected the man, cold and empty of any personal effects except for the framed university degrees hanging on the walls.

I studied Erhall, trying to see the resemblance between us. I spotted a hint of it in the angle of his cheekbones and the slope of his forehead. It wasn't obvious enough strangers would look at us and guess we were related, but it was there if one looked closely enough.

I blinked, and the resemblance disappeared, replaced by a pinched visage and cold, calculating eyes.

"So." Erhall steepled his fingers beneath his chin, his lips as pinched as the rest of his face. "The crown princess herself visiting me in my office. To what do I owe the honor?"

"I have an agenda item for Parliament's next session." Bridget radiated authority, and pride flashed through me. She'd come a long way since the day we sat in her hotel suite in New York, watching Nikolai's abdication on TV. She'd looked like she wanted to throw up during his speech, but there was no trace of that scared, uncertain girl today. "Open the motion to repeal the Royal Marriages Law."

Erhall stared at her for a second before laughing. Loudly.

A snarl rumbled in my throat, but I forced myself to remain silent. This was Bridget's show.

"I thought this was another citizen write-in issue," Erhall said. "I'm afraid I can't do that. The law is one of the oldest in Eldorra, and as...*moving* as your press conference was, it's tradition. Not to mention, we have far more important issues at hand, including the water pollution problem *you* brought to our attention last month. You want clean drinking water for the people of Hedelberg, don't you?"

Bridget smiled, not blinking an eye at his heavy-handed threat. "I'm afraid *you* misunderstand *me*. That wasn't a request, and I trust Parliament is competent enough to handle more than one issue at a time. If it's not, I suggest a change in how you run the chamber, Mr. Speaker...or a change in the Speakership altogether."

Erhall's chuckles vanished, and his face hardened. "With all due respect, Your Highness, Parliament consults the Crown as a courtesy, but no one, not even His Majesty, dictates the law."

"Then it's a good thing I'm not dictating the law." Bridget crossed her legs, her posture flawless as she stared him down. "I'm telling you to repeal one. It is outdated and holds no practical value for the country or the people. Without value, tradition is nothing but an imitation of the past, and the people agree. A recent poll put public approval for a repeal at ninety-three percent."

Erhall's chest puffed with indignation. "I beg to differ. Tradition is the foundation of this country, this office, and *your* office. We cannot go about tearing it down willy-nilly. So no, I'm afraid I cannot bring the motion to the floor. No matter how many souvenir T-shirts they're selling with Mr. Larsen's face on them," he added with a small sneer.

Bridget and I exchanged glances.

Are you sure?

Yes. Do it.

Short, succinct, and silent. The most efficient conversation we'd ever had.

"You should care more about Mr. Larsen's public profile," Bridget said, her mild tone giving no warning before she dropped the bombshell. "Considering he's your son."

Most explosions were deafening, rattling teeth and eardrums with the sheer force of the energy expelled. This one was silent but a hundred times deadlier, its shock waves slamming into Erhall before he ever saw it coming.

I could pinpoint the moment the impact hit. His face drained of color, and the smug self-satisfaction disappeared from his eyes as they bounced between me and Bridget. Back and forth, back and forth, like two ping pong balls stuck in a pendulum.

"That's—he's—that's a lie," Erhall sputtered. "I don't have a son."

"Michigan, summer of eighty-six," I said. "Deidre Larsen."

I didn't think it was possible, but Erhall's face paled further until it matched the color of his starched button-down.

"Judging by your reaction, you remember her." I leaned forward, my face creasing with a grim smile when he scooted back an inch in response. A faint sheen of perspiration glistened on his forehead. "She's dead, by the way. Turned to alcohol and drugs after a piece of shit lowlife abandoned her when she told him she was pregnant. Overdosed when I was eleven."

I thought I caught a flash of regret in Erhall's eyes before he covered it up.

"I'm sorry to hear that." A muscle worked in his jaw, and he reached for his tie only to lower his hand before making contact. "But I'm afraid I don't know a Deidre Larsen. You have me mistaken for someone else."

My hands flexed into fists. Bridget slid a hand onto my knee, her touch cool and reassuring, and I expelled a long breath before I forced myself to relax.

I wasn't here to beat down on Erhall, at least not physically. We had a more important goal to accomplish.

"That's not what the DNA tests say." I reached into my pocket and slapped the papers, courtesy of Andreas, on the desk with a thud that made Erhall jump. "Take a look if you don't believe me."

He didn't touch them. We both knew what I said was true.

"What do you want?" Erhall recovered some of his composure. "Money? A title?" He raised an eyebrow. "Monthly bonding activities?"

Despite his mocking tone, he stared at me with a strange expression that almost...

No. The day I willingly engaged in any form of "bonding" activity with him was the day icicles formed in hell.

"Her Highness already told you." I tilted my head in Bridget's direction. Shes sat calmly next to me, her expression neutral, almost bored, as she watched our conversation. "We want you to open the motion to repeal the Royal Marriages Law."

"And if I don't?"

"You might find the news about your long-lost love child splashed across the front page of the next *Daily Tea*," Bridget said. "Hypothetically speaking, of course. Journalists can get their hands on the darnedest things." She shook her head. "It's too bad they won't wait until after the elections. You have quite a strong opponent this year. Just a hint of a scandal could tip things in his favor. But what do I know?" Her smile returned. "I'm just a 'pretty face.'"

Erhall's face changed from chalk white to bright purple in zero-point-two seconds. It would've been alarming had it not been so satisfying. "Are you *blackmailing* me?"

"No," Bridget said. "I'm encouraging you to do the right thing. Because you *will* do the right thing, won't you, Mr. Speaker?"

I could tell he was struggling to hold back some choice epithets as the wheels spun in his head.

If he refused, he risked losing his political career over the scandal an illegitimate child would cause. He represented one of the most traditional counties in the country, and his voters would not respond well to the news he had a child with an American waitress out of wedlock.

If he caved, he would lose the power play, because that's what this was. It wouldn't take much for Erhall to bring the motion to the floor, but doing so meant Bridget gained the upper hand. Politics was a game and losing a match—especially to someone Erhall deemed inferior for no other reason than her gender—had to sting.

The grandfather clock ticked in the corner, the passing of seconds deafening in the silence.

Finally, Erhall's shoulders slumped, and a thrill of victory darted through me. "Even if I bring the motion to the floor,

Parliament will never pass it," he said spitefully. "Public opinion only takes you so far."

Bridget's smile didn't waver. "Let me worry about the rest of Parliament. You do your part, and the world never has to know about your indiscretion. You might even sit in the Prime Minister's seat one day. But remember, Mr. Speaker, I'm going to be queen. And I will still *be* queen long after your political career is over and you're hawking your memoir about your glory days on morning talk shows. So, it's in your best interest to work with me and not make things difficult. Don't you agree?"

Erhall was an asshole, but he wasn't an idiot. "Fine. I'll open the motion at the next session of Parliament," he said, tone sullen.

"Excellent." Bridget rose from her seat. "I do love a productive meeting. Mr. Larsen, is there anything else you'd like to add?"

I stared at Erhall. While certain things he said and did pissed me off, my overall feelings toward my father had shifted from loathing to indifference.

Whatever hold he had over me, it was gone.

"I spent my life building you up in my mind," I said. "You were the decision that changed two lives irrevocably, the monster who changed my mother into the monster *she* became. I could've found out your identity a long time ago, but I chose not to. I told myself it was because I didn't trust myself enough not to kill you for what you did"—Erhall flinched and scooted back another inch—"but the truth is, I was scared of facing the ghost that had haunted me my entire life, even when I was convinced ghosts weren't real. What was he like, the man that was technically one half of me? How would he react when he found out I was his son?"

The muscle in Erhall's jaw jumped again.

"Well, I finally faced him, and you know what I realized?" I looked him straight in the eye. Not an iota of anything other than apathy passed through me. "He's not a monster. He's a sad, pathetic little man who was too much of a coward to own up to the consequences of his actions, and I wasted decades letting him have more power over my life than he deserved. So no, I don't and will never want your money, your title, or any form of relationship with you. As far as I'm concerned, my father is dead. He died when he walked away thirty-four years ago."

Erhall flinched as I, too, stood, my height throwing a shadow over his hunched form. I nodded. "Have a good day, Mr. Speaker."

Bridget and I made it halfway to the door before he said, "Arranged marriages aren't only for royals, Mr. Larsen. People have been forced into loveless marriages long before Her Highness was born."

I paused and looked back, my eyes locking with Erhall's. I glimpsed another flash of regret, but it wasn't enough. Not for what he did to Deidre, and not for what he did to me. There was no excuse for how he'd handled the situation.

Instead of responding, I closed the remaining distance to the exit and left him there, sputtering and alone in his cold, oversized office.

Bridget waited until we entered the elevator, away from the prying ears and eyes of Erhall's assistant, before she spoke. "We should make our rounds on the speech circuit," she said. "We'd make a killing."

A laugh rumbled in my throat. A heavy weight had lifted off my chest, allowing my laughter to flow more freely.

"Hard pass for me. I'm not typically a speech kinda guy."

"You did good in there." Bridget squeezed my arm, the movement conveying more than any words could, before a glint of mischief lit up her eyes. "I thought Erhall would rupture an artery. Imagine if we'd mentioned Andreas too."

Andreas had been adamant about never letting Erhall know the truth about him. He had more to lose than any of us if the truth about his parentage came to light, and I had no problem keeping the secret—partly because I respected his choice, and partly because it kept him in line. Even if he didn't want the crown, he was still on my watch list. Anyone who could possibly threaten Bridget was.

"So. Battle number one won," I said as the elevator stopped on the ground floor of the Parliament building. "What's next?"

Bridget's mischief gave way to determination. "Next, we win the war."

"Damn right we will."

I held out my hand, and she took it, her small, soft palm nestling perfectly in my bigger, rougher one.

The doors whooshed open, and we stepped out to a frenzy of camera flashes and reporters shouting questions over each other.

Out of the shadows and into the spotlight.

I'd never expected global recognition, but I meant it when I said I would follow Bridget anywhere—including into the middle of a media firestorm.

You ready, Mr. Larsen?

Born ready, princess.

Bridget and I kept our hands clasped together as we walked through the storm.

One battle down, one war to win.

Good thing I was, and always will be, a soldier for one queen.

48

BRIDGET

For the next month, I launched into campaign mode to woo, or threaten, enough ministers into voting yes on a repeal. Some were an easy sell, others not so much. But one hundred phone calls, eleven in-person visits, twenty-three media interviews, and countless public appearances—both scheduled and "candid"—of me and Rhys later, the big day finally arrived.

Rhys and I sat in my suite, watching the vote play out on TV. I'd stress-ate my way through two packs of Oreos while he sat next to me, his face impassive but his body vibrating with the same restless energy tunneling through my veins.

The current vote count: ninety yay, thirty nay, and two abstentions, with fifty-eight more votes to go. We needed one hundred thirty-five yays for a repeal. It looked good, but I wasn't counting my chickens until they hatched.

"Lady Jensen." Erhall's sour voice rang through the mahogany-paneled chamber on-screen.

"Yay."

"Lord Orskov."

"Yay."

I squeezed Rhys's hand, my heart thumping. I'd slotted Orskov into the *maybe* column, so his vote was a big win.

"They'll pass it." Rhys's quiet confidence soothed the frayed edges of my nerves. "If they don't, we have our backup plan."

"Which is?"

"Burn down Parliament."

I huffed out a laugh. "How's that supposed to help?"

"I don't know, but it'd be damn satisfying."

Another laugh, another easing of nerves.

Fifty-seven down. Fifty-six. Fifty-five.

The vote continued until only two ministers were left and we were one yay short of a repeal. If either of them voted yes, we were home free.

I squeezed Rhys's hand again as Erhall called on the next minister.

"Lord Koppel."

"Nay."

I deflated while Rhys let out a stream of curses. I hadn't expected Koppel to vote yes, but it was disappointing nonetheless.

Regret rose in my throat. I should've dug out the blackmail file on Koppel. I'd tried to keep my campaign aboveboard, never outright threatening any of the ministers except Erhall, but perhaps I'd miscalculated. I wouldn't be the first person in history who'd gotten screwed over by their conscience.

You did what was right.

The hairs on the back of my neck prickled. I straightened and looked around my suite, but it was empty save for Rhys and me. Still, I could've sworn I heard a soft female voice whisper to me...a voice that sounded suspiciously like my mother's, based on the old tapes I'd watched of her.

This is what I get for staying up late. I'd been too wired to sleep much last night, and I was clearly delirious from exhaustion.

On-screen, a smug smile slashed across Erhall's face, and I could *tell* he was praying for the repeal to fail. He'd opened the motion as promised, but his glee had been visible every time someone voted nay.

"Lady Dahl."

I gnawed on my bottom lip.

Dahl was the last minister left. She had one of the most unpredictable voting records in Parliament, and she could go either way. None of my calls to her had yielded anything more than a polite *Thank you, Your Highness. I'll think about it.*

The restless energy emanating from Rhys tripled until it was near audible in the thick silence of my suite. The Oreos sloshed in my stomach, and I wished I hadn't binged on so much sugar in such a short time.

Dahl opened her mouth, and I squeezed my eyes shut, unable to watch the moment that would change my life—for better or for worse.

Please, please, please...

"Yay."

Yay. It took a minute for my brain to process that one word. When it did, my eyes flew open in time to see an irritated-looking Erhall say, "With a final vote count of one hundred thirty-five yay, forty nays, and five abstentions, Parliament officially declares the Royal Marriages Law of 1723 repealed. The chamber..."

I tuned out the rest of what he said. I was too buzzed, my skin racing with tingles of electricity and my head dizzy with disbelief. My stunned gaze met Rhys. "Did that really happen?"

His eyes crinkled into a small smile. "Yeah, princess, it did." Fierce pride and relief lined his face.

"We did it." I couldn't wrap my head around it. The law had been the bane of my existence since I became crown princess, and now, it was gone. I could marry whomever I wanted without giving up the throne. I could marry *Rhys*.

The import of what happened fully sank in.

"*We did it!*" I squealed and flung myself into a laughing Rhys's arms. Everything went blurry, and I realized I was crying, but I didn't care.

So many months of agonizing over the law, so many early mornings and late nights and conversations that made me want to tear my hair out...all worth it, because *we did it.*

I'm proud of you, honey. The soft female voice returned, and emotion welled in my throat.

It didn't matter whether the voice was real or a figment of my imagination. All that mattered was it was there, closer than it'd ever been.

Thanks, Mom. I'm proud of me, too.

Rhys, my grandfather, and Nikolai had all reassured me I could do my job as queen, but I hadn't quite believed them until now. My first real victory in Parliament. I hoped my relationship with the ministers would be more cooperative than combative, but I wasn't naïve enough to think it'd be smooth sailing from here on out. There'd be plenty of uphill battles to come, but if I won once, I could win again.

Rhys captured my mouth in a deep, tender kiss. "*You* did it. I'm just along for the ride."

"Not true." I snuggled closer to him, so euphoric I would've floated right off the ground had he not secured his arms around my waist. "You were there for everything, too."

The interviews, the meetings, the public appearances. All of it.

A deep sound rumbled in Rhys's chest. "Looks like you're stuck with me, princess." He grazed his knuckles over my spine. "Should've thought this through."

"Am I?" I adopted a thoughtful expression. "I could always break up with you and date someone else. There's a movie star I've always—" I squealed again when he stood and tossed me over his shoulder.

"Rhys, put me down." I was smiling so big my cheeks hurt. "I have calls to answer." I waved my hand in the general direction of my phone, which had been vibrating with new messages and calls since the vote concluded.

"Later." Rhys's palm landed with a hard smack on my ass, and I yelped even as heat seared through me at the impact. "I need to teach you a lesson about joking with me. Especially about other men."

Was it wrong my panties dampened at the way his voice lowered into a possessive growl? Perhaps. But I couldn't bring myself to care as he kicked the door to my bedroom fully open and tossed me on the bed.

"What kind of lesson?" I was already so wet my thighs were sticky with my arousal, and Rhys's dark smile only made me wetter.

"Get on your hands and knees," he said, ignoring my question. "And face the headboard."

I complied, and my heart crashed against my ribcage when the bed dipped beneath Rhys's weight. He yanked my skirt up with one hand and my panties down with the other, the movement so forceful I heard the unmistakable *rip* of silk tearing.

I needed to set aside a monthly budget to replace all the underwear he'd ruined, but I wasn't complaining.

"We'll celebrate the vote later." Rhys dragged his finger through my slickness and over my sensitized clit, and a tiny whimper escaped my mouth. "But for now, let's see if you still think you're funny after I'm done with you."

That was the last warning I received before a loud *thwack* filled the room, and a blush of pain mingled with pleasure burst onto my skin.

I lowered my head just in time to stifle my scream with my pillow before another burst of sensation joined the first.

He was right. We could celebrate the vote later. For now, we needed to work off all the tension and anxiety from the past month, and—

I gasped when Rhys filled me from behind, and soon, every thought melted away except for the bliss of his touch and the fullness in my heart.

49

BRIDGET

WE SPENT THE REST OF THE DAY AND NIGHT IN MY ROOM, only surfacing for food, but the next morning, reality intruded, and I was forced to extricate myself from Rhys's arms.

As high as I was riding from our victory, I had one big issue left to deal with. I'd waited until after the vote because I couldn't afford to be distracted before then, but it was time to face it once and for all.

Rhys stayed in the bedroom while I waited for my guest in the sitting room.

I heard a knock before Mikaela poked her head in. "You wanted to see me?"

"Yes. Please, sit."

She walked in and plopped into the seat next to me. "I've been *dying* to talk to you, but you didn't answer my calls yesterday. I assume you were...*busy*, but oh my god, the vote! We have to celebrate! That's ama—"

"Why did you leak the photos of me to the press?" I skipped the buildup and got straight to the point. I couldn't stomach small talk with the proverbial black cloud hanging over us.

I kept my voice neutral, but I dug my nails so deep into the couch cushion they left tiny indentations.

I hadn't wanted to believe it when Rhys told me. Part of me still hoped he was wrong. But Mikaela's pale face and panicked eyes told me all I needed to know.

It was true.

Betrayal stabbed at me with sharp talons, puncturing my previously cold calm.

I didn't have a lot of friends in Eldorra. I had acquaintances and people who sucked up to me because of my title, but no real *friends*. Mikaela had been the one constant by my side, and I'd trusted her.

"I...I don't know what you're talking about," Mikaela said, avoiding my eyes.

"Rhys's old company traced the photos back to *your* IP address." Rhys's old boss Christian was apparently a computer genius, and Rhys had asked him to help find the leaker's identity. I'd known for weeks Mikaela could be the culprit, and I'd had to pretend nothing was wrong until I confronted her.

If the royal thing didn't work out, I might have a second calling as an actress.

Mikaela opened her mouth, closed it, then opened it again. "I thought I was helping you," she said weakly. "She told me it would help."

"I know."

The talons of betrayal dug deeper.

Christian had found some...interesting text messages when he'd looked into Mikaela's correspondence with *The Daily Tea,* and they had thrown me for as much of a loop as the discovery Mikaela was technically the leaker.

The fact it hadn't been Mikaela's idea didn't lessen the sting. She should've known better.

I heard another knock.

"Come in." I didn't take my eyes off Mikaela, who looked like she wanted to sink into the couch and never come back up.

Elin walked in, sleek and polished in her white Escada suit and three-inch pumps. Her eyes flicked over Mikaela before settling on me. "You requested to see me, Your Highness."

"Yes. We were discussing the leaked photos of Rhys and me." I finally tore my gaze away from my friend—ex-friend—and met Elin's cool blue one. "Might you know anything about that?"

Elin wasn't dumb. She picked up on my insinuation immediately, but to her credit, she didn't feign ignorance or make excuses.

"I did it to help you, Your Highness," she said after only one missed beat.

"By leaking *private photos* of me? How was that supposed to help?"

"They were not private photos." Annoyance crept into her tone. "They were perfectly innocent photos framed in a suggestive manner. I would've never leaked truly incriminating images. But if I hadn't done that, you and Mr. Larsen would've continued carrying on your reckless actions, and something more scandalous *would've* popped up. It was only a matter of time. Don't think I didn't notice what you two tried to hide beneath my nose. I didn't hold this job for so long by being oblivious."

Dammit. I should've known Elin would catch onto our affair.

She was right. We *had* been reckless, too caught up in our honeymoon phase to take the usual precautions. But that didn't make what she did right.

"And the video?"

I'd finally told Rhys about the video from Nikolai's reception a few weeks ago. He'd been upset I kept it a secret for so long, but since nothing had come of it, he'd calmed down after, oh, five days. He had, however, also asked Christian to look into who'd sent it, and when I learned Elin was behind the video as well, I'd nearly fallen out of my seat.

The surprises never stopped coming.

Mikaela's eyes bounced between me and Elin. "What video?"

We ignored her, too locked in our stare down.

"It's a crime to plant cameras in a private residence," I said. "Especially a private *royal* residence."

"Prince Nikolai knew about the cameras." Elin didn't so much as blink. "The security chief convinced him to install secret surveillance while the house was under renovation. Too many contractors going in and out. It was a precautionary measure."

I paused, absorbing the information, before I said, "Blackmail is also illegal."

"I didn't blackmail you, nor would I ever do so." Elin's brows drew into a tight frown. "I sent you the video hoping it would prompt you to break off your relationship with Mr. Larsen. When you didn't, I had to leak the pictures."

"You didn't *have* to do anything. You could've talked to me about it first," I said coldly. "For a communications secretary, you're not great at communicating."

"It wouldn't have changed a thing. You're stubborn, Your Highness. You would've told me you were ending things and gone right back to him. I had to force your hand. Plus, *The Daily Tea* reporter we sent the photos to had already been snooping around, hoping to find dirt. Security found him trespassing on the grounds. He was quite persistent, that one, almost like he has a personal grudge." Elin tilted her head. "Hans Nielsen, formerly of *The National Express*. Ring a bell?"

Several. Hans was the paparazzo whose camera Rhys had destroyed in the cemetery last year. Apparently, he'd moved up the career ladder *and* held a grudge.

I flashed back to a few weeks ago, when Rhys told me he suspected someone had snooped around his guesthouse while he'd been living there. I bet it was Hans, considering it happened before Rhys and I had gotten together and Elin hired a photographer to trail us.

I didn't tell Elin any of that, though.

"Regardless, the pictures satisfied him and kept him from digging further," Elin said when I didn't respond. "I must say, in hindsight, your press conference was inspired, and you and Mr. Larsen made it work. Yesterday's vote was a big win, so no harm, no foul."

Funny she called the press conference inspired *now* when she'd thrown a massive fit over it.

"No harm, no foul?" I repeated. "Elin, you went behind my back, created a scandal, and dragged Mikaela into it!"

Mikaela, who'd been watching the rapid-fire exchange between us with wide eyes, lowered her head.

"I needed a go-between. I couldn't have the photos traced back to me." Elin heaved a deep sigh. "Honestly, Your Highness, it all worked out. I fed the press a smaller scandal so they wouldn't stumble onto a larger one. I was protecting the royal family. That has always been my number one goal."

"Perhaps." I steeled my spine. "I appreciate your service to the family over the years, but I'm afraid it's time we part ways."

Mikaela squeaked while the color leached from Elin's face.

"You're *firing* me? You can't fire me. His Majesty—"

"Has given me the authority to make whatever staffing

changes I see fit," I finished. I pressed my hands tight against my thighs to keep from shaking. Elin was one of the palace's longest-serving employees, and I'd always been slightly terrified of her. But while she was great at the external part of her job, I needed someone who worked *with* me, not someone who snuck around behind my back and tried to dictate my actions. "You stepped over the line, and you lost our trust. Mine *and* the king's."

Elin clutched her phone, her knuckles whiter than her suit. Finally, she said, "As you wish. I'll have my desk cleared out by the end of the week." A muscle twitched beneath her eye, but otherwise, she showed no emotion. "Is there anything else, Your Highness?"

Brisk and efficient to the end.

"No," I said, feeling strangely melancholy. Elin and I had never been close, but it was the end of an era. "You're dismissed."

She gave me a tight nod and walked out. She wasn't one for dramatics, and she knew me well enough to know when I'd set my mind on something.

"You too," I told Mikaela.

"Bridget, I swear—"

"I need to think things through." Maybe I would forgive her one day, but her betrayal was still fresh and nothing she said right now would penetrate the hurt. "I don't know how long that's going to take, but I need time."

"Fair enough." Her chin wobbled. "I really *was* trying to help. Elin was so convincing. I didn't believe her at first when she said you and Rhys had something going on. But then I thought about the way you looked at each other, and that time you took so long to answer the door at your office...it all made sense. She said you would get in huge trouble if—"

"Mikaela, please." I pressed my fingers to my forehead. It hurt almost as much as my heart. If I were old Bridget, perhaps I would've let what she did slide, but I couldn't afford to let things slide anymore. I needed people I could trust around me. "Not right now."

Mikaela swallowed hard, her freckles stark against her pale skin, but she left without trying to make excuses again.

I expelled a sharp breath. The conversation had been shorter but harder than I'd expected, even after weeks of mental preparation.

I supposed nothing could fully prepare someone for firing one of their longest-serving employees and saying goodbye to one of their oldest friends in the span of half an hour.

I heard Rhys come up behind me. He didn't speak. He just swept his palms over my shoulders and massaged the muscles with his thumbs.

"I'd hoped you were wrong." I stared at where Mikaela had sat, the sting of betrayal lingering on my skin.

"Princess, I'm never wrong."

I released a half laugh, breaking some of the tension. "I can think of a few instances when you were."

"Yeah? Like when?" Rhys challenged, a hint of amusement shining through.

I deepened my voice to mimic him. "*One, I do not become personally involved in my clients' lives. I am here to safeguard you from physical harm. That is all. I am not here to be your friend, confidant, or anything else. This ensures my judgment remains uncompromised.*" I reverted to my regular voice. "How'd that work out for you, Mr. Larsen?"

He stopped massaging my shoulders and curled one hand around my throat. My pulse jumped as he lowered his head until his lips grazed my ear. "Mocking me? Do you need a refresher lesson already, Your Highness?"

Another piece of tension cracked.

"Maybe. You might want to brush up on your teaching skills, Mr. Larsen," I said, playing along. "The lessons should last longer than a couple hours."

Another laugh escaped when Rhys picked me up and swung me around until we faced each other, and my limbs wrapped around his neck and waist.

"I knew you were trouble the moment I saw you." He squeezed my ass, hard, but those steel-gray eyes were soft as he examined me. "You did what you had to do, princess."

Despite the gruff delivery, his single short sentence comforted me more an entire speech from someone else could.

"I know." I rested my forehead against his, tightness ballooning in my chest. "But there are so few people I can turn to here, and I just lost two of them in one day."

Too much was changing too fast. Some of it was good, some of it was nerve-wracking. Either way, I could barely keep up.

"You have me."

"I know," I repeated, softer this time.

"Good. And for the record..." Rhys's lips tilted up into a small smile. "I've never been happier to be wrong. Fuck *personally involved*. That's not good enough. I want to be in your mind, in your heart, and in your fucking soul the way you are in mine. You and me, princess..."

"...Against the world," I finished. The tightness in my chest no longer had anything to do with Elin and Mikaela.

"That's right. You're never alone, princess," he whispered against my mouth. "Remember that."

Rhys and I hadn't officially celebrated yesterday's victory yet, but as he kissed me, I realized we didn't need champagne and fireworks. We'd always been best when it was just us, no pomp and circumstance required, and the best celebration was *being* together without having to hide.

No shame, no guilt, no impending vote or tough conversations with soon-to-be ex-friends and ex-employees hanging over our heads.

Just us.

That was all we needed.

50

RHYS

"You can't sit by a queen's side if you don't know which fork to use. You'll embarrass yourself at state functions." Andreas crossed his arms over his chest. "Did you not look at the diagram I sent you?"

"They're. All. Forks," I bit out. "They serve the same function."

"I'd like to see you try to use an oyster fork to eat steak."

A dull ache throbbed at my temple. We'd been reviewing dinner etiquette for the past hour, and I was one second away from stabbing Andreas with one of his beloved forks.

He'd officially moved out of the palace and back into his townhouse last week, after the parliamentary vote, and we were reviewing place settings in his kitchen.

I'd asked him to help me acclimate to the whole royal life-style thing. Diplomatic protocol, who's who in Eldorran society, and so on.

I already regretted it, and we hadn't even finished our first lesson.

Before I could respond, the doorbell rang, saving Andreas from death by utensil.

"Study the diagram," he said before answering the door.

My temple throbbed harder. I should've asked the palace's protocol office for help instead. They were humorless automatons, but at least I didn't want to murder them every five minutes.

I heard faint voices, followed by the sound of footsteps.

"Rhys?"

I looked up and saw Bridget standing in the doorway with Booth. I wasn't sure who was more surprised, her or me.

"What are you doing here?" we asked at the same time.

"It seems I'm now the most popular person in the family." Andreas stepped around Bridget. "Ironic."

She walked to me and gave me a quick kiss before sliding a cool glance in Andreas's direction. "You're not the most popular person anywhere except in your head."

I didn't bother hiding my smile. Snarky Bridget was one of my favorite Bridgets.

Andreas arched an eyebrow. "Care to explain why you're here then, Your Highness? I assumed you'd be too busy to visit little ol' me."

Good question. Bridget was supposed to be at a coronation planning meeting.

"My meeting ended early, so I thought I'd come by to say thank you. I didn't get a chance to say it before, but I appreciate you helping Rhys with Erhall." It came out grudgingly. Bridget's relationship with Andreas had warmed a few degrees since she found out he'd been trying to help her in his own fucked-up way, but they would never be best friends. They were too different and had too much history.

Andreas's face broke out into a devious grin.

"Don't be a dick," I warned.

"Me? Never." he drawled before turning to Bridget. "I appreciate the gratitude, cousin dearest. Does this mean you owe me a favor in the future?"

She narrowed her eyes. "Don't push it."

Andreas shrugged. "It was worth a shot. While you're here, maybe *you* can explain place settings to your boyfriend. I drew a perfect diagram, but alas, it's not enough."

Bridget's confusion morphed into amusement when I explained the situation, glaring at Andreas the whole time.

"He doesn't know his forks," Andreas said after I finished. "I'm trying to civilize him. Imagine using a salad fork to eat pasta." He sniffed with disdain.

"I know them enough to stab you with one of them," I said.

Booth snorted from the doorway.

"The violence is another thing we have to work on." Andreas finished his whiskey and set it on the counter. "You're dating a princess now. You can't go around stabbing people."

"Oh, I think people will understand once they find out who I'm stabbing."

Bridget laughed. "Forget about him," she told me. "I'll help you." She turned to Booth. "I'm fine here. Rhys is with me. I believe there's a football match you want to watch?"

Football as in soccer, not American football. It was one of the thousand small things I had to get used to.

Booth's face lit up. "If you wouldn't mind, Your Highness."

Since it was getting late and Andreas had no groceries except for milk and eggs, we ordered takeout while Booth watched his game in the den and Bridget and Andreas fought to teach me about place settings. Eventually I got the hang of it, and we moved on to nobility ranks. It wasn't hard to remember. After the royal family, dukes and duchesses ranked highest, followed by marquesses, counts, earls, and barons. Eldorra had a similar hierarchy to Britain.

"You might make a good Prince Consort after all." Andreas wiped his mouth with a napkin and checked the clock. "If you'll excuse me, I have a call with an old friend from Oxford. Don't destroy the kitchen while I'm gone."

"Good to hear. You know how I live for your approval," I deadpanned.

"I do." He clapped me on the shoulder on his way out, and my annoyance ratcheted up another notch.

I couldn't believe I shared DNA with that guy.

When I turned back to Bridget, she was trying, and failing, to suppress a smile.

"What's so funny?"

"You and Andreas. You bicker like Nik and I do." Her smile widened at the incomprehension on my face. "You bicker like siblings."

Siblings.

It didn't hit me until that moment. I'd known Andreas was my brother, but he was my *brother*. A real, albeit annoying, one I saw regularly. We argued all the time, but maybe that was just what siblings did, like Bridget said.

I wouldn't know. I'd been alone all my life...until now.

My stomach swooped with the oddest sensation.

"I still don't trust him fully," I said. Cynicism was hardwired into my DNA, and while Andreas hadn't done anything shady since I confronted him about being my brother, it'd only been two months.

"Neither do I, but let's stick with optimism for now. Besides, it'll be nice for you to have a brother here. Even if I wish he were less..."

"Andreas-y?"

Bridget laughed. "Yes."

"Hmm. We'll see."

I drew her closer and kissed her forehead. I could hear

Booth's football game in the den, and our takeout containers lay scattered on the kitchen island along with Andreas's empty whiskey glass and the rumpled diagram he'd drawn for me.

It didn't look like a royal gathering. It looked like a normal Wednesday night at home.

And as Bridget wrapped her arms around my waist and Andreas returned, grumbling about a delayed bachelor trip to Santorini, I finally identified the odd sensation gripping me.

It was the feeling of having a family.

51

RHYS

THREE MONTHS LATER

"Rhys!" Luciana's face creased into a huge smile. "*Como estas?*" She looked Bridget over with a twinkle in her eye, and when she spoke next, her words held a teasing note. "*Es tu novia?*"

I laughed and tangled my fingers with Bridget's. "*Si, es mi novia.*"

"I knew it!" Luciana said with delight. "*Finally.* Come, come. I have food for you."

She ushered us to the same table we'd sat at during our last trip to Costa Rica. I couldn't believe that had only been a year ago. So much had changed since then.

Hell, so much had changed in the past three months alone. Bridget and I could finally enjoy *being* together, even as preparations for her coronation ramped up and I slowly acclimated to the spotlight. I didn't enjoy the attention, but I was more comfortable with it, and that was the best I could hope for.

"This was a good idea." Bridget sighed with happiness

when Luciana brought out a feast of meat and rice. "I needed a vacation."

I smirked. "I always have good ideas."

Bridget hadn't wanted to go on a trip until after her coronation, but I could tell she was buckling under the stress. She needed a getaway to reset. Plus, my mouth could be pretty damn persuasive, especially when I used it for purposes other than talking.

It was our first vacation as an official couple, and I'd chosen Costa Rica not only for sentimental purposes but because no one in town knew or cared Bridget was a princess. Even after all the recent press coverage, they treated her as they would anyone else—warm and friendly, sometimes inquisitive, but never prying.

"Five days in paradise," I drawled. "Swimming, sunbathing, fucking—"

"*Rhys.*"

"What, you don't like the itinerary?"

"Lower your voice," she hissed, her face the color of the tomatoes on her plate. "People will hear."

"No one's listening."

We were the only ones on the trip. No Booth, no entourage. It took a helluva lot of convincing, but the palace finally agreed to my plan. I was still qualified to guard Bridget, even if I was no longer officially employed in that capacity.

Since I quit working for Christian, I'd taken on a few freelance security consulting gigs. I didn't need the money—Harper Security had paid *very* well, and I wasn't a big spender—but I'd go out of my mind with boredom if I didn't have something to occupy my days.

"You don't know that." Bridget tucked a strand of hair behind her ear. She wore a tank top and shorts, and her skin already glowed from the sun. No makeup or fancy clothes, and she was still the most beautiful sight I'd ever seen. "People could definitely be listening."

"Trust me. I know." The closest people to us sat three tables over, their eyes glued to the soccer game on TV. "Even if they are, ain't nothing wrong with fuck—"

"*Rhys.*"

I chuckled but stopped trying to get a rise out of her lest her face explode from embarrassment. It never failed to amaze me how prim Bridget was in public compared to how wild she was in bed. It made our sex even hotter, knowing I got to see a side of her no one else did.

After lunch, we walked around town for a bit before I convinced her to return to the villa.

I couldn't wait much longer.

"I have a surprise for you," I said as we drove up the hill. I couldn't resist dropping a hint, and talking kept my focus off the knot of nerves in my stomach.

I wasn't used to being nervous.

Bridget perked up. "I love surprises. What is it?"

I kept one hand on the steering wheel and twined the fingers of my other hand with hers. "It wouldn't be a surprise if I told you."

"I like surprises I'm prepared for," she said. "Just a hint?"

I shook my head with a grin. I'd been doing a lot more of that lately—grinning.

Something had changed over the past few months. The dark, heavy cloud that'd hung over me all my life had dissipated. It still came back now and then, but sunny days were the default now, not thunderstorms.

It was...strange. The darkness had been a protective shield, and without it, I felt stripped bare. Defenseless, which was not something I ever wanted to feel. But in moments like this, when it was just me and Bridget, I didn't need defenses. She'd broken through all of them, anyway.

"Here we are." I parked in front of the villa. "Surprise."

Bridget looked around slowly. "Okay..." She shot a confused glance in my direction. "I hate to tell you this, but we've been here before, remember? Luggage drop-off this morning? Bucket list number four?"

"Trust me, that's not something I'll ever forget." My mouth quirked up at the warm rose creeping over her cheeks. "But that's not the surprise. This is." I held up a set of keys. "I bought the house."

Her mouth fell open. "What?"

"My buddy was thinking of selling anyway. He and his family are moving further down south. So, I bought it." I shrugged.

We could stay in the nicest hotels in the world, but I wanted a place that belonged to us.

"Rhys, you can't..." Bridget's eyes darted to the villa. "Really?"

"Yep." My grin widened when she squealed in a decidedly unprincess-like manner and jumped out of the car.

"We're coming here every year!" she yelled over her shoulder. "And we need more hammocks!"

I followed her inside, a laugh rumbling from my chest as she visited every room like they were long-lost friends.

I loved seeing her like this, wild and carefree, her guard down and her face lit with a smile. A *real* one.

"I love this place." She slid open the glass door to the terrace and sighed when she saw the pool. "Perfection."

"Why do you think I bought it?"

A teasing sparkle brightened her eyes. "Rhys, are you a secret romantic?"

"I don't know." I reached into my pocket and pulled out a

small velvet box, the knot of nerves in my stomach doubling. Bridget sucked in an audible breath, but otherwise everything hushed—the wind, the birds, the roar of the Pacific in the distance. It was like the entire world held its breath, waiting to see what happened next. "You tell me."

I opened the box, revealing the glittering diamond ring that had burned a hole in the back of my dresser drawer for two months. I'd wanted to wait until the perfect moment. Now it was here, and I felt like an eighteen-year-old walking into Navy training for the first time again, determined but scared as hell about how the next chapter of my life would unfold.

A proposal was inevitable. I knew it, Bridget knew it, the world knew it. But just because something was inevitable didn't mean it wasn't important, and this was the most important moment of my life.

"I'm not the best at flowery language, so I'll keep it simple." Fuck, was my voice shaking? I hoped not. "I never believed in love. Never wanted it. I didn't see the practical value and, to be honest, I was doing just fine without it. But then I met you. Your smile, your strength, your intelligence and compassion. Even your stubbornness and hardheadedness. You filled a part of my soul I always thought would be empty, and you healed scars I never knew existed. And I realized...it's not that I didn't believe in love before. It's that I was saving it all for you."

A half sob bled through the hand pressed to Bridget's mouth.

I took a deep breath. "Bridget, will you marry me?"

The question hadn't fully left my mouth before Bridget threw her arms around me and kissed me. "Yes. Yes, yes, a thousand times *yes!*"

Yes. One word, three letters, and it filled me up so completely I was sure I'd never hunger again.

I slipped the ring on her finger. It fit perfectly.

"There's no taking it back," I said gruffly, hoping she couldn't hear the hitch in my voice. "You're really stuck with me now."

Bridget let out another half sob, half laugh. "I wouldn't have it any other way, Mr. Larsen." She curled her fingers around mine. "You and me."

A deep, pleasurable ache spread in my chest, warming me more than the late afternoon sun ever could.

I didn't know what I'd done to deserve her, but she was here, she was mine, and I was never letting her go.

"You and me." I cupped her face and brushed my lips over hers. "Always."

EPILOGUE

RHYS

Six months later

"Do you solemnly promise and swear to govern the People of Eldorra according to their respective laws and customs?"

"I solemnly promise so to do." Bridget sat in the coronation chair, her face pale but her hand steady on the King's Book as she took her official oath. Her grandfather stood beside her, his face solemn but proud, and the rest of the cathedral was so quiet I could feel the weight of the occasion pressing into my skin.

After months of planning, the big day was finally here. In a few minutes, Bridget would be crowned Queen of Eldorra, and I, as her fiancé, would officially be the Prince Consort in waiting.

It wasn't something I'd ever dreamed of or thought I wanted, but I would follow Bridget anywhere, from the smallest, shittiest town to the grandest church. As long as I was with her, I was happy.

I stood with Nikolai, Sabrina, Andreas, and the other von

Aschebergs in the front row, closest to the coronation. The ceremony took place in the sprawling Athenberg Cathedral, which was packed with thousands of high-profile guests. Heads of state, foreign royals, celebrities, billionaires, they were all there.

I clasped my hands in front of me, wishing the archbishop would speed things up. I hadn't talked to Bridget all day, and I was itching to get to the *coronation* ball so we could have some alone time.

"Will you to your power cause Law and Justice, in Mercy, to be executed in all your judgments?" the archbishop asked.

"I will."

Pride seeped through me at Bridget's strong, clear voice.

She completed her oath, and a collective hush fell over the cathedral when the archbishop lifted the crown from Edvard's head and placed it on hers.

"Her Majesty Queen Bridget of Eldorra," the archbishop declared. "Long may she reign!"

"Long may she reign!" I repeated the words along with the rest of the guests, my chest tight. Beside me, Nikolai dipped his head, his face shining with emotion; next to Bridget, Edvard stood ramrod straight, his eyes suspiciously bright.

The archbishop finished the ceremony with a few verses from the King's Book, and it was done.

Eldorra officially had a new ruler and its first female monarch in over a century.

A low, electric hum replaced the hush. It skittered through the soaring hall and over my skin as Bridget rose for the exit procession; judging by the way the other guests shifted and murmured, I wasn't the only one who felt it.

It was the feeling of watching history being made.

I caught Bridget's eye during her procession, and I flashed her a quick grin and a wink. Her mouth curved into a smile before she tamped it down, and I fought back a laugh at her overly serious expression as she left the church.

"That was the longest ceremony ever." Andreas yawned. "I'm glad I wasn't the one who had to sit up there."

"Good thing you'll never sit up there, then." My relationship with Andreas had developed into something resembling genuine friendship over the months, but his personality still left a lot to be desired.

He shrugged. "*C'est la vie.* Let Bridget shoulder the burden of a nation while I live like a prince with none of the responsibilities."

Nikolai and I exchanged glances and shook our heads. While Andreas and I never missed an opportunity to sneak a dig at the other, I had a much easier relationship with Nikolai. Another brother, albeit by marriage rather than blood, and I didn't want to murder him half the time.

After the formal exit procession, the guests filed out of the cathedral, and soon, I found myself in the palace ballroom, impatiently waiting for Bridget to arrive.

Only five hundred people received invites to the coronation ball compared to the thousands at the ceremony, but that was still too many people. All of them wanted to shake my hand and say hi, and I indulged them half-heartedly while eyeing the door. At least my lessons with Andreas came in handy—I remembered everyone's titles and greeted them accordingly.

My pulse kicked up a notch when the Sergeant at Arms' announcement finally rang through the ballroom. "Her Majesty Queen Bridget of Eldorra."

Triumphal music played, the doors opened, and Bridget swept in. She wore a lighter gown than the ornate affair she'd donned for the ceremony, and she'd replaced her crown with a more wearable tiara.

She waved to the crowd, her public smile firmly in place, but when our eyes met, a hint of playfulness crept in.

I excused myself from my conversation with the Prime Minister of Sweden and made my way through the crowd. For once, I didn't need to use my height or build—everyone parted when they saw me approaching.

The perks of being the future Prince Consort, I supposed.

By the time I reached Bridget, she had half a dozen people fighting for her attention.

"Your Majesty." I held out my hand, cutting off a woman who'd been gushing over her dress. The crowd fell silent. "May I have this dance?"

A grin played at the corners of Bridget's mouth. "Of course. Ladies, gentlemen, if you'll excuse me."

She took my hand, and we walked away with six pairs of eyes burning into us.

Bridget waited until we were out of earshot before saying, "Thank the Lord. If I had to listen to Lady Featherton compliment my outfit one more time, I would've stabbed myself with the spikes from my tiara."

"We can't have that, can we? I very much like you alive." I rested my hand on the small of her back as I guided her across the dance floor. "So, you're officially queen. How does it feel?"

"Surreal, but also...right." She shook her head. "I don't know how to explain it."

"I understand."

I did. I felt much the same way. I wasn't the one who'd been crowned, of course, but we'd waited and planned for so long it was strange to have the ceremony behind us. We'd also had time to get used to the idea of Bridget being queen, and now that she was, it felt right.

We always end up where we're meant to be.

"I know you do." Bridget's eyes glowed with emotion before

she made a face. "I can't want to get out of this dress, though. It's not as bad as my coronation dress, but I swear it still weighs ten pounds."

"Don't worry. I'll rip it off you later." I lowered my head and whispered, "I've never fucked a queen before."

A chuckle rose in my throat at the deep blush spreading over Bridget's face and neck.

"Do I have to stop calling you princess now?" I asked. "*Queen* doesn't roll off the tongue quite as nice."

She narrowed her eyes. "Don't you dare. By royal decree, you're never allowed to stop calling me *princess*."

"I thought you hated the nickname."

I spun her around, and she waited until she was in my arms again before saying, "As much as you hate when I call you Mr. Larsen."

I used to. Not anymore.

"I was joking." My lips grazed her forehead. "You'll always be my princess."

Bridget's eyes shone brighter. "Mr. Larsen, if you make me cry at my own coronation ball, I'll never forgive you."

My smile widened, and I kissed her, not caring if PDA was against protocol. "Then it's a good thing I have the rest of our lives to make it up to you."

BRIDGET

Three months after my coronation, Rhys and I returned to the Athenberg Cathedral for our wedding.

It was as grand and luxurious as one would expect of a royal wedding, but I worked with Freja, the new communications secretary, to keep the reception as small as possible. As queen, I couldn't have a friends-and-family-only party for diplomatic reasons, but we cut the guest list from two *thousand* to two hundred. I considered that a major victory.

"I'm jealous," Nikolai said. "You only have two hundred people to greet. My hands nearly fell off at my reception."

I laughed. "You survived."

We stood near the dessert table while the rest of the guests ate, drank, and danced. The actual wedding ceremony had gone off without a hitch, and as much as I enjoyed seeing my friends and family let loose, I was counting down the minutes until I could be alone with Rhys, who was currently talking to Christian and a few of his friends from the Navy.

He hadn't expected his military buddies to come, since he hadn't spoken to them in so long, but they'd all showed up. Whatever worries he might've had about seeing them again, they seemed to have disappeared. Rhys was smiling and laughing and looked perfectly at peace.

"Barely," Nikolai joked before his smile faded. "I'm glad things worked out for you and Rhys," he added softly. "You deserve it. When I abdicated, I didn't think...I never wanted to put that kind of pressure on you. And when I realized what it meant...what you had to give up..."

"It's okay." I squeezed his hand. "You did what you had to do. I was upset when you first told me, but it all worked out, and I enjoy being queen...for the most part. Especially now that Erhall is no longer Speaker."

Erhall had lost his seat by half a point. I'd be lying if I said the news hadn't given me immense pleasure.

I had, however, worried Nikolai would be upset or jealous about the repeal. Would he be bitter I got to stay with Rhys *and* keep the crown? But he'd been nothing but supportive, and he'd admitted he enjoyed his new life more than he'd expected. I think part of him was actually relieved.

Nikolai had grown up thinking he wanted the throne

because he didn't have a choice to *not* want it, and now that he was freed from those expectations, he was thriving. Meanwhile, I'd taken up the mantle and grown into the role.

Ironic, the way things turned out.

"Yes, he was a bit of a toad, wasn't he?" Nikolai grinned and glanced over my shoulder. "Ah, it seems my time is up. I'll talk to you later. I need to save Sabrina before Grandfather forces her to name our baby Sigmund after our great-great-uncle." He hesitated. "Are you happy, Bridget?"

I squeezed his hand again, a messy clog of emotion tangling in my throat. "I am."

Did I feel like the weight of the world was on my shoulders sometimes? Yes. Did I get angry, frustrated, and stressed? Yes. But so did a lot of people. The important thing was, I no longer felt trapped. I'd learned to master my circumstances instead of letting them master me, and I had Rhys by my side. No matter how terrible of a day I had, I could go home to someone I loved who loved me back, and that made all the difference.

Nikolai must've heard the sincerity in my voice, because his face relaxed. "Good. That's all I need to know." He kissed my cheek before he beelined to where a five-months-pregnant Sabrina sat with our grandfather, who'd spent his post-ruling days fussing over his future great-grandchild and trying to find a suitable hobby to fill his time.

Edvard had forced Rhys to teach him how to draw for a few weeks before it became clear his talents did not lie in the artistic realm. He'd since moved on to archery, and I'd had to add a hazard pay bonus for the staff accompanying him to practice.

I turned to see what had made Nikolai leave, and my face broke into a smile when I saw Rhys approaching.

"Long time no see," I teased. We'd only had one dance

together before we were pulled away by various friends and family.

"Don't remind me. My own wedding, and I barely see my wife," he grumbled, but his frown eased when he drew me into his arms. "We should've eloped."

"The palace would've had something to say about that."

"Fuck the palace."

I stifled a laugh. "Rhys, you can't say that. You're the Prince Consort now." The King Consort title didn't exist in Eldorra, so even though I was the queen, he was called the Prince Consort.

"Which means I can say it even more than before." Rhys grazed my jaw with his lips, and goosebumps of pleasure dotted my arms. "Speaking of Prince Consort...what benefits come with the position?"

"Um." I tried to think through the fog in my head as he caressed the nape of my neck. "A crown, a lovely room in the palace, medical benefits..."

"Boring. Boring. Even more boring."

I laughed. "What do you want then?"

Rhys lifted his head, his eyes gleaming. "I want to bend—"

"Hi guys, I'm so sorry for interrupting." Ava appeared beside us. She looked lovely in her mint green bridesmaid dress, but her face was etched with concern. "Have you seen Jules and Josh? I can't find them anywhere."

"She's afraid they've murdered each other," Alex added, coming up behind her.

Ava rolled her eyes. "You're exaggerating."

"Not by much. I saw Jules with a knife earlier."

"I hope they haven't. Bad press if there's a murder at my wedding," I joked. "But no, I haven't seen them. Sorry."

Still, I swept my eyes around the room just in case.

Booth, whom I'd insisted attend as a guest instead of a guard, was deep in conversation with his wife and Emma, who'd flown in a few days ago so we could catch up before the wedding. Apparently, she'd gotten more attached to Meadow's cuddliness and Leather's foul mouth than expected, and she'd adopted both from the shelter. I was delighted, especially when Emma promised to send me pictures and videos of them often.

Steffan was dancing with Malin. I'd called him after my press conference to apologize for not giving him a heads up, but he hadn't been upset at all. He said it'd given him the courage to stand up to his father, and considering he was attending the most publicized event of the year with Malin, it must've all worked out.

Christian stood in the shadows, chatting with Andreas, but his eyes strayed to something—*someone*—on the dance floor. I followed his gaze and winced when I saw Stella.

That's not good. Or maybe I was reading too much into the situation.

Even Mikaela was in attendance, hanging out with some of our old school friends. I'd invited her as an olive branch, but it would take a while before I trusted her again.

Almost everyone who played a major role in my life was there...except Jules and Josh.

"I haven't seen them either," Rhys said.

Ava sighed. "Thanks. I just wanted to check. Sorry for bothering you, and congrats again!" She dragged Alex away, probably to look for her brother and Jules, even though Alex looked like he would rather eat nails.

"Well, that ruined the mood," Rhys said dryly. "We can't even have a conversation without getting interrupted."

"Perhaps we should wait until after the reception because that'll keep happening. I already see Freja coming toward us. Unless..." I lowered my voice, a spark of mischief kindling inside me. "We hide."

We stared at each other for a beat before a slow smile spread across his face. "I like the way you think, princess."

Rhys left first, slipping out under the auspices of using the restroom, and I followed soon after. We couldn't be gone long, but we could steal a few moments for ourselves.

"Your Majesty!" Freja called as I passed her. "Where are you going? We need to discuss—"

"Ladies' room. I'll be back." I quickened my steps and contained my laughter until I reached the small drawing room where Rhys was waiting.

"It's like we're sneaking around again." I shut the door behind me, my heart racing with the twin thrills of finally being alone with him and doing something we weren't supposed to do.

"Just like old times," he drawled. The lights were off, but enough moonlight filtered through the curtains for me to see the carved planes of his face and the tender heat in his eyes.

"So, tell me." I looped my arms around his neck. "Was this where you expected to end up as a kid? Hiding in a royal drawing room with your wife on the night of your wedding?"

"Not exactly." Rhys brushed his thumb over my bottom lip. "But someone once told me we always end up where we're meant to be, and this is where I'm meant to be. With you."

Forget butterflies. An entire flock of birds took flight in my stomach, soaring into the clouds and taking me with them. "Mr. Larsen, I do believe you're a secret romantic after all."

"Don't tell anyone." He cupped my ass and squeezed. "Or I'll have to spank you again."

I choked out a laugh right before his mouth crashed down on mine and everything else—Freja, the reception, the hundreds of people gathered in the ballroom just a few doors down—ceased to exist.

Kidnapping, blackmail, betrayal...our path to where we

were now was anything but conventional. I wasn't a storybook princess, and Rhys wasn't Prince Charming.

I didn't want us to be.

Because while what we had wasn't a traditional fairytale by any means, it was ours. And it was forever.

THE END

He hates her...almost as much as he wants her.
Preorder Twisted Hate now for a steamy enemies to lovers romance featuring Josh and Jules.

For a sweet/sexy bonus scene of Rhys and Bridget's first Christmas Eve as husband and wife, type this link into your browser: https://BookHip.com/CZSVZXV

Want to discuss my books and other fun shenanigans with like-minded readers? Join my Facebook reader group, Ana's Star Squad!

Thank you for reading *Twisted Games!* If you enjoyed this book, I would be grateful if you could leave a review on the platform(s) of your choice.

Reviews are like tips for author, and every one helps!

Much love,
Ana

TWISTED SERIES
A series of interconnected standalones

Twisted Love
Twisted Games
Twisted Hate
Twisted Lies

IF LOVE SERIES

If We Ever Meet Again (Duet Book 1)
If the Sun Never Sets (Duet Book 2)
If Love Had a Price (Standalone)
If We Were Perfect (Standalone)

STANDALONES

All I've Never Wanted

Scan to easily access all of my books:

Keep in touch with Ana Huang

Join my Facebook reader group, Ana's Star Squad, to get the latest updates and talk about books, Netflix, and more!

https://www.facebook.com/groups/anasstarsquad

You can also find Ana at these places:

Website:
http://www.anahuang.com

Bookbub:
http://www.bookbub.com/profile/ana-huang

Instagram:
http://www.instagram.com/authoranahuang

Goodreads
http://www.goodreads.com/anahuang

ACKNOWLEDGMENTS

Thank you to everyone for reading Bridget and Rhys's story! This couple has consumed me for months, and now that they're finally out in the world, I hope you love them as much as I do!

I especially want to thank the people who've helped make this book a reality:

To my alpha and beta readers Brittney, Brittany (with an a), Yaneli, Sarah, Rebecca, Aishah, and Allisyn for your constructive feedback. You helped make the story shine, and I am so grateful for your honesty and attention to detail.

To my PA Amber for keeping me sane and always being there when I need a second opinion. What would I do without you?

To my editor Amy Briggs and proofreader Krista Burdine for working with me on my ever-changing and sometimes tight deadlines. You are rockstars!

To Amanda at E. James Designs for the stunning special-edition cover and the teams at Give Me Books and Wildfire Marketing for making release day a dream.

And a HUGE thank you to every reader and blogger who've shown this series so much love! I am blown away by all the reviews, gorgeous edits, and DMs. You truly deserve the world.

xo, Ana

ABOUT THE AUTHOR

Ana Huang is an author of primarily steamy New Adult and contemporary romance. Her books contain diverse characters and emotional, sometimes twisty roads toward HEAs (with plenty of banter and spice sprinkled in). Besides reading and writing, Ana loves traveling, is obsessed with hot chocolate, and has multiple relationships with fictional boyfriends.

Made in the USA
Middletown, DE
14 July 2022